Stardust

Also by Hope C. Tarr

AMERICAN SONGBOOK SERIES
 Book 1: IRISH EYES
 Book 2: STARDUST

Stardust

HOPE C. TARR

Shine Bright!

Hope C. Tarr

LUME BOOKS
A JOFFE BOOKS COMPANY

Lume Books, London
A Joffe Books Company
www.lumebooks.co.uk

First published in Great Britain in by Lume Books

Copyright © Hope C. Tarr 2025

The right of Hope C. Tarr to be identified as author of this work has been asserted in accordance with the Copyright, Designs and Patents Act 1988.

This book is a work of fiction. Names, characters, businesses, organisations, places and events are either the product of the author's imagination or are used fictitiously. Any resemblance to actual persons, living or dead, events or locales is entirely coincidental. The spelling used is British English except where fidelity to the author's rendering of accent or dialect supersedes this.

No part of this book may be used or reproduced in any manner for the purpose of training artificial intelligence technologies or systems. In accordance with Article 4(3) of the Digital Single Market Directive 2019/790, Joffe Books expressly reserves this work from the text and data mining exception.

Cover design by Jarmila Takač

ISBN: 978-1-83901-598-4

*To my grandmother,
Henrietta ("Hattie") Magdalene Carey (née Preuer)
May 31, 1904–March 12, 1999
To me, forever "Granny."
And to all the grandmothers, never underestimate the powerful
difference you make in a child's life.*

Love is now the star dust of yesterday.
The music of the years gone by.

Stardust: music and lyrics by Hoagland "Hoagy" Carmichael, 1927

PART ONE: 1938–1939

"If you are lucky enough to have lived in Paris as a young man, then wherever you go for the rest of your life, it stays with you, for Paris is a moveable feast."

Ernest Hemingway

Chapter One

June 1938, Paris, France
Even after all that has come to light since, I refuse to remember my first meeting with Coco Chanel as anything other than magical. I can still see myself moving through her flagship boutique and atelier on rue Cambon as if watching a film, my grandmother Rose smartly turned out in a brown and off-white speckled tweed Chanel suit, her still mostly ginger-colored curls swept into a chignon. At fifty-eight, she was a strikingly attractive woman, her Irish peaches-and-cream complexion only lightly lined, her whiskey-brown eyes exuding the same keen intelligence and zest for life that had attracted Grandpa Adam to her all those years ago on Inishmore.

As the matriarch of our family, and the founder of Kavanaugh's department store in Manhattan, she didn't find it easy to get away. That early summer trip to Paris was in celebration of both my high school graduation and eighteenth birthday as well as an opportunity to scout out the competition – *Au Bon Marché*, *Galeries Lafayette*, and *La Samaritaine*, for starters. Opening a Kavanaugh's in Paris, the fashion capital of the world, had long been Gran's ambition.

That first morning over breakfast on our balcony at the Hôtel Lutetia looking out onto the Eiffel Tower, a croissant and café crème for me, and black tea and toast for Gran, she announced she had a surprise birthday present in store. No amount of my wheedling could get it out of her.

"Fine, it's a secret then." Still hoping to trip her up, I reached for Monmarche's latest illustrated guidebook, *On Foot in Paris,* lying closed atop our table. "What shall we do first?" I fished, sure that my "surprise" must be somewhere in those printed pages.

I'd flipped through the book on the ocean liner leaving from New York, looking mostly at the photographs, and hadn't opened it since we had docked at Le Havre the previous day. The Louvre, Napoleon's Tomb in Les Invalides, Notre Dame Cathedral – I knew I should be panting to see those and other important historic places and yet what I really wanted was to go shopping!

Expression sheepish, she admitted, "I have one tiny bit of business to tick off, and then the rest of the day is all yours."

Gran was what decades later would be known as a workaholic. Owing to her tenacity and smarts, Kavanaugh's had shaken off its humble beginnings as a dry goods store on Grand Street in Lower Manhattan to become one of Manhattan's leading luxury department stores, on a par with Lord and Taylor, R.H. Macy & Co, and Saks Fifth Avenue. From the first time I'd toddled inside, my chubby baby hand wrapped around Gran's pinkie, I had adored every inch of it. The rose marble floors and cathedral ceilings. The sprays of freshly cut pink roses on every floor, another hat tip to Gran. The weak-kneed thrill of riding the glass elevators six floors up to the rooftop restaurant. The Steinway grand piano, the centerpiece of the central foyer, where a succession of tuxedo-clad pianists tickled the ivories from opening to closing. I had been helping on weekends since high school, starting in giftwrap and working my way through the various departments, absorbing the magic of the place, a retail emporium where a humble housewife, secretary or shopgirl could walk through the etched glass entrance doors and be treated like a queen.

"Why not come with me to my meeting and then we'll start our vacation straight after?" Gran suggested.

Inviting an eighteen-year-old to tag along to a business meeting might sound strange, but by then Gran made no bones about me being her successor. Fortunately, no one in my family was remotely interested in fighting me for the throne.

Certainly not my mother, Moira, busy from dawn to dusk running her law practice from a ground floor office in one of the new highrises on the Grand Concourse in the Bronx.

Nor was her younger half-brother, Blake, Kavanaugh's chief financial officer and Gran's son by Grandpa Adam, though my uncle had grown up believing that her first husband, Joe Kavanaugh, was his father. A natural introvert, he spent most days cocooned in his darkpaneled office down the hall from Gran's, poring over ledgers and stock reports and dictating serious-sounding letters to his secretary.

My brother, Neil, was another such lone wolf. The artist of the family, he had dropped out during his freshman year at the San Francisco Art Institute for reasons yet unknown to the rest of us. Back in New York and working as a window dresser in Kavanaugh's display design department, he seemed content as a nine-to-fiver.

That left me. At the risk of seeming to brag, I had always been Gran's favorite. As more cynical minds than mine hadn't hesitated to point out, her love for me was on par with Narcissus falling head-over-feet for his reflection. Unlike my blonde-haired, blueeyed brother, who favored our father, I was the spitting image of a young Rose O'Neill. Same creamy complexion, with the unfortunate tendency to freckle. Tawny brown eyes. Turned-up nose. Full mouth, a tad too wide but topped with a near-perfect bow. All of it, *the lot*, as Gran would say, framed by a cap of ginger-colored corkscrews impervious to straightening and sufficiently thick to tear the teeth off most combs. Keeping up the reputation of redheads, I'd inherited Gran's ironclad will as well. Once I made up my mind to something, I pursued it come hell or high water and pity the person who tried to stand in my way.

It wasn't until later, when the two of us had settled in the back of the Renault taxi, that Gran let the cat out of the bag about my surprise.

"31 rue Cambon," she instructed the driver.

For a dazzling few seconds, I wondered if I had heard right.

Thirty-one rue Cambon was the address of Maison Chanel. The flagship fashion house was a temple to haute couture. Its founder, Gabrielle "Coco" Chanel, had been my idol since I'd saved up my allowance and bought my first issue of *Vogue*.

I knew her origin story by heart. Like Gran, she had lost her mother at an early age. Both women had grown up poor, Gran on Ireland's Aran Islands, and Chanel in rural France. Both had started out designing women's hats, but dresses were the dream. Chanel's cotton jersey dress, launched in 1914 when fine fabrics were scarce due to the Great War, had placed her in the pantheon of great designers. Since then, she had singlehandedly transformed the landscape of women's fashion from boned corsets and hobble skirts to fisherman's sweaters and tailored trousers, cardigans paired with pleated skirts, and chic little black dresses. More than two decades later, women the world over embraced her signature sartorial simplicity.

Catching her sideways smile, I said, "Gran, really?"

"Yes, really," she confirmed, reaching across the seat to squeeze my hand, hers covered in wrist length cotton gloves that hid scars from a terrible fire in a hotel where she had worked as a chambermaid not long after coming to New York. "You are to select one outfit, my darling, whatever your heart desires."

"Oh, Gran, you're too good to me," I gushed, feeling dizzy with my great good fortune.

I had adored clothes all my life, since the days spent dressing my dollies in miniature couture replicas sewn by Kavanaugh's seamstresses, their splashy ensembles putting my friends' Raggedy Anns and Kewpie dolls to shame.

"That, my love, would be impossible."

Cruising along the Champs-Élysées, an early summer sun gilding the Arc de Triomphe, my window rolled down partway so that the warm breeze ruffled my hair like playful fingers, I felt like the luckiest girl alive.

We came to the corner of the rue St-Honoré and rue Cambon where the road opened onto a square in front of a large domed church. Our driver turned right onto rue Cambon, and my heartbeat picked up in anticipation. Craning to look past Gran to the view outside the passenger window, I counted five consecutive Chanel storefronts, at numbers 23, 25, 27, 29 and the flagship, number 31. Unlike New York, where we were frightfully fond of neon signage, discreet black lettering called out "CHANEL" from above plain white awnings.

Our taxi drew up to the curb, and I scrambled out, inelegant in my hurry, my skirt catching on the door handle. I managed to extricate myself without damage, and Gran and I approached the entrance to the boutique.

A doorman stood sentry, a big pink-cheeked fellow in a green ulster who looked like he'd be more at home on Gran's native Aran

Islands than at a fancy French fashion house. He touched his forelock in an old-fashioned show of respect and held the door for us to enter.

Feeling as if I were about to step upon sacred ground, I followed Gran inside, the boutique smaller than I'd envisioned and thrillingly chic, a cocoon of cream-colored walls, glass cases, and mirrors, the air perfumed with what I instantly recognized as Chanel No. 5. Black-clad saleswomen circulated, assisting shoppers and tidying the displays of handbags, shoes, gloves, hats, scarves, and the costume jewelry that Mademoiselle had popularized for daywear – long ropes of faux pearls and glass beads, chunky cuff bracelets, statement brooches and dramatic gold chains.

Gran approached a salesgirl stationed at the perfume counter near the front of the shop. Behind her, mirrored shelves held bottles of No. 5, by then the world's most famous fragrance.

"Mrs. Rose Kavanaugh Blakely and Miss Daisy Blakely from New York," Gran said, and that's when it hit me.

We weren't only here to shop. Gran's "tiny bit of business" was with the great Chanel herself!

They had met once before in 1931 when Chanel came to America to design costumes for the movie mogul, Samuel Goldwyn. Disgusted with the vulgarity of Hollywood, she had left after a month and taken a train to New York where she had spent several days touring the major Manhattan department stores, including Kavanaugh's. Gran couldn't have been more thrilled if royalty had visited.

"Mademoiselle Coco is expecting you, madame. *Un instant, s'il vous plaît.*" She picked up the handset of a gold and black house telephone and dialed.

A husky female voice issued forth from the phone. A few words were exchanged in French, and then the girl set the receiver back in its cradle and stepped out from behind the counter.

"Come with me, *s'il vous plaît*."

We followed her through a discreet inner doorway connecting the boutique to the atelier.

"Mademoiselle Coco will be down shortly," she told us and left.

We stood inside a gallery of unadorned ivory walls and shiny-black floors. Racks of white-cotton garment bags hung from gilt rails, veiling what remained of the most recent couture collection, or so I supposed.

A mirrored spiral staircase sprung from the room's center. I'd seen that staircase before, photographed for fashion magazines. It was from those beige-carpeted steps that Chanel staged her biannual fashion shows.

Feeling as if I were dreaming, I drifted over. The sense of being watched had me raising my gaze. A dark-haired pixie of indeterminate age stood at the top, one hand resting on the banister. Seeing me, she began her descent, the faceted mirrors multiplying her slight, chicly clad form, which seemed to float toward me.

La Grande Mademoiselle herself. Of course, she would make an entrance.

She wore one of her famous flecked tweed suits, and a bolero hat pinned atop her wavy chin-length bob. Both wrists were garlanded with gold bracelets that jangled with each downward step. Hanging around her slender neck, threaded on a white grosgrain ribbon, was a pair of silver scissors, along with a necklace of pearls the size of quail eggs.

She stopped at the second to last step and seized my shoulders, her grip so steely that I very nearly dropped my handbag.

"*Grandes épaules, une beauté!*" she exclaimed, the ferocity of her dark gaze bordering on frightening.

I caught "big" and "beauty" but not the rest and looked to Gran for guidance.

Coming to my rescue, she explained, "Mademoiselle Chanel says you have great shoulders and are a beautiful young woman."

Chanel's scarlet lips spread into a smile. "You know French, Madame Blakely?"

Ever modest, Gran admitted, "I've picked up a word or two over the years and have encouraged Daisy to do the same."

Though I was a lackluster student, French was the one high school subject to which I'd applied myself, if only so I could decipher the fashion captions in the issues of *Vogue France* when I got my hands on them.

Gran gestured to me. "Allow me to present my granddaughter, Daisy Blakely."

"*Enchantée.*" Chanel held out her hand.

Square palmed and big knuckled, it didn't quite fit with her petite, svelte frame and yet I was so awed to be in her presence that for half a minute I considered kissing her ring.

Gran's nudge brought me back from my stunned state. I took the offered hand, her steely grip swallowing mine in a brief but firm shake.

"It's an honor to meet you, *Mademoiselle*." I hesitated and then volunteered, "We almost met once before."

"*Vraiment?*" Dark half-moon brows steepled; the black-brown eyes beneath stayed skeptical.

"When you visited our store in New York," Gran answered for me. "Daisy was just eleven years old, and adamant that she must meet *La Grande Mademoiselle*. Unfortunately, she came down with chicken pox the day before your visit."

Gran's Irish charm worked its usual wonders. Mademoiselle's face softened.

"And now the bud has flowered into a beautiful young woman." Stepping off the landing, she ran her gaze over me as if cataloging every freckle, which no amount of Coty's Air-Spun face powder could conceal for long.

Looking from me to Gran, she said, "We will have lunch and get to know each other, but first I will take you on a little tour."

She turned and started up the beige-carpeted stairs.

Following her up, Gran behind me, I saw that each mirrored vertical pane was set at a different angle, fracturing our reflections as if we were the subjects of a Surrealist painting.

We stepped off onto the third-floor atelier where she employed more than one hundred seamstresses known as *petites mains*, "little hands." She led us into the first of several workrooms, large and square with tall windows overlooking rue Cambon. Seamstresses in black work smocks and neatly pinned back hair sat at their workstations, their fingers flying.

The babble of French subsided when they saw us. Chanel walked to the front of the room and announced, "*Voici* Madame Rose Kavanaugh Blakely and her granddaughter, Mademoiselle Daisy Blakely of Kavanaugh's Department Store in New York."

Murmured greetings in French chorused, mostly *bonjours* and *enchantées,* and then she introduced her senior staff, starting with Madame Angèle Aubrey, her right-hand woman for more than thirty years, and Madame Giselle Millet, her *première atelier*, chief seamstress, for nearly as long.

"Not everyone can qualify as a *petite main*," she told Gran and me afterwards. "Only those who have completed their studies. An average of ten years of experience is required to attain the professional level," she added with palpable pride.

"Such diligence and discipline," Gran remarked. "You are to be commended, mademoiselle."

Chanel accepted the compliment with a spare nod and led us back out to the stairs. We descended one flight to her private residence guarded by mirrored double doors.

A dark foyer led into the apartment. Passing a Louis XVI-style chaise longue upholstered in white satin, I recognized it as the one Mademoiselle had posed in for *Vogue* the previous year, and a shivery thrill shot through me. The famous German American fashion photographer, Horst P. Horst, had captured her in profile, looking dreamily off into the distance, dressed all in black, a hairbow atop her wavy, chin-length dark hair, an artful tangle of gold chains carelessly cascading below her breasts. Holding a half-smoked cigarette between her thumb and index finger as a man might do, she epitomized the modern woman I desperately aspired to be.

Like the boutique, the apartment was more compact than I had expected, three rooms furnished in a palette of cream and beige: a dining room, parlor, and pocket-sized study with a rolltop desk and shelves of books, their tooled leather spines picking up the golden hue of the wallpaper. Unlike so many successful self-made people who lard their homes with impersonal luxury, Mademoiselle Coco seemed to have an intimate connection to every object on display. Before sitting down to lunch, she took us through, pointing out her treasures.

A gilded Russian icon was a gift from the composer, Stravinsky.

"I first met Igor in 1913 when his ballet, *Le Sacre du Printemps*, premiered at the Théâtre des Champs-Élysées," she told us, straightening the picture frame. "It was as if the theater had been visited by an earthquake, the boos, hisses, and shouted insults at times drowning out the music. The critics called it the work of a madman, but I recognized his genius even then."

The oil painting of a single shaft of wheat hanging above the beige suede sofa was by Salvador Dalí.

"Salvo stays at La Pausa, my villa on the Riviera, when he needs quiet to work," she said.

The burgundy lacquered Coromandel screens in every room were from Chanel's great love, the English polo player, Arthur "Boy" Capel, who had died in 1919 when his motorcar crashed at Puget-sur-Argens on his way to Cannes to spend Christmas with her.

"Boy knew I detested doors, "she said, her expression wistful. "I use them to hide all the exits so my guests will forget to leave."

Conspicuously absent was a bedroom.

As if reading my thoughts, she said, "I like my privacy; I never sleep where I work. I keep a suite at the Ritz for sleeping." She walked over to the floor-to-ceiling window and pulled back the drapes. "Come look."

It took me a minute to realize she meant me.

At Gran's nudge, I joined her at the window. Looking out across rue Cambon, I saw the back of a massive building of gleaming limestone and royal blue canopies.

"Voilà, the Hôtel Ritz. The Place Vendôme side where I have my suite was an eighteenth-century *palais*. But I always go in and out through the rue Cambon side. That way I do not have to see the *Italienne's* vulgar shop," she added, making a face as if a noxious odor had invaded the room.

"The *Italienne*?" I echoed, again looking to Gran for guidance.

"I believe Mademoiselle refers to Elsa Schiaparelli," Gran answered evenly. "She has her atelier on Place Vendôme."

Mademoiselle Coco let the curtain drop and turned back to us. "She calls me the Hat Maker, can you imagine?" She sniffed, shaking her head in disgust. "I ought to call her the Sweater Maker."

I had read somewhere that the Italian born Schiaparelli had got her start in New York, where she had lived for six years in a shabby Greenwich Village walkup supporting herself and her polio-afflicted daughter by selling her hand-knit sweaters.

"But I am talking too much," Mademoiselle continued. "I talk vehemently, I know I can be unbearable," she insisted, despite Gran and me assuring her it wasn't so. "You must be hungry. Americans are always hungry, always obsessed with food, eating too much, and eating badly. Come, we will eat well."

A square walnut table dominated the dining room, a brace of bronze lions set at its center. On impulse, I reached out and patted their heads.

Slipping into her chair at the head of the table, Chanel said, "I am Leo, the fifth house of the zodiac."

We took our seats. Two maids materialized through a side door carrying platters of food, followed by a butler who circulated with a white cloth-wrapped bottle of champagne, a decadence Gran declined but which, being newly turned eighteen, I accepted with enthusiasm.

The lunch was delicious, a feast and very French. Several dishes like duck liver pâté and a savory bacon and cheese pie called Quiche Lorraine were new to me. Salad Niçoise I'd had before, though *never* one this tasty. There was also an assortment of cheeses, a few of which I recognized or thought I did. I tried some of each, skipping back and forth between soft and hard and mild and pungent selections, not then knowing I was meant to sample them in order. Helping myself to more of the brie, I caught Mademoiselle Coco watching me.

"You are enjoying your *déjeuner*, mademoiselle?" she asked, smiling thinly.

Mouth full, the best I could do was nod.

Gran saved me by speaking up. "Your chef is superb. I wonder if he might be persuaded to share some of his recipes?"

Sipping her wine, Mademoiselle Coco admitted, "I have everything brought over from the Ritz. I must. I have no kitchen."

Dessert consisted of shell-shaped miniature sponge cakes called madeleines and apple and caramel tartines. Mademoiselle Coco took a bite of tartine and then pushed her plate away.

Reaching into her jacket pocket, she brought out an octagonal silver-and-gold cigarette box engraved with a coat of arms. She nonchalantly slipped a cigarette between her scarlet lips and lit it, and I fought to keep my mouth from falling open.

Both Gran and my mother were adamant about no smoking at the table. Whenever Grandpa Adam and my dad indulged in the occasional cigar, they were banished to the study or patio.

Mademoiselle Coco held the case out to me. "Like one?"

Gran answered for me. "Daisy doesn't smoke."

"How very American," Mademoiselle remarked, blowing an acrid jet toward the high curved ceiling.

Afterwards, she took us to the mirrored couture salon where three folding chairs were set out. Pleasantly tipsy from the single glass of champagne I'd drunk, I sat next to Gran, my brain blanketed in a lovely, soft buzzing that made everything seem mellow and right.

Glancing over my shoulder, I saw Madame Aubrey roll in a Victrola on casters. Outside the door, Madame Millet marshaled a group of models to fall into line.

Chanel slipped into the empty chair on my left. At her signal, a record started up, "Isn't It Romantic?" sung by the French crooner and actor, Maurice Chevalier.

Heart racing, I watched as the mannequins entered one by one and made their way to the front of the room. Tall and willowy, swan-necked and slim-hipped, each girl was more lovely and graceful than the last, their sleek, cropped coiffures putting my shoulder-length mop to shame, their perfectly penciled eyebrows and red lips straight out of a glamour magazine.

But it was the clothes that I coveted, Chanel creations from previous collections, some of which I had seen in magazines. There were jersey suits, dresses with matching jackets, daytime-to-cocktails ensembles, and lastly, an off-the-shoulder sleeveless gown in white lace I couldn't take my eyes off.

Leaning in, I whispered to Gran, "It's like a dream. I keep feeling like if I pinch myself, I'll wake up."

She reached over and squeezed my hand. "Not a dream, darling girl. Every young lady should spend some time in Paris. This is *your* time. Savor every moment."

The last model reached the front of the room, and I popped up from my seat, clapping like I was in the stands at Yankee Stadium.

Chanel rose and joined her models at the front of the room. "*Avec plaisir*, I welcome Mademoiselle Blakely to our Chanel family. In one week, she will begin as my apprentice, assisting with the spring and fall collections."

Wondering if the champagne had hurt my hearing, I whipped my head around to Gran.

Beaming at me, she said, "Happy birthday, darling."

Chapter Two

That night Gran and I recalled our day over tea and macarons in her suite, the two of us lounging on the sofa in our pajamas, my new Chanel gown hanging in a white-cotton garment bag in the wardrobe.

"*Bit of business*, my foot!" I exclaimed for the umpteenth time, the magnitude of her surprise taking its time to sink in. "You certainly kept your cards close to your chest. I never suspected a thing."

"It wouldn't have been a surprise if you had," she pointed out.

I picked a pink macaron from the tiered chinaware tray on the tea table and popped it into my mouth. "Eight whole months in Paris. I still can't believe you got Mom to agree."

Their mother-daughter relationship hadn't always gone smoothly. Both possessed strong personalities and were as different as night-and-day. Mutual admiration had taken its time in coming, but when it did, it stuck, cemented by a shared personal tragedy – the loss of my mother's beloved twin, Joey, killed fighting in France during the Great War.

My favorite photograph of Mom was a studio photographic portrait taken before that sad event, when she was about my age. Wearing suffragette white, a sash slung across her breast emblazoned with "Votes for Women Now," her straight, dark hair reaching her waist, she seemed poised to march out of the picture: a glorious, force-of-nature female for whom her future daughter's preoccupation with pretty dollies and party dresses and later, "frivolous fashion magazines," would land as a bit of a blow. A founder of the Bronx Women's Bar Association, Mom had devoted her life to paving the way for other women to enter the professions. That I, her only daughter, had absolutely no interest in being a doctor or lawyer was tough to take.

Gran sucked her teeth, bringing me back from my musings. "I presented it to her as your year abroad," she said. "And promised that you'd enroll in business school as soon as you're back."

I groaned. Business college was the compromise I had hammered out with my parents after high school graduation and which I had dreaded every day since. Four more years of sitting in classrooms with dull professors droning on and assigning readings from dry-as-dust textbooks – how would I stand it?

"I don't see why I should. I already know what I want to do with my life. Work with you on setting up a Kavanaugh's here in Paris. Surely an apprenticeship at a famous French atelier beats any stuffy old business school."

Gran arched a brow. "Darling girl, Kavanaugh's isn't going anywhere, and neither am I. A deal's a deal."

Rather than press my luck, I changed the subject. "Tell me more about this feud Mademoiselle Coco has with Elsa Schiaparelli."

"Oh, they're old rivals. The bad blood peaked two years ago when Schiap, as she's known to her friends, did the unpardonable." She paused to sip her tea.

Sensing there was more, I waited. Being Irish born, Gran knew how to spin out a story. Rushing her rarely got me anywhere.

Setting the cup and saucer aside, she picked up where she had left off. "She partnered with Chanel's artist friend, Salvador Dalí."

"The one who painted the chaff of wheat we saw?"

Gran nodded. "A departure from his usual Surrealist style but yes. Together, they created a couture collection inspired by his artwork: A mirror suit with trompe-l'oeil pockets in the shape of boxes and buttons made of drawer handles; a handbag in the form of a telephone; a skirt with flaps that looked like lips; an evening dress skirt with a life-size lobster printed on it. No one, including Chanel, had ever seen anything like it. The searing colors, the outrageous designs were the antithesis of her trademark simplicity – and clients went wild for it. They still do."

"What happened after?" I asked.

"Chanel took Mr. Goldwyn up on his offer: one million dollars to come out to Hollywood and design costumes for his leading ladies, including Gloria Swanson. A staggering sum, to be sure, but those in the know have speculated that Mademoiselle's going was more to do with saving face than making money."

"Paris wasn't big enough for her and Schiaparelli both?" I surmised, feeling terribly sophisticated and grown up to be having such a conversation.

"It seems so," Gran said. "Only Hollywood wasn't ready for Chanel. Her designs weren't sufficiently flashy for the silver screen. The relationship with the studio soured. After a month of gowning starlets in Tinseltown, she took the train to New York and then a ship back to Paris to take up where she had left off, including her rivalry with Schiap."

It seemed even the *Grande Mademoiselle* had her challenges.

Gran hesitated. "But Daisy, don't you go getting caught up in all that. Allegiances in the fashion world are notoriously fickle. Friends turn to foes with the snap of a finger. Better to ignore gossip and concentrate on learning everything you can."

Her serious tone had me sitting up straighter. "I'll work hard and make you proud, I promise."

"I know you will, dear, you're my blood after all, but I also want you to take time to enjoy yourself. Eavesdrop on conversations in cafés. Walk the streets F. Scott Fitzgerald, Ernest Hemingway, and Djuna Barnes trod in the twenties. It's no coincidence that the most brilliant minds of the new century flocked here after the Great War, a lost generation seeking to make sense, and art, from catastrophe. Soak up everything you can, the beauty and the grit. We're only young once."

"Mademoiselle Coco certainly seems to have drunk from the fountain of youth," I mused aloud, unable to resist bringing the conversation back to Chanel. "I've never met anyone like her."

The famous designer, then fifty-five years old, had run circles around her staff. By the time we had left that afternoon, she was still brimming with vitality, more like a young girl than a woman in the latter half of life.

Gran picked up the teapot and topped off our cups. "I can't say I have either," she admitted, "and I've lived a good deal longer than you. By the by, before we left, I had her promise to keep an eye out for you."

"Oh, Gran, you didn't?" I said, momentarily mortified that Mademoiselle Coco might see me as a baby in need of sitting.

"Only until you find your footing. Paris is very different to New York, and this is your first time abroad, after all. For the record, her response was *avec plaisir*."

For the first time since we'd stepped off the boat train from Le Havre, Gran looked less than sure of herself.

"I wasn't wrong to spring this on you, was I? The apprenticeship is meant as an opportunity for you to learn the ins and outs of the French fashion trade from a master, but you don't have to stay if you don't want to. I can come up with an excuse, and you'll go back to New York with me at the end of the week without anyone being the wiser."

Panicked that my present might be snatched away, I rushed to reassure her. "No, please don't. I'm thrilled, really, I am. And so lucky. The luckiest girl in the world."

Her face softened. "It's me who's the lucky one. From the moment you were old enough to walk and talk, I knew you'd carry on Kavanaugh's after I'm gone." She reached over and squeezed my hand, my fingers sticky from the sweets.

"Don't say such things! You're young yet," I insisted.

A world without my grandmother wasn't one I cared to contemplate.

She tucked a loose curl behind my ear. "Don't fret, I'm not looking to punch my ticket just yet. But I do want you to know what a comfort you are to me."

Mollified, I settled back against the sofa cushions.

"Enough shoptalk," she announced, picking up the Monmarche guidebook from the table and cracking it open. "We have six whole days of vacation before I leave for home, and you start at Maison Chanel. Let's make good use of them."

As all good things do, our week together in Paris flew by. Whether smiling back at the Mona Lisa at the Louvre, riding a glass-cage elevator to the top of the Eiffel Tower or sitting on the deck of one of the tour boats gliding along the Seine, the City of Light provided endless entertainments.

More than any sightseeing attraction, it was the Parisians who fascinated me most. The women in their colorful silk scarves and casually upswept hair seemed chicer and more confident than we did in New York. The men looked dignified yet relaxed.

On Gran's last day, we lunched *en plein air* at Les Deux Magots, the Left Bank café that was a legendary gathering spot for famous artists and writers. Lingering over glasses of chilled white wine and plates of escargot served in savory garlic herb butter, we got a kick out of watching our fellow patrons passionately arguing over politics, art or which café served the best *crème brulée*.

"Your grandfather swears the Left Bank is the real Paris," Gran said. "The Paris of artists, philosophers and writers."

Looking around at the several patrons lunching solo, sketching or scribbling earnestly in their moleskin notebooks, I was inclined to agree.

Afterwards, Gran suggested we stop in at Shakespeare and Company bookstore, a short walk away at 12 rue de l'Odéon, to pay our respects to the American proprietor, Sylvia Beach. With the encouragement of her French friend, Adrienne Monnier, Miss Beach had opened Shakespeare and Company in 1919 as an English language bookstore and lending library. According to Gran, Miss Beach was a great friend to all writers but especially to American expats, such as Ernest Hemingway, F. Scott Fitzgerald, and E.E. Cummings, who had poured into Paris in the postwar Prohibition years.

We crossed the cobblestone street, and I spied Grandpa Adam's latest novel among the new books in the store window. I pointed it out to Gran, who smiled and took out her Kodak camera to snap a picture.

"Your grandfather will consider this as great an honor as being named on the *New York Times*' bestseller list," she exclaimed, slipping the camera back in her handbag.

The shop bell announced our entry with a soft trilling. Books lined the walls from floor to ceiling. More were shelved in freestanding bookcases or displayed on tables according to subject. Framed photographs of famous writers, living and dead, were hung about. Several plump, threadbare armchairs were arranged around a big coal stove, which must make everything wonderfully cozy in the winter. I could imagine patrons coming in from the cold, knocking snow from their hats and coats, and pulling up a seat to read.

A young woman stood on a ladder in the stacks, reshelving books from a trolley. Gran walked up, introduced herself as Mrs. Adam Blakely from New York, and asked if Miss Beach was in.

At the mention of "Blakely," the girl's face lit up, and she quickly descended. "I will let her know you are here."

She disappeared into a curtained-off area at the back of the store, and we used the wait to browse. I spotted *Ulysses* by the Irish writer, James Joyce and recalled Grandpa Adam saying that Miss Beach was a heroine in literary circles for publishing the novel at her own expense after the U.S. and Joyce's native Ireland banned it as obscene.

"I still don't see what could be so bad about a book," I said, pulling the heavy volume from its place on the shelf.

Though a copy held pride of place in Grandpa Adam's study, so far, I had only flipped through its eight hundred pages, searching without success for the naughty parts.

Gran thought for a moment. "Not bad, different. Freedom must always be defended, Daisy. Not only bodily freedom but spiritual and intellectual freedom, too."

Before I could ask more, a twig-like woman of middle age stepped out from the back of the shop. She wore her wavy brown hair shorn to her ears and with a deep side part. Lively brown eyes looked us over. Me being me, my attention turned to her clothes, a full, tweedy skirt such as a schoolmarm might wear, a high-collared white blouse, and a baggy cardigan that looked like it was meant for a man, with pockets that drooped as if she'd shoved her hands inside one time too many. Miss Beach, I presumed.

Face wreathed in smiles, she walked up to my grandmother and stuck out her hand. "Mrs. Blakely, what an absolute delight to see you again."

"It's Rose, please, and I'm surprised you remember me, Miss Beach. When last I was here, it was on honeymoon with my husband nearly sixteen years ago."

"Nonsense, you're aging like a fine wine," Miss Beach answered, gaze going over Gran's svelte figure, shown off to advantage by the tailored navy Chanel suit.

Miss Beach pulled a volume off a shelf labelled "American Fiction." The Kelly-green book jacket was battered, and coffee stained, and yet I knew that novel as well as I knew my grandmother's face.

My Wild Irish Rose by Adam Blakely.

Grandpa Adam's debut novel was a fictionalized retelling of his and Gran's love story, from their first meeting on the Aran Islands when Grandpa was a young soldier wounded fighting the Spaniards in Cuba, and Gran a barmaid at her family's pub on Inishmore.

"Still one of our most frequently borrowed books," Miss Beach said, returning it to its prominent place on the shelf.

"Adam will be so pleased," Gran said. "Although he has written six novels since, he still swears it's his favorite."

"We have them all." Miss Beach gestured to a row marked as "B" where Grandpa Adam's more recent works were shelved. Her gaze shifted to me. "And who might this be?"

"Allow me to introduce my granddaughter, Daisy. Starting next week, she'll apprentice at Maison Chanel," Gran added with palpable pride.

"How long are you staying in Paris, dear?" Miss Beach asked me.

"A whole eight months, lucky me. I'll get to help with both the August and February collections."

Maison Chanel released two collections a year, summer and winter, always on the fifth of the month, five being Mademoiselle's lucky number.

"A splendid opportunity," Miss Beach agreed. "Prepare to have the time of your life. As my great friend Mr. Hemingway is fond of saying, Paris is a movable feast. Adrienne and I must have you to one of our dinner parties once you're settled. It won't be formal at all; it never is in our house; people don't dress up. But it's always an interesting evening; one never knows who might drop by. By the by, where will you be living?"

Amid trying to keep up with her rapid-fire speech, I realized I hadn't given any thought to lodgings. "I have absolutely no idea," I admitted, looking to Gran. So much for being grown-up and independent.

"I'd planned to put Daisy up at the Ritz, so she can be close to the atelier," Gran answered.

"A five-minute walk along rue Cambon, you couldn't ask for greater convenience," Miss Beach agreed, though I sensed there was a "but" coming. "But I do wonder if that might not be too close. The Ritz is divine, the best hotel in Paris, but it can be a bit of a fishbowl, if you take my meaning."

Gran considered that for a minute. "We'd be grateful for any recommendations."

Miss Beach glanced between us. "I know a widow, Madame LeBrun, with an apartment house on rue Saint-Lazare in the eighth. Nothing extravagant, but it's clean and decent, and she provides a hot breakfast and supper. And it's a short bicycle ride to Maison Chanel." She looked at me. "Bicycles, autobuses and the Métro are how the real Parisians get about. I can give you her address if you like."

"Do, please," Gran said.

Miss Beach pulled a notepad from her pocket. Taking the pencil from behind her ear, she scribbled down the address and handed it to Gran.

"We'll call on Madame LeBrun directly. Thank you, Sylvia."

"Not at all. We Yanks must stick together." Her gaze flickered back to me, and she clasped my hand in both of hers. "Should you ever find yourself lonely or in the slightest difficulty, know you can call on Adrienne and me anytime, day or night."

"That's very kind of you, Miss Beach. I will, thank you."

"We don't stand on formality here. You must call me Sylvia."

"Yes, Miss ... Sylvia."

Wine at lunch and now addressing adults by their first names. Stepping out to join Gran on the sidewalk, I had a strong feeling I was going to like living in Paris.

Chapter Three

Less than an hour later, we stood outside what must have been an elegant limestone manse at one time, the blue painted shutters peeling, though the window boxes on the upper balconies spilled forth with a profusion of flowers – geraniums, hydrangeas, roses, and others I recognized but didn't know the names of.

Several knocks brought a sharp-featured, apron-clad Frenchwoman to the door, presumably the proprietress, Madame LeBrun. Judging from the fragrant smells wafting our way and a smudge of what looked like flour on her cheek, we had interrupted her baking.

Sizing us up, she asked in English, "What can I do for you?"

"Mademoiselle Beach of Shakespeare and Company mentioned you might have a flat for let," Gran began.

At the mention of Miss Beach, Madame LeBrun's demeanor softened. "Come in," she said, stepping back to make room for us.

We entered a dark foyer with a central staircase leading upwards and a chipped console table piled with mail.

Madame LeBrun clicked her tongue. "I *had* an apartment, a small one. I just let it to an English girl. *Je suis desolée.*"

Not as *desolée* as I was. What terrible timing!

"That is a pity," Gran agreed. She glanced at me. "My granddaughter is in Paris for the next eight months for an apprenticeship at Maison Chanel."

Creaking boards brought my attention back to the staircase where a pretty, plump young woman with a sandy blonde bob, broad forehead and bright pink lipstick was making her way down.

She stepped off the landing and walked up to me.

"You're starting at Maison Chanel?" she asked in Cockney-accented English.

"I am," I admitted. "And this location would have been perfect but ... well, *c'est la vie*."

I started to turn away, but she reached out and grabbed my arm. "Me, too. I'll be working in the boutique as a salesgirl, I mean *vendeuse*." She giggled and I glimpsed the gap between her front teeth, the slight flaw adding to her cheeky charm.

"Paris is a small world, I guess. Well, congratulations on the job and the apartment." I looked over at Gran, not wanting to waste any more of our last day together.

"This may sound mad but what if we were to share?" She looked from Gran and me to the landlady.

"There are two beds," Madame LeBrun said.

Gran intervened. "Before anything is decided, we'll have a look first, with your permission, madame."

The landlady gestured to the stairs. "*Après vous*."

We took the stairs to the fifth floor, the English girl, who introduced herself as Bridget Ponsby, leading the way.

"Cracking, isn't it?" she exclaimed, charging inside as if she had moved in already.

I followed her in. A painted screen separated the main living area from the bedroom. A hotplate and coffee press sat out on a small kitchen table. There was an old sofa and ottoman, both patterned in faded fleur-de-lis, and a pedestal sink, the porcelain chipped in places, but no toilet, at least none that I could see. When Gran tested the taps, it took a while for the rust to clear.

She shut off the water and walked back to me. Dropping her voice, she said, "It's not too late to reconsider. I haven't released the room at the Ritz. You'd have it all to yourself. En-suite bathroom, too."

As if sensing she was about to lose our business, Madame LeBrun spoke up. "There is a *toilette* and bath down the hall. You would share it with only one other lodger, Monsieur Levy, a widower, very quiet and regular in his habits. My son Olivier and I live one floor below."

"Splitting will make things easier on us both," Bridget chimed in, having no way of knowing that I, or at least my family, was rich.

I stepped around the screen and looked into the bedroom. A nightstand and table lamp sat between two narrow beds outfitted with faded quilts and lumpy-looking pillows. There was also a dresser painted green and chipped in places, and a walnut wardrobe that stuck when I tried to open it.

Addressing Gran, Madame LeBrun said, "For both girls, I will charge only a few francs more. For the breakfast and the *dîner*. And the linens," she clarified in response to Gran's sharp look.

"How few exactly?" Gran asked, still a thrifty Irishwoman to her core and not about to be taken advantage of.

She and Madame LeBrun retreated to a corner to haggle, and I chewed my lower lip, pondering. If I stayed at the Hôtel Ritz or another similarly glitzy hotel, I would remain a tourist, always somewhat removed from the city, knowing that merely by picking up the house telephone I could secure room service, laundry service, car service and whatever else I desired. If I lived here, there would be mishaps and messiness and confusion, but I would be forced to find my own way in this fascinating and thoroughly magical city.

Gran walked up, breaking into my thoughts. "It's your decision, Daisy. You're the one who'll be living here. What do you think?"

I took a last look around. No doubt about it, the flat was dark and dingy and down-at-heel, the opposite of the comfort I had grown up with. But there was also a tall window that opened onto a wrought-iron balcony. Stepping out, I saw it had its very own window box sprouting a flourish of flowers as well as a view worthy of a postcard.

Turning back, I answered, "I think it's perfect."

The next morning, a hotel porter loaded Gran's luggage into the trunk of one of the taxis lined up outside the hotel entrance. To stretch out our time together, we had agreed that I would accompany her as far as the train station.

We settled into the backseat, and the taxi nosed into the traffic on boulevard Raspail.

Gran fretted her lower lip as she sometimes did when she was puzzling out a problem. "I hope we did the right thing in taking that room," she said.

It wasn't like her to second-guess herself. Not wanting her to worry, I rushed to reassure her. "Bridget seems nice and outgoing. She's been in Paris a few weeks already, so she knows the lay of the land. I'll have a ready-made friend in the city. An *English-speaking* friend, though her French is loads better than mine. With both of us working at Maison Chanel, we can look out for one another there, too."

Her expression eased, and she patted my hand. "I'm sure you're right, and it will all work out. And if it not, we can always put you up at the Ritz or another nearby hotel. Which reminds me, I'll telegraph Blake from the ship and have him wire you the money."

"What money?" For the first time it occurred to me to wonder if my apprenticeship was unpaid.

"You'll receive a small wage from Maison Chanel, but it won't be sufficient to live on," she said.

This from a woman who had come to New York with hardly a penny in her pocket.

"I'm sure I can manage."

All my life, I'd fought against being pigeonholed as a poor little rich girl. Meeting someone like Bridget, who had gotten herself to Paris under her own steam only fueled my determination to be more independent. More like Gran had been at my age.

Gran's brow furrowed. "I don't like to think of you over here alone and purse pinched. Take it, for my sake."

"Thank you," I said, though I vowed then and there not to touch so much as a penny.

It wasn't until the taxi let us out at Gare Saint-Lazare that reality sank in. I wouldn't be seeing Gran or the rest of the family for eight months. Standing outside the entrance to the classical-style stone station, I couldn't seem to stop hugging her.

Pulling back, I pleaded, "Sure you can't stay longer?"

She sighed. "Your grandfather might have something to say about that."

I recalled the telegram Gran had received at the hotel desk that morning, the third from him in a week. "Missing you, is he?"

She nodded. "The muse overseeing his latest book doesn't seem to be cooperating. If he'd come along, he would have spent most of his time holed up in the hotel room writing, or so he says."

Reading between the lines, I asked, "You don't believe him?"

She hesitated. "I believe he knows what this trip means to us and didn't want to be in the way. That's the measure of true love, Daisy. Knowing when to hold on and when to let go."

I gave her a final, hard hug and stepped back. "Send me a telegram once you're settled aboard?"

"I will." She framed my face between her gloved hands. "Write us every week and call home at least one Sunday a month, more often if you're lonely."

I struck a smile to make up for my damp eyes. "I will, I promise."

She picked up her valise, the same threadbare, needlepoint satchel she'd brought with her from Ireland in 1898, when a change of linens, sewing kit, and my late Great-Uncle Danny's rosary were the sum of her worldly possessions.

"Look after yourself, darling. And remember, if you change your mind, you can always come home."

"Goodbye, Gran."

Eyes shining with unshed tears, she shook her head. "No, darling girl, not goodbye. It's bad luck. Better we say, 'go safely for now'."

Chapter Four

My first week at Maison Chanel was in every way a trial by fire – and Mademoiselle Coco the flamethrower. Her moods were mercurial, seesawing from extravagant displays of affection to foot-stamping furies.

Within the first hour of my first day, she announced that I would be known as Marguerite, the French for Daisy. In her mind, my willingness to answer to the translated version of my name was never in doubt, but then she was accustomed to those around her bending to her will. Why should I, an upstart heiress from America, be any different?

As prearranged by Gran, my principal assignment was to shadow Mademoiselle Coco in the atelier, but I would also help out in the boutique as I had at Kavanaugh's. I quickly fell into a routine, my days patterned according to our opening and closing hours. Unlike Gran, Mademoiselle Coco was not an early riser. After a leisurely breakfast, she emerged from the swinging back doors of the Ritz, crossed rue Cambon, and made the five-minute walk to No. 31, rarely arriving before 11 a.m.

One of the *vendeuses* stood sentry at the boutique entrance to alert us. "*Elle vient!*" She is coming!

We would all snap to attention, the models madly putting on their makeup, the *vendeuses* spritzing the entrance and grand staircase with atomizers of No. 5.

As if oblivious to the behind-the-scenes fuss, Mademoiselle would sail inside, bid us a collective "*bonne journée*" and head up the mirrored staircase, issuing directives in husky French.

Once inside her workroom, she was all business. A cigarette dangling from her scarlet mouth, she began by selecting fabrics, pairing them with various trimmings, and then discarding what she didn't like.

Next came the design. I never once saw her sketch anything in advance. Instead, she began by draping fabric over the mannequin, adjusting as she went, wielding the silver shears on the ribbon around her neck. More than once, I held my breath as her flying blades cut close to the model's collar, making me fear the poor girl would lose an ear tip. No one ever did.

Draping, pinning, cutting, looping – the process often went on for hours, with the rest of us standing in absolute silence. Only once she was satisfied did she turn the mockup over to the pattern makers. The next day, they presented the completed sample for her approval. If it didn't satisfy, she ripped it apart and had the *cabbage* carried away, no matter how costly the materials. If it did, she proceeded to tuck and pin, and then the finished sample was sent back to the senior seamstresses to sew the final garment.

Fascinated, I couldn't get enough of watching her.

Catching my steady stare from the side of her eye, she snapped, "Marguerite, your eyes will fall out."

Despite her curt tone, I sensed she appreciated my studious devotion.

I quickly came to appreciate the recurrent design features that underscored her celebrated simplicity: a high armhole, narrow sleeves, and a small shoulder; the latter to make the wearer appear more svelte.

At 1:30 p.m., we broke for lunch, which she often took in the Ritz dining room with its towering blue ceiling, cream-colored walls, and arched windows draped in gold satin. Around three o' clock, she returned to her atelier apartment for a catnap on the sofa. Twenty minutes later, she emerged refreshed and ready to pick up where we had left off.

Unlike Kavanaugh's, no one at Maison Chanel punched a time-clock. We knew we were done for the day when Mademoiselle Coco removed the ribbon with the scissors from around her neck and broke her silence, usually something along the lines of: "Now ... there you are ... it's not so tacky, is it? Not too bad, don't you think?"

Going between the atelier and the hotel delivering messages, confirming appointments, whatever errand I was given, I quickly became acquainted with the senior hotel staff. The managing director, Claude Auzello, a short wisp of a man with a pencil mustache and a dignified demeanor that would have come off as stuffy for an American but for a Frenchman seemed just right. Working with him was his American wife, Blanche, a brassy bottle blonde and former film actress who adored juicy gossip and dry martinis. Olivier Dabescat, the obsequious maître d'hôtel, ran the hotel dining room as if it were a battleship. Jacques, the doorman in top hat and black overcoat, rang the boutique every morning to tip us off when Mademoiselle was on her way.

At the end of my first week, Mademoiselle Coco invited me to join her for a drink at the Ritz.

"I am an ogre, and yet you are still here. We must celebrate your fortitude," she insisted, her voice carrying to the workroom's four corners.

While over the moon at this clear mark of her favor, I was also acutely aware of the envious looks veering my way. Avoiding Madame Millet's gimlet gaze, I collected my handbag and followed Mademoiselle down the mirrored stairs.

We entered the Ritz from the rue Cambon rear entrance, stepping inside a boutique size lobby. Bellhops and porters and other members of staff went about their day, everyone dressed in smart royal blue uniforms and spotless white gloves.

Flanking either side of the reception area were the bar and ladies' lounge. Without thinking, I headed for the lounge.

Mademoiselle Coco caught my arm. "That is for dull women who hide away and play bridge. We are *bon vivants, femmes nouvelles*. For us, the American bar."

We entered the wood-paneled barroom, a cozy enclave of backgammon tables and plush club chairs, with a polished ebony bar backed by an enormous hunting mural. Mademoiselle walked up to the bartender, leaving me to follow.

"Frank, this is my new apprentice, Mademoiselle Daisy Blakely from New York," she said, the first time in a week I'd heard my given name on her lips. "Daisy, Monsieur Meier, head barman at the Ritz and the author of *The Artistry of Mixing Drinks*."

Looking to be in his early fifties, Monsieur Meier was built like a boxer, his stocky frame smoothed out by a pristine white bar jacket, his dark hair meticulously oiled and parted in the center. A salt-and-pepper chevron mustache sat atop a friendly smile.

"A pleasure, *mademoiselle*. What may I get you ladies this evening?" he asked in English, with a trace of Germanic accent.

Never having been to a bar before, I looked to Mademoiselle Coco.

"Champagne," she said without having to think about it.

He inclined his head. "I have a very nice Château Latour on ice."

Having no idea what that was, I figured that if the Ritz served it, it must be good. Not just good. *Ritzy*.

We took a table facing the door, and Frank brought our drinks over, two fizzing flutes carried on a silver tray along with a crystal bud vase that held a single pink rose. Seeing it made me think of Gran and Kavanaugh's, and I felt a stab of homesickness.

"*Santé*," Mademoiselle said, saluting me with her flute.

We had just gotten our first sip down when a party of five bounded in, all talking at once, their flushed faces and high-pitched babble, in French, of course, driving my suspicion that they'd started drinking already. I recognized the dark-haired beauty in her early forties and the older man with the waxed handlebar mustache as the French film stars Arletty and Sasha Guitry. I had seen their movie, *The Pearls of the Crown*, when it had played at the World Theater on West 49th Street in New York.

The slender man with the long, thin face and poof of fluffy auburn hair was tougher to place. It wasn't until Chanel leaped up from her chair and exclaimed, "*Le Prince Frivole est arrivé!*" that my memory kicked in. Jean Cocteau, the poet, playwright, and novelist sometimes known as the Frivolous Prince after the title of one of his many works. I had seen his author photograph on the book jacket of Grandpa Adam's copy of his novel, *Les Enfants Terribles*.

I had met the big-boned, florid-featured older woman with frizzy red hair earlier in the week when she'd stopped by the atelier. The Polish-Russian socialite, Misia Sert, divorced from her third husband, a Spanish muralist. Chanel had introduced her as her best friend from their youth when she was an up-and-coming designer and Misia the toast of bohemian Paris.

The quintet crowded around us, speaking in rapid-fire French I couldn't begin to follow and cheek-kissing as if they hadn't seen each other in months, years, instead of days. A junior barman I hadn't noticed before, whose name pin read "Georges," came over to serve us. Squeezed out of my seat, I looked on as additional chairs were carried over and tables pushed together. A fresh bottle of champagne was brought out and glasses poured and passed around. When Mademoiselle Coco announced she was hungry and wanted canapés for the table, I seized on the excuse to go over to the bar and place the order myself.

I recited our selections to Frank, who passed them on to yet another junior barman to give to the kitchen.

When he turned back, I still stood there, gripping the bar rail like it was a lifeline and, I am sure, looking rather forlorn.

"They can be a bit overwhelming, can't they?" he said, not really a question.

I hesitated, and then admitted, "My French isn't good enough yet to keep up. It's very different from the French I learned in New York."

His warm smile put me immediately at ease. "Wonderful city, New York. I miss it." He picked up a Turkish towel and began buffing an already spotless piece of stemware as if he had all the time in the world.

"Were you there long?" I asked, grateful to have someone to talk to, in English no less.

"Ten years." He slid the wine glass into the overhead rack and reached for another. "I trained at the Hoffman House."

I leaned in and whispered, "The grand hotel on Broadway with the … naughty mural behind the bar?"

I had never seen the infamous mural myself, but from what I'd heard it depicted naked nymphs frolicking with a rather ... well-endowed faun. Sadly, the Hoffman House had been demolished to make way for an office skyscraper, so I would never have the chance to see its wicked splendor for myself.

"The very one," he replied, a glimmer in his eye.

"What brought you to Paris?" I asked.

"Prohibition. Not much call for barmen once the Volstead Act became law."

Taking in his starched collar and pristinely knotted tie, his white bar jacket without a smudge on it, I surmised that slinging rotgut in a speakeasy wouldn't have been his style.

"When the Ritz family asked me to open an American-style bar, I jumped at the chance," he added.

"Well, I'm glad you did. This champagne is delicious," I said, then silently kicked myself, for he hadn't done more than pour it.

If he was amused by my silliness, he didn't show it. "You'll have to try my cocktails one of these days. I've invented several. The Bee's Knees is one of my favorites."

"I look forward to it," I said, though I had never drunk anything stronger than wine in my life and that was only since coming to Paris.

But then Paris wasn't only a new city. It was opening a whole new world for me. If I was to hold my own here, I would have to grow up quickly.

The impromptu party broke up a bit before nine. I assumed Mademoiselle would also call it a night. Instead, owl-eyed and energetic, she lit yet another cigarette and insisted on showing me around the hotel, opulent even by New York standards. Awed to have no less than the *Grande Mademoiselle* herself as my guide, I followed her through, taking it all in.

A long corridor known as the Hall of Dreams connected the two sections of the hotel, and was lined on both sides with glass-fronted cabinets. The illuminated shelves displayed a sumptuous array of French luxury items including Louis Vuitton leather goods, gold-filled Cross pens, and sparkling gemstone jewelry designed by Van Cleef & Arpel

In the Place Vendôme wing, I admired the tapestried walls and tall ceilings, which dripped with crystal chandeliers and were trimmed with lacy confections of ornamental plasterwork, like icing on a birthday cake. In the main *salle*, a spectacular winding grand staircase, carpeted in royal blue and banded by a shiny-black wrought iron railing, led to the upper floors. At Mademoiselle's insistence, we climbed it to her third-floor suite.

Stepping inside, I breathed in the heavy scent of No. 5 and felt like I was back in the boutique.

Standing in the center of the main room, she waved her arms to encompass the sleekly restrained surroundings, all creams and beiges and plush upholstery with touches of gilding and pops of color from the bowls of pink roses.

"Fashion is not something that exists in dresses only, Marguerite," she exclaimed. "Fashion is in the sky, in the street. Fashion has to do with ideas, the way we live, what is happening. Do you understand?"

Put on the spot, I did my best to be a good pupil.

"I … I think so," I said.

By then, the champagne had begun to wear off. Along with a slight headache, I was starting to feel nervous again.

"You *think*? There is no thinking, only *knowing*." She dropped her arms and marched over to the window.

Pulling back the drape, she demanded, "What do you see?"

I hesitated, wondering if it was a trick question. "The ... Place Vendôme."

A brusque nod, "What else?"

"The uh ... obelisk ... with the statue of Napoleon on top," I added, proud of myself because I'd never been much good at history.

"And what does this obelisk remind you of, hm?"

I scrambled to think of something to say, something witty and sharp and unexpected, but my mind drew a blank.

Her drawn-out sigh confirmed I was proving a poor student already. "It is the shape of the glass stopper in every flacon of No. 5."

A few nights later, we were once again sipping champagne, that time in her atelier apartment, with her Great Dane, Gigot sprawled at her feet. Out of the blue, she picked up the lesson by telling me the origin of her perfume business.

"In the summer of 1920, I was with Grand Duke Dmitri Pavlovich, first cousin to the late tsar and living in exile after the filthy Bolsheviks took over Russia. Knowing I wanted to make a perfume, a fragrance unlike any other, Dmitri introduced me to Monsieur Ernest Beaux, known as *Le Nez*, the Nose, for having been the perfumer to the Russian royal court."

Fascinated, I waited to hear more.

She reached for her Gitanes and slipped a thin stick into her mouth. Lighting it, she took a deep drag before continuing.

"I told Monsieur Beaux to make me a scent that smelled like a woman, not a rose, and that is what he did," she recalled with a smile. "He presented me with *cinq* samples, and I chose the fifth."

"What was it about No. 5 that made it stand out from the other four?" I asked, eager to learn all I could from her, not only the business side of things, but the artistry, the magic of it all.

"One must have a nose. Do you have a nose, Marguerite?"

I paused. "I'm not sure," I admitted.

She picked up the cube-shaped flask of No. 5 from the coffee table and pulled out the stopper, the *octagonal* stopper. "What do you smell?" she asked, leaning forward and flagging the bottle beneath my nose.

Closing my eyes, I tried hard to concentrate. There was a subtle floral fragrance, but the predominant aroma was earthy, almost … grassy.

I had it on the tip end of my tongue to say so but fearing to offend, I went with the safe choice. "Flowers? Camellias, maybe," I added, knowing they were her favorite.

I opened my eyes. Seeing the disappointment on her face, my heart slumped.

She stoppered the bottle and set it aside. "The secret formula contains more than eighty ingredients. The most important is Jasmine Grandiflorum, found only in Grasse on the Riviera."

I had been right, or close to right, but as usual hadn't trusted my gut. Feeling as if I had failed her, I picked up my champagne and drank.

Her serious look lifted, and she let out a sharp laugh. "I will let you in on a secret, *chérie*. With money, you do not need a nose. With money, you can buy all the noses you like as I bought Beaux's."

She took another puff of her cigarette and blew a jet of smoke up towards the ceiling.

"His true genius is as a chemist. He experimented with the new synthetic chemical compounds called aldehydes. They make scent stay on the skin, not like the old perfumes that fade after a few hours."

Feeling as if I were receiving a true education, I wished I had thought to bring my new moleskin notebook.

"How did you go about advertising it?" I asked, thinking of Kavanaugh's, both the New York store and the one planned for Paris.

She snorted. "I didn't. We launched in the boutique on the 5th of May 1921, no reporters, not even a party. I gave away bottles to all my friends and had my *filles* spray the entrance and all the dressing rooms as we do today. *C'est tout.* Women adored it; their men went mad for it. Our small laboratory in Grasse could not keep up with the demand. Théophile Bader, cofounder of Galeries Lafayette, wanted to sell it, but we could not make enough. That is when he introduced me to Pierre Wertheimer. With his brother, Paul, Pierre owns Bourjois, the largest manufacturer of cosmetics and perfumes in France."

"And the three of you incorporated as Parfums Chanel," I broke in, keen to show her I had done my homework.

Instead of looking pleased, her face mottled, and her dark eyes narrowed to slits.

"I was cheated," she insisted in a rage-choked voice, stamping out her cigarette although it was only half-smoked. "Those greedy Wertheimers tricked me into signing over seventy percent of my shares to them. That *salaud*, Bader, took another twenty and sold it back to Pierre."

"That's terrible," I said, though a part of me, the nagging voice that lived in my gut, not my head, asked if maybe there wasn't another side to the story.

She inhaled heavily, then blew out her breath. "*C'est pas juste.* That is why I won't rest until I have my company back, *all* of it. Since 1928, *les frères* Wertheimers have had to keep a lawyer on staff to deal with my lawsuits," she said as if it were a point of pride.

Glimpsing the gleam in her gaze, I resolved then and there to never do anything that might get me on her bad side.

"But what was it about No. 5 that made you choose it?" I asked, hoping to steer the story back to the good part.

As the future head of Kavanaugh's, I would be required to think on my feet, at times to make split second decisions, as I had seen Gran do on any number of occasions. Whether firing a saleslady on the spot for refusing to wait on a Black customer or launching a new marketing campaign when the old one was no longer working, once Gran made up her mind, she rarely second-guessed herself.

Brave and bold, Mademoiselle Coco was cut from similar cloth albeit on an international scale. So far, I had gotten the bold part down, mainly when it came to speaking my mind. Bravery, which I suspected came from a deep, unwavering self-trust, was proving more elusive.

She took out another cigarette and slipped it between her scarlet lips, the corners of her mouth lifting ever so slightly.

"*Cinq*, it is my lucky number."

Chapter Five

July 1938
Despite the long hours I put in at Maison Chanel, I took Gran's advice to heart and found time to enjoy Paris. Fortunately for me, Bridget was a peach of a roommate as well as a built-in best friend: good-natured, reasonably tidy and always game for a good time.

We spent our first Bastille Day stacked like sardines along the Champs-Élysées for the parade, cockades pinned to our blouses and waving miniature French tricolors on sticks every time a new marching band went by. Then we were off to the Champs de Mars with our blanket and baguettes to carve out a postage-stamp-sized parcel of lawn for viewing the fireworks over the Eiffel Tower. Instead of going home afterward – the next day, Friday, was a workday, after all – we joined a party on the deck of one of the picturesque houseboats moored along the Seine, drinking wine from the bottle being passed around and singing the *Marseillaise* until our throats were raw. By the time we made our way back to Madame LeBrun's, arms linked to keep ourselves upright, darts of dawn light were shooting through the sky. A few hours later, we woke up with sore heads but smiles on our faces, certain we were living our dream lives.

If our accommodations proved less than dreamy – breakfast was often cold bread and cheese left over from the previous day, the linens were left to pile up, and Madame LeBrun's son, Olivier, was a nasty little Peeping Tom prone to barging in on us in the bathroom – at least it gave us something to laugh about. Laugh we did. And why not? We were young and pretty and let loose in the world's most romantic city. The world might not be our oyster, but Paris certainly was.

Amid all the fun and silliness, Bridget took a practical approach to life that I couldn't help but admire. As one of six children raised in a three-room flat in Bethnal Green, she knew how to stretch a franc, steering us to the cafés that served the heartiest *plats du jour* and filled the carafes of wine to the brim. Above all, she was determined not to follow in her mum's footsteps by marrying young and having "a horde of kids" by the time she was thirty.

"What'll you do after?" she asked me one sultry late July evening as we sat sipping white wine outside La Maison Rose, a pretty, pastel-pink café on the corner of rue de l'Abreuvoir and rue des Saules in Montmartre.

"After what?" I asked, lifting my hair off my damp neck to better catch the breeze.

"After all this." She spread her arms in the air as if to encompass the city and its endless charms and pleasures.

I didn't have to think. "Go back to New York, suffer through business college, and then go to work for my grandmother at our store."

I made a point of saying "store" instead of "department store." I still felt funny about the disparity in our circumstances. By then, I knew that Bridget's father worked in a government munitions factory in Woolwich, and her mother had gone back to hairdressing once their littlest was weaned. Bridget had left school at sixteen, starting out at a penny sweets shop in Lambeth and working her way up to selling gloves at Selfridge's saving her pennies to take French classes in the evening. When she had first come to Paris, she had lived out of a single suitcase in a hostel in La Villette where the stench from the slaughterhouse was so thick that it had seeped inside even with the windows shut. For weeks, she had taken the green autobus into the first arrondissement and pounded the pavement until Madame Millet hired her.

"They like to keep one Brit on the salesfloor for the Teddies and the Yanks, and the girl they had quit a few days before I walked in," she'd told me.

The contrast between our circumstances humbled and embarrassed me. Whereas Bridget's gumption had put her in the right place at the right time, my apprenticeship had been arranged by Gran. As a birthday gift, no less.

But money could be a double-edged sword. It had a way of driving a wedge between people. If I were to admit I was the heir to a retail empire, it would change things between Bridget and me. So far, I had played my cards close to the vest, telling myself that holding back the truth wasn't the same as outright lying.

"What about you?" I asked, taking another sip of wine.

Midway into my second glass, my brain was a blurry buzz of contentment.

"Dunno." She thought for a moment, then her face lit up. "Go back to London, marry some bloke and have a horde of kids before I'm thirty."

She burst out laughing and so did I, snorting wine up my nose – so much for my aspirations to Parisian sophistication.

"Where to next?" I asked, not ready to end the evening.

She thought for a moment. "What would you say to us treating ourselves to a proper night out? I've been dying for a look inside Chez Joséphine."

"The cabaret owned by Josephine Baker?" I asked.

By then Josephine Baker was a household name. The Black American song-and-dance sensation had taken Paris by storm in the twenties with her banana dance where she cavorted in a short skirt of rubber bananas and not much else. International stardom had fast followed. As the headliner at the *Folies Bergère* with a parade of hit songs like "*J'ai Deux Amours*," and starring roles in four films under her belt, La Baker was accounted to be the richest Black woman in the world.

Bridget nodded. "We'd have to go home and change."

"Do we have time?" I asked.

"Loads," she assured me. "Clubs like that don't get going much before midnight."

Throwing caution to the wind, I polished off the rest of my wine. "Count me in."

Later that night, we stood in line outside the cream, white and gilded club at 40 rue Pierre Fontaine, a stone's throw from the Moulin Rouge's red windmill. Though the wine from earlier had worn off, my excitement hadn't. That night would be my first time setting foot in a fancy, grownup nightclub. While New York had no shortage of such establishments – The Cotton Club, the Stork Club and El Morocco to name a few – I had always been too young to go.

I looked over at Bridget, her usual confident self in a sleeveless low-cut lavender mermaid gown that hugged her bust and hips. The dress wasn't couture or even particularly well made and yet she wore it like a queen.

I had planned to wear the Chanel gown Gran had given me, but Bridget had talked me out of it, swearing that wearing all white would make me look too much like a bride. Knowing that she was saving her pennies to purchase a Chanel handbag, and that her one precious couture cocktail dress had so far stayed in the closet awaiting a "special occasion," I hadn't wanted to make an issue of it. In the end, I had settled on a teal-blue satin gown with covered buttons to the shoulders and back, the neckline modestly filled in with a cowl neck, the bias cut helping to camouflage the few pounds I had put on from all the French wine and pastries. Glancing around at the bare shoulders and sequins surrounding us, I felt a little dowdy.

"Do I have lipstick on my teeth?" I asked in a whisper.

"I can't very well tell with your mouth closed, now, can I?"

I stretched my lips into a stiff smile.

"Teeth are fine, but your face is all shiny. Powder your nose."

"Here?" I asked, imagining what my mother would say if she knew I was wearing makeup at all, let alone applying it in public.

Bridget had talked me into letting her make me up. For the first time in my life, I wore what she called a "full face" – pancake foundation, rouge, cake mascara, shimmery eyeshadow, and noir red lipstick.

Bridget snorted. "And why not? You want to make a grand entrance, don't you?"

I unclasped my beaded clutch purse, took out my compact, and blotted my face.

A few minutes later, a liveried doorman unhooked the velvet rope and let the two of us in. I followed Bridget through the double doors.

The interior was larger than I'd guessed, the entryway dominated by a massive mural of La Baker wearing a red-lipped grin and her infamous banana skirt. We walked through to the clubroom, the white walls and pillars trimmed in gold paint, and the stage built to accommodate a full orchestra.

A maître d' led us to our table in the back and handed us cocktail menus.

"I should probably stick with wine," I said, raising my voice over the roar of big band music and collective conversations.

Bridget made a face. "Pooh, what fun is that?"

A waiter approached to take our order.

Bridget blurted out, "Soixante Quinze" and held up two fingers.

"Why seventy-five?" I asked the waiter, wondering what Bridget was getting me into.

"It is named after the French 75mm field gun used in the Great War," he answered, snapping up our menus.

While we waited for our drinks, I took it all in. Cut glass mirrors surrounded the stage, reflecting the dance floor from multiple angles and making me think of Maison Chanel's mirrored staircase. Blue chandeliers bathed the dancers in cerulean light, the patrons a mix of Blacks and whites, young and old.

Our cocktails arrived. I took a sip from my champagne flute and nearly choked. Now I understood why it was named after a field gun. It wasn't only strong. It was deadly.

"Lovely." Bridget downed half her drink in a single swallow. "Bring us two more," she told the waiter.

"Bridget!"

She drained her glass and popped up from her chair. "Don't be a fuddy-duddy. Drink up and let's dance."

"What the heck." I finished my drink and followed her out onto the dance floor.

The night passed in a boozy blur of blue lights and bare shoulders. A little before one o' clock, Josephine Baker swept in, jaw-droppingly stunning in a skimpy beaded champagne-colored evening gown, her short hair worn smooth and parted to the side, several artfully arranged pin curls framing her piquant face, her slender neck and wrists draped in precious gems. On my fourth French 75, I saw that what I'd at first taken to be a diamond bracelet was in fact the gem-studded loop of an animal's leash.

I whipped my head around to Bridget. "Is that a—"

"A pet cheetah," she confirmed, a lot better at holding her liquor than I was. "She's named it Chiquita even though it's a boy. I heard she took it with her to the Opera, and it sat on her lap the entire time."

A retinue of servants with more animals trailed in, including a potbellied pig, a goat, and a Great Pyrenees, all on flashy leashes.

Miss Baker handed off the cheetah to one of her people and began going table to table, playing up to the men, the homely ones especially, chucking chins, stroking bald heads, and drawing the shyest out to dance. Watching her twirl and gyrate to the jazz beat, I felt dizzy and not only because I was more than a little drunk.

By the end of the night, the entire club was out on the dance floor – the waiters, cooks, cashier, errand boys, and several pet animals, including the pig. Bridget and I danced with them, makeup melting and dresses plastered to our dripping skin.

In the middle of a lively swing number, a scream pierced the music. We swung around to the stage where the cheetah, leash dragging, prowled the orchestra pit.

The musicians threw down their instruments and scattered. Panicked patrons ran for the exits.

Bridget gripped my arm. "Better call it a night."

We grabbed our purses off the table and joined the stampede up the aisle, dodging elbows and shoulders and feet running over ours.

Outside, clubgoers poured out onto the pavement. Now that the danger was past, it was as if we were all let in on the same hilarious joke. Standing around in the balmy air, people laughed and danced and made funny growling noises, several slurping the dregs of drinks they'd somehow managed to hold onto. Someone passed me a half-drunk bottle of champagne. I tipped it back and took a swig, too buzzed to bother that it was flat and lukewarm.

Bridget eased it out of my hand and gave it back. "If we hurry, we can make the last Métro train." She hooked her arm through mine and started steering us toward what I vaguely remembered was rue Lepic.

I sighed, more than a little slushy and in no rush to be home. "Bridge?"

She firmed her hold on me. "Yes, Daise?"

"I wish tonight didn't have to end. Ever," I said, past caring that my thick tongue made the words come out slurred.

With my best friend by my side and the balmy night breeze brushing my face, I felt like I was living a modern-day fairy tale. A delicious, enchanted dream I never wanted to wake up from.

Her chuckle tickled my ear. "Stick with me, ducks. We'll have loads more."

Chapter Six

As we approached the deadline for the August collection, tempers at the atelier spiked, especially Mademoiselle Coco's. She routinely ripped apart finished pieces and started from scratch, stormed through the workrooms threatening to fire everyone if they didn't pick up their pace and smoked nonstop. At day's end, even the most seasoned seamstresses were wringing their hands.

"It is because of Schiaparelli," Madame Millet muttered after one particularly brutal outburst.

Chanel's archrival had gone with shocking pink for her collection. Her bold color choice and avant-garde designs, the antithesis of Chanel's pared-down simplicity, had earned rave reviews from the Paris fashion critics.

The centerpiece of Chanel's collection was a stunning scarlet crêpe de chine evening gown. Only perfection would do and yet something about the gown remained stubbornly off.

The last Monday morning in late July, Mademoiselle Coco had taken us all by surprise by coming in early instead of her customary 11 a.m. Bridget and the other *vendeuses* had barely had time to put away the atomizers of Chanel No. 5 when she stomped into the boutique, clearly in a state.

Summoned to the mirrored salon, I stood by her side while she fussed with the evening gown. Nothing and no one suited her. Lunchtime came and went. Stomachs, including mine, rumbled and still we were no closer to finishing the gown than when we'd started.

I studied the gown modeled by Yvette, her slender shoulders starting to slump. The scarlet fabric was stunning, but was it stunning enough to stand up to hot pink?

Chalking up my courage, I said, "What if we tried it in gold lamé instead? It would pair beautifully with those silk georgette sleeves."

Gran had always said I'd inherited her eye. The past six weeks at Maison Chanel had not only sharpened my fashion sense but it had also bolstered my confidence. When I took my turn working in the boutique, I often knew what customers wanted before they did. Despite my iffy French, my sales numbers were double those of any other *vendeuse* except for Bridget.

The workroom went silent. Madame Millet's mouth dropped. Chanel's dark gaze drilled into mine, and for a stomach-churning minute I wondered if I had overstepped.

"Do it. Quickly," she added, waving me off.

Relieved, I hurried to the stockroom where the accessories were kept. Looking around, I spotted the bolt of gold lamé half-hidden on an upper shelf. I dragged the step ladder over, slipped off my shoes, and climbed up. Reaching the top rung, I pulled the fabric to me, heavier than it looked. Wrestling it down, a wave of wooziness hit. The workroom teetered, taking me with it.

I came to lying on my side on the floor, coughing and sputtering.

Someone, Bridget, held a vial of something astringent beneath my nose. "Gorm, Daise, you gave me a fright."

I pushed the smelling salts away and elbowed myself upright. "W-what happened?"

Bridget braced her arm around me. "You fainted and cut yourself a nasty gash, that's what."

I reached up to my throbbing forehead. When I brought my hand away, my fingers were bright red.

Horrified, I turned my head and saw that the bolt of gold lamé had hit the floor with me. Dribbles of blood dotted the costly fabric.

Mademoiselle Coco rushed up with Millet and Aubrey as Bridget helped me to my feet. Guiltily thinking of the spoiled fabric, I braced myself for another tirade.

Instead, she cupped my face between her hands, tenderly like a mother might. "*Ma pauvre fille*, you must see a doctor at once. A good one, a plastic surgeon."

"I don't want to be a bother," I protested, feeling worse than if she had yelled at me.

Ignoring me, she turned to Madame Millet. "Bring a clean cloth and ice and call for the car to take her to the American."

Confused, I looked back to Bridget.

"The American Hospital in Paris," she clarified, handing me her hankie.

As I was about to find out firsthand, the hospital was in a western suburb of Paris, fewer than six miles from the city center. Funded by wealthy Americans living in Paris, it had opened in 1909 to serve the expat community.

Standing at the dressing mirror, I dabbed the blood. "It's such a small cut, surely anyone can stitch it," I protested although with less enthusiasm than before.

Truth be told, the wound had begun throbbing. That and the surprising quantity of let blood was threatening to bring up my breakfast.

Mademoiselle's frowning face joined mine in the mirror. "You must not entrust your beautiful face to some brute with big hands and beer on his breath. My driver will take you there and bring you home."

A short while later, fortified by a half tin of Selfridges chocolate biscuits courtesy of Bridget, I sat in the back of Chanel's powder blue Rolls Royce holding a blood-soaked hankie to my head as her driver navigated through the heavy midday traffic on the Champs.

The twenty-minute drive took us out of Paris proper into the broad, tree-lined boulevards of Neuilly-sur-Seine. The stately, gated stone villas reminded me of the few Gilded Age mansions left on Upper Fifth Avenue, only these were preceded by long driveways and verdant carpets of lush lawns.

We turned onto boulevard du Château, and the hospital complex came into view, a trio of vast château-like pink brick and limestone buildings with terraces and mansard roofs facing a front lawn bordered by box hedges. It wasn't until the chauffeur passed through the arched ironwork entrance and pulled up to the porte-cochere to let me out that it hit me. I was in a foreign country and going to see a doctor, a *surgeon*, all alone. Until then, the only doctor I had seen by myself was the dentist.

Inside the main hospital building, I consulted the departmental directory, the listings in both English and French, and took the patient lift to the surgical floor. Stepping off, I followed the signs for "*Chirurgie Plastique*/Plastic Surgery," the "surgery" part making the consequences of my mishap feel frightfully real.

Walking the scrupulously clean corridor, a strong smell of carbolic in the air, I consoled myself that the hospital seemed to be up to American standards of cleanliness and modernity. I passed several nurses dressed in spotless, all-white uniforms, their nursing caps making me think of nuns' veils, and two doctors wearing lab coats and conferring in hushed, serious tones.

A stern-faced French nurse presided over the surgical reception desk. Looking up from the stack of patient charts she had been organizing, she asked, "*Que puis-je faire pour vous, mademoiselle?*"

In halting French, I launched into an account of my mishap.

Wincing at my butchering of her native tongue, she interrupted me. "In English, mademoiselle."

I started again. "I fainted at work and cut my head. I know this all must seem terribly silly, it's just a cut, but my ... employer, Mademoiselle Chanel insists I be seen by a plastic surgeon."

She gave a sharp shake of her head. "Without an appointment, it is not possible. The doctors have been in surgery all morning. Our chief resident, Dr. Jacob, is the only one seeing patients, and he has no more appointments. The accident department will be able to help you."

It seemed I had come across the one person in Paris for whom the name Chanel held no sway. If my mother were here with me, she would fight like a lioness, refusing to budge until I was seen by a specialist. But Mom wasn't here, nor was Gran, and the pain and queasiness and ... *foreignness* of everything suddenly seemed more than I could manage on my own.

On the verge of tears, I was about to accept defeat and ask directions to the accident department when a tall, young doctor in a rumpled lab coat, dark hair mussed and beard stubble blanketing his lean face, stepped out from one of the examining rooms. Beneath thick, arched black brows, his dark brown eyes studied me.

He looked from me to the nurse. "*Ce qui s'est passé?*"

She summarized my situation in French. At her mention of Chanel, the corners of his mouth dipped.

I waited, expecting him to dispatch me to the accident ward, too. Instead, his gaze skimmed my wound and then dropped to my eyes, fixing there with such intensity that I felt faint again despite the biscuits in my belly.

"You will have to wait," he finally said, his tone curt but not unkind.

I blinked, the sound of his voice bringing me back to myself. "Yes, of course. Thank you. I mean, *merci beaucoup*."

He grabbed a clipboard from the desk and turned away.

I gave the nurse my details and then walked into the patient lounge. She hadn't exaggerated how busy they were. Nearly every seat was taken. I found one at the back of the room and took it.

I had just sat down when an older Frenchman approached the admittance desk, about my father's age, his salt-and-pepper hair neatly side parted. After exchanging a few words with the nurse, he entered the patient lounge in search of a seat. He hesitated and then took the empty chair across from mine. I looked up to send him the obligatory social smile and that's when I saw.

His face wasn't a face at all but a painted copper mask. From across the room, the flesh tones and features had looked lifelike, but up close the carefully curated illusion collapsed. Only the eyes moved inside the punched-out holes; the nose, cheeks, jaw, and mouth were all a metal mold.

I grabbed a magazine from the rack and pretended to peruse it despite it being a medical journal and all in French.

Finally, the man was called up for his appointment. I peeked around to see the young, dark-haired doctor greet him warmly, calling him by his first name and asking after his family. Coward that I was, I slunk lower in my seat until they disappeared into an exam room.

Once they had, I traded in the medical journal for a copy of *Collier's* dated January 15th. Flipping past an article by the war reporter Martha Gellhorn on American volunteers fighting in the Spanish Civil War – too serious, too sad – I was soon deep into a short story: "The Mummy That Walked" by Sax Rohmer.

I had just come to the part where the main character, a mystery-solving magician, was about to bring the ancient Egyptian queen Cleopatra and her court back to life when a woman called out, "Miss Blakely."

Startled to hear a midwestern American accent, I looked over.

A young American receptionist had replaced the French nurse. Then again, this was the American Hospital, so I suppose I oughtn't to have been surprised that Americans also worked here.

"Doctor Jacob will see you now," she said.

I replaced the *Colliers* in the rack and stood, my anxiety rushing back.

A nurse led me back to the exam room. The dark-haired doctor from earlier sat on a swivel stool consulting a chart, mine I supposed.

He stood when I entered. "Mademoiselle Blakely?"

"*C'est moi*," I said, my eye going to the medical cart where an array of alarming looking surgical instruments sat out on a metal tray.

"*Américaine?*" he asked, though it didn't sound much like a question.

"Yes, from New York."

"You fainted at work?" he asked, switching to English.

"I forgot to eat lunch," I admitted, expecting a scolding.

Instead, he gestured for me to take a seat on the exam table.

I climbed onto the crisp, white cover and sat, arranging my skirt over my knees, my legs dangling over the side making me feel like a little kid. "The bleeding seems to have stopped. Perhaps I don't need stitches after all," I suggested.

"You need them." He slipped on rubber gloves and doused a gauze pad in a clear liquid. "Saline solution," he said, answering my unspoken question.

Leaning in, he blotted the dried blood on my forehead. Amid the stinging I caught his scent, lavender and vanilla overlaid with the spiciness of tobacco.

He dropped the soiled gauze into a waste bin and looked down at my hands, tightly laced in my lap. "You are one of Chanel's *petites mains*? You do not have the hands of a seamstress."

He took my hands and turned them palm up, his own fingers long and tapered, the nails neatly clipped. A shiver shot through me though the room was warm. In New York, I had held hands with many a boy who had angled to walk me home, their palms unpleasantly moist, their grip too loose or too tight, but this was my first time on the receiving end of such a firm yet gentle cradling.

"I'm at Maison Chanel as an apprentice learning about the business side of haute couture." Pride had me adding, "My family owns a department store in New York. Kavanaugh's. Someday soon, you'll see our marquee here in Paris."

Giving me back my hands, he studied me, his eyes fringed with thick lashes that made me think of paintbrushes. "Does the world need more stores for the rich to shop?"

His question, clearly rhetorical, caught me off guard. I had never thought of it that way.

Before I could come up with a reply, he set his hand on my shoulder. "Lie back."

Feeling foolish, I settled on the exam table while he left me to go to the glass fronted medicine cabinet.

When he turned back, he wielded a glass syringe tipped with a long needle. Staring at the oh so sharp point, I felt my heart flip.

"A few quick pricks and then you will feel pressure but no pain," he promised, shifting to stand over me.

"Scout's honor?" Catching his confused look, I explained, "An American expression for telling the truth."

Serious brown eyes bored into mine, bringing back the lightheaded feeling I'd experienced out in reception. "I always tell the truth. And I promise I will be very fast."

Digging my nails into my palms, I closed my eyes and made myself hold still.

He hadn't lied. The quick, sharp pricks took me back to the time I'd been stung by a bee in Central Park. Not pleasant by any stretch but bearable.

I opened my eyes to see him toss the needle into the trash receptacle.

Turning back, he probed the area with his fingers. "What do you feel?"

I hesitated. "Nothing."

"*Bon*, I am an honorable scout."

That time he smiled, and I caught myself staring at his mouth, the top lip a perfect ribbon, the lower lip full and pillowy, the teeth straight and beautifully shaped albeit slightly tobacco stained.

I studied the white-painted pressed tin ceiling while he laid out his instruments. "I feel a little silly bothering you for such a small cut,"

I admitted, thinking of the man with the copper mask who clearly had greater claim to a surgeon's care than I did.

"Not silly. Most *médecins généralistes* will use catgut to close the wound, but catgut is unpredictable," he told me. "Sometimes it dissolves, and the wound can reopen. And there is the problem of scarring. I use only synthetic sutures. No surprises and minimal scarring."

Spotting the surgical scissors and slender hook and thread in his hand, I snapped my eyes shut. He went to work, and I felt a pulling sensation but, as he had promised, no pain.

"You have been in Paris long?" he asked.

"Just since June."

"How do you find it here?"

The question took me aback. While I was no stranger to boys showing an interest, having a grownup man asking about my thoughts and opinions, an *attractive* man, was a novel experience.

Feeling myself blushing, I took a moment to answer. "The city is spectacular, so dreamy and romantic. A different world from New York."

"In what way different?" he asked, again as if genuinely curious to hear what I had to say.

Again, I considered the question. "Here, everyone takes their time. Whether eating, walking or working, no one's ever in a rush."

"And in New York?"

"We are *always* in a rush."

"*J'ai fini.*"

I opened my eyes. "That's it?"

"*Oui, c'est tout.* You will have a small scar for a little while, but it will fade."

He dabbed some sort of soothing salve on the sutures, covered the wound with gauze and then helped me to sit up, his hand lightly holding my elbow.

Now that the worst was over, I relaxed and looked around. For the first time, I noticed a large glass-fronted cabinet on the far wall, the shelves holding a dozen or so plaster face casts, all young men and so grotesquely disfigured they might have been props from a Bella Lugosi movie.

Following my gaze, he said, "We call them *gueules cassées*. It means 'broken faces.'"

Fighting a shiver, I asked, "Are they all from the war?"

In New York on Decoration Day and the Fourth of July, veterans of the Great War were a fixture at military parades, many with missing limbs, some disfigured. But the masked man in the waiting room was my first time seeing one up close.

He nodded. "The war made more than 15,000 *gueules cassées* in France. Trenches shield bodies better than heads; steel helmets protect brains but not faces."

I thought of my uncle, Joey killed at the Battle of Château-Thierry. From the few details I had been given, I gathered that his death had, at least, been a quick one.

He released a heavy breath. "If Hitler has his way, soon there will be more broken faces. More broken everything."

The ominous remark raised the hairs on my nape. "From everything I've heard, he's out to reunite Germans who lost their citizenship under the Treaty of Versailles. Surely now that he has Austria, he'll be satisfied."

Admittedly, I had never been much of a newspaper reader. What I knew of world affairs came from the Pathé newsreels shown in movie theaters before the main feature. That March, while waiting to see *Jezebel* with Bette Davis and Henry Fonda, I had sat in the darkened cinema and watched Adolf Hitler ride through Vienna in an open car greeted by a rabidly cheering pro-Nazi crowd. As chilling as the scene was, the threat had felt far away, like something that might take place on Mars or the moon.

One dark brow lifted. "*Faute de grives on mange des merles*? Half a loaf is better than no bread?"

"Something like that, yes."

He sucked his teeth. "I think that for such a man, a megalomaniac, nothing but the whole loaf will satisfy."

Thinking we were finished, I started to scoot off the table, but he stopped me with another of those strangely stirring touches.

"You fainted. I think this is not the first time."

Again, not a question.

"Sometimes I get lightheaded when I uh, have my ... monthly," I admitted, feeling myself flushing, that time from embarrassment.

My family doctor in New York was balding, bushy browed, and old enough to be my grandfather. Discussing my ... lady parts with the young and handsome Dr. Jacob was nothing less than mortifying.

If he noticed my reddening face, and I didn't doubt that he did, he was kind enough not to remark on it. "I suspect you are anemic. Your nail beds are very pale. But I would like to be certain."

Stomach knotting at the prospect of yet another poke, I let him slide up my sleeve.

"Make a fist," he directed. "A good one like you are going to punch someone," he added, furling my fingers.

I did, and he probed the inside of my elbow with gentle fingers.

"You have very small veins," he remarked, searching out a suitable one.

"Is that a compliment?" I quipped.

Golly, was I flirting? I must have lost more blood than I'd thought. He had ten years on me at least. And he was blunt speaking if not exactly rude. Surprisingly, I liked it. I liked *him*. Unlike the smooth-talking boys back home, who only told girls what they thought we wanted to hear, he spoke his mind without apology or reservation but also with conviction. With *passion*.

The corners of his mouth twitched. "An observation."

He tied a tourniquet above the site and swabbed the spot with alcohol. Seeing him pick up a vial tipped with another lethal looking needle, I quickly turned my head. Keeping my arm steady, I distracted myself by counting backward from ten in my head. He slipped the needle out without my feeling it, kept pressure on for a moment, and then covered the puncture with a Band-Aid.

"Make an appointment to return in ten days to have the stitches removed. I will give you the results of the blood test then." He stripped off his gloves and held out both hands to help me up.

I took them and stepped down, the press of his flesh against mine thrilling, my mind picturing all the wicked things those lovely, long-fingered hands might do when they weren't wielding needles.

"I will, thank you."

He released me and stepped back. "Ten days, do not forget."

"I won't," I promised, feeling breathless and shaky and not quite myself.

At the door, I looked back, but he'd already moved on to the next patient chart.

No matter, I told myself, heart skipping beats. *I'll see him in ten days.*

For the first time in my life, I was looking forward to visiting the doctor.

Chapter Seven

Chanel's chauffeur drove me back to my apartment. I was home just long enough to plug in the floor fan when Bridget walked in. She dropped her handbag inside the door and rushed over, enfolding me in a sweaty Chanel No. 5 scented hug.

Pulling back, she scrutinized my bandage. "Was it awful? Are you in terrible pain? Will you need to wear a fringe?"

I shook my head. "It throbs a little, but not too badly. Dr. Jacob says it won't scar."

Something in the way I said his name must have tipped her off.

She eyed me. "Fat and fusty, was he, balding with veiny hands and carbolic for cologne?"

I hesitated. "He's a surgical resident, and quite fit, with a full head of hair. Maybe twenty-eight or twenty-nine."

She perked up. "Married?"

"I don't think so. He wasn't wearing a wedding ring."

"You can't go by that. A lot of men, Frenchmen especially, don't. What else?"

Smoothing a hand over my wrinkled skirt, I said, "Nothing, that's it."

She lightly swatted my arm. "Oh, Daisy, don't be such a dark horse. I've been locked up in that stuffy boutique all day with all *women*. Tell me *everything*."

"There's really not much to tell," I insisted.

Apart from my overly active imagination, it was the truth.

Bridget being Bridget, she would get it out of me sooner or later. She poured us each a glass of red wine, shepherded me over to the sofa and put my feet up on the ottoman, then plunked down beside me.

I'd barely got my first sip of wine down when she demanded, "Out with it."

Surrendering, I filled her in on what she insisted on calling my "medical adventure," painting a picture of Dr. Jacob that included tousled dark hair, velvety brown eyes, and full lips.

I finished, and she sat back with a sigh. "He sounds scrumptious. When are you seeing him again?"

"In ten days to get the stitches out."

She lobbed me a look. "I meant *outside* of the hospital. You gave him our phone number, didn't you?"

Madame LeBrun kept a telephone in the downstairs hallway, an old-fashioned candlestick model with the mouthpiece mounted at the top of the stand, but we were only allowed to use it to make "necessary" calls. When I'd made the first of my monthly Sunday night calls home to the family, I'd done so from the Ritz. It was easier that way and a lot more private. Sundays were slow with most weekly guests checking out. Madame Auzello, who insisted I call her Blanche, had taken a shine to me and let me use her husband's office when he wasn't in it.

I shook my head, the throbbing dulled by the wine.

She rolled her eyes. "Daisy Blakely, have I taught you nothing these past weeks?"

Seeking to redeem myself, I volunteered, "I did mention I work at Maison Chanel."

She brightened. "Think he'll drop by?"

Recalling his opinions on the fashion industry, I said, "I doubt it."

And yet when I went to bed that evening instead of counting sheep, I quieted my buzzing brain with imagining scenarios for how Dr. Jacob and I might bump into each other.

The next day, I was back at work. To my relief, no one brought up my accident or questioned me about my hospital visit. Likely they were too harried with pushing out the collection to give my mishap much thought. Madame Aubrey informed me that I'd be helping in the boutique, which meant a lighter load than the pressure cooker that the atelier was in the runup to the August 5th showing. Though I'd been looking forward to having another crack at the stubborn gown, I felt too guilty about ruining the fabric to argue.

Before opening, Bridget and I went around with atomizers of No. 5 spraying the entrance, dressing rooms and staircase. Taking advantage of it being only the two of us, she dropped down on the tufted beige dressing stool.

"We're supposed to be *working*." I darted a look around, imagining Madame Millet or worse, Chanel herself, walking in on us.

She rolled her eyes at me. "Millet is too busy upstairs to pay us any mind and Mademoiselle Coco won't be in for another hour at least."

She raised her wrist and brazenly squirted perfume on the inside.

I grabbed her arm. "Bridget, what are you doing!"

"Don't be a ninny. I'm on the sales floor. It's my job not to just look nice but smell nice, too."

She sprayed her other wrist as well, and then rubbed the two together.

"You're supposed to dab it, not bathe in it," I pointed out.

She snorted. "Can't have too much of a good thing. If only mum and dad could see me now, up to my ears in No. 5." She held out her wrist, and I drew a dutiful whiff though by then we both had it all but coming out of our pores. "Rolls off the tongue a sight smoother than No. 22."

"What are you talking about?" I asked.

Her hazel eyes widened. "You don't know?"

"Know what?"

She patted the cushion and after another nervous look around, I squeezed in beside her.

Dropping her voice, she said, "Mademoiselle's nose, Monsieur Beaux created *two* series of sample scents: one through 5 and 20 through 24. Mademoiselle's first pick was No. 22, but sales were middling, so she went back and picked No. 5."

"That can't be right," I protested. "She told me specifically that she settled on No. 5 because it's her lucky number."

Bridget shrugged. "Makes for a better story, don't it?"

"I suppose so," I said, feeling like I had the day my brother told me there was no Santa Claus *and* no Tooth Fairy.

The conversation stuck with me throughout the day. Chanel's doctoring the origin story of her famous fragrance was a white lie at worst, clever marketing at best. She wouldn't be the first luminary to have a hand in shaping her legend. Still, thinking of Gran and how scrupulously honest she always was, the situation didn't sit quite right with me, the nagging voice inside of me demanding to know what other truths the *Grande Mademoiselle* might bend if the situation suited her.

Chapter Eight

August 4th–5th, 1938

The day before the showing, the entire atelier worked through the night. As demanding as Chanel was of us, she asked even more of herself. More than once during that long night, I saw her lie on her back on the beige carpet to check that a hem was perfect. Though she had food brought in from the Ritz for the staff, she subsisted on cigarettes and sips of water.

Around 9 p.m., she called for all the designs to be carried back upstairs to the atelier. A cigarette hanging from the side of her mouth, she began ripping away at the stitching, cutting, and reshaping, adding trimming and then removing it.

"*Je suis fini*. This is my final collection!" she declared, snipping the stitches of an armhole with her ever-present scissors, then using pins to reposition the fabric point by point.

I caught Madame Millet's eye. "It is the same with every collection," she mumbled, and I took heart and kept working.

Two hours before the showing, the folding chairs were set up in the salon and several Coromandel screens were brought downstairs for the backdrop. Meanwhile, upstairs in the atelier, the workroom was in an uproar, with everyone talking at once. Boxes of accessories, handbags and hats spilled over the worktables.

Mademoiselle Coco paced the four corners like a caged tiger, smoking cigarette after cigarette and lamenting that the clothes weren't ready; she wanted to change them all.

"Better to cancel than be a laughingstock," she said to anyone within earshot.

Worst of all, the gown that was to be the grand finale of the collection still wasn't quite right. Though she'd taken my suggestion to redo it in gold lamé, something was missing.

Face tense, Mademoiselle Coco plucked at the columned skirt. "Monstrous," she declared, reaching for her scissors.

Panicked, I spoke up. "What if we did away with the bow?"

My suggestion drew a scowl, but at least the scissors stayed where they were. "And leave it plain?" she demanded. "A nothing gown to be worn by a nothing woman?"

Out of the side of my eye, I spotted Madame Millet walking up. For a fraught few seconds, I considered backing down and slinking off. But would Gran back down? Would Chanel? Not when they knew they were right, as I suddenly knew I was.

I might not have a "nose", but what I did have was an eye for detail. A vision.

I braced myself to be brave, no matter that the inside of my mouth was suddenly sawdust dry, and my palms were sweating. "Not plain. We could finish it with ... a little something extra? A flourish of silk camellias perhaps?"

Camellias, Chanel's favorite flower, were a frequent motif in her designs, though she hadn't used them in the current collection.

Mademoiselle Coco studied me for an agonizingly long moment, then whipped around to Madame Millet. "Call down to the accessories counter," she said, and then strode off to check the next ensemble.

Madame Millet glared at me. "Who do you imagine you are, *Mademoiselle*?"

Watching her stomp off, I asked myself the same. If the gown with the camellias was a flop, I could see myself sent back to New York in disgrace, a failure. But I couldn't worry about that now. Not when there was a show to put on.

Two hours later, I joined Chanel atop the mirrored staircase where she sat looking down onto the salon. Filling the seats were senior editors from *Vogue* and *Vogue Paris*, *Harper's Bazaar*, *Marie-Claire*, *Le Nouveau Luxe*, *Le Miroir Du Monde* and other French and American fashion magazines as well as a select number of distinguished clients, many of them Chanel devotees for decades. Hair combed and fresh lipstick applied, she gave no sign of the nervousness I had seen on display earlier. I, on the other hand, was a wreck, checking my watch and chewing my nails, my fast-beating heart feeling like it might break through my chest at any minute.

Madame Millet led the mannequins to the top landing where they lined up for the *defilé*, the descent down the mirrored stairs. Yvette started down first. The other models sashayed past at intervals, and I grasped the genius behind Chanel's seating herself on the fifth step. From our birds' eye vantage point, we could see the clothes from every angle in the mirrored panels as well as observe the audience's reaction without ourselves being seen.

Yvette reached the stage, and it struck me. I wasn't reading about a Chanel show in a fashion magazine, I was *living* it! No matter how the show was received, this moment was mine to hold onto. Forever.

I began to relax, enjoying not only the beautiful clothes I'd had a hand in helping create but the pageantry of it all. It felt like I was at the Met Opera House watching a ballet, the mannequins gliding downward with their necks stretched long, shoulders rolled back, hips thrust out, one hand slipped into a pocket or set on a hip, the other hand holding up a card with the style number. One by one, they made their way to the podium between the Coromandel screens and struck a final pose, smiling out onto the audience.

I glanced over at Chanel. Taking in her tightly laced hands lying in her lap and the tense set of her shoulders, I had the impulse to put my arm around her. But that would have been a terrible breach. Back in New York, I was Miss Daisy Blakely, granddaughter of Rose Kavanaugh Blakely, but within the four walls of Maison Chanel, I was Marguerite, another of Mademoiselle's *filles*. It was all well and good for her to pinch our cheeks and straighten our collars like an imperious mother might, but the unspoken boundary between us didn't go both ways.

The show finale, the gold lamé gown with my improvised camellias on the waist, drew a standing ovation.

Chanel rose and started down the stairs, calm and perfectly poised as if success were never in doubt. She reached the dais amid the flash and pop of cameras. Listening to her speech, at times humble and humorous, I felt a swell of pride to have been part of something so much larger than myself.

I waited until she had finished and then followed her down. When I reached the salon, she was surrounded by well-wishers.

From the Paris bureau of *Harper's Bazaar*, Marie-Louise Bousquet approached and air-kissed both her cheeks. "You have done it again, Coco. *Magnifique. Absolument magnifique.* The gold lamé – the camellias give it *un petit quelque chose en plus.*"

A little something extra.

Pulse pounding, I waited for Mademoiselle Coco to acknowledge me.

Instead, she kept her gaze on Marie-Louise. "Camellias have always been my favorite flower. Beautiful and resilient, they weather the frost and come out stronger. Like me," she added with a chuckle.

They chatted a moment more, and then Marie-Louise drifted off.

Mademoiselle Coco bent her head to my ear, and I waited. A private thank you from the world's greatest couturier was as good or better than a hundred public accolades, or so I told myself.

Her cigarette-scented breath tickled the inside of my ear. "You see, Marguerite, women do not want to look like lobsters. They do not want to dress in pink like little girls. They want to look and dress like women."

It was a dig at her rival Elsa Schiaparelli. Even at the pinnacle of her glory, Mademoiselle Coco was not one to let go of a grudge.

Afterwards in the atelier, champagne was passed around, the *petites mains*, models, all of us laughing and talking and toasting like we had come through a battle. In a way we had. By then, I had shrugged off most of my hurt feelings, the nagging voice inside me muted by the bubbly. Sipping, I tried telling myself that my expectations for being credited had been out of line, or at least naïve. The gold lamé gown bore the Chanel label. With or without the camellias, whether in brilliant gold or bold scarlet, it would have been a hit as all Chanel's creations were.

Mademoiselle Coco popped in for a quick toast before heading out for a celebratory dinner at Maxim's. Looking at her, bright-eyed and vibrating with vitality, no one would suspect she had been up all night.

I, on the other hand, felt like a balloon stuck with a pin. Now that the heady rush was over, my single glass of champagne had finished me. I helped Bridget put away the chairs and close the shop. When she suggested stopping off at Café Voisin, close by on the corner of rue Saint-Honoré and rue Cambon, I pleaded a headache and went home ahead of her.

The next day, more than one fashion reviewer praised the gold lamé gown, with its cannily placed camellias, as Chanel at the height of her powers. Only Madame Millet, who had done the final hand-stitching, knew I was responsible, and she resented me far too much to credit me for my part, which was fine by me. By then I was content to keep my small victory to myself, as confirmation that I wasn't only learning design and the business of haute couture. I was learning to trust myself.

Chapter Nine

With the August collection behind us, the atelier quieted. As summer softened into early autumn, I took advantage of the lull to spend more time outdoors. The Luxembourg Gardens on the Left Bank in Saint-German-des-Prés had been a favorite spot since I had first explored them with Gran. Though the Tuileries Garden was a short walk from both Maison Chanel and the Ritz, the more bohemian Left Bank held a special magic for me. Strolling the park's gravel paths, sometimes stopping to watch old men playing pétanque, I fantasized about bumping into Dr. Jacob there, though I never did.

When I had gone back to the American to have my stitches removed, I had dressed to the nines in a belted chiffon Chanel day dress from the summer 1937 collection, my hair swept up in a sophisticated chignon I was sure made me look twenty-five at least. I was crushed to learn that Dr. Jacob had been called away to assist with an emergency surgery. Another resident snipped my stitches and read me my blood test results, which confirmed mild anemia, prescribed me iron pills and sent me on my way.

Walking to the elevators after my appointment, I had caught myself dragging my feet, which was ridiculous. Ridiculous as well as a great deal of fuss over a man who had shown no interest in me beyond my being his patient. And yet beyond his good looks, there was something about him, something earnest and enigmatic and a bit dark, that had hooked me and wouldn't let me go. A *coup de foudre*, the French called it, the sensation of being struck by lightning.

A different sort of storm seemed poised to strike Europe. By late September, the leaders of Great Britain, France and Italy met Hitler in Munich and signed an agreement granting Germany the Sudetenland region of Czechoslovakia. The shameful concession was meant to appease Germany and keep the peace, but I kept going back to Dr. Jacob's certainty that a tyrant like Adolf Hitler would always want more. At the Ritz, Frank and Blanche worried aloud that the Führer had his eye on Poland next.

Jewish refugees from Germany, Czechoslovakia, and now Poland poured into the United States, England and France. Many of those who came to Paris found work at couture houses, which went to show that the fashion industry didn't only benefit the rich who wore its clothes. I longed to throw that fact in Dr. Jacob's handsome face but short of falling off another ladder, I didn't see how I would ever get the chance.

The first Monday in October, I returned to the atelier with pastries from Angelina, Chanel's favorite patisserie on rue de Rivoli, to find Madame Millet arguing with a young woman off the street, Eastern European judging from her accent. Knowing Millet's English to be poor, and surmising that the girl didn't have any French, I set down the box of macarons and Mont Blanc pastries and walked up.

"Perhaps I can help?" I offered, first in French and then in English.

Hearing English, the girl's light brown eyes brightened. "I come about the position for seamstress. I bring these to show you." She swept a chapped hand over the dozen embroidery and appliqué sample squares spread across the cutting table.

A glance confirmed the workmanship was very fine.

Looking up, I asked, "You sewed all these?"

She nodded, so hard I thought her round cloche hat might topple off. It was as out-of-date as the rest of her outfit, the ensemble clearly cared for and clean. "My father has ... had a tailoring shop in Warsaw. He teaches me from the time I am little girl."

Small and thin, with pale blonde hair wound into a tight bun and earnest brown eyes, the girl couldn't have been much older than I was. Though she was neat as a pin, I couldn't help noticing her frayed collar and cuffs. What courage it must have taken for her to show up at the atelier in her shabby clothes and mended stockings. A similar courage to Gran's in coming to New York, also as an immigrant without family, friends, or references.

"I'm Daisy ... Marguerite Blakely, an apprentice to Mademoiselle Chanel." I held out my hand.

She took it in her ungloved one, which felt cold and rough. "Hanna Kaminski."

"It's a pleasure to meet you, Miss Kaminski." I glanced over at Madame Millet, her white knuckled fist planted atop the counter. "A word, madame?"

She gave a grudging nod, and we stepped to the side.

"Mademoiselle Coco has begun designing for the February collection. Perhaps we could use an extra pair of hands," I ventured.

If I'd had any hope of melting her, her dark look dashed it to the ground.

"There are many fine Frenchwomen in Paris in need of work," she snapped.

The remark, and its ugly implications, made me that much more determined.

Rather than stand around arguing with her, I turned away and walked back to Hanna. "May I borrow these?" I asked, gesturing to the sewing squares.

She nodded.

"Wait here, please." I grabbed the samples and hurried to the salon.

Mademoiselle Coco stood at the triple mirror with Yvette, pinning what was shaping up to be a day dress in jersey, still Mademoiselle's preferred fabric. With a cigarette dangling from her mouth and silver scissors flying, she was in deep concentration, her full attention on the creation taking shape.

I hesitated, courage flagging. Not even her most senior employees dared interrupt her when she was working. I hung back, waiting for her to notice me, hopefully before Miss Kaminski gave up and left.

Just when I was on the verge of breaking her number one rule and speaking up, she asked, "Marguerite, why are you lurking there? Come closer."

I approached.

"*Avec ceinture ou sans ceinture?*" she asked, gesturing to the model's waist.

Ordinarily, her asking my opinion would have shot me over the moon, but I was in too much of a hurry to savor it.

"Without a belt, I think."

She rolled her eyes. "You *think* or you *know*?"

Funny, how she could be the most indecisive of anyone, changing a design the night before a show or spending a week on a dress only to decide it was *merde* and tearing it apart, and yet she couldn't tolerate the slightest wavering in us, her staff.

"Without, definitely," I amended, mindful to be less wishy-washy. Seizing my moment, I added, "There's an applicant for the *petite main* position downstairs. She brought these." I held out Miss Kaminski's samples.

Letting the scissors drop around her neck, she took them, turning them over to examine the stitching from the underside.

"Very nice work," she said, handing them back.

I steeled myself. "I was thinking we might bring Miss Kaminski on for the February collection."

She frowned. "Madame Millet does the hiring for the atelier."

"Yes, but she seems ... reluctant to hire her. I think perhaps because she is Polish."

She turned back to Yvette, who hadn't moved a muscle. "As I said, it is for her to decide."

"But these samples show she can do the job." Lowering my voice, I added, "Women around the world adore your clothes, your accessories, your perfume. They adore *you*. Denying someone work because of her nationality isn't only unjust. It isn't ... Chanel."

I was going out on a very large limb, and for a girl who was, until a few minutes ago, a total stranger. And yet the similarity of Miss Kaminski's circumstances to Gran's wouldn't let me give up.

Mademoiselle Coco's dark eyes bored into mine. "You are certain the samples are hers?"

I thought back to Hanna's handshake, the roughened fingers and callused thumb. The hand of a seamstress, no doubt about it.

Meeting her gaze, I said, "I am."

She slipped the cigarette from her mouth. "We will try her for one week. If she satisfies, Millet will put her on ninety days probation with the offer of a permanent position after."

"Thank you, thank you! *Mille mercis*," I amended, for she liked me to speak in French during work hours. "You won't be sorry."

She waved me off and I beat a hasty retreat, knowing I had better quit while I was ahead.

Back in the atelier, I found Madame Millet standing guard over the girl as if worried she might steal something.

I handed back the samples, and Miss Kaminski's shoulders drooped like a flower losing its petals.

"Thank you for trying to help, mademoiselle." She folded the squares and slipped them back into her bag.

Spotting Madame Millet's smug face out of the side of my eye, I repeated Chanel's terms, doing my best not to gloat. Finished, I asked, "How does that sound?"

The girl's wan face glowed. "Thank you! You will not be sorry."

Looking back to Madame Millet, whose own face had fallen like a soufflé baking in an overheated oven, I kept my voice cool and said, "I'm sure we won't. But you will need to learn French, enough to take instruction in the atelier and read the patterns."

"I will do it!" she exclaimed.

Madame Millet finally unscrewed her tight lips and spoke. "Be here tomorrow morning at eight o' clock, and do not be late. Maison Chanel does not tolerate shirkers."

Miss Kaminski bobbed her head. "I will be here. You will not be sorry," she said, that time to us both.

Watching her all but float off, I felt my mouth lifting in a smile. I couldn't help every refugee pouring into Paris, but I had helped this one, and doing so felt good, wonderful, in fact, no matter that Madame Millet would almost certainly find a way to make me pay for it later.

Spotting her fuming face in one of the mirrors, I quickly wiped mine of any suggestion of satisfaction. "I'll take these pastries upstairs, madame," I said, summoning my most demure voice.

Picking up the box, I seized on the excuse to make myself scarce.

Chapter Ten

Hanna sailed through her trial week in the atelier with flying colors. As a *petite main*, she only needed enough French to take instruction. By the end of the first week, she'd memorized many of the more frequently used sewing terms such as *avantbras* (forearm), *coutures* (seams), and *surpique* (top stitch). For the rest, she had made herself a cheat sheet, the French terms neatly copied out with their Polish translations.

The other employees kept their distance, a few making cutting comments at her expense. Along with her Polish accent, her shabby appearance set her apart. I made a point of inviting her to lunch with Bridget and me. Knowing she couldn't afford to eat at cafés, I started packing an extra baguette and cheese and suggested to Bridget that we take advantage of the mild fall weather to picnic on the steps of La Madeleine or Place Vendôme.

One warmish day at the end of September as the three of us were getting ready to leave for lunch, I noticed Hanna admiring my handbag, a Chanel flap bag from the previous year.

Caught staring, she blushed. "Very nice."

Lacking a proper purse, she carried her things in a dingy needle-point pouchette.

Bridget looked back from the threshold. "Are you coming?"

"Go on without us," I said. "We'll catch up."

I waited for Bridget to walk off, then said, "It doesn't really suit me. Why don't you have it?"

Hanna drew back. "I cannot accept."

"A trade, then. I'll take yours and you take mine."

She hesitated, and I could see in her eyes how dearly she wanted that handbag. "You are certain?"

"Absolutely."

I had several Chanel handbags given to me as gifts over the years. I would hardly miss this one. But for Hanna, having something smart of her own, a Chanel design, might help her feel more confident.

Upstairs in the atelier, we emptied our bags atop one of the worktables, laughing at the odds and ends we found at the bottoms. We finished our swap, and Hanna held the Chanel purse on her lap, smoothing a reverent hand over the quilted lambskin. Seeing her smile brought me more satisfaction than any handbag ever had.

I glanced at the wall clock. Changing out the handbags had taken longer than I'd anticipated. "We might as well take our lunch here," I said. "That way we won't have to hurry back."

Hanna was still on probation and with Madame Millet monitoring her every move, looking for a reason to discredit her, she couldn't afford to be late.

"What of Bridget?" she asked.

"She'll understand," I assured her.

Though shy at first, between bites of bread and cheese, Hanna shared snippets of her life in Warsaw before the threat of Nazi invasion had sent her family fleeing: Picnics on the banks of the Vistula River; concerts at the Philharmonic Hall, movies at the Atlantic

Cinema. The picture she painted of cabarets and nightclubs, one with a revolving rubber dance floor, was of a city similar to Paris where the arts thrived, and nightlife glittered.

Listening, I was doubly glad I had given her the handbag. Already I could see a difference in her. She sat up straighter, and her eyes had lost their hunted look.

Finished, I dusted crumbs from my fingers and gathered up our baguette wrappers. Standing up from the table, I picked up the pouchette, mine now.

"The others will be back soon. I'm going downstairs to the *cabine* to put this away. I can take yours too if you like."

During work hours, purses and other personal items were stowed downstairs in the model's lounge, not in lockers but on open shelves. At Maison Chanel, we were a family, Chanel insisted, and what need did a family have for locks?

She paused, then passed me the flap bag as if reluctant to part with it. "*Dziękuję.* Thank you."

Down in the *cabine*, I placed our purses side by side on an empty shelf, took a moment to refresh my lipstick, and went back upstairs.

At 3:30 p.m., Chanel walked in from lunch at the Ritz. We had just picked up where we had left off in the atelier when Madame Aubrey burst in, face flushed.

"A flacon of No. 5 is missing from the boutique," she announced to the workroom.

Given how quickly we blew through the stuff, the fuss struck me as melodramatic. "Perhaps it was sold," I suggested. "Or used to fill the atomizers."

Vehement, she shook her head. "I checked the receipts myself. We sold six bottles today but seven are missing from the case. And the atomizers were filled last night before closing. We have a thief among us."

All of us were herded into the salon, the mirrors reflecting our tight, anxious faces.

Bridget, Hanna and I stood together.

Catching Hanna's worried look, I leaned in and whispered, "I'm sure they'll get to the bottom of this, and then we'll all have a good laugh."

Madame Millet was summoned to weigh in. She insisted that every employee in both the atelier and boutique submit to having her handbag searched.

"The honest have nothing to hide," she told us, tone dour.

The purses were brought up from below and crowded onto the worktables for inspection. When Madame Millet's assistant tried handing me my former purse, reflexively I reached out to take it, then I remembered about the switch and picked up the pouchette instead.

"We switched," I explained.

Hanna reached for the flap bag, but Madame Millet grabbed it away and opened it.

"*Voilà!*" She brought out a bottle of Chanel No. 5, the box still sealed.

Hanna shrank back. "I do not know how it got there."

Madame Millet snorted. "Your sticky fingers put it there, mademoiselle."

Hanna turned imploring eyes on me, and I didn't hesitate to jump in.

"She's telling the truth. I carried our purses downstairs myself, and there was no perfume in either bag. Someone must have slipped it in after we went back to work. As a nasty prank," I added, picking up on the snickers and whispers among several of the other girls.

Had one of them slipped the perfume inside intending to retrieve it at the end of the day? That anyone would risk her livelihood for a flacon of perfume was hard to imagine. Then again, a bottle of No. 5 sold for six hundred francs, the equivalent of twenty U.S. dollars. The steep price put it out of reach for a typical Parisian shopgirl.

Or perhaps the goal was to get Hanna in trouble, fired. Amid the tensions with Germany, resentment against the refugees, many of whom were Jewish, was growing. But I was reasonably sure no one had seen us swap handbags.

Uncharacteristically quiet until then, Mademoiselle Coco walked up to Hanna. "Gather your things and go. I will not tolerate *voleurs* working for me."

Horrified, I said, "Any one of us could have slipped the perfume into the handbag. Did anyone *see* her steal?"

Bridget gave me a warning nudge, but I was too caught up to heed her.

Chanel's face contorted, her mouth twisting. "I opened this atelier in 1918 and not once has so much as a hatpin gone missing. And now this Polish girl arrives and bottles of *parfum* disappear."

It was only one bottle, but I was prudent enough not to nitpick.

"That's circumstantial evidence at best," I countered, more my lawyer mother's daughter than I'd known.

Chanel's black eyes burned into mine. "This is not New York, not your 'melting pot.' You are a guest of France. *My* guest. Forget your place again and you will find yourself on the next ship back."

Shaken, I stood by as Madame Millet and Madame Aubrey escorted Hanna out. The rest of us were told to get back to work.

Below in the boutique, I went through the motions of my day, but the stricken look on Hanna's face as she was led away stuck with me.

I was folding scarves and brooding when Bridget walked up.

"Cheer up, Daise, this will all blow over. You'll be back on the tit in no time."

"I'm not so sure," I said glumly.

"You mustn't take it all so to heart. Mark my words, by tomorrow, it'll be as good as forgotten. People like Mademoiselle Coco are a different breed to us."

Despite the dust-up, I found myself defending her. "She's not the same as Misia Sert and the others," I said. "She started with nothing and worked hard for everything she has."

Bridget snorted. "She's worked hard all right, shagging toffs like the Duke of Westminster. Bendor, he goes by, after his *racehorse*. Oh, don't give me that look. I'm not saying anything that isn't already known. The Chanel textile factory in Huddersfield that her nephew, Monsieur Palasse, used to oversee, the house in Mayfair, the duke set it all up for her to keep her in England with him."

In enough trouble already, I shushed her and darted a look around.

Dropping her voice, she carried on. "I'm not saying I fault her for it. I wouldn't mind having a beau with deep pockets, would you?"

Fortunately for me, Bridget was called away before I had to come up with an answer.

Guiltily thinking of the money I had sitting in the Bank of France, I finished folding and walked off to straighten a display of handbags.

It was a relief to finally turn the shop sign to *Fermé*. Ordinarily, I stayed on to help Bridget tidy, and then we walked to the Métro together. When she insisted that I go home ahead, I didn't put up a fight.

I'd just crossed to the other side of rue Cambon when I spotted

Hanna standing under a lamppost, the Chanel purse dangling from her wrist.

I walked up. "Hanna, what are you still doing here?"

Forlorn eyes looked into mine. "How can I go home, mademoiselle? How can I tell my parents that I am dismissed for a theft I did not commit?" She hesitated. "Would you come with me? You could help explain."

Though I'd been looking forward to getting home and having some time to myself, I didn't see how I could say no. "All right, if you think it will help."

A half-hour walk brought us into the Marais, the Jewish quarter that straddled the third and fourth arrondissements. This was a side of Paris I'd never seen before. Unlike the gleaming limestone mansions and broad boulevards that formed the backdrop for outdoor fashion shoots, here the roofline was a jagged jumble of mansard, gabled, and flat styles, the streets narrow and twisty like those in a medieval city, the sidewalks uneven, the stone buildings densely stacked. Like the Lower East Side of New York, where Gran had lived when she had first come to New York, but which I had only ever driven through, most of the storefront signs were in Hebrew. I stuck close to Hanna, who clearly knew her way around.

We came into a small square on rue Pavée, noteworthy for a handsome synagogue in the Art Nouveau style; otherwise, the street appeared gritty and down-at-heel. Hanna pointed out her building, a tall tenement with a bright persimmon painted door and heavy, weather-beaten masonry. We entered the dark, musty foyer and Hanna led us up a creaking set of wooden stairs.

Mr. and Mrs. Kaminski sat in the small parlor of their fifth-floor apartment listening to the radio. Hanna's mother was a worn version of her daughter, slender with pale hair turned silver and light brown eyes bracketed by worry lines.

Mr. Kaminski perused a periodical in Polish. Round-faced, bespectacled, and mostly bald with a thin combover and thick sideburns, he wore a tweed suit, vest, and trousers, the tailoring fine though the fabric was threadbare.

Hanna's mother took one look at their daughter's blotchy face and red eyes and threw down her darning. "What has happened?" she asked in English. "And who is this?"

Struggling not to cry, Hanna managed to introduce me. Between the two of us, we summed up the situation at the atelier, with me emphasizing the unfairness of Hanna's dismissal.

"I feel responsible. I was the one who insisted we switch handbags," I admitted.

"Is there any chance the true thief may come forward?" Hanna's father asked, looking at me.

"It's doubtful," I answered, not wanting to give false hope. "The entire staff was called together and given the opportunity to confess, and no one did."

He blew out a heavy breath. "In Warsaw, I had my own tailoring shop. It was my father's and his father's before him. When the Germans took the Sudetenland, the talk was that Polska would be next. We have seen how the Nazis treat the Jews of Germany and Austria. We came here to begin anew, but the Nazi anti-Semites have a long reach."

Desperate to make things right, I found myself saying, "My family owns a department store in New York. Kavanaugh's. We have a team of seamstresses and tailors on premise to make alterations. I can wire my grandmother first thing in the morning and see if a place can be found for Hanna. And also, for you, sir, if you like."

Once again, I was stepping out on a very large limb, and I knew it. But also knew that Rose Kavanaugh Blakely had never turned away a person in need in her life. I couldn't imagine that she would turn down the Kaminski family.

He shook his head, his expression weary. "You are kind, but it took all our savings to come here."

I hesitated. Perhaps the money I had in the bank could be put to use after all?

"Let's see if there's a job first and if there is we'll work out the details."

Hanna's mother took my hand and kissed the top. "You are angel."

Mortified, I pulled away. "Please, I haven't done anything yet."

"But you are willing to try," she said. "You have the good heart."

"My wife and I have lived our lives," Mr. Kaminski said. "It is not for ourselves that we worry." He turned damp eyes on his daughter. "Hanna is everything to us, our gold."

They asked me to stay for supper, but I declined, not wanting to take food from their mouths. After the disaster of a day, all I really wanted was to go home, make myself a cup of tea, and crawl under the covers.

Outside, the narrow, winding streets were a maze to me. Unlike Bridget, who seemed to have a built-in compass, I had never had much of a sense of direction. After ten minutes of wandering in circles, other than a dime-sized blister on my toe, I had nothing to show for my trouble.

Almost everyone on the street was an Orthodox Jew, the men in broad black hats, beards with side curls and long black coats. The women with their hair hidden beneath scarves, wigs, or hats and modestly attired in long sleeves, three-quarter hemlines, and thick hose. Catching snippets of their conversations, I realized most were speaking in languages other than French.

I was scraping up my courage to approach a young mother out walking with her family when I spotted a tall, dark-haired man in a camel-colored suit and bowler stepping out from a barbershop.

My heart lifted. "Dr. Jacob," I called out, waving to catch his eye, my purse swinging.

He walked up, and I caught a minty whiff of what must be shaving lather. "You are a long way from rue Cambon, mademoiselle."

Thrilled that he remembered me, I stammered out, "Yes, well, I was visiting a friend and got a bit ... turned around."

"You are lost," he said, cutting to it. His gaze homed in on my forehead, the gash slimmed to a fine, white scar just as he'd predicted. "It is healing nicely."

I felt myself flushing and reminded myself that it was his handiwork he was admiring, not me.

"Thanks to your suturing it is. And you were right about the anemia. The other doctor I saw prescribed iron pills," I put in, wistfully thinking of the beautiful dress and sophisticated hairstyle wasted on a stranger.

"I know, I read your chart," he said, and my heart stupidly lifted even though him keeping tabs on me was probably nothing more than professional protocol. "You are taking them?" His knowing look dared me to fib.

"Yes ... when I remember," I hedged. "And I make certain to eat lunch no matter how busy we get."

"Take more meat and leafy green vegetables. And not too much coffee. Or too many cigarettes. Like me," he added with a sheepish look that landed as utterly charming.

"I don't smoke at all," I admitted, which since coming to Paris felt like a failing.

He looked down at the tops of his shoes and then back up at me. "Have you had dinner?"

Thinking he meant the question as a scold, I admitted, "It's been a rotten day, and I haven't had the chance yet."

"I know a place, not too far from here, simple but good."

Surprised, I fought back a smile. "Are you asking me to dinner, doctor?"

He shrugged. "You are hungry. I am hungry. Why should we not break bread together?"

Meeting his gaze, maddeningly inscrutable, I wondered if he was asking me on a date. Or was his invitation merely a mission of mercy to keep me from fainting again? There was only one way to find out.

I set my hand in the crook of his arm, thrillingly firm beneath the fine tailoring. "Lead the way."

Chapter Eleven

We settled into an outside table at a kosher café on rue des Écouffes.

Watching me, expression amused, he asked, "Not what you are used to, I think?"

"You do realize, Dr. Jacob, that I grew up in New York City. Both Manhattan and Brooklyn have large Jewish populations."

On the way to the café, we'd passed his apartment house on rue des Rosiers, one of the better kept buildings on the block, low rise by New York City standards, with small balconies jutting from the street facing windows.

"Jean-Claude," he corrected me. Picking up a menu, he asked, "Do you mind if I order for us?"

Many men then took for granted that it was their right to do so. I liked that he asked first.

"Please do."

Our waiter approached, and Jean-Claude gave him our order in what I recognized as Yiddish. Gran's friend, Rivka Katz, had taught Neil and me a few words and phrases when we were kids.

Soon after, a carafe of white wine arrived, followed by a large platter of pickled herring and the savory potato pancakes known as latkes.

He served me first, placing a generous portion on my plate and filling my wine glass.

Hungrier than I'd realized, I tucked in, adding a dollop of sour cream to my latke, which was golden brown and as good or better than any I'd had in New York. I was more skeptical of the pickled fish, but the herring turned out to be tender with just the right amount of briny bite to it.

Big bowls of fragrant chicken soup followed, topped off with a trio of savory dumplings that I knew from Mrs. Katz were called matzo balls.

Served with the meal was the mainstay of every French table: a baguette.

Jean-Claude broke off a hunk of bread and passed it to me. "French *and* kosher," he pointed out.

"Delicious," I said, dunking a corner in the soup.

I'd worried we might not have much to say to each other outside of the hospital, but conversation flowed easily as we progressed through the meal. When he asked me about my life in New York, homesickness had me telling him all about my family. My stalwart lawyer mother who'd championed underdogs all her life. Dad, modern minded and loyal as a Labrador, who had served us bowls of cold cereal and plates of burned toast on nights when mom was working late. Neil, my artist brother, restless and still searching for his place in the world. Uncle Blake, smart and steadfast and always a little aloof. Grandpa Adam, a bestselling novelist whose literary debut was a thinly veiled version of his youthful romance with my grandmother. And lastly, Gran, the founder of Kavanaugh's and the fulcrum of our family.

Midway through the meal, I realized I had done most of the talking.

Embarrassed at being such a chatterbox, I asked, "How did you decide on plastic surgery as your field?"

His gaze shuttered, and instantly I regretted my question.

"I didn't mean to pry. It's none of my business."

He flagged a hand, sweeping away my apology. "*Non*, it's all right. My father is … was a *guele cassée*. A broken face."

I hadn't expected that. "I'm so sorry," I said sincerely.

He reached for the carafe and topped off our wine. "He was born in Luxembourg, but his family came to Paris when he was a child. When war broke out with Prussia, he was conscripted into the French army and received the Croix de Guerre for his courage at the First Battle of the Marne."

"You and your family must be very proud," I ventured, thinking of Uncle Joey who no number of medals could ever bring back.

He raised his wine glass and took a drink. "He served France far better than she did him. When we visited Papa in the auxiliary hospital, my little sister, Rachelle, ran screaming from the room. To her, he was a monster. The night before he was to be released to come home to us, he hanged himself."

On impulse, I reached across the table and touched the top of his arm. When he didn't pull away, I let my hand lie for a moment before taking it back.

He sent me an apologetic look. "Now you see what a misanthrope I am."

"After today, I'm feeling a bit misanthropic myself," I admitted.

His warm brown eyes looked into mine. "Sometimes it helps to talk."

I told him about Hanna's unfair firing and how the missing perfume had been pinned on her largely because she was Polish.

"This seamstress, she is also Jewish?" he asked once I'd finished.

"I believe so, yes," I said, recalling the mezuzah I'd seen affixed to the right side of the outer door of the Kaminski's apartment.

Expression grim, he reached for his cigarettes, not the Gitanes that Chanel smoked but Gauloises. "We wag our fingers at the Nazis, but we should look to ourselves first. Hatred of Jews is not new to France."

I remembered Mr. Kaminski saying something similar.

Shaking the light blue pack, he pulled out a cigarette, hesitated, and then slid it back in.

"Go ahead, I don't mind," I rushed to reassure him. "I'm used to it by now. Mademoiselle Coco smokes all the time."

A grunt was all the reply I got. As I had when we had first met at the hospital, I got the strong feeling that he didn't approve of Chanel.

Before I could prod him for his reasons, our waiter came back to clear our plates.

Jean-Claude looked over at me. "Would you like dessert? The apple tart is *très bon*."

Though I didn't see how I could squeeze in another bite, I wasn't ready for the evening to end. "Perhaps we could share?"

"*Bonne idée.*" Jean-Claude nodded to the waiter and then lit his cigarette, careful to direct the smoke away from me despite my insistence that I wasn't bothered by it.

Dessert came. Jean-Claude forked up a morsel and held it out to me. "The first bite is always the best."

Looking into his eyes, I opened for him. The fork sliding between my lips set off a strange, fluttery feeling inside me, not in my stomach but lower, in the private place between my legs.

"It is good?" Reaching across, he brushed a crumb from the corner of my mouth, and I thought I saw his hand tremble.

"Delicious," I answered, though lost in his eyes, his scent, these *feelings*, the pastry might have been cardboard for all I cared.

After the meal, he hailed a taxi to take me home. Holding the door for me, his hand brushed the small of my back, and more shivery warmth jetted through me. I turned back to him for *la bise*, the customary French bumping of cheeks I was still mastering. Grazing my cheek against both of his, the skin smooth from his recent shave, I couldn't help thinking what it would feel like to share a real kiss instead.

Stepping back, I said, "Thank you for dinner. And for saving me from wandering around in circles."

He inclined his head. "Thank you for saving me from eating alone. I forget how pleasant it can be to share a meal with a companion."

Meaning he must not have a girlfriend!? I held my breath and waited, certain he was working up to ask me out.

The taxi driver honked his horn.

Jarred, I took a stumbling step back. "*A bientôt*," I said, French for *see you soon*. I hesitated, and then asked, "Will I ... see you soon?"

His eyes clouded, and his gaze veered away. "*Bonne nuit*, Daisy. Get home safely."

I spent most of the taxi ride home kicking myself for being too forward, too *American*, and frightening him off. Perhaps I had read too much into him feeding me the tart, which had felt more intimate and romantic and ... sensual than any kiss I had ever had.

Back in the apartment, I turned my mind to the missing flask of No. 5. The perfume hadn't dropped into my former handbag by itself. Someone had put it there but why? To get Hanna in trouble because she was Jewish, and an immigrant, was the conclusion I'd leaped to. But no one had been around to see me give her the purse.

The answer was so blatantly obvious that I marveled I hadn't come to it earlier. Someone at Maison Chanel had hidden the perfume in what they believed to be my handbag to get *me* in trouble. Millet had never forgiven me for going over her head to get Hanna hired. I'd figured she would get back at me somehow, but hadn't imagined she would go to such lengths.

The next morning, I stopped in at the Ritz before work to send a telegram to Gran about the Kaminskis. Blanche was covering the front desk when I walked up, wearing a bold print dress I recognized in a glance as a Schiaparelli.

She greeted me with her customary smile. "Daisy, what can I do for you?" she said, never missing an opportunity to speak English with me.

"I'd like to send a telegram to New York."

I reached into my handbag for my wallet to pay, but she wouldn't have it.

"Put your money away. We New Yorkers have got to stick together," she added with a wink.

Giving up, I gave her the text of the telegram, which she keyed in. When I came to the part about Hanna being wrongfully fired from Chanel, I thought I heard her mutter "bitch" beneath her breath.

Afterwards, I thanked her and left the hotel by the back entrance. Crossing rue Cambon, I felt like a soldier bracing for battle.

"Where's Millet? Aubrey?" I asked Bridget, busy wiping down the glass top display counters.

"Well, good morning to you, too," she said with a smirk, then waved her Turkish cloth toward the staircase.

I climbed the mirrored stairs, my ears hot as coals. Walking into the third-floor workroom, sure enough I came across Madame Millet and Madame Aubrey huddled in a corner. Seeing me, they fell silent, but their smirks stayed in place.

Fed up, I marched over to them. "I know it was one of you who put the flask of No. 5 in the flap bag."

Millet's eyes narrowed. Aubrey sucked her teeth.

"You are making up stories, mademoiselle," Millet insisted.

"Take care who you accuse," Aubrey warned.

Their vehement denials didn't begin to make me doubt myself.

"You can play innocent all you like but your nastiness has gotten an innocent girl fired," I said, too righteous in my outrage to care that I was shooting myself in the foot. "I hope you can live with that. I wouldn't want to."

Turning my back on their stunned faces, I walked away with what I flattered myself was an admirable display of dignity.

Later that morning, Mademoiselle Coco breezed in at her usual time. I girded myself for a reprisal of the previous day's tirade.

Instead, all smiles, she beckoned me over. "Marguerite, *chérie*, I need your opinion on a new design I came up with this morning."

Startled, I nodded. "*Oui, mademoiselle.*"

She brushed by and sailed up the mirrored stairs.

Following her up, I told myself that she hadn't fired Hanna for being Polish or Jewish. She'd fired her because Madame Millet had convinced her that the girl had stolen. If there was a villain in the story it was the *première atelier*, not Mademoiselle Coco. And yet the nagging voice in my head, which had started sounding an awful lot like Gran, asked if I wasn't drawing the wool over my own eyes.

A chuckle brought me back to the moment. I looked over my shoulder at Bridget holding her atomizer. "Back on the tit," she said with a grin.

The next day when I stopped in at the Ritz, I had a telegram from Gran. As luck would have it, her head tailor had retired recently and one of the seamstresses was leaving at the end of the month to get married. Relieved, I used my lunch break to take my passbook to the bank and withdraw the funds to cover the ocean liner tickets to New York for Hanna and her parents. Back at Maison Chanel, I stuffed the money in my shoe rather than entrust it to my handbag.

As soon as work was over, I took a taxi to the Kaminski flat. A flood of happy tears greeted my good news, with Mr. Kaminski swearing to pay me back every centime as soon as he and Hanna started working. That time when they asked me to supper, I accepted. A bottle of Krupnik was opened, and glasses poured and passed around. The meal was merry, one toast leading to another. When I finally got up from the table, my nose was numb.

Afterwards, with the honey-sweetened liquor singing through my veins, I made my way to rue des Rosiers where Jean-Claude lived, hoping to run into him again. After our lovely time together at the impromptu dinner, I had been sure he was going to ask me out on a real date. If only that taxi driver hadn't honked his horn. If only I hadn't shot off my big mouth, maybe he would have.

The adage that lightning doesn't strike twice proved sadly true. Though I managed to find the barbershop where I had spotted him and the café where we had dined, there was no more sign of him than if he had been a ghost.

Chapter Twelve

Christmas Eve 1938
Fall slipped into winter and before I knew it, Christmas was upon us, my first away from home. Shop windows shone with colorful displays, patisserie shelves overflowed with decadent desserts like cotillon Christmas chocolate cake, mille-feuille, and traditional *Buches de Noël* (Yule Logs). The façade of Galeries Lafayette was illuminated with an electric light display of elves decorating a Christmas tree. Magical as it all was, I missed New York.

I hadn't seen or heard from Jean-Claude since our impromptu dinner and had come to conclude that my upset over Hanna's firing had led me to misread his friendliness as flirtation. The depressing prospect left me feeling even more lonesome. When a fat packet of letters arrived from my family, I ripped it open and read the contents in a single sitting.

Everyone sounded well and mostly the same, Mom going on about the latest case she was trying and dad tinkering with his ancient Rolls Royce every free moment he got, the car a relic from his and Mom's courting days. Gran's letter was mostly about Kavanaugh's, which had taken *The Nutcracker* as its Christmas theme, the dazzling store windows dressed by my brother, who seemed to finally be finding his footing.

The Ritz was likewise magnificently ornamented for the holidays, including an enormous Christmas tree set to the side of the curved grand staircase, its limbs festooned with exquisite crystal and glass ornaments and fat red velvet bows, its evergreen scent filling the air. Every year, Marie-Louise Ritz, widow of the hotel's founder, hosted a Christmas Eve cocktail hour and buffet supper for hotel residents. Though I had been looking forward to a cozy night at home with Bridget, when Chanel invited me along as her guest, I didn't see how I could say no.

A few hours before the event I was frantically searching for something to wear.

Pulling my head out of the crammed closet, I looked over at Bridget. "I feel awful leaving you on Christmas Eve."

Dressed in a housecoat and with her hair in rollers, she shrugged. "I'll be all right. A few of us *vendeuses* are meeting up at Café Voisin." She shoved in beside me. "What are you wearing?"

I brought out the white lace Chanel gown Gran had got me for my birthday, still in its linen garment bag. "This, I think."

I drew down the zipper and lifted out the gown, feeling a bit nervous and not only because I was running late. Until then, Bridget had never seen the gown in full, at least not that I knew of. While she had saved enough to buy several Chanel day dresses and accessories from older collections, an evening gown was out of her reach. Not wanting to show her up, until then I had left mine in the closet.

Bridget whistled. "Gorgeous but a bit summery, don't you think?"

"I do," I agreed, draping it over my arm, "but it's all I've got."

Though I could have tapped into my bank account and bought out the boutique, other than paying for Hanna and her parents' passage to New York, I had kept my promise to myself and lived solely on my small salary.

An hour later, I entered the Ritz bar where the cocktail portion of the evening was in full swing. Chanel was nowhere in sight, but I glimpsed several familiar faces, including the millionaire French industrialist, Charles Bedaux and his Michigan-born wife, Fern, Arletty, and Madame Ritz in an Edwardian era gown greeting guests while her two Belgian griffons roamed the room sniffing out scraps of fallen food. Awash in a sea of jewel-toned satins and brocades, in my lovely, lightweight dress, I felt very much a fish out of water.

"You look lost, mademoiselle."

I turned to see a golden-haired gentleman in his early forties, slender and of medium height, impeccably dressed and raffishly handsome, smiling with the casual confidence of a man who knows he's irresistible to women. Most women, anyway.

"May I offer my assistance?" he asked me in English, his voice carrying a trace of a German accent.

"I'm a guest of Mademoiselle Chanel," I said, annoyed at being cornered. Despite his chivalry and good looks, something about him rubbed me the wrong way.

"Coco and I are great friends," he said and though his Teutonic features remained arranged into a polite mask, I had the sense that he was laughing at me. "I have it on good authority that she will be down shortly, time enough for us to enjoy a glass of champagne while we become better acquainted."

Before I could think how to refuse, he snagged two flutes off the tray of a passing waiter and handed me one.

"*Prost.*" He saluted me with his fizzing flute.

I lifted my glass. "*Sláinte.*"

"You are Irish?" he asked, his gaze grazing my face and bare shoulders.

I sipped my champagne. "On my mother's side."

His sensual mouth spread into a smile. "You must be Coco's Marguerite. The department store heiress from New York?"

I hesitated, disappointed to hear that was how she had described me.

"Daisy Blakely." I held out my hand and he took it, his lips brushing the top of my glove.

"Baron Hans Günther von Dincklage at your service, Fräulein." He bowed at the waist, then straightened. "Or perhaps you prefer miss?"

"Mademoiselle, please. What brings you to Paris, baron?"

Before he could answer, Mademoiselle Coco walked up.

That evening's ensemble was a stunning black sequined evening gown and matching slit cape. In the softening light of the candles, she looked a good decade younger, calling attention to her lively dark eyes and full lips.

"I see you've met Spatz," she said, setting a possessive hand on the baron's forearm.

Young and inexperienced though I was, I recognized a woman staking her claim when I saw it.

"Spatz?" I echoed.

"It is 'sparrow' in German," he explained. "A small name from childhood."

He didn't strike me as particularly sparrow-like. More of a peacock, I would have said, not that I knew all that much about birds beyond New York City pigeons.

"The baron and I met through mutual friends in Toulon. Or was it Monte Carlo?" she asked, looking over at him.

"My dear Coco, I find it impossible to remember a time when I did not know you."

The suave reply saw her simpering like a schoolgirl.

"Spatz is a special attaché to the German embassy in Paris," she told me, sounding proud.

A propogandist for the Nazi regime, no wonder I had taken such a strong, immediate dislike to him! Kristallnacht, the Night of Broken Glass, was still fresh in all our minds. Bridget and I had listened to the British Broadcasting Corporation's, BBC's, harrowing account of how, in early November, the Nazis had launched a brutal pogrom against the Jews of Germany and Austria, torching Jewish businesses and synagogues, desecrating cemeteries, and dragging families from their homes to be beaten and, in some cases, butchered. Some thirty thousand Jewish men were believed to have been arrested for no reason and interned at Nazi concentration camps. When I had telephoned home the following Sunday, Grandpa Adam mentioned that President Roosevelt had recalled the U.S. ambassador to Germany over the incident.

I took another sip of champagne. "You speak English like a Brit," I observed, too young to know what an ass I was making of myself. "You hardly have any German accent at all."

He accepted my "compliment" with a spare nod.

Mademoiselle Coco scoffed. "Spatz isn't German, not really."

I glanced back at him. Blond and blue-eyed with a pale complexion and classically sculpted features, he might have stepped out of a Nazi propaganda poster.

"My mother was English," he admitted.

"It must be difficult for you having family on both sides of the current troubles," I said, curious as to what he would say.

He shrugged. "The bonds of blood between Germany and England run deep. The British royal family only took the surname of Windsor in the last war; before, they were the house of Saxe-Coburg. German. Among the British aristocracy, there are many who applaud the measures the Führer is taking to rebuild Germany."

"He's doing a lot more than rebuild," I countered. "Overtaking sovereign nations, butchering innocent women and children, not to mention imposing his absurd Aryanism."

He lifted a sandy brow. "Was it not we Germans who helped to settle your American West?"

"I have nothing but admiration for the German people," I said, feeling the urge to defend myself. "It's your Führer I'm not a fan of. His detestable actions don't appear to leave much room for diplomacy."

"I prefer to believe that there is always room for diplomacy. And hope," he added with another of his smooth smiles.

Monsieur Dabescat rang the dinner bell, putting an end to further back and forth, which was just as well since I was clearly outmatched.

"Shall we, ladies?" the baron said, his gaze encompassing both me and Mademoiselle Coco.

"I'll be along in a minute," I lied.

Watching them walk off to join the others filing out toward the Grille Room, I contemplated slipping out and joining Bridget at Café Voisin.

"You did not do too badly."

I whirled to find myself facing yet another German, also blond and blue-eyed but young, in his early twenties and a looker. Topping six feet, his broad shoulders stretching the seams of his white dinner jacket, he reminded me of Buster Crabbe, the Olympic swimmer turned Hollywood movie star.

Seeing sympathy in his aquamarine-colored eyes, I bristled. "You were eavesdropping."

My accusation drew a dazzling smile that surfaced a dimple in his jaw, making him even more ridiculously handsome. "It is a party. Everyone eavesdrops."

He had me there.

"You were brave to take him on," he continued. "Baron von Dincklage has made diplomacy and international relations his career."

"Propaganda, you mean?" I said, not yet ready to lay down my sword.

He gave me a measuring look. "It would be a pity to spoil such a pleasant evening arguing politics. I much prefer discussing literature. Tell me, what is your opinion of *My Ántonia*?"

His question floored me. "The Willa Cather novel? I've never read it."

He looked disappointed. "I was going to ask you if you thought it an accurate depiction of the American pioneer life."

"I've never been out west, so I can't say," I admitted.

Before coming to Paris, I'd never been farther from home than Connecticut. For the first time, it occurred to me that Gran may have had other objectives in sending me overseas besides learning to judge the cut of a sleeve or the swing of a skirt. If I was serious about taking Kavanaugh's international, and I was, first I had some growing up to do.

He took a step back. "I am being rude. We have not been introduced. Friedrich Augustus Eberhardt." He clicked his heels together in that oh so German way and bowed, though coming from him the gesture seemed more courtly than dictatorial.

"That's quite a serious-sounding name," I said, smiling despite myself.

His own smile widened, and I saw that he had perfect teeth, straight and white and worthy of a Pepsodent ad. Unlike Jean-Claude, he must not be a smoker.

"I come from a very serious, very old Prussian military family," he admitted, eyes dancing as if he were sharing a secret. "But please, call me Fritz."

I held out my gloved hand. "Daisy Blakely, though Mademoiselle Chanel prefers Marguerite."

He took my hand, pressing it briefly. "And what do you prefer?"

It had been a while since anyone had asked me that.

"I'll answer to either," I said, figuring I had taken enough stances for one evening.

Caught up in talking to him, suddenly I saw that the bar had emptied. Other than the staff, we were the only two remaining.

"Would you do me the honor of allowing me to escort you to dinner, Mademoiselle Daisy Marguerite Blakely? I hear they are serving choucroute, an Alsatian recipe for sauerkraut served with sausages and potatoes," he added, no doubt in response to my blank look. "I would hate for it to grow cold." Bringing his face close to mine, he dropped his voice to a whisper. "I will let you in on a secret – it is not *gut* cold. In fact, it is terrible."

"I'll pass on the pickled cabbage, but I am hungry." I surrendered my empty champagne flute to a passing waiter and gave him my hand.

I spent a very pleasant Christmas Eve in Fritz's company. Attentive and mannered, well-read and well-traveled, he was also easygoing and movie-star handsome. Like me, he missed his family, especially his school age sister. We both adored Paris, with its cafés and public gardens and gleaming limestone buildings and monuments.

At midnight, we toasted the holiday, with several couples stealing kisses beneath the mistletoe. Fritz didn't try to kiss me, though loosened up by several glasses of champagne, I wouldn't have minded if he had.

Not that the brush with Baron von Dincklage didn't still rankle. I couldn't say what infuriated me more: that he had gotten the better of me or that he clearly had enjoyed doing so. I was determined that the next time I found myself face to face with him, or someone like him, I would be better prepared.

That Christmas morning while Bridget was still sleeping, I slipped out to the newsstand around the corner and bought copies of every paper and broadsheet I could get my hands on.

Chapter Thirteen

January 1939

The start of 1939 was damp and raw, and Madame LeBrun stingy with her coal, but with my internship set to end after the February 5th collection, I was determined to make the most of every frosty moment. Bridget and I went ice skating at the Piscine Molitor, the public pool by the Bois de Boulogne converted to an ice rink in winter, and roller-skating at the Vélodrome d'Hiver, the winter sports stadium near the Eiffel Tower known to locals as the Vél d'Hiv.

A packet of letters arrived from home. One weekday evening when Bridget was out on a date, I huddled in blankets on the sofa and settled in for a leisurely read-through. As usual, I opened Gran's first.

> *Darling Daisy,*
> *Another year gone by; can you believe it? Hopefully I'm not the first to let the cat out of the bag, but the news is so delicious and long overdue that I believe I'll risk it. Both your uncle and brother have lady friends!*

I felt my mouth fall open. As far as I knew, Uncle Blake hadn't stepped out with anyone in two years, not since his former fiancée, Valerie, called off their wedding and presumably broke his heart, though the rest of us saw it as a lucky escape from a lifetime of henpecking.

As for Neil, though he was tall and blonde and decent ... okay, *good* looking, the spit of our father as a young man, other than going to prom, which Mom had pushed him into, he had always been too shy to ask a girl out.

> *Blake met his Henrietta – she goes by Hattie, how charming, don't you agree – when she came into Kavanaugh's to convince us to start carrying Madam C.J. Walker products in our cosmetics department Miss Madge Quigley, the department head, was about to call in security to escort her out (the nerve!) when Blake gallantly interceded. I am happy to report that our cosmetics counter now carries the full Madame Walker line alongside the latest makeups by Max Factor, Elizabeth Arden, Helena Rubinstein, and Revlon. As for Miss Quigley, I presented her with her walking papers.*

I paused there, grinning from ear to ear. Miss Quigley was a forked-tongue shrew who had delighted in chewing out her subordinate staff, though with customers butter wouldn't melt in her mouth. White customers, at any rate. Gran had been angling to catch her in the act for years now. I was only sorry I hadn't been there to see her get her comeuppance.

> *Neil's amour is a bit of a mystery. All the dear boy will say is that she is Italian, her parents hailing from Sicily, and that*

she lives with them and an older brother, a police officer, on Staten Island. Your mother is determined that he will bring her by the house before the month runs out, and as we both know, when my Moira sets her mind to something, it almost certainly comes about.

Speaking of which, she's begun looking into business schools on your behalf. A gentle reminder, dear girl, after the 5th of February, like Cinderella with the clock chiming midnight, your lovely time in Paris draws to a close. In the interim, don't let Mademoiselle Chanel work you too hard. Find time to enjoy these final five weeks. Selfishly, I cannot wait to have you in my arms again. Until that happy time, I remain …

Your loving grandmother,
Rose Kavanaugh Blakely

I slid the letter back in its envelope with a sigh. Five more weeks in Paris, how final it sounded.

By then I had as good as given up on hearing from Jean-Claude. As Bridget never missed an opportunity to point out, there were plenty of other fish in the sea. Though I hated to admit it, she was right. It would be stupid if not criminal to waste what little time I had left in Paris pining for someone who hadn't lifted a finger to see me again.

I was, however, seeing a good bit of Fritz. Unlike Jean-Claude, Fritz was a fast mover. The day after Christmas, he had invited me to New Year's Eve supper at the Ritz. When at midnight he moved in to kiss me, I had let him. Only at the last moment, Jean-Claude's face flashed through my mind, and I kept my lips closed. What might have led to a passionate kiss stopped at a friendly peck.

Later, I kicked myself, sure my cold fish treatment would mean the end of things. Instead, Fritz invited me to join him the following Sunday afternoon for a walk. It turned out we both loved the Luxembourg Gardens. Bundled up to our ears, we strolled the gravel paths, talking of everything and nothing. Near to me in age, good-natured, and whip-smart without being pretentious, he was fun and easy to be with and, despite the disappointing kiss, clearly still smitten with me. After Jean-Claude's rejection, his adoring looks were balm to my bruised ego. When at the end of the date he kissed me, on the cheek that time, and asked if he might call on me the following Sunday at Madame LeBrun's and take me walking again, I didn't have to think about my answer.

Despite the hectic preparations for the February collection, the week seemed to drag by. Sunday finally came, and Fritz arrived at the agreed-upon noontime. Bridget followed me downstairs to Madame LeBrun's parlor where he waited. Coming up on the open doorway, we saw him perched on the edge of the faded couch, his broad shoulders dwarfing the dainty camelback.

Bridget grabbed my arm, her fingers pinching. "Gawd, Daise, he's a dish," she whispered though seeing Fritz's pinkening cheeks, I was sure he'd heard her.

She wasn't wrong. Even with his golden hair hidden by a cap and a thick muffler reaching up to his ears, Fritz was a looker. I was sure Bridget wasn't the only other girl in Paris to think so.

An hour later, Fritz and I strolled up to the Medici Fountain, one of our favorite spots even though it was drained for the winter.

"Bridget was quite taken with you. For a moment, I thought I was going to have to fight her off," I teased.

Solemn faced, he shook his head. "You would not have to fight."

Meeting his earnest eyes, it was my turn to feel embarrassed and not only because my playful remark had held a hint of real jealousy. Fritz wanted me and not only as a friend. Seeing him through Bridget's eyes made me realize I wanted to be more than friends, too. But did I want him enough to completely give up on Jean-Claude? Until I figured that out, it wouldn't be right to lead him on.

Turning the topic, I said, "You seem very at home in Paris."

He shrugged. "Sometimes. My mother was from Alsace-Lorraine. She spoke French to us at home as well as German." He hesitated. "She died of tuberculosis when I was seven."

I reached over and touched his sleeve. "It must have been hard on you and your sister growing up without her."

"I was away at school, and Klara was too young to remember much." Changing the subject, he asked, "How is the February collection coming?"

I shrugged. "It's the usual mayhem, but I'm getting used to it."

When I'd first come to Paris, Chanel's every cross word or black look had sent me into spasms of panic, but I had grown a thicker skin since. Whatever mood she was in, it usually passed quickly.

"You like working for Mademoiselle Chanel?" he asked.

I didn't have to think about it. "I do, very much. My grandmother arranged my apprenticeship, and I'm learning a lot."

Shadowing Mademoiselle Coco continued to be an education. Lately, she'd had me accompany her to clothing shops that sold *prêt à porter* copies of her designs. Like a child playing dress-up, she insisted on traveling incognito, tying a scarf over her chin-length hair and hiding her dark eyes behind huge sunglasses. After perusing the clothing on racks and scribbling in a pocket-sized notebook, she would fling off her disguise and reveal herself to the flabbergasted shopkeeper. Some days she was generous, offering advice for improving the pirated products. Other times, especially if she had been brooding over her "stolen" perfume company, she would call out her imitators as *voleurs*, thieves, and threaten to seek justice in the courts. By then, I had accepted that everything about her was always in conflict, almost as if two people inhabited the same body.

"But you will return to New York soon?" Fritz asked, expression wistful.

"After the fifth of February," I admitted, though lately I had begun asking myself if I really had to.

As homesick as I still sometimes got, leaving Paris would mean sacrificing my independence as well as my friendship with Bridget. And saying goodbye to not one but two men: Fritz and Jean-Claude, or at least the dream of him.

His glum look mirrored my mood. "I will be sad to see you go but perhaps it is for the best."

"If Hitler invades Poland, you mean?" I pressed, breaking our unspoken agreement to steer clear of Franco-German politics.

I had listened to enough BBC news reports to know that if Germany seized Poland, a cornerstone country in the Treaty of Versailles, her allies Britain and France would have little choice but to declare war.

Rather than reply, he pulled the scarf from his neck and wrapped it around mine, the tender gesture warming me as much as the wool did. "There is a good café on rue Notre Dame des Champs. We can eat something and warm up."

"I'd like that," I said. "Afterwards, do you mind if we stop in at Shakespeare and Company? I promised my grandmother I'd keep up my acquaintance with Miss Beach."

The mention of the bookstore brought a smile to his face. "Of course. Perhaps my copy of *My Ántonia* will be in. She promised to order it."

I had brought Fritz by the week before. Though he never wore his uniform on our outings, his Teutonic looks marked him as German. It didn't help that he stood a head taller than most Frenchmen. If Miss Beach ... Sylvia disapproved of me socializing with a German soldier, neither she nor Miss Monnier gave any sign of it. Both women were the souls of hospitality, never failing to invite us to their upstairs apartment for tea. That Sunday was no exception.

After my date with Fritz, I stopped in at the Ritz to make my monthly Sunday call home to New York before it got too late there. I had spoken to my parents and Neil the month before, which made it Gran's turn. I spent most of the call talking a mile a minute, pleading my case for why I ought to be allowed to extend my stay in Paris through a second summer, highlighting all the marvelous contacts I was making, shamelessly namedropping Charles and Fern Bedaux, the Duke and Duchess of Windsor and John Cocteau, all clients or friends of Chanel. Then there was the indisputable knowledge of design and merchandising I was picking up, and the self-reliance I was learning by living off my wages. Surely the hands-on experience of working for the world's most celebrated couturier trumped enrolling in some fusty old business college.

Finally, I stopped for air.

Gran's sigh reached me through the receiver. "No promises, Daisy, but I'll speak to your parents and see if something can be worked out."

Under the circumstances, it was the best I could hope for. "Thank you, Gran. Give my love to everyone."

Feeling hopeful, I stepped out of the office into the lobby.

"Marguerite."

Only one person in Paris called me that.

I turned to Mademoiselle Coco walking toward me from the Hallway of Dreams, wearing a black jersey dress, its simplicity offset by a profusion of long gold and glass-beaded necklaces.

"Join me for a drink," she said, beckoning me to the bar.

Though I had been looking forward to a cozy evening at home with Bridget, taking in her melancholy expression, I didn't see how I could say no, especially as I was hoping to stretch out my internship.

"I'd love to," I said.

A few minutes later, we were tucked into a table with flutes of champagne, the rest of the bottle chilling in the footed ice bucket beside us.

She took a sip of champagne and reached for her cigarettes.

"I miss being in love. Life is so terribly boring without it," she lamented. Lighting a cigarette, she took a deep drag and looked out to the bar, empty except for the two of us and Frank. "I need to find myself another Englishman. English men are strong, virile. Boy was English and after him there was Bendor, the Duke of Westminster. I was with him for almost ten years. The whole time he showered me with jewels, houses, and holidays on his yacht, and yet … I never wanted to weigh more heavily on a man than a bird. And then there was my dear Paul Iribe, to whom I was engaged. He dropped dead three years ago while the two of us were playing tennis."

"I'm so sorry," I murmured.

Given these brooding reminiscences, I gathered things must not be going so well with Baron von Dincklage.

As if reading my mind, she said, "Spatz likes to say his mother is English, but though she spent time in England, she is German. If war comes to France, he will fly back to Germany like a sparrow." She pantomimed a fluttering motion with her cigarette hand, dropping ash onto the tabletop.

For all her fame and wealth and glittering friends, in moments like this one, her life struck me as awfully lonesome and more than a little sad.

"Have you ever been in love, Marguerite?"

I thought of Jean-Claude, who had made no effort to see me again, and Fritz, who seized every opportunity to do so. If it wasn't for him being a German soldier at a time when Germany and France were edging toward war, he would have been the perfect boyfriend. Unlike Jean-Claude who was brilliant and dedicated but also dark and brooding, Fritz was even-tempered and fun and made no secret of his feelings for me. I had liked him from the start, not the *coup de foudre* I had felt for Jean-Claude, a dark storm that threatened to sweep me away, but more of a slow stirring.

My hesitancy wasn't lost on her. Those sharp eyes missed nothing, not an infinitesimal piece of lint on a dress and certainly not the awkward prevaricating of an inexperienced American girl.

"You have a lover; I can see it in on your face!" she exclaimed.

Cheeks on fire, I shook my head.

"A *tendresse*, then?"

I hesitated, then admitted, "There is a man, around my age, who I like very much."

I left off mentioning Fritz was a German soldier, though our dating was hardly a secret. As Miss Beach had warned when we had first met, the Ritz really was a fishbowl.

"And the other man?" she asked, reading between the lines.

"He's older by ten years and doesn't seem to see me in the same way as I do him," I admitted.

"And yet you burn for him?"

Embarrassed at being so transparent, I settled for nodding.

She sent me a commiserating look and took another drag of her Gitane. "The two men I've loved, Boy and Paul, I think they must remember me even in Heaven. Men always remember a woman who caused them concern and uneasiness."

Chapter Fourteen

My second summer in Paris felt a little like playing hooky from school. Giving in to my pleas, Gran had stepped in to smooth things over with Mom. The result was even better than I had hoped for. I was allowed to stay on for the August *and* February collections.

"But then it's back to New York, no more foot dragging," Gran told me over the telephone, sounding sterner than I had ever heard her. "Otherwise, your parents will have my head, and I won't blame them."

Knowing I was living in Paris on borrowed time doubled my determination to milk every moment.

That July 14th, Bastille Day, Bridget and I again joined the jubilant crowds lining the Champs-Élysées for the military parade, the broad boulevard festooned with both France's Tricolor and Britain's Union Jack. I would have loved to have brought Fritz along, but with tensions building over Hitler's insistence on annexing Poland, he couldn't very well come out with us.

Thirty thousand French and British troops marched in the bright sunshine; a mighty show of unity meant to recall the victory parade of the Great War after Germany's embarrassing total defeat. Afterwards, combined units of the French and British Air Forces flew in formation from the Arc de Triomphe to the Obelisk, a dramatic display of international unity to make Hitler sit up and take notice.

Later, we joined the thousands packing the lawn of the Champ de Mars for the fireworks over the Eiffel Tower. That year marked the one hundred and fiftieth anniversary of France's independence as well as the fiftieth anniversary of the tower, originally built as a World's Fair exhibit. As before, we stayed out late dancing and drinking wine with other young people in Trocadéro Square, the plaza splashed in multicolored lights from the Venetian lanterns strung about. Unlike the previous year, I tempered my tippling, knowing I would be needed in the atelier the next day to help push the collection.

The August 1939 collection showed a series of "gypsy" dresses in silk, cotton, and rayon with loose-flowing sleeves and full skirts. As with Chanel's Russian period in the twenties, the folk inspired outfits were a hit. In a nod to patriotism, the collection included a flouncy ivory organdy gown with red, white and blue floral embroidery.

By the end of August, Paris began bracing for a possible German invasion. Workmen took down the stained-glass windows of the Sainte-Chapelle. Curators of the Louvre began cataloging and crating the museum's treasures to be sent into hiding outside the city. Monuments and other landmarks were piled with sandbags as fortification against bomb blasts. The government evacuated thirty thousand French children to the provinces and handed out gas masks to anyone staying in the city. Streetlights were turned off as a precaution against German air raids. A dark cloud settled over the city. With every passing day, the luminous Paris I'd fallen in love with seemed to lose a little more of her light.

At the Ritz, workers dug a bomb-proof cellar in the hotel's walled garden. Jackhammers drilled from dawn to dusk, driving Chanel to declare that if they didn't finish soon her head would split. More so than the noise, worrying over her nephew, André Palasse, among the tens of thousands of Frenchmen called to guard the Maginot Line, likely accounted for her headaches. The 280-mile-long string of fortifications had been built after the Great War to defend against future German attacks.

When Fritz left a note asking to meet at the Medici Fountain at the Luxembourg Gardens in the middle of the week, I didn't have to wonder what it was about.

I found him waiting for me at the foot of the grotto-style fountain, the sculpture of "Polyphemus Surprising Acis and Galatea," a mythological star-crossed couple, visible behind him.

Walking up, I fought to put on a brave face. "You're leaving, aren't you?"

Though I had known this moment was coming, I hadn't realized until then how much our time together had meant to me. Fritz's departure would leave a huge hole in my life.

His sad eyes met mine. "The German embassy has advised all Germans to leave France immediately, and the ambassador has been recalled to Berlin."

"We'll be on opposite sides, enemies," I said, feeling miserable about it.

He drew me to him. "I could never be your enemy."

I set my cheek against his chest while he stroked my hair. When he gently tipped up my chin and leaned in to kiss me, I met him. Unlike the few boys who had kissed me back in New York, with acne spots and chewing gum they sometimes forgot to spit out, Fritz was always patient and thoughtful and thorough. That time was no different. But *I* was different. Knowing I would likely never see him again, I let myself go. My lips flowered beneath his, my body melting into his muscled heat, my hands moving over his shoulders and back, the heat from my palms causing his shirt to cling.

For the first time, Fritz was the one to break our embrace. He lifted his mouth from mine and slipped his arm from my waist. "Once the war is over, there are things I wish to say to you. Until then, go home to your family in America. You will be safe there."

Regret rushed me. All these many months I hadn't given us a chance, not really. Instead, I had wasted our time together mooning over a man who had forgotten all about me. And now the war was here, and it was too late for us.

Heart in my throat, I settled for a nod. "Please take care of yourself," I said, a poor substitute for all that I was feeling.

Rather than risk breaking down in front of him, I turned and walked quickly away.

Chapter Fifteen

By the start of September, German forces had surged into Poland. The next day, France closed its border with Germany and drafted more than five million Frenchmen, including 19,000 doctors. I had to think Jean-Claude was among them. Though I hadn't seen him since our dinner, I still thought of him from time to time. And Fritz? Despite promising to seek me out after the war, I doubted I would ever see him again. Even if I did, given the evil regime he was fighting for, could I really pick up where we had left off?

Two days later, Britain and France declared war on Germany.

Like most people, I seesawed between worry and a funny sort of relief. After all the months of waiting and wondering, the war had finally come to us.

Bridget dug in her heels and declared she wasn't budging. Throwing her arms around me, she begged me to stay, too.

"If you go back to New York, I'll have to find another roommate, and I couldn't bear it. Say you'll stay and ride out the storm with me. Through thick and thin."

"Through thick and thin," I echoed, hoping I was making the right decision.

Declaring that war was no time for fashion, Chanel announced that she would close her couture business, not only the Paris atelier and boutiques but also those in Deauville and Biarritz. Four thousand employees stood to lose their jobs – the artisans who cut her gowns, the *petites mains* who stitched each creation from scratch, the *vendeuses* like Bridget who assisted customers in her boutiques, and the mannequins who modeled her creations.

"Those greedy ingrates!" she hissed when I ventured to point out that war was a terrible time to be out of work. "Why should I care if they starve? I show them the same loyalty they showed me three years ago when they went on strike and locked me out of my shop. They are getting what they deserve."

As she'd demonstrated with the Wertheimer brothers, Chanel was more than capable of carrying a grudge against anyone she felt had betrayed her.

In the end, she decided to keep one store open, the flagship boutique at 31 rue Cambon. Whittled down to a skeleton staff of five: Millet, who made alterations for existing clients, Aubrey who did the books, Bridget who manned the perfume counter, and me, the shop would continue to sell No. 5 along with hats, handbags and other fashion accessories. Meanwhile, twelve other couturiers continued to release their collections including Chanel's archrival, Elsa Schiaparelli.

A blizzard of letters and telegrams arrived from New York, everyone including Gran pleading with me to come home. With the atelier closed for the foreseeable, no one would have faulted me for giving my notice and doing exactly that. And yet every time I thought about going back on my word to Bridget and booking my passage to New York, I couldn't bring myself to.

It wasn't only Bridget I hated to think of leaving. Frank, Blanche and the rest of the Ritz staff were like a second family to me. And then there was Chanel. By then I knew her well enough to recognize the fragility beneath her imperious armor. Amid all her successes, her life had been marked by tragic deaths – first her mother, her sister who'd committed suicide, Boy Capel and more recently Paul Iribe. Now she risked losing another dearly loved one, André. Since he'd been sent to fight on the Front, the vial of Seconal she used as a sleep aid had nearly run out. What would happen to her if I left, too?

A few days after war was declared, an unexpected visitor showed up at the shop.

With Bridget out on an errand, I had taken over the perfume counter, though with all the upheaval, so far, we hadn't seen a single customer. The boutique door opened. Expecting Bridget, I looked up from counting our stock of No. 5 and felt my heart skid to a stop.

Jean-Claude entered. Seeing him, every word of every speech I had rehearsed since the previous fall fled my mind.

He took off his hat and approached the perfume counter. "You are still here. When I saw you coming out of the Métro the other day, I was not certain it was you."

So, we *had* run into one another, though I hadn't known it.

I reached up to touch my hair, which I'd recently let Bridget chop off into a shoulder-grazing bob. "Yes, well, it's been a while," I said, keeping my voice cold.

His gaze dropped to his hat, which he gripped with both hands.

Fingering the felt as if he were out to wear holes in it, he said, "The American has been mobilizing to operate as a military hospital as it did during the Great War. With so many on staff called to the Front, and the Americans leaving, we are short-staffed." He hesitated, shifting his feet on the beige carpet. "You will be going back to New York soon? I am surprised you have not left already."

"At the moment, my plans are up in the air," I said. "Is there something I can help you with? A *flaçon* of No. 5 perhaps?" I asked, flinging a hand to the shelved bottles behind me. "With the war on, these will be second to gold soon."

"You are angry with me," he said, not a question.

"Not angry ... All right, yes, angry. You led me on, feeding me ... apple tart and acting like you wanted to kiss me, and then I never heard from you again. If you weren't interested, why not skip the swoony dinner and put me in a cab from the start?"

Furious with him as I was, his gaze going over me did funny things to my insides. "Who says I am not interested?" he asked.

"If you are, you have a strange way of showing it."

He blew out a heavy breath. "You were so young. You *are* so young."

That time, I crossed to the front of the counter. "Not so young that I don't know my own mind." *Or heart*, I added, silently to myself.

Bridget chose that moment to walk in.

Gaze bugging, she looked between us. "I'll just pop upstairs and see if Madame Aubrey needs anything," she said, heading off toward the stairs.

Jean-Claude looked back at me. "If the Germans make it through the Maginot Line, go to the hospital. It will be the safest place."

After all this time, he'd gone out of his way to come see me at the boutique because he was concerned for me. Because he *cared*.

With nothing to lose, I asked, "Do you make a point of inviting all your former patients to shelter with you at the American?"

His dark gaze burned into mine. "Not all of them."

Before I could think what to make of that, of any of it, he turned and walked out, as much a puzzle as he had ever been.

Chapter Sixteen

A few days later, I presented myself at the American, not to seek shelter but to offer myself as a volunteer on my days off. I'd like to say that patriotism for my adopted country and a deep loathing of Nazism were all that motivated me, but that was only part of it. In coming to the boutique, Jean-Claude had shown he had feelings for me. With both of us working in the main hospital building, I would have a chance to discover how deeply those feelings ran.

After the blitzkrieg, "lightning war," Germany had rained down on Poland, razing Hanna's beloved Warsaw to rubble, we had steeled ourselves for a massive airstrike. Now that the war was on, I had envisioned myself rolling bandages and writing letters home for wounded soldiers and spooning up broth for those too ill to lift their heads – all the things that noncombatants did in wartime. Instead, the months that followed felt oddly anticlimactic.

The French started referring to the war as La Drôle de Guerre. Brits, including Bridget, called it the Phony War. There were some skirmishes at sea, but little actual fighting on land or in the air. Still, we had to treat it as real.

The hospital organized a team of women ambulance drivers to ferry patients between Neuilly and the three field hospitals set up at Fontainebleau, Angoulême, and Châteauroux. A typical New Yorker, I had never learned to drive. Instead, I spent my shifts helping prepare civilian patients for transport to other facilities, unpacking and stocking medical supplies, working in the blood bank, filing medical records, whatever was needed.

By the end of September, we received our first battlefield patient. More wounded began trickling in. One Sunday afternoon during my shift, Jean-Claude walked up to the dressing station where I stood assembling field hospital care kits.

He leaned his shoulder against the doorframe, watching me. "You have been here since eight o' clock this morning."

I made myself keep working. "So have you," I said, pleased he had noticed my comings and goings.

"There is something I want to show you." He gestured for me to join him out in the hallway.

Intrigued, I said, "All right, I'll finish here and be along in a minute."

We took the staff elevator up to the fourth floor where senior medical personnel were housed. As chief surgical resident, Jean-Claude had a room there as well though of course I had never seen it.

"This way," he said, starting down the narrow hallway.

I followed him to the stairwell and up the steep flight of narrow stairs that led to the rooftop.

He held the door, and I stepped out onto the fenced terrace, which spanned the length of the building.

Thrilled, I rushed up to the rail. "You can see all the way to the Eiffel Tower!"

"The best-kept secret in Paris," he agreed, coming up behind me.

He took off his lab coat and settled it over my shoulders, his hands lingering longer than was necessary. Enveloped in the deliciousness of lavender, vanilla and tobacco, and with the mellow autumn sunshine striking down on our faces, for a fleeting few minutes I knew what it was to be completely content.

Standing beside me, he rested his forearms on the rail and looked out.

"Mont Valérien," he said, pointing to the left, "and that is Ville de Suresnes." He gestured to a hilly cluster of trees.

"Beautiful," I said, sneaking a sideways peek at his profile, the high forehead, aquiline nose and stubborn chin unspeakably dear to me. "If I were you, I'd come up here every chance I got."

Shaking his head, he admitted, "I cannot remember the last time I did."

"Not even on Bastille Day?"

Looking across to the Eiffel Tower rising above the treetops, I couldn't imagine letting such a splendid view of the fireworks go to waste.

He turned to face me, rolling his eyes. "We French call it *La Fête Nationale*, and Dr. Jack asked me to assist with removing a urinary tract obstruction, so *non*, I did not."

Dr. Jack was Dr. Sumner Jackson, the big, bluff urologist and surgeon from Maine whom everyone on staff called by the shortened version of his name.

"Well, I'm honored you invited me up. Why did you?" I asked, hoping to draw him out.

A shrug met my fishing. "We should enjoy it while we can."

His cryptic words brought me back to the world's present

problems, admittedly a lot weightier than one American girl's romantic longings.

"Do you really think the Boches will break through the Maginot Line and invade?" I asked.

Since Fritz had gone, I'd adopted the derogatory slang term for the Germans, which roughly translated to "cabbage heads." The epithet probably derived from the fermented cabbage, sauerkraut, that was a staple of the German diet, although nobody seemed to know for certain.

Still gazing out, he nodded. "You have only to look at a map to see where we are vulnerable. West of the line are four-hundred kilometers of unprotected borderlands with Belgium and the Netherlands. De Gaulle has warned for years that we cannot withstand attack from a modern army, but his superiors, puffed-up old men like Pétain, still live in the trenches of the Great War."

Having become a newspaper reader over the past year, I knew a bit about *Maréchal* Phillippe Pétain. Revered by the French as the hero of the Battle of Verdun, the eighty-two-year-old Great War veteran was Vice Premier in Prime Minister Paul Reynaud's Third Republic government. Colonel Charles de Gaulle had been his protégé until the two men fell out. Many French, including Mademoiselle Coco, considered de Gaulle to be an alarmist.

Given the Nazis' violent persecution of Jewish citizens in Germany as well as the conquered countries of Austria, the Sudetenland and now Poland, I trembled to think what would happen to Jean-Claude if France were invaded.

Jean-Claude interrupted my thoughts with, "Your family cannot be happy that you are still here."

Looking away, I admitted, "Now that the war's on, they're clamoring for me to come home. I just got another letter from

Mom this morning. She wants me to enroll in business school at Brooklyn College."

I was still composing my reply in my head, which would emphasize that the current conflict wasn't a real war, but a phony one.

Gaze brushing my profile, he asked, "What do *you* want?"

I didn't have to think about it. "Not to waste four more years in school when I already know what I want to do with my life."

"Opening your Paris department store," he said, that time with a smile in his voice.

I nodded. "After more than a year apprenticing at Maison Chanel, I have a much better understanding of the French market. The Parisian sense of style is very different from ours in New York or Los Angeles, less glitzy, more boutique. Once the war's over, I'd like to stay on in Paris and oversee the design, the building, the staffing, all of it. I can make a success of it, I know it."

Just as Gran had taken her modest dry goods emporium and grown it into a grand department store, I was determined to turn my Parisian vision into reality. Lately, when I pictured my future self, whether in Paris or New York, I'd started seeing Jean-Claude at my side.

"Then we must hope for a swift German defeat," he said, but his eyes told me he didn't hold out much hope of it.

That evening, we biked back to the city together. Though Jean-Claude slept at the American most weeknights, Fridays were the sabbath. Whenever possible, he went home for Shabbat dinner with his family.

Drawing up outside Madame LeBrun's, we got off our bicycles.

"I'd ask you in, but my landlady would have my head," I said.

"I must get home. It is almost sundown."

When he leaned in for the customary bussing of cheeks, the

devil on my shoulder had me turning my face and giving him my mouth instead.

He brushed his lips across mine, the muted kiss leaving me wanting. Wrapping my arms around his neck, I pressed closer.

He untangled my arms and stepped back, shaking dark hair out of his eyes.

Reading the regret on his face, I felt like I had been slapped. "If you don't want me, just say so," I said, schooling my voice not to shake.

He sent out a heavy sigh. "I *do* want you. You know I do. But Daisy, in these terrible times, we cannot. We must not."

"Everyone else is going on with their lives. Why not us?" I demanded.

"If the Nazis come, having a Jewish lover will put you in danger."

Tears pushed at the backs of my eyes, but I was too stubborn to shed them. "Maybe de Gaulle is wrong. Maybe the Line *will* hold."

He reached out and touched my cheek. "Maybe it will," he said, though I could tell by his tone he didn't really believe it. "Until we know how the war will finish, we must be patient."

He stepped away and got back on his bicycle. Heart in my throat, I stood on the sidewalk until he turned the corner and disappeared.

I remembered that Bridget had a date. In no mood to be alone, I got back on my bicycle and rode to the Ritz.

As I'd hoped, Frank was behind the bar when I walked in.

"Bee's Knees or gin fizz?" he quizzed me, gesturing to the cocktail he'd just made.

It was a game we played.

By then, I knew that both cocktails were made with gin, a testimony to what a barfly I'd become.

Noting the egg white foam topping the drink, I said, "I'll go with gin fizz."

He nodded his approval. "Your usual glass of champagne?"

Pulling up a barstool, I admitted, "I could use something stronger tonight. Why don't you surprise me?"

"I have just the thing," he said, reaching for his mixing glass.

I watched him fill the shaker with ice and then add a dash of sweet vermouth, French vermouth and lastly rye whiskey, eyeballing the measurements rather than using a gigger, as a less experienced barman might. After giving the mixer several brisk shakes, he strained the liquid into a chilled martini glass.

He dressed the finished drink with a single brandied cherry and set it on a blue-monogrammed bar napkin in front of me.

Lousy as I'd walked in feeling, I couldn't help but smile. "A Manhattan?"

It seemed even Frank was nudging me to go home to New York.

There's a reason we're cautioned against drinking alone. Frank's delicious cocktail went down entirely too smoothly. When he set a plate of finger sandwiches in front of me, I ate them all and called for *l'addition*.

Coming out into the rue Cambon lobby, I ran into Blanche at the front desk.

"Daisy, what terrific timing. A telegram just came in for you."

She handed it to me. Knowing how she prided herself on being the eyes and ears of the hotel, I thanked her and slipped the tan-colored card into my purse.

I waited until I was outside and took it out to read under the light of the lamps.

GRAN HIT BY CAR (STOP) IN COMA (STOP) DOC SAYS IS TOUCH AND GO (STOP) COME HOME SOON AS YOU CAN (STOP) WIRE TRAVEL ARRANGEMENTS TO KAVANAUGH CORP OFFICE (STOP) NEIL

Chapter Seventeen

I can't say how long I stood there rereading those same sparse lines as if expecting a different conclusion, the shock more sobering than a river of black coffee. That my indomitable Irish grandmother had survived a deadly hotel fire, the loss of a beloved son in the Great War, and a worldwide influenza epidemic only to succumb to a careless automobile driver seemed beyond belief.

I glanced at my wristwatch. It was pushing seven o' clock. Any travel arrangements would have to wait until the morning.

Depending on how I found things with Gran, there was no telling when I'd be back in Paris. Before I left, I had to see Jean-Claude and say goodbye. If I waited until morning, I might miss him.

Thirty minutes later, I stood outside the door to his family's flat, gaveling away with the brass knocker.

A woman a few years older than me answered, a lace scarf pinned to her shoulder-length brunette hair. Jean-Claude's younger sister, Rachelle, I presumed.

"I'm sorry to trouble you, but I'm a ... friend of Jean-Claude's. Is he in?" I asked, peering past her to the candlelit apartment.

She ran her gaze over me, and I got the impression that she didn't much care for what she saw.

Turning back inside, she bellowed, "*Frère, il y a une femme ici pour te voir.*"

Jean-Claude emerged from the dining room, wearing a yarmulke and a concerned look. "Daisy, *ce qui s'est passé?*"

I took Neil's telegram from my pocket and showed it to him.

He looked back up, expression stark. "I am so sorry. I know you love her very much."

Until then, I'd managed to hold myself together. But the compassion in Jean-Claude's eyes proved to be my undoing. The tears I'd been holding back since reading Neil's telegram suddenly spilled over.

"Before I came to Paris, she ... she was my w-world." My bottom lip trembled so violently I could barely get the words out.

He took my hands and led me into the living room. "When will you go?"

I drew a shuddering breath. "First thing in the morning. Gran needs me and so does my family. I want to be there with them," I added, though that was only half true.

As in Josephine Baker's ballad, "*J'ai Deux Amours,*" I had two loves now, Gran and Jean-Claude, no matter that he was determined to keep me at arm's length, at least until the war was over.

"Have you booked your passage?"

I shook my head. "By the time I got the telegram, it was too late."

I'd come to him straight from the Ritz bar. No wonder the sister had given me dirty looks. I must smell like a speakeasy.

"You have your passport?"

His question brought me back to myself.

"It's back at my flat."

He nodded. "We will get you a ticket first thing in the morning."

We. I liked the sound of that. Despite the pride I took in my newfound independence, in that moment I was grateful to have someone strong and practical to lean on.

"Thank you."

I turned to go, wishing he were coming with me. But with the war on, no matter how phony or *drôle* we cared to call it, he couldn't very well up and leave the country. Not even if I were his girl, which I desperately wanted to be.

The press of his hand on my shoulder had me turning back. "Stay and eat with us. Maman always cooks too much."

"*C'est vrai, je le fais.*"

I looked past him to a stately older woman standing in the dining alcove, a sheer black scarf draped over her steel-gray hair. Dressed in an old-fashioned, high-necked black dress with jet buttons and a hemline that reached to her ankles, she was slender and straight-backed and nearly as tall as her son.

"*Mille mercis*, Madame Jacob, but I've imposed on you enough already."

She crossed the carpet to me. "Nonsense, we are about to recite *kiddush*. Please, stay as our guest."

"You see, you are outnumbered." Jean-Claude said, the tender expression on his face making my decision for me.

He cupped my elbow and led me into the dining room, the table beautifully set with polished silver and crystal goblets.

Both he and his mother were gracious and patient in guiding me through the Shabbat rituals, including lighting the two candles on the table – to see through the darkness, Madame Jacob explained; the *kiddush* prayer recited by Jean-Claude while holding a cup of wine, and the breaking of the challah, a delicious, braided bread from which we tore off bits and dipped them in salt. Despite the sandwiches I'd had at the Ritz, I managed to do more than pick at the excellent Sabbath supper, which consisted of a fish course, followed by chicken soup and beef bourguignon with noodles.

Between rituals, Jean-Claude and his mother kept the conversation flowing, which helped take my mind off Gran for a little while at least. Several times I looked across the table to find Rachelle regarding me with suspicious eyes.

Afterward, Jean-Claude walked me out to the street and hailed me a taxi. "I will come for you in the morning, and we will make a plan," he said.

I hesitated to get in, my thoughts flashing back to our dinner a year ago when summoning a taxi had led to him vanishing from my life. Now I was the one of us set to disappear.

"Promise?" I asked, feeling on the verge of tears again.

He brushed the hair back from my eyes; his fingertips grazing my temple was all it took to turn me into a pool of yearning. "I am an honorable scout."

Warmed that he remembered, I admitted, "Sometimes I wish you were less honorable."

A sad smile answered. "So do I." He lifted my hand and pressed a kiss to my palm. "Try and get some sleep."

By the time I got back to the apartment, Bridget was home from her date. Holding out Neil's telegram, for the second time that night, I burst into tears.

"Daise, I'm so sorry," she said, hugging me hard. "Your gran will pull through, I know she will, and then you'll be back in a jiff." She pulled back to look at me. "You are coming back, aren't you?"

I hesitated. "Honestly, Bridge, I don't know anything for certain."

What I did know was that there was one more person I needed to say goodbye to.

The next morning after a sleepless night, I rose as soon as the sun was up and dressed. Bridget was still sleeping when I let myself out.

I got on my bicycle and rode to the Ritz. Ordinarily Mademoiselle Coco wouldn't be up for hours, but I had to see her before I left. Fortunately, by then, everyone on staff knew me. I waited for the overnight duty manager to telephone up to her suite. It took several rings, but finally she answered and told him to send me up.

A few minutes later, I stood outside her door.

She answered it wearing champagne silk pajamas and a matching robe, her hair covered with a Chanel silk scarf. It was the first time I'd seen her without lipstick. She looked younger and softer without it, almost like a little girl.

"Don't stand there, come in," she said.

I entered, and she closed the door behind me.

"What is so important it could not wait?" she asked.

I told her about Gran, that time managing to stay dry-eyed. She waited for me to finish and then, to my shock, took me in her arms.

I hugged her back, her small body birdlike. Standing barefoot, her head came just above my shoulder.

"Your *grand-mère* is a strong woman," she said, rubbing my back as a mother might. "Being strong myself, I recognize this trait in others." She pulled back to look at me. "Go to New York to be with your family but know there is always a place for you at Maison Chanel if you choose to return."

Comforted, I kissed her on both cheeks and then made my way back to Madame LeBrun's. I'd just got there when Jean-Claude bicycled up, wearing a sharkskin weave wool suit and a black felt fedora. We stowed our bicycles, and I ushered him inside to the guest parlor.

Sitting on the sofa beside him, I shared the travel plans I'd been working out in my head overnight.

My first thought was to book a seat on one of Pan American Airways' boat planes. The company's Boeing B-314 clipper had made its inaugural intercontinental flight earlier that year. Ordinarily, the luxury aircraft was the province of heads of state, wealthy industrialists, and celebrities. Thanks to Gran, I could afford it.

"You could do that, yes," he agreed without raising a brow, for unlike Bridget, he had always known I came from money. "But Le Bourget airfield is in Marseilles, four hours by train. And you do not know if they will have a seat for you."

In the end, I resigned myself to a standard four-to-five-day ocean voyage, praying Gran would hold on until I got there.

I hadn't expected Jean-Claude to accompany me to Le Havre, but he surprised me by doing just that. We settled into our train seats, and he slipped his arm around me. Laying my head on his shoulder felt like the most natural thing in the world. I turned my cheek into the warm wool of his coat and breathed in his scent of vanilla, lavender and cigarettes. If it hadn't been for Gran lying in a hospital bed an ocean away, I would have been content to stay as we were. When an elderly passenger commented on what a beautiful young couple we were, rather than correct her, he smiled and set his head against the seatback to sleep.

Surprisingly, I joined him. I awoke with my head still pillowed on his shoulder and our train steaming into the station. Jean-Claude brought my suitcase down from the rack, and we headed to the ticket office where I bought a one-way ticket on an ocean liner leaving later that afternoon.

Rather than take the next train back to Paris, he waited with me at a dockside café, my suitcase tucked beneath our table. Nursing a cup of tepid tea, suddenly it hit me. I was leaving France with no definite plan for returning.

"I'm coming back," I said, the out-of-the-blue announcement as much a promise to myself as him.

"To open your big, shiny American department store?" he teased, though his expression stayed tender.

"Before that. As soon as my grandmother is back on her feet," I said, refusing to let myself think about the black dress packed in my suitcase.

He looked out to the harbor, gulls shrieking in the gray washed sky. "Maybe you should stay in New York. College might not be so bad. You will meet boys your own age. There will be time again for Paris when you are older."

His comment landed like a fist in my throat. I didn't want boys. I wanted him.

Swallowing hard, I said, "Trying to get rid of me?"

He turned back to me, anguished eyes meeting mine. "You know I am not. But I care for your safety. You are so young still. And with the war on, our lives are so complicated."

Past caring that we were in public, tables of other passengers all around, I leaned closer. "Then start making them simple. Kiss me."

"So American," he said, shaking his head, but his gaze slid to my mouth where it stayed as if stuck there.

From there, it was as if everything slowed to a stop, except for my heart, which broke into a gallop like Sea Biscuit at the 1937

Preakness. Like that plucky, longshot racehorse, I wasn't willing to hold back, not any longer.

I set my hands on his shoulders, his suitcoat bunching beneath my fierce fingers, and slid to the edge of the seat.

"Kiss me, I dare you." I lifted my chin and waited, taking in the flaring of his nostrils, the V-shaped vein pulsing in the center of his forehead, the slight hitch to his breathing.

That time, he dipped his head and kissed me, *really* kissed me, his lips moist and pillowy soft, his tea-flavored tongue raising a beautiful, bittersweet ache.

When he finally lifted his mouth from mine, I pulled my head from the clouds, astonished to find my feet still planted on the pier.

He brushed a kiss over the faint scar on my forehead. "It will go away, I promise."

I looked into his eyes, searching for answers he wasn't ready to give. "I don't want it to go away. I don't want to go away either. I don't want to leave you."

"I do not want that either, but we … we do what we must." Expression grave, he pushed back from the table and stood. "*Bon courage,* Daisy. And *bon voyage.*"

Chapter Eighteen

Four days later, my ship sailed into New York Harbor. Standing on deck bundled against the blustering winds and foamy spray, I looked from the Statue of Liberty to the Battery ahead and felt a lump land in my throat. The skyline had altered from Gran's day, with modern skyscrapers springing up in place of many of the grand old buildings, the Empire State Building topping them all; otherwise, it wasn't so very different from what Gran would have seen when she had first come to New York forty years ago, a brave young Irishwoman striking out on her own with hardly a nickel to her name. Now she lay in a hospital bed, in a coma, perhaps never to wake up again.

It seemed to take an eternity for the gangplank to be lowered. Once we passengers were let off, I didn't wait around to regain my land legs. I caught a taxi from Pier 54 and went directly to Lenox Hill Hospital on East 77th Street, the closest hospital to where Gran's accident had happened. Looking out the taxi window, I took in the soaring office towers of midtown, the Brooklyn and Manhattan Bridges, and the sidewalks and crosswalks paved with people, all of them moving along at a brisk clip, not the sauntering gait I had become accustomed to in Paris.

Once at the hospital, I lugged my suitcase through the accident ward, the carbolic smell as familiar to me as Chanel No. 5. Coming up to the nurse's station to ask the way to Gran's room, I was jarred to hear everyone speaking English, their New York accents striking a harsh note in my ear.

I found Gran not comatose at all but sitting up in bed, a bandage wrapped around her head, one side of her face stained greenish yellow, and her right leg encased in a plaster of Paris cast.

Her eyes lit when she saw me. "Daisy!"

Hearing my name on her lips, the waterworks I'd damned up for most of the transatlantic trip burst. Eyes streaming, I dropped my luggage and hurried over, stopping short of hugging her.

Striking a smile, she opened her arms. "Darling girl, if a New York City taxicab can't break me, you certainly won't."

I put my arms lightly around her and for the first time since I'd gotten Neil's telegram, I felt like I could breathe.

Grandpa Adam, looking haggard but happy, stood from his bedside chair. "Daisy, sweetheart, you're a sight for sore eyes."

He came over for his hug, his trousers hanging loose around his waist, his shoulder blades showing beneath his pullover.

Beaming at us, Gran fussed, "Have a care, Adam. You'll squeeze the poor girl's bones to powder."

He let me go with a laugh. "Your grandmother's been bossing me around since she woke up yesterday."

She grinned. "While I'm at it, perhaps you could find that nice young orderly and see if he might scrounge up a second chair for our Daisy?"

"I'll do one better. How about I take myself off for a cup of coffee and let you girls catch up?"

He and Gran shared a warm look.

"That'd be grand, sweetheart," she said. "You deserve a break."

At the door, he stopped and looked back at me. "S'good to have you home, kid."

"Thanks, Gramps. It's good to be home," I said though I was still acclimating to the ... *Americanness* of everything.

He went out into the hallway, pulling the door closed behind him.

I took the chair he'd vacated and clasped Gran's hand between both of mine. "Tell me what happened, unless it's too upsetting."

"Honestly, I don't remember much. I was crossing Fifth Avenue at Seventy-Sixth Street to meet with our banker, and the next thing I knew I woke up here, your grandfather holding my hand. The darling man hasn't left my side this entire time. Your mum's been here, too, and Neil, sweet boy. And Blake comes evenings after the store closes. He's bringing his lady friend Hattie by later."

"How much longer until you're released?" I asked.

She hesitated. "I sustained a nasty skull fracture though, as your grandfather will attest, my head is the thickest part of me." She glanced down at her cast. "My right femur is fractured as well. I'll be in this cast for six to eight weeks and then I'll graduate from crutches to a cane. Me with a cane, can you imagine! In the meantime, I'm stuck here having this horrid hospital food."

She gestured to a meal tray sitting out on the side table, with a congealed bowl of what might be chicken soup and an untouched dish of lime Jell-O.

"But don't mind me, prattling on. With everything that's been going on, I'm relieved to have you home safe. And I want to hear everything you've been up to in Paris. Your last letter mentioned Mademoiselle Chanel was closing her atelier. I don't imagine that working in the boutique takes up all your time. What else have you been doing with yourself?"

I told her about my friendship with Fritz, cut short by the war, and my volunteering at the American Hospital, a surprising source of satisfaction considering I'd been squeamish all my life. I left off mentioning Jean-Claude. Much more than a friend but not quite a boyfriend, I wasn't sure what to call him.

Brushing my hair back from my forehead, she asked, "Oh, dear, what happened here?"

I had kept my fainting mishap out of my letters and phone calls, not wanting to worry anyone. Left with no choice, I told her the story, referring to Jean-Claude as the brilliant young surgical resident who'd fixed me up and who I often assisted at the American.

Her knowing gaze met mine. "Your young man sounds very special. Has he a name?"

Trust Gran to cut to the heart of things.

"Jean-Claude Jacob, only he's not 'my young man,' not yet anyway. But I'm working on it."

I could tell she didn't like the sound of that. "He's not toying with you, is he?"

Thinking back to our passionate parting at Le Havre, I shook my head. "He has feelings for me, I know he does, but he's worried on account of the war and him being Jewish."

I might have said more but a knock on the door cut me off. Before I could get up to open it, Mom, Dad, and Neil poured in.

Mom's gaze flew to me and stuck there as if she couldn't quite believe I was real. "We ran into Adam downstairs, and he said that Daisy ... Oh, never mind about all that now."

The next thing I knew I was in her arms, and she was rocking me against her, her dark hair, more silvered than when I had left, tumbling down from its haphazard bun, her hold fiercer and tighter than I ever remembered it being.

Finally, she pulled back, holding me at arm's length, her teary eyes taking me in. "You're so ... grown up."

Dad and Neil tackled me next, passing me back and forth like a football.

"You're a sight for sore eyes," Dad said, lifting me off my feet.

Neil poked me in the ribs. "What the heck, skinny minnie, don't those Frenchies feed you over there?"

"I missed you, too, lamebrain," I said, making a point of messing up his pomaded hair. "When do I get to meet this girl of yours?"

"Soon," he said, looking away.

By the time Grandpa Adam got back, Uncle Blake had joined us with his girlfriend, Hattie, a petite stunner dressed in buttercup yellow, who I learned wasn't only a cosmetics saleslady but also a performer at the Cotton Club, the legendary Harlem hotspot that had moved to the Theater district a few years ago.

"I sing and dance backup in the chorus," she explained.

"Hattie is being modest," Uncle Blake cut in, taking her hand. "You should hear her sing Cole Porter. Ethel Merman can't hold a candle to her."

"Blake, please." Hattie's cheeks darkened, and she swatted at his arm, but his grin only broadened.

"Sounds very glamorous," I said, hiding a smile to see my starchy uncle in what looked like real love.

Since Valerie, he'd hidden himself behind an armoring of staid suits and a pencil pushing sense of duty. Clearly Hattie brought something out in him, something that until now the rest of us, his family, had missed. Having tasted it with Jean-Claude, I recognized it when I saw it.

The *something* was passion.

"Blake tells me you're working at Chanel in Paris," Hattie said, turning the conversation back to me. "Now *that* sounds glamorous." Her expression sobered. "How is it living over there with the war on?"

Knowing my Paris residency was a sore spot with my family, I hesitated. "It's fine, really. Mademoiselle Chanel takes good care of me," I said, catching Gran's eye. "I also volunteer at the American Hospital, but so far, we've only had a handful of casualties. The biggest complaints are dysentery and boredom," I made sure to add, deliberately downplaying the situation.

"Thank your lucky stars you're back home before it gets any worse," Mom said. "Daisy will be enrolling in business school in the spring," she informed the room at large. Looking back at me, she added, "If you go to Brooklyn College, you'll be close enough to work at Kavanaugh's part-time."

Not so long ago, her dangling Kavanaugh's like a juicy carrot might have brought me in line but working at Chanel had toughened me to such trivial manipulations. In the hard knocks school of her atelier, I had learned to stand my ground and, equally importantly, pick my battles. Rather than risk turning Gran's hospital room into a battleground, I settled for silence.

Fortunately, Gramps stepped in.

"I don't know about anyone else, but I could use some ice cream. Neil, why don't you take Daisy down to the cafeteria and see if you two can't rustle up some Rocky Road. Make it double scoops. We're celebrating." He looked around the room, stopping at me, a tear in his eye. "Our girl is home."

* * *

By the time the ice cream was procured and passed around, visiting hours were almost over. We left Gran to get some rest, with me promising to come back in the morning. Exhausted, I went home with my parents in dad's Rolls Royce. When he pulled up to our townhouse on East 93rd Street, I was already asleep in the back.

"Some things never change," mom said, helping me inside and pulling off my shoes, then tucking me into bed like she had when I was little.

When I woke up the next morning, feeling like Rip Van Winkle, all three of my family members had left for work, mom and dad to their respective offices and Neil to Kavanaugh's. I would stop by the store later, but first I wanted to get back to Gran. With all the excitement the night before, we hadn't gotten to finish our conversation.

I made myself coffee and got dressed, then took a cab to the hospital.

Gran was finishing up breakfast when I got there. I waited for the orderly to take away her barely touched meal tray and leave before passing her a handled paper bag.

She reached inside and pulled out the freshly baked bagel I'd picked up from Zabar's appetizing store on my way over.

"Darling girl!"

The cabbie had given me a hard time about the extra stop but the look of pure delight on Gran's face made it worth it.

I sat in the bedside chair and made light conversation while she ate.

"That was heavenly," she said, sweeping the last crumbs into the bag and setting it aside.

Settling back against the banked pillows, she looked me over. "We're all so thrilled to have you back."

I looked down at my folded hands.

"You are back, aren't you?"

I braced myself with a breath and lifted my gaze to hers. "I know I've had this second year in Paris thanks to you. You went to bat for me with Mom, and that can't have been easy. I swore to come back here after this February and apply to business school, and really, I meant to, only … Paris started out as a lark but somewhere along the way I … I've made a life there. A life I love. And if I don't go back and see it through, I'll never forgive myself."

She sent me a knowing look. "The city isn't all you've fallen in love with, is it?"

"It's early days yet, but yes, I … I love Jean-Claude." There, I'd said it. "I love him, and I can't imagine being with anyone else. I don't want to imagine it. I know it's not ideal, being in a foreign country at war, but I feel about him the way you do about Grandpa Adam."

She sent out a sigh. "If the Nazis take France, he and his family will be in dreadful danger. Selfishly I don't want that danger to rub off on you. Promise me you'll take care."

"I'll be as careful as I can." Short of lying to her, which she would see through in a New York minute, it was the best I could offer.

She thought for a moment, fretting her lower lip. "It's not what I would have chosen for you, but you're a grown woman and your life is yours to make. When will you leave?"

"I'll stay another few weeks, I think. Long enough to help get you settled at home and to spend time with everyone. Mademoiselle Coco promised me my job back, though with the atelier closed, there's not all that much to do."

"That's good of her," Gran said.

"It is," I agreed.

For all her faults, Chanel could be loyal to those who stuck by her. Madame Millet, Madame Aubrey, her maids, and now me.

Gran reached out her hand, and I took it.

"I'll miss you terribly and so will your mother," she said. "You're going to have to tell her, you know. And your father."

I would just as soon face down Hitler's panzers as Mom, but Gran was right. It had to be done.

"I will. I just have to find the right time."

She arched a brow. "There is no right time. There never will be. Tell her what you've told me. Speak from your heart. She won't like it, but she'll come around eventually. After all, she was a young woman once, making her way in life, not so very different to you."

Chapter Nineteen

November–December 1939

The Paris I returned to that November 1st seemed more somber than the city I had left. Or maybe being away from the Phony War and thrown back into the bustle of New York had given me a fresh perspective. Bridget flew to the flat door to greet me, hugging me as if years had gone by, and then whisking away my suitcase and refusing to let me lift a finger for the rest of the night. While making us tea, she brought me up to date. To ensure the soldiers guarding the Maginot Line were provided for, the French government had instituted rationing. Coffee, tea, spirits, and petrol were now luxury items that only the well-off could afford. Seeing her reuse her teabag for a second cup, both cups drunk without milk or sugar, I was shocked at how much had changed since I'd left. And yet even with a war on, it was good to be *home*.

The next morning, I accompanied Bridget to Maison Chanel. If I was going to stay in Paris on my dime and not my family's, I would have to work. Mademoiselle Coco had promised there would be a place for me when and if I returned. Having a job waiting had helped me break the news to my parents. But with the war dragging on, and

Mademoiselle Coco's tendency toward changeability, I worried that the situation might have altered in my absence.

I found *La Grande Mademoiselle* in her apartment above the boutique, reading a book or trying to. Fortunately, my fears proved unfounded. She greeted me warmly, kissing me on both cheeks, and swore that the atelier hadn't been the same without me.

"There is nothing worse than solitude, Marguerite," she lamented, once the initial welcome was out of the way, and we'd taken seats. "It can help a man realize himself, but it destroys a woman."

The air raid drills grated on her nerves, and she fretted over André, serving on the Front. Above all, she missed being in love, or the feeling of being in love, which she seemed to see as one and the same. Von Dincklage had left the country with the rest of the German embassy officials and staff back in September. Though Chanel rarely mentioned him by name, I sensed she missed him, or at least the attention he'd paid her.

Thinking of the baron brought my mind back to Fritz. I wondered where he was serving. Hitler's chief general, Field Marshal Erwin Rommel had announced that he would wage a clean war, one without hate. Was such an ideal truly achievable? Had it ever been?

A few days after I got back, Winston Churchill visited Paris as Britain's new Lord of the Admiralty. In town for talks with the French Naval Commander, he made time to see his old friend, Coco. They dined in her suite at the Ritz, the food and wine brought up by elevator from the hotel kitchen. The next day, a relieved Chanel told anyone who would listen that Winston had assured her that Britain and her allies were well-equipped to defend France.

It didn't take me long to fall into a new routine, dividing my time between volunteering at the American on Sundays and one weekday and working at Maison Chanel where my responsibilities had expanded to helping Madame Aubrey keep the accounts. Neither she nor Madame Millet were exactly warm to me, but I did sense a thawing as if they respected me for returning.

I saw Jean-Claude on my first Sunday back. Coming out of surgery and still wearing his scrubs, he stopped in his tracks when he spotted me. Reserved at work, he didn't grab me, kiss me and pull me into the nearest supply closet as I might have wished, but the warmth in his eyes and the slow smile spreading over his face told me I had been missed. As with mesdames Millet and Aubrey, I sensed a new respect. I hadn't had to come back. I had chosen to. Hopefully he would finally realize that my feelings for him ran far deeper than a crush.

By December, the American's two hundred and fifty beds were filling up with French soldiers injured from shelling along the Maginot Line. A few days before Christmas, we received a very special early holiday present – a private performance by Josephine Baker. Dressed in pilot's coveralls, not the slinky evening gown of my memory, she sang "Dinah," "I Love My Baby," and "Stardust," finishing with her signature song, "*J'ai Deux Amours.*" Afterwards, she walked along the rows of patient beds, squeezing hands, plumping pillows, and kissing foreheads.

The hospital held a modest reception in the main salle of the Memorial Building. Libations and light refreshments were passed around. Pajama-clad soldiers, many in wheelchairs, toasted Miss Baker beside a large Christmas tree decorated with garlands and ornaments handmade or contributed by the staff and volunteers.

Feeling eyes on me, I turned to Josephine Baker walking up.

"Why do you look so familiar?" she asked, looking me over.

Surprised to be singled out by an international celebrity, it took me a moment to find my tongue. "I'm Daisy Blakely. My friend and

I came to your club once before the war. It was the night your pet cheetah escaped."

Given all that had happened since, that night felt worlds away, the girl who'd drunk four French Seventy-fives and danced until the wee hours almost a stranger.

She laughed. "Honestly, honey, that happens *a lot* of nights. You wouldn't happen to be any relation to Rose Kavanaugh Blakely, would you?"

"She's my grandmother," I said, feeling the usual pride.

Her smile widened, revealing a slight and thoroughly adorable overbite I hadn't noticed before. "That explains the resemblance. Before I came to Paris, I was in New York doing 'Chocolate Dandies' with Ethel Waters, and I needed something to wear to the wrap party. Your grandmother helped me find a gown when none of the other department stores would let me through the door, never mind in the dressing rooms. When one of her saleladies refused to help me, she fired her on the spot and waited on me herself."

I had heard the story a time or two, but never that the customer was Josephine Baker. But then Gran wasn't one to namedrop or to make a fuss over her own good deeds.

"I'll be sure to tell my grandmother that I met you, Miss Baker. She'll be tickled pink that you remembered her."

"Call me Jo, please. How long have you been nursing?"

"Oh, I'm not a real nurse. I'm just a volunteer. My regular job is at Maison Chanel."

Her eyes widened. "You're one of Coco's *filles*? That's interesting."

"More of an apprentice," I said. "Before the war, my grandmother arranged for me to work at the atelier and learn the fashion business. Now that it's closed, I'm helping in the boutique and with the books."

"I'll have to stop by and do a little shopping one of these days."

"Please do."

I might have said more but Dr. Gros, the hospital's chief of staff, walked up and guided her away.

I found Jean-Claude by the punch bowl. In honor of the British pilots, the kitchen had tapped into the hospital's reserves of red wine to make wassail.

He ladled the warm, mulled wine into a punch glass and passed it to me, then filled one for himself.

I hesitated. "I'm still on shift."

"A sip to salute the holiday." He raised his glass. "*Joyeux Noël*."

I lifted mine. "*Joyeux Hanoucca*."

We touched glasses and drank.

I nearly spat my wassail back into my cup. "That's—"

"Horrible," he confirmed, taking back my glass, and setting it and his aside. "How do the Teddies drink it?"

Thinking of Bridget, I said, "I suspect theirs is a lot tastier."

He gestured to the garland above our heads. "Is that …"

"Mistletoe," I said, feeling my hopes lift.

His gaze slipped to my mouth. "What is the English expression for when you must delay taking something that you badly want to do until another time?"

Not above torturing us both, I bit my bottom lip and then soothed it with my tongue, savoring how his eyes darkened. "We call it a rain check."

PART TWO: 1940–1941

"The only thing necessary for the triumph of evil is for good men to do nothing."

Edmund Burke

Chapter Twenty

May–June 1940

By May, men were back to fishing in the Seine. The outdoor cafés, never entirely empty even on the sharpest of winter days, were full again, the square tables spilling out onto the sidewalks. Mimes and other street performers returned to the parks and Métro stations. Old men and boys again played pétanque in the Tuileries and Luxembourg Gardens.

The Paris nightlife, which Bridget and I had thrown ourselves into our first year in the city, had lost its allure, for me at least. On Saturdays, my one day off, I liked to take boulevard St. Germaine to the Luxembourg Gardens where the horse chestnut trees had come into blossom and the Medici and Léda fountains were once more filled and running. Walking the gravel paths, my thoughts invariably turned to Fritz. Though he was the enemy now, I couldn't help hoping he was staying safe.

Afterwards, depending on my mood, I sometimes stopped in at Café Deux Magots for a café crème or a glass of crisp Chablis. I still got a kick out of the bohemian patrons earnestly scribbling or sketching in their moleskin notebooks. Lately, I'd begun carrying a notebook myself, jotting down everything from bistro dishes I wanted to suggest to Gran for the restaurant at Kavanaugh's, to shop window displays that caught my eye as something Neil might appreciate. He wasn't much of a letter writer but according to Gran and mom, he was still seeing his mystery girl, Maxine, whom they'd yet to meet.

The following Wednesday, business at the boutique was slow, and Madame Millet let me off early. I took the opportunity for a leisurely stroll along the quay. Leaning against the stone balustrade and looking out onto the sparkling Seine, it was hard to believe there was a war on.

In no hurry, I stopped to browse the bookstalls. Though still not much of a reader, I was always on the lookout for something Grandpa Adam or my father might like. When I came across a first edition copy of *My Ántonia*, the brown dust jacket somewhat the worse for wear, I snapped it up. A silly, sentimental thing to do as I almost certainly wouldn't be seeing Fritz again, and yet I paid my francs and slipped it into my bag anyway.

On my way to catch the autobus home, I came across a clutch of a half-dozen old men gathered about a newspaper kiosk gesticulating and speaking in rapid French.

"*Nous sommes finis.*" We are done for.

"*La France est la prochaine.*" France is next.

"*La Ligne Maginot nous sauvera.*" The Maginot Line will save us.

Walking up, I pushed my way through and scanned the papers on the rack. My gaze homed in on the front-page of *Paris Soir*, and my stomach dropped to the sidewalk.

L'Allemagne lance une blitzkrieg contre les Pays-Bas, la Belgique et le Luxembourg.

* * *

Germany's surprise blitzkrieg attack on the neutral nations of Netherlands, Belgium, and Luxembourg brought the Drôle de Guerre to a dramatic end. The same day, the British prime minister Neville Chamberlain, who had pursued a policy of appeasement prior to the war, resigned from office. Winston Churchill took the reins of government.

The next day, the Germans pushed into eastern France, plowing through the dense Belgian Ardennes Forest and crushing French border outposts. As Jean-Claude had predicted, they didn't have to knock down the Maginot fortifications. In many cases, they simply went around them.

The American began filling with casualties. Staff surgeons, including Jean-Claude, operated round the clock. Coming off grueling back-to-back surgeries, his scrubs splashed with blood from resecting the bowel of a gut shot French soldier and then reconstructing the shattered jawbone of another, he shuffled out of the operating theater, a week's worth of beard stubble blanketing his drawn face. Seeing him sway on his feet, I abandoned the trolley of biscuits I'd been pushing to patients and hurried over.

"*Ça va bien*," he insisted.

"Clearly you're not fine," I answered, bracing my arm around him. "You need sleep. Please, lie down for a bit. Even an hour would help."

"One hour," he agreed, and it was a testimony to how exhausted he was that he didn't fight me harder.

Rather than take him all the way up to his room, I found him an empty cot in a staff breakroom, pushed him down onto the narrow mattress and helped him off with his shoes. He settled onto his side with a sigh, out before his head touched the pillow.

"*Dors bien, mon amour.*" Pulling the blanket over him, I pressed my lips to his cheek.

Bicycling back that evening beneath a smoke-charred sky, my first, panicked thought was that the Germans had broken through and were putting Paris to the torch. Fortunately, the tattoo of artillery and the boom of bombs remained in the distance. The only people I encountered on the road were fleeing French, their belongings strapped onto horse carts and lorries, many carrying bundles on their backs.

After two days straight at the hospital, I was shocked to see how Paris had emptied. There wasn't a taxi to be had. The cafés were deserted, the tables and chairs taken inside. On rue Cambon, the storefronts, including Maison Chanel, were buried behind heavy street-level shutters. Bits of charred paper carried on the breeze, the streets and sidewalks feathered with black ash. Once I got home to Bridget, she explained that the diplomatic missions and French ministries had been burning documents all day to keep them from falling into the enemy's hands.

By early June the Germans had stepped up their offensive. An aerial attack killed more than two hundred and fifty Parisian civilians and wounded another six hundred and fifty Afterwards, I left Mademoiselle Coco in the Ritz bomb shelter and hurried back to the hospital to do what I could to help.

My days and nights blurred together. Bathing patients, carrying cups of water and bone broth to those who could swallow, preparing dressing kits to free up nurses needed to do the work of doctors, like everyone else I subsisted on stale coffee and the determination not to give in to fear.

My birthday came and went. It wasn't until the day after that I glanced at a calendar and realized I'd turned twenty. Thinking of the whirlwind eighteenth birthday celebration that had brought me to

Paris, I was struck by how much had changed in two years, including me. While I still appreciated beautiful clothes, fashion was no longer my be-all and end-all.

A few days later, the French government fled to Tours. U.S. Ambassador William Bullitt declared Paris an open city to save it from destruction. Finding one of the few remaining working telephones in the American embassy on Avenue Gabriel, he had managed to get his message through to Berlin.

Every hour, medics brought in more wounded. The doctors, nurses, orderlies, and we volunteers could barely keep up. Bleeding soldiers lay on gurneys moaning in pain and sobbing for their mothers. Once spotless white medical uniforms bore badges of vomit and blood.

In the middle of helping Jean-Claude change a patient's dressing, I was called away to the nurse's station for an urgent phone call.

Chanel's voice rose above the static. "We are leaving for Corbère today. Pack a bag and meet me at the Ritz at one o' clock."

"But I'm needed here. I can't just—"

"I promised your *grand-mère* I would take care of you. Would you make a liar of me?" she demanded.

I thought back to my own promise to Gran to be as careful as I could and felt the fight drain out of me.

Surrendering, I said, "I'll go, but I have to bring Bridget."

Over the line, I heard what sounded like the striking of a cigarette lighter.

"Who?"

"My roommate, the British girl. The *vendeuse* you kept on."

"If you can get her here by one o' clock, we will take her, too."

The line went dead.

Jean-Claude walked up as I set the receiver in its cradle.

"Chanel wants me to take me with her to her nephew's château in Corbère," I said, miserable about it.

He took my hand and ferried us into the nearest supply closet.

Shouldering the door closed, he folded me into his arms and kissed me. Past caring about the gore on my smock, I kissed him back, desperate and wanton and greedy, my arms wrapped around his neck, my breasts crushed against his chest. Unlike the other sweet moments that we'd stolen since I'd got back – a lingering look or brush of hands in passing, a passionate embrace between shifts – this one was weighted with uncertainty. As with our parting in Le Havre, there was no guarantee we'd ever see each other again.

Lifting his lips from mine, he said, "Chanel is right to take you away before the Germans break through."

"What about you?" I demanded, shuddering to think of him, a Jew, left behind in Paris.

"I will work better knowing you are safe." He rested his forehead against mine. "The roads ... I want to send someone with you, but there is no one left."

Making up my mind to be brave, I stepped back to look at him, resolved to memorize every detail of his haggard but handsome face. "I'll be all right. Go back to your patients. They need you."

I turned to go, but he caught me to him, an arm braced around my waist, his lips laying a trail of fevered kisses along the side of my neck, his stubble grazing my skin. "*A bientôt*," he murmured, and I managed a watery smile, remembering.

Outside, I got on my bicycle and pedaled as fast as I could back to the city, dodging craters made by bomb blasts, an overturned cart, and dead animals sprawled on the side of the road.

When I got to Madame LeBrun's, the apartment was ominously

empty. Bridget's bedcovers were mussed, but since she wasn't one to make her bed, I couldn't know when she'd last slept there. The best I could hope for was that she was sheltering somewhere safe.

I threw underwear, clothes, and toiletries into an overnight case and headed down the stairs.

Stepping off one floor below, I knocked on Madame LeBrun's apartment.

Coming to the door, she looked down at the case in my hand.

"Mademoiselle Chanel asked me to go with her to Corbère," I explained.

She gave a weary nod. "The country, it is the safest place. I sent Olivier to my late husband's sister in Provins."

Mindful of the ticking clock, I said, "I'm sure he will do very well there. Mademoiselle Ponsby is supposed to come, too. Have you seen her?"

"Not for a few days."

I opened my purse, counted out five hundred francs, and handed her the money. If I couldn't find Bridget in time to take her with us, at least I could make sure she had a roof over her head when she got back.

"Two months' rent. Please hold our flat. Bridget is still in the city, and I plan on coming back as well."

She nodded and slipped the money into her apron pocket.

Outside, I strapped my case on the bicycle rack, climbed on and pedaled as fast as I could to the Ritz.

I found Chanel on the Place Vendôme side outside the sandbagged main entrance, her Louis Vuitton luggage being loaded into the trunk of a rusted Cadillac.

"Thank you for making room for me," I said sincerely.

Though I'd fought coming, the bicycle ride back from the American had been sobering. I suspected it was only a matter of days or even hours until Paris fell to the Nazis.

"Germaine and Jeanne have gone back to their village and my chauffeur has deserted me, too, to fight the Boches," she said as if the poor man had any say in being conscripted.

She gestured with her cigarette to the beefy Frenchman closing the car trunk.

"The concierge found me this … Marceau Larcher to take his place, but he refuses to drive my Rolls through the refugees. He says it will attract the wrong sort of attention. So, we are to make the journey in this ancient monstrosity."

The drive south was hot, tedious, and terrifying. Sitting in the backseat with Chanel, a case of No. 5 rattling on the cracked leather cushion between us, I felt every bump and rut in the road. Going town to town, we never knew when we might encounter German panzer tanks. Mostly, we inched along narrow country lanes clogged with automobiles, trucks, horse-drawn drays, and refugees on foot. Abandoned luggage, blown out tires and sundry furniture and household items littered the roadsides, the debris worsening the farther we got from Paris.

Mademoiselle Coco spent most of the more than four-hundred-mile journey smoking and staring out the rolled-down window. I'd never known her to be so quiet. As one hour bled into the next, her silence unnerved me almost as much as the news reports on the car radio did.

By then, the Germans were hours away from entering Paris. Broadcasting live from Paris, Columbia Broadcasting System correspondent Eric Sevareid warned, "No American after tonight will be broadcasting directly to America, unless it is under the supervision of men other than the French."

Once we crossed the river Garonne at Agen, the congestion let up. Larcher took the winding roads as if we were at the Grand Prix. More than once, I closed my eyes, certain the next hairpin turn would send us hurtling over the cliffside.

At Doumy, we turned east onto country roads that led to the Palasse château in Corbère. A modest manor house with a mansard roof, turret, and ivy climbing the front, it promised to be a homey sanctuary from the chaos of Paris.

A small but enthusiastic party of family and neighbors was on hand to greet us: André's Dutch wife Catharina, their daughters thirteen-year-old Gabrielle, named after Chanel, but called Tiny, and twelve-year-old Hélène. Both girls spoke fluent English, having spent much of their childhood in Mayfair when their father was overseeing Chanel's business interests in England. Joining them were Chanel's former lover, Étienne Balsan, and his wife, Victorine. Apparently, the couple had an estate nearby.

A short while later, we sat sipping aperitifs on the terrace. Catharina showed us the postcard from the Swiss Red Cross informing the family that André was alive but ill. One of 300,000 French troops captured when the Germans broke through the Maginot Line fortifications, he was being held in a stalag in Germany. A prisoner of war, at least he was alive.

The mood that first evening was one of relief. The food was fresh and plentiful, most of it from the estate. After our harrowing travels, we all enjoyed several glasses of the crisp, white *vin du pays* produced on the property. Surrounded by bounty, I couldn't help thinking of Bridget and Jean-Claude back in Paris.

The next morning, Marie-Louise Bousquet, the Paris editor of *Harper's Bazaar* whom I'd met at my first Chanel showing, drove over from Pau. Tiny and I smothered our laughter as we watched Marie-Louise navigate the cobblestone courtyard in her pencil-thin high heels.

A few days later, mesdames Millet and Aubrey took the train down from Paris. Once Nazi tanks had rolled into Paris, they'd been glad to get out. Rather than find rooms for them at the château with the rest of us, Catharina put them up in an annex where they also took their meals.

At noon on the following Monday, French radio interrupted its regular programming to broadcast the new head of French government, *Maréchal* Pétain's address to the fallen nation.

> *"You, the French people, must follow me without reservation on the paths of honor and national interest ... it is with a heavy heart that I tell you that today we must stop fighting."*

Catharina quietly stood and switched off the radio.

"Better Hitler than Stalin and the Communists," Balsan offered to the stunned room.

Someone gave a half-hearted murmur, otherwise no one answered.

The next day, de Gaulle broadcast his own address from London where he'd gone into exile. Unfortunately, the BBC neglected to record it, viewing the recently promoted general as a minor figure in the landscape of the war. But the four-minute speech proved so stirring that he was invited to repeat it. That time the broadcast was recorded and reached many of us in France.

> *"France has lost a battle but not a war ... Whatever happens, the flame of French resistance must not be extinguished and will not be extinguished ... "*

Résistance. We couldn't know then the power that word would hold. That over the Occupation years, it would spark a movement that would grow from scattered pockets of brave foot soldiers to a sophisticated intelligence and operations network tens of thousands strong.

Chapter Twenty-One

The following week, Hitler arrived in Compiègne to sign the armistice, which divided France into two zones: *La Zone Occupée* in the north including Paris, controlled by the German military, and *La Zone Libre* in the south under Pétain's French State government, now headquartered in Vichy. The next day, he made his victory progress through Paris riding in an open car. German film crews cataloged every stop of the tour, including the Opera, the Champs-Élysées, the Arc de Triomphe, Place du Trocadéro, and Les Invalides where he lingered over Napoleon's tomb.

Chanel was inconsolable. She paced the courtyard smoking nonstop and drinking absurd amounts of wine, bemoaning the "filthy Boches" sullying her city and fretting over her beloved André rotting in a German stalag. Through the International Red Cross, we'd received a letter from him assuring us he was safe but battling a cough that the camp doctor believed to be tuberculosis.

"My mother died of tuberculosis," she confided to me one evening after supper, her eyelids weighted with wine. "I must get André home to France where he can be treated. I *must*."

Amid everything, her gilded dressing table set arrived. A gift from the Duke of Westminster, I'd seen it in her suite at the Ritz. She must have arranged to have it shipped before we'd left Paris. It seemed we were staying for a while.

Mail service resumed. In the *Zone Libre*, all you had to do was add the correct stamp and take your letter to the post office, no different than before the invasion, only now Vichy censors combed through every word we wrote. I sent off letters to Gran and my folks assuring them I was safe in the countryside and that Mademoiselle Chanel was keeping her promise to take very good care of me.

I wrote to Jean-Claude and Bridget, too, but the postal rules were a lot stricter in the Occupied Zone, so I wasn't sure if my letters got through.

Grateful as I was to be in the relative safety of the countryside, I was a city girl at heart. Keeping country hours, where people rose and went to bed with the sun, took some getting used to. After my first week in Corbère, my relief ran to boredom. I missed Paris with its bustling boulevards, chic shops, and vibrant cafés, but I reminded myself that the city as such didn't exist anymore.

June slipped into July. Bastille Day came and went unmarked and uncelebrated. I thought back to how Bridget and I had kicked up our heels the previous two years and felt myself sinking into self-pity.

In such moments, I reminded myself how lucky I was. Tucked away on the Palasse estate, we could go for weeks without seeing a German soldier. Walking the grounds and surrounding woods, enjoying meals made by Catharina's excellent cook, it was tempting to think the war couldn't touch us.

One sultry morning in late July, I was coming back from the henhouse with Tiny, who'd thought it great fun to show me, *une fille de la ville*, how to gather eggs. Carrying our full baskets lined with straw, we ran into Chanel coming out of the stable. Wearing riding breeches tucked into high boots and a loose-fitting equestrian jacket that I suspected had been borrowed from her nephew's closet, a silk cravat loosely knotted at her throat, she was just back from a ride, her first since we'd arrived at the château. The exercise seemed to have done her good. There was a healthy pink in her cheeks that didn't come from rouge, and a light in her eyes that I hadn't seen since the Nazis invaded. I could imagine how she must have looked a decade ago when she was still with the Duke of Westminster, presiding over his country house parties and going riding, fishing and hunting with the likes of Churchill.

"Auntie Coco!" Tiny ran up to Chanel as if she hadn't seen her in eons.

"*Bonjour, chérie.*" Chanel leaned down and kissed both her cheeks. Straightening, she said, "Be a good girl and take those eggs to Cook and tell her I want an omelet, a big one. Can you do that for me?"

Ever eager to please her great-aunt, Tiny took my basket and tore off toward the kitchen.

As soon as she was out of earshot, Chanel announced, "Marguerite, pack your bags. We leave for Vichy after breakfast."

At Mademoiselle Coco's insistence, Larcher covered the two hundred and seventy miles to Vichy in a single day. Marie-Louise joined us on the journey, which necessitated transferring the box of perfumes to the trunk. I sat sandwiched between her and Chanel in the back of the Cadillac, straining to see out the passenger windows.

German tank battalions and infantry were everywhere. At a checkpoint outside of Lourdes, we were stopped and made to show our papers, including the *laissez-passer* now needed for traveling between the two zones.

"*Danke schön, fräulein,*" the young soldier said, handing me back my documents.

Torn between anxiety and anger, I didn't answer beyond a nod. Such studied politeness didn't fool me. I sensed our conquerors were only getting started and that more crackdowns were to come.

We arrived in Vichy after eight o' clock at night. Sticky, dusty and travel worn as we were, it was a relief to get out of the Cadillac and stretch our legs.

Before the war, Vichy was a sleepy spa town where people came for the medicinal mineral waters. Now it teemed with politicians, Nazi soldiers, diplomats, bureaucrats, and hangers-on, the former casinos and hotels requisitioned as government offices and flying the flag of the Third Reich, a red background with a black swastika on a white disk.

The remaining hotels and guesthouses were full up. Fortunately, Chanel had a friend, André-Louis Debois, with an empty hotel room we could use. A senior official in the French Ministry of the Interior, he had been fired for helping French Jews obtain visas for America.

The first night had the festive feeling of a slumber party, the three of us making a meal of bread and cheese and passing around a bottle of wine. Afterwards, Marie-Louise and Mademoiselle Coco shared the bed, and I took the chaise longue. The only damper on the evening was when Chanel took her zippered toiletry kit from her suitcase and filled the hypodermic needle from the glass vial of Sedol.

Catching me watching her, she said, "I need it to sleep."

The next day, Saturday, Misia came down by train from Paris. I couldn't say I was happy to see her. Chanel dabbled in drugs, as I was learning many creatives in Paris did, but Misia did more than dabble. Once at a dinner party in Chanel's apartment, I'd seen her open her evening purse, calmly take out a syringe and inject herself in the thigh.

A boozy Saturday ensued with Misia determined to drag us into every seedy café, cabaret, and brothel we went by, and Chanel and Marie-Louise equally determined to stop her. It was a relief to finally return to the room. By then, my companions were three sheets to the wind, and I wasn't far behind. I took an aspirin and went to bed, stopping my ears with my fingers until their chatter finally fell off.

The next morning, Sunday, Misia couldn't be roused. After assuring ourselves she was breathing, Chanel, Marie-Louise, and I put on our Chanel straw boaters and went out without her.

Our hotel was a short walk from the Hôtel du Parc, the headquarters for the new collaborationist French State government. At Chanel's insistence, we joined the massive crowds gathered outside for the changing of the guard. Afterwards, Pétain appeared in full dress uniform with his pro-Nazi deputy prime minister, Pierre Laval, a stocky man with a black handlebar mustache who reminded me of a bandit in a cowboy movie. While a military band played patriotic music, the two men walked along the barricades gladhanding adults, kissing babies, and accepting flowers from little children.

After that we stopped for lunch at the hotel's terrace restaurant. Even on a Sunday, it was a popular spot for government officials, Wehrmacht officers, and civil servants. We had to wait to be seated and once we were it took a while for the waiter to make his way over. Between us, we ordered the *soupe au pistou*, a hearty pesto soup of white beans, green beans, and tomatoes, *salade Niçoise*, and bouillabaisse made the local way with rockfish, sea robin, and European conger.

Sipping chilled white wine, a soft breeze stirring the sultry air, after the melodramatics of the morning I was looking forward to a relaxing lunch.

Seated at an adjacent table, a French couple had finished their food and were working their way through a second bottle of champagne. Taking in the man's cheap suit, tacky tie, and bad combover, I pegged him as a minor bureaucrat. The woman, a buxom brunette wearing a huge, silly-looking hat, too much rouge, and no wedding ring, was clearly the dominant one in the relationship. With each slug of champagne, her voice seemed to rise a decibel. That and her frequent hyena-like laugh made it impossible to ignore her.

I glanced over at Chanel, mouth drawn tight and an angry blue vein beating in her temple, signs she was close to losing her temper.

"It's not too late to cancel our order and go somewhere else," I offered, hoping to head off a scene.

Chanel pretended not to hear me. "*Alors*, it is the height of the season here," she called out at a volume calculated to carry.

The woman in the awful hat shot us a scowl and then resumed her monologue even more loudly than before, that time clearly out of spite.

A German in a straw fedora and tan woven silk suit joined her and her companion at their table. The woman leaned in to say something to him, that time in a whisper, and the trio turned to glare at us.

"You have something to say, *fräulein*?" the German demanded in guttural French, his icy eyes homing in on Mademoiselle Coco.

I cut a look at Marie-Louise tracing a finger around the rim of her sweating waterglass, her face drained of color.

Chanel let out a gay laugh. "*Pas de tout*. I was just remarking on mademoiselle's festive hat and wishing ours were not so plain."

Apparently placated, they left us alone and went back to talking among themselves.

Our food arrived. We bolted it down and called for *l'addition*, all of us eager to leave.

It was the first time I'd ever seen Chanel back down. But then we were no longer in Paris. No longer at Maison Chanel where she reigned supreme, a benevolent tyrant, or so she had been before the invasion.

The lesson for me was clear. Under the new Nazi order, even the *Grande Mademoiselle* must pick her battles.

Other than meals, I was left on my own, a state of affairs that suited me. After the confinement of long car trips and tight hotel rooms, I appreciated the solitude. By then I knew better than to ask where Chanel disappeared to every morning after breakfast. I was confident I knew the reason for her absences. André. We were in Vichy so that she could advocate for his release.

I knew that she was friendly with Josée de Chambrun, an occasional customer at the boutique and the wife of Comte René de Chambrun, Chanel's lawyer in her ongoing legal battle with the Wertheimers. Josée's father was none other than Pierre Laval. I can't say whether Chanel's connection to Josée led to a meeting with Laval or his deputies, but the box of No. 5 in our room was three-quarters empty and there was still no sign that she had made any headway.

A few days later, she came across me at a café near our hotel nursing a glass of chilled Chablis and nibbling on a fruit and cheese platter. At an adjacent table, a group of red-faced German soldiers in feldgrau uniforms and shiny belts barked orders in badly accented French and banged their beer steins on the table. Though too stubborn to get up and leave, I was relieved not to be alone with them any longer.

She pulled up a chair, hailed the beleaguered waiter, and ordered a glass of champagne with a splash of pastis. In the unforgiving sunlight, I noted the crow's feet bracketing her eyes and the sallowness of her olive complexion. Until then she'd always seemed ageless to me. Seeing her so beaten down drove home that she wasn't a young woman. The past few months of agonizing over André had taken a toll.

"Eat something, just a bite," I urged, sliding the platter toward her.

Expression bleak, she pushed it away. "I am too tired to chew." Planting an elbow on the table, she held her cheek in her hand.

"No luck?" I asked, hoping to nudge her back to the easy confidences of my early days in Paris when nothing about her life had been too intimate to share with me.

She swept her elbow off the table and straightened. "What do I need with luck? I have friends, good friends, in Paris. Important people who know how to get things done. It is time to return. I have left my business too long."

Stunned, I dropped the grape I'd been about to pop in my mouth. "But I thought you meant to stay closed until Paris is free?"

"Not all Germans are gangsters," she snapped, as if she hadn't spent the last six weeks railing against the filthy Boches. "*La guerre est finie. We must all get back to our lives.*"

Though I knew better than to argue with her, I sensed that far from being over, the war for France's soul was just beginning.

Chapter Twenty-Two

August 1940

We returned to a Paris awash in red and black swastika flags. Looking out as Larcher drove us through streets and avenues sullied with Nazi soldiers, I felt as if my heart were breaking. My beautiful Paris reduced to *this*. The detested swastika flew from the Eiffel Tower, the Hôtel Ville, the Arc de Triomphe and every other public building and monument of note. On the main boulevards, German street signs in Gothic script replaced the French ones. All the clocks were set to Berlin time. Banners proclaiming *Deutschland siegt an allen Fronten* – Germany everywhere victorious – were draped over archways and buildings as if Paris and her treasures were one big, extravagant early Christmas present the Führer had given himself.

Reaching rue Cambon, we confirmed that Maison Chanel remained shuttered and seemed to have been left alone. Rather than stop off, Mademoiselle Coco had Larcher drive us directly to the Ritz. After the long, sticky journey, she wanted a bath, a meal, and a nap.

We turned the corner onto the Place Vendôme where German tanks were parked at the plaza's four corners. Scarlet banners emblazoned with swastikas bled down all four sides of the grand hotel, and miniature Nazi flags were placed at intervals along the curved mansard roof. It hurt me to see them there. After two years of daily back and forth between it and the atelier, the Ritz felt like a second home, Frank, Blanche and Jacques more like family than hotel employees.

Larcher let us off at the sandbagged main entrance. Instead of Jacques in his top hat, a German trooper guarded the double doors, a rifle butt resting on his shoulder. Taking in his smooth, babyish face, I suspected he was even younger than me.

"Heil Hitler," he barked as we approached, making the Nazis' silly, stiff-armed salute.

When we tried going inside, we were told in no uncertain terms that the hotel was requisitioned by the Wehrmacht. As civilians, we could only enter as guests of a German officer.

Chanel's face mottled. "I am no one's guest! I live here. I am Coco Chanel, and I keep a suite in the Place Vendôme wing. Number 305, since *1934*," she emphasized as if that ought to matter to him.

"The Place Vendôme wing is reserved for senior officers of the Wehrmacht," he said.

At that point, most in her position would have given up and walked away, but not Mademoiselle Coco.

Fists planted on her narrow hips, she sallied forth with, "The Hôtel Ritz is Swiss-owned, and Switzerland is neutral, is it not?"

That time the sentry flushed. "It does not work that way, Frau Chanel."

"*Mademoiselle*," she snapped. "You are in France now, so speak French!"

She pressed on in that fiery vein, until he finally relented and agreed to let us inside, albeit by the rear entrance on rue Cambon, now the civilian wing of the hotel. Cutting through the pocket-sized lobby,

Mademoiselle stormed up to the reception counter, catching Claude Auzello coming out of his office.

Amid copious apologies, he confirmed what the sentry had said, adding that Chanel was far from the only guest to give up her room. Hitler's second-in-command, Reichsmarschall Hermann Göring, was now installed in the Imperial Suite formerly occupied by the wealthy American widow, Laura Mae Corrigan.

"This is outrageous," Mademoiselle Coco said. "I will move to another hotel that appreciates my patronage."

"*Je suis désolé*, but it is out of my hands," Monsieur Auzello answered with admirable reserve. "It is not only the Ritz that has been requisitioned. The Majestic, the Lutetia, all the luxury hotels in Paris have been taken over by the Wehrmacht. We alone are fortunate to be allowed to accommodate civilian guests."

"Where are my things, my screens, my …" Her voice trailed off on a tremor, not from fear, at least I didn't think so, but because she was so spitting mad.

"Mademoiselle must speak with the *Kommandant*, Colonel Speidel."

"All dirty like this?" She looked down at herself and then back at him. "I'll go when I'm clean."

After several more rounds of back and forth, he agreed to show us to a temporary room where she could wash up.

"You go to the *Kommandant* and tell him that Mademoiselle Chanel has arrived. Return for me in fifteen minutes," she ordered him.

Ordinarily, ferrying a guest around the hotel would have been beneath him, but Mademoiselle Coco wasn't any guest. She was the *Grande Mademoiselle*, the world's most celebrated couturier, and she didn't intend to let anyone forget it, not even the Nazis.

He slipped out and closed the door, leaving us alone.

She looked over at me, the corners of her lips twitching. "It is better to be clean when one is asking for something."

I sank into the nearest seat, torn between awe at her tenacity and fear of what it might lead to.

She stepped behind the dressing screen. "*Ma pauvre* Marguerite, this is not what you expected of your time in Paris, is it?" she asked, peeling off her blouse and draping it over the top of the partition.

I let a shrug stand as my answer.

She emerged with her camisole tucked into her skirt, her pencil-thin arms firm as a girl's, and went into the small adjoining bathroom.

I heard her turn on the sink taps, singing softly to herself – "*Qui Qu'a Vu Coco?*" "Who Has Seen Coco?" By then, I recognized it as the song she'd sung as a young cabaret performer in Moulins and the origin of her nickname.

When Monsieur Auzello returned exactly fifteen minutes later, she emerged fresh as a rose, her face and neck bathed, her hair combed, and her mouth wearing a fresh coating of crimson lipstick.

"Reste ici." Stay here, she told me, and then followed him out, head held high.

I trained my gaze on the small bronze-encased Swiss wall clock and waited. The minutes passed, each tick seeming to echo my heart's panicked pounding. Chanel was wealthy and internationally known, but the dust-up at lunch in Vichy had showed she was as subject to Nazi rule as the rest of us. And we weren't in the Free Zone anymore. We were in Paris, the heart of the occupied territory. Though we'd only been back about an hour, it was clear you couldn't take a step without encountering a German in uniform. In demanding to see the ranking Nazi in charge, had Chanel overplayed her hand?

Forty minutes later, she returned, not a hair out of place.

Relieved to see her in one piece, I bolted to my feet.

"It is settled," she announced, and taking in the tight set of her mouth I gathered the outcome wasn't entirely satisfactory.

In a few clipped sentences, she explained that a small suite had been found for her on the top floor of the rue Cambon wing, now considered the civilian side of the hotel. We waited for her things to be moved over and then Monsieur Auzello returned to collect us. I thought he looked as wrung out as I felt but to his credit his professional demeanor never faltered.

We followed him out to the small elevator set across from the manager's office and piled into the closet-sized car, barely big enough to fit us all.

"Six," Monsieur Auzello told the elevator operator, a young man in hotel livery and white gloves who punched the brass buttons from his perch on a high stool.

The elevator rose with a clank. I silently counted off the floors, aware of Chanel standing ruler straight beside me, her jaw tight and hands fisted.

We ground to a bumpy stop and stepped off into a long hallway of guestrooms, the passageway noticeably narrower and dimmer than those in the Place Vendôme wing.

Monsieur Auzello turned to the door directly across from the elevator and took a key from his coat pocket.

"Voilà," he announced, unlocking it.

Holding my breath, I followed Mademoiselle Coco inside.

We were in a modest two rooms, a small sitting area and a bedroom, both sparsely furnished and austerely white. Looking around, I suspected it had served as staff quarters before the war. Though the wood-burning fireplace would be lovely in the winter and the window presented a pleasant view of the hotel garden bordered by boxwoods and blessed with chestnut trees, it was nonetheless quite a comedown from her former accommodations.

The hotel director cleared his throat. "Madame Ritz is also lodged on this floor as are Mademoiselle Arletty, Monsieur and Madame Charles Bedaux, and *la famille* Dubonnet."

The widow of the hotel founder along with a French film star, a millionaire industrialist and his American socialite wife, and a fabulously wealthy family of aperitif winemakers – not exactly a shabby set of neighbors, and yet Mademoiselle Coco hadn't said a word.

We two watched in tense silence as she prowled the four corners like a panther, running her fingers along the stark white walls, taking inventory of the simple furnishings, going to the window and pulling back the sheer white curtain.

Letting it drop, she turned around to us. "*C'est magnifique.*"

Monsieur Auzello exhaled audibly. "The dining room will commence dinner service at five o' clock. Shall I have Monsieur Dabescat reserve your usual table?"

By then, she had moved on to opening the dresser drawers, inspecting her clothing, which had not only been brought over but folded exactly as she liked.

She acknowledged him with a distracted nod. "*Mille mercis.*"

Palpably relieved, he bowed at the waist and backed out of the room.

The outer door had barely clicked closed when she began pulling clothes from the wardrobe and draping them over chairs and tables.

"Tonight, I will wear all white," she announced. "White is clean, pure. The opposite of these dirty Boches, is it not Marguerite?"

The same Boches that in Vichy she'd sworn were not all gangsters? Struggling to find my footing, I settled for a nod. Her changeability baffled and unsettled me, and yet I couldn't help but admire her unflappable courage.

She disappeared into the white-tiled bathroom to draw a bath.

"Larcher has taken your valise to your apartment," she called out over the running water. "I will see you at the boutique tomorrow. We will show these Boches they cannot keep Paris down."

"*Oui, Mademoiselle.*" Eager to get home to see Bridget and have a bath of my own, I edged toward the door.

Whatever else she was – groundbreaking couturier, adoring aunt, passionate lover – Mademoiselle Coco was a survivor.

Chapter Twenty-Three

The elevator opened to the ground floor. Distracted by searching my handbag for the apartment house key I feared I'd left behind in Vichy, I stepped off – and plowed into a hard-muscled human.

My *laissez-passer*, lipstick, comb, and the elusive key spilled out over the marble.

"*Excusez-moi.*" I dropped to my hands and knees on the floor.

"Daisy?"

I craned my neck to look up, and for a handful of heartbeats a surge of giddy gladness suffused me. Fritz, back in Paris and in one piece, not dismembered or dead as I'd sometimes imagined him. His blond hair, cropped close on the sides, was mostly hidden beneath a thickly braided officer's cap. My gaze slipped to the feldgrau tunic with the distinctive Wehrmacht collar flashes and the detestable symbol of Nazi Germany, an eagle clutching a swastika in its talons, and an icy wave of anger broke over me.

I finished shoveling my things back in my bag and got up, pointedly ignoring his outstretched hand. "Showing your true colors, Herr Eberhardt?"

"Hauptmann Eberhardt," he corrected me, handing me my lipstick, which I snatched back and dropped in my purse without so much as a thank you. "Though I hope you will call me Fritz when I am off duty."

"I won't be seeing you off duty," I said.

He took that in.

"I suppose your boss, von Dincklage is back as well?" I asked, noting the brown leather attaché case he held.

When we'd first met, his posting as an assistant to a German embassy attaché when relations with France were moving toward war should have set off warning bells. At the time, I had been too besotted with Paris and my exciting new life to put two and two together. Now that I did, it seemed likely he had been spying on us, or at least helping von Dincklage to do so.

"The baron is in Paris, yes," he confirmed, tone neutral.

"As an embassy attaché? Or should I say propaganda master? Do we really need those in wartime?" I asked, not bothering to mask my sarcasm.

"Baron von Dincklage's official duties are to oversee textile production for the war effort."

"And his unofficial duties?"

He didn't answer, not that I'd expected him to.

Instead, he said, "I am billeted at the Hôtel Lutetia. Should you find yourself in need of anything, you can contact me there."

"Don't hold your breath."

That time, his stoic mask slipped. "Daisy, please, this doesn't have to change things."

"It's Mademoiselle Blakely to you. And *this* ..." I swept a hand to indicate the despised uniform and all that it symbolized, "changes *everything*."

Leaving him standing there, I took off toward the exit.

* * *

By the time I stepped out of the Métro and walked the few blocks to Madame LeBrun's, I felt like Chanel must, my feelings a twisted tumult of contradictions. Happy to be back in Paris but hating what the Nazis were doing to it. Grateful to find Fritz alive but hurt and angry over how easily he had slipped into the role of occupier.

I had a tearful reunion with Bridget, followed by a truly miserable supper with Madame LeBrun and Olivier, back from the countryside and as bratty as before.

Afterwards, Bridget and I retreated upstairs and set about getting rip-roaringly drunk. Sitting on the floor with our backs to the dingy wallpaper, we passed a bottle of brandy back and forth.

"Better enjoy it. It's the last of my stash," she told me.

"Whaddaya mean?" I asked, slurring after my first few sips. "I'll get us more."

Always better at holding her liquor than I was, she shook her head. "You won't, not unless you buy it on the *Marché Noir*. The Boches banned selling liquor in the shops. It's beer and wine from now on, for us commoners, at least. I expect you'll be drinking champagne and Bee's Knees at the Ritz with Mademoiselle Coco like you did before the war."

Though her tone was matter-of-fact, I didn't miss the undercurrent of resentment.

"Bridge, I'm so sorry I had to leave you. I came to get you and bring you with us, but you weren't here, and Madame LeBrun didn't know where you were or when you'd be back. I had to go; I couldn't wait any longer. If I had, I would have been left behind, too."

She snorted. "Can't have that, can we?"

"I know it sounds cowardly and maybe it is, but I promised my grandmother I'd be careful if she let me come back."

"S'all right," she said, taking a long pull from the bottle. "Thanks again for paying the rent. Two whole months. Someone's flush."

Too lily-livered to look her in the eye, I focused on the far wall, the plaster buckling under a blot of moisture.

"I'm not flush, but my family is," I admitted, wishing I were drunker. "My grandmother owns Kavanaugh's department store in Manhattan. Someday I'll inherit it along with my brother and mother and uncle, but Gran's picked me to run it all. She wants to open a store here in Paris, too, so she arranged with Mademoiselle Coco for me to intern at Maison Chanel and learn the French fashion trade. Mademoiselle promised to keep an eye on me for her, which is why I couldn't say no to going with her to Corbère."

There, I had done it, as good as admitted I had lied to her for the past two years.

She stayed quiet, which wasn't like her.

I turned my head to look at her, her profiled face unreadable, her hands with their chipped nail polish wrapped around the brandy bottle.

"Bridge, say something, please."

She turned to face me. "I know. I've known for a while now."

I felt my mouth fall open.

"Nothing stays secret for long in an atelier. *Petites mains* are as gossipy as hairdressers. I always thought a Chanel evening gown was quite a birthday gift, even if it was a leftover sample. When Yvette let slip that Mademoiselle Coco had them put on a whole fashion show just for you, I thought she was pulling my leg. But you switching handbags with that Polish girl cinched it. No one who'd saved up for *months* for a Chanel purse would trade it for a grubby pouchette, no matter how nice a person they are. But then you didn't have to save up, did you? Yours was given to you."

Caught out, I hung my head. "I don't know what to say."

"You could have told me, you know. All this time pretending to scrape by when you were fixed. Why?"

Tears filled my eyes. She was my only friend in Paris, and the best friend I'd ever had. The girls I'd buddied around with back in New York were mostly silly debutantes. I supposed I was a silly deb, too, but I hadn't wanted to be, not even then.

"Money has a way of coming between people. When you told me how hard you'd worked to get yourself to Paris, I felt ashamed of how easy I've had it. I've spent the past two years trying to be more like you – brave and resourceful and independent. Can you ever forgive me?"

I waited, heart in my throat.

She brought the brandy to her lips and took another drink.

"No more secrets." She passed me the bottle.

Relief made a ragdoll of me. I took a swig and slumped back against the wall.

"No more secrets," I promised, using my sleeve to blot a dribble of brandy from my chin.

I couldn't know then that the promises dearest to our hearts are the hardest ones to keep.

Chapter Twenty-Four

My first morning back, we were awakened by blaring martial music and pounding jackboots as Wehrmacht troopers goose-stepped down the Champs to the Place de la Concorde. Loudspeakers ensured the din reached us no matter where we were in the city.

Head splitting from the previous night's tippling, I turned on my side and looked across at Bridget, a sleep mask covering her eyes.

"They've conquered the country. What's left to celebrate?" I groused.

She pulled down her mask. "Don't shoot the messenger, but they do this *every* morning."

I carried my towel down the hallway to the bathroom where I washed my face and brushed my teeth. By the time I came back, Bridget had put on a pot of coffee, or the ersatz version that passed for it under the new rationing program. It tasted like burned acorns, especially without sugar or milk to put in it, but at least it was hot. I poured myself a cup and sat down to peruse the newspaper. Thumbing through the morning edition of *Le Figaro*, a mouthpiece for Nazi propaganda as all French media was by then, I spotted a short news article buried in the back.

The Vichy government had declared that only those with French fathers could practice the professions, including medicine. The Paris Prefecture of Police had come up with a list of nine hundred and fifteen physicians who fell into the non-French category, which apparently included those whose fathers were naturalized citizens. I remembered Jean-Claude mentioning his father was born in Luxembourg and my heart dropped.

I pulled on clothes, popped an aspirin, and got on my bicycle to Neuilly. Pedaling through the somber city streets, I passed boarded townhouses, the flowers withering in their window boxes, graffitied storefronts with broken windows, and trash gathering in the gutters. Several cafés had reopened but the tables were taken up by German soldiers. I couldn't help feeling like the City of Light had had her soul snuffed out.

I came up to the hospital's gated archway, steeling myself for a Nazi flag flying from the ramparts. Instead, I saw the flag of the *Croix Rouge Française* – the French Red Cross.

By then I was sticky with sweat, my blouse plastered to my back. I entered the main building by the staff entrance, stowed my bicycle in the wire cage locker and took the elevator to the plastic surgery department. Other than the stern-faced French nurse, who'd softened to me since I'd started volunteering, the floor looked empty.

"Is Jean ... Dr. Jacob in?" I asked, bracing myself to hear he'd been dismissed on account of the new law.

"He has just returned from ward rounds," she told me.

Relieved, I made my way back to his office. Standing outside his closed door, I smoothed a hand over my unruly hair and knocked.

"*Entrez*," he called out, and I realized how much I'd missed hearing his voice.

I entered, pulling the door closed behind me, unsure what to expect after six weeks away. When I'd left, France was still a free, independent nation. Now she was a conquered country, her citizens vassals of Nazi Germany.

He stood from his desk, his lab coat as rumpled as I remembered it, his dark hair curling around his collar, badly in need of a trim.

"You are back."

Before I could answer, he rounded the desk and drew me into his arms, dropping kisses on my temple, my cheek and lastly, my lips.

When we finally broke apart, my heart was pounding, and my knees were weak. "We got in yesterday afternoon from Vichy."

At my mention of the spa town now synonymous with the French puppet government, his mouth tightened.

"I read about the new law banning 'non-French' doctors and wanted to make sure you were all right," I explained. "Are you … all right?"

Resting his hands on my shoulders, he blew out a long breath. "There is an exemption for those whose fathers served in the First World War. I am saved – for now."

"That's a relief," I said, though I didn't much like the "for now" part.

Then again, in our current fraught circumstances, the present moment was as far ahead as any of us could foresee. So far, we had been lucky. Since the war started, I had found my way back to Paris, and him, not once but twice. Going forward, I swore to myself that I would savor whatever time we got to share.

His hands fell away from me, and he flagged me to a chair, but I shook my head and stayed standing.

"I saw the Red Cross flag outside," I said. Being under the aegis of a neutral international organization boded a lot better than being under the Nazi administration, or so I had to think.

He nodded. "Before going back to America, the hospital board of governors appointed General de Chambrun as governor general. Like Pétain, Chambrun served with distinction in the Great War. It does not hurt that his son, René, is married to Pierre Laval's daughter."

René de Chambrun was also Chanel's lawyer against the Wertheimers, but there was nothing to be gained by bringing up that sore subject.

"He used his influence with the Vichyites to save us from being requisitioned by the Nazis," he continued. "In exchange, we agreed to provide medical care to the British and French *prisonniers de guerre*."

The American was now a hospital for POWs. I let that sink in.

"Mademoiselle Chanel is reopening the boutique, but the atelier will stay closed, so I won't be needed full-time."

His forehead creased. "You are planning to stay?"

I didn't hesitate. "I am."

"Most Americans have left or are making plans to. Dr. Gros suffered a stroke and was evacuated to Pennsylvania. Dr. Bove leaves for New York at the end of the month. Your family must worry for you."

According to Bridget, who had posted two letters so far to her family in London, mail from the Occupied Zone had to be smuggled to the Free Zone and then sent on from there. Luckily, before leaving Vichy, I'd taken advantage of the liberal postal system to write to my family. Before dropping off the letter, I had reread it so many times I had it memorized.

Dear Family,

Mademoiselle Coco is returning to Paris to reopen her boutique, and I'm going with her. I'll be back living with Bridget at Madame LeBrun's, so I won't be alone or lonely.

I'm also hoping to resume volunteering at the American Hospital. I won't know for sure until I get there, but I suspect every pair of hands is needed now more than ever.

I realize my decision to stay must seem baffling to you, foolish, even. I've struggled to explain it to myself and the best I can come up with is this:

Paris has my heart. She has ever since I stepped off the boat train with Gran. Not only the physical place – the cafes, the monuments, the buildings – but the people. I can't desert them in their hour of need. If I did, I'd regret it for the rest of my life.

This may be the last letter from me for some time, but please know that I am keeping well and holding each one of you in my heart.

Yours always,

Daisy

I lifted my chin. "I wrote from Vichy, so they know I'm safe. I'm sure they're not happy about me staying on, but I'm twenty now, old enough to decide these things for myself," I made sure to add, wanting him to know I was out of my teens, officially a grownup. "Do you think the hospital will take me back as a volunteer?"

"You are determined," he said, and I detected a grudging admiration in his voice. "We can use volunteers with experience. See Madame Allard in Administration. Tell her I sent you." He looked past me at the wall clock. "I wish I had more time to spend, but I have a rendezvous."

"That's all right," I said. "I'll drop in on Madame Allard."

I turned to go, disappointed that our reunion was so brief but consoling myself that there would be plenty of opportunities to see each other in the days ahead.

To my surprise, he called me back. "Would you want to come with me?"

I stopped and turned around. "To your patient exam?"

He let out a laugh. "My rendezvous is not with a patient but a pig." He shucked off his lab coat and went to hang it on the door hook. "You are coming?"

I would have jumped on any excuse to stay with him longer, but I was also intrigued. "Lead the way."

We took the lift to the ground level canteen and cut through the kitchen. The lunch service was in full swing, with women in hair nets and aprons ladling out large vats of soup and taking out trays of bread from a baking oven. Sitting atop a counter used for assembling patient meal trays, a box brimmed with *Cartes Individuelle d' Alimentation*. Ration cards.

Following my eye, Jean-Claude explained, "To be fed, patients must bring their ration cards."

Shocked, I asked, "Are your storehouses *that* low?"

"Ah, *oui*. The Nazis are diverting as much of France's food and wine as they can to Germany to feed their army. Under the new Ministry of Agriculture and Supply, French adults are allowed only twelve hundred calories a day, the elderly eight hundred and fifty."

In Corbère, I hadn't given a thought to my next meal. With most everything produced on the Palasse property, there had always been plenty. I had been back in Paris less than a day, but already I was seeing that life in the Occupied Zone was a whole other ballgame.

"Twelve hundred calories aren't enough to keep healthy people fit, let alone ailing ones," I protested. "Are there no exceptions made for them?"

His brow knitted. "It is not only Jews they hate. The Nazis want to weed out the weak and ill. Starvation is a slower means of murder but cleaner than bombs and bullets."

On that grim note, we stepped out to the garden. Jean-Claude led us up a pebbled path that ended in a small gardening shed. He took a key from his pocket and slipped it into the padlock. The door opened on rusted hinges. Entering, he pulled the chain of the single lightbulb dangling from the center of the low ceiling.

I followed him in. Dust motes floated like fireflies in the close, musty air. Everything was coated in a thick, white film. Shovels, rakes and other rusted gardening tools were heaped into corners. Two long wooden troughs took up the center of the floor, one piled with burlap bags of potatoes, the other lined with salt, ice and straw but otherwise empty.

"You weren't joking. It really is a pigsty," I observed, fighting sneezing.

"Once a week, a farmer from outside Paris makes deliveries," he said. "In this way, we are able to feed our patients and staff."

He went on to explain that Dr. Jackson, who'd taken over as the hospital's chief medical officer, had bartered with a local landowner to trade the hospital's surplus wine for cheap potatoes.

"As you know, the American has two hundred and fifty patient beds," Jean-Claude continued. "The authorities allow each hospital patient one-half liter of wine a day. We give the farmer five hundred liters of wine. In return, he takes five *thousand* kilos of fertilizer and *voilà*." He gestured to the bin of potatoes.

It was, I admitted, an ingenious arrangement.

"In a little while, three hundred kilos of salt pork from the *Marché Noir* will be delivered," he added, a gleam in his eye.

I gave up the fight against smiling. "The pig you have your rendezvous with?"

He nodded. "The German authorities sometimes conduct on-the-spot inspections of the hospital, so we hide the food out here until they leave."

"Why are you telling me this?" I asked.

He shrugged in that oh-so-French way that made me weak-kneed but only when he did it. "Three hundred kilos are … a lot of pig. Perhaps you will help?"

Until then, we'd almost always been together at the hospital or bicycling back to Paris, surrounded by people, busy and in a rush. There was something about standing alone with him in the stillness, the shed's thin walls and tar paper roof cocooning us from the garden and hospital beyond, that made me bold.

"Perhaps I will but only if you can meet my price," I said, shamelessly flirting as I once wouldn't have dared do.

He took a step toward me, the corners of his eyes creasing in a smile. "*Dites-moi*. Tell me."

I set my palm on his chest and felt his heart racing a mile a minute, a match for mine. "Another kiss, and make it count."

"*À votre service, mademoiselle*." Spanning my waist with his hands, he drew me to him.

Chapter Twenty-Five

September–October 1940

With the new government installed in Vichy, the prevailing sentiment was that life would settle down to normal. And yet after a month back in Paris, normalcy was the last thing I found.

The Nazis controlled almost every aspect of our lives. A 9 p.m. to 5 a.m. curfew was imposed after which the city went dark. Women were banned from buying cigarettes, though Chanel and her wealthy friends like Misia and Arletty continued smoking like chimneys courtesy of the Black Market. Works by Picasso and other modernist artists were declared degenerate and prohibited from public display. To feed the Nazi war machine, nearly everything was rationed from basic foodstuffs to petrol and fabric.

Restrictions on textiles made it a tricky time for fashion. Silk was prioritized for parachutes, wool for uniforms, leather for boots, and linen for bandages. Floor-length gowns disappeared from collections. Design houses that stayed open had the Nazis breathing down their necks. They tightened limits on fabric, imposed prudish restrictions on skirt lengths, and warned couturiers like Madame Grès on pain of closure to stop designing in red, white, and blue, the colors of the

French flag. Given the scarcity and creative suppression, I began to think Chanel had been right to close.

Other than popping in to say a quick hello to Frank, I hadn't been back to the Ritz bar since returning to Paris. Chanel had invited me a time or two, but I had always found a reason to decline, not wanting to risk running into Fritz. Or von Dincklage. Though the baron wasn't sufficiently high up to be housed at the hotel, according to Frank and Blanche, he was a frequent fixture in the bar and restaurant where he and Mademoiselle Coco dined together nearly every night.

With our favorite cafés overtaken by German soldiers, Bridget and I became homebodies. Every night at six o' clock, we put on our pajamas and switched on our now illegal wireless radio. With Nazi censors controlling all printed and broadcast news, the BBC's *Radio Londres* was our sole source for trustworthy information. On September 8th, we learned that the German Luftwaffe had launched a large-scale aerial bombing campaign, a *blitzkrieg*, on British industrial cities including London, sending civilians to seek refuge in basements, cellars, and the Underground.

I switched off the broadcast and went over to give Bridget a hug. "When was your last letter from your family?"

Bravely holding back tears, she said, "More than a month."

A week later, another BBC broadcast announced that the United States had instituted a draft. Starting September 16th, American men between the ages of twenty-one and forty-five would be required to register, a significant step toward mobilizing for war as well as a shot across the bow to the Germans. My heart sank. I had to believe Uncle Blake's mild heart murmur would disqualify him from active duty, but if America entered the war, Neil would almost certainly be called up. Thinking of all the beautiful young Frenchmen I'd seen carried in on stretchers at the American, some maimed, others dead, and others kept prisoner at Drancy, I shuddered to think of my gentle artist brother exchanging his paints and colored pencils for a rifle and hand grenades.

As the citizen of a still nominally neutral nation, I didn't have to rely solely on BBC reports or smuggled letters. I could call home. At the Ritz, Blanche had resumed my phone privileges albeit with a warning. The hotel's French switchboard operator had been replaced with a German girl. Instead of Marie from Paris, we had Helga from Berlin listening in. But even a carefully worded phone call was better than no phone call at all.

The next Sunday, I called my parents from Claude's office. As usual, Mom picked up.

"It's only a matter of time before America joins the war," she said, the tremor in her voice cutting through the crackling over the connection. "Once that happens, the Germans will take the gloves off when it comes to any Americans left in France. With your brother having to register with the draft board, don't your father and I have enough to worry about without imagining you being hauled off to some horrid ... stalag, or worse?"

Even though I doubted it would make any difference, I tried again to make her understand. "When you were younger than I am, you were out marching for women to get the vote even though you could have been arrested."

"I was never arrested."

"But you *could* have been," I pointed out. "And Gran let you go anyway."

"Because she knew I was doing my part to make a difference."

"So am I," I answered, more hotly than I'd meant to.

The phone was passed to Dad and Neil shortly thereafter, both of whom did their best to smooth things over with small talk and amusing anecdotes, but the upsetting exchange with my mother stayed with me long after we had hung up.

Later that month, the news went from bad to worse when imperial Japan invaded French Indochina, joining the war on the side of Germany and fascist Italy and upping the odds that America would have to step in and fight. By then, I was spending more and more time at the American, taking on extra shifts as my boutique schedule allowed. In keeping with the hospital's deal with Vichy, on any given day, the wards were filled with ailing French and British POWs, most from La Muette, the prison at Drancy on the northeastern outskirts of Paris. Whether wheeling in meal trays, helping change a wound dressing, or writing letters home for a soldier too ill to put pen to paper, I felt like I was doing something important, something that mattered. Still, it was maddening to stand by and watch a recovered patient turned over to the Nazis, knowing that filthy conditions and poor diet would likely land him back in the hospital, or worse, the morgue.

Brave physicians like Dr. Jackson and Jean-Claude did what they could. Doctoring patient charts to make a malady look worse on paper, handing out diagnoses of tuberculosis to men with minor coughs or chest colds, and making backdoor deals for rationed medicines, medical supplies and equipment were among the illegal activities for which they routinely risked their lives.

Volunteering allowed me to keep tabs on Jean-Claude, whom I worried about constantly. By mid-October, signs reading *Interdit aux Juifs*, No Jews, began appearing at the entrances to restaurants, theaters, and businesses around Paris. Under the *Ordonnance d'Aryanisation*, all Jews in the Occupied Zone were required to register with their arrondissement's prefecture of police or face arrest.

One weekday when Jean-Claude didn't show up for his usual shift, I imagined the worst. When he finally walked in, disheveled and out of sorts, I felt weak with relief.

I looked back to the English patient I'd been reading to, rail thin and recovering from a stubborn case of dysentery. "We'll pick this up tomorrow," I said, closing the cover on Dickens' *Great Expectations*.

I set the book back on the bedside table and got up from my chair to make my way over to Jean-Claude.

Standing at the nurse's station, he slipped on his lab coat, then ran a hasty hand through his hair.

Wishing we were back in our garden shed so I could throw my arms around him, I lowered my voice and asked, "Where were you? I was worried."

In a few terse words, he told me how he, his mother and sister had stood in line for hours outside their local commissariat de police at 27 boulevard Bourdon. Finally, called up to the counter, they'd had to give their street, nationality, and occupation to be recorded in the police ledger.

Trying not to panic, I asked, "Did they say why they wanted the information?"

He tossed me a look. "*Non*, but it is obvious they are preparing to round us up like cattle and ship us off."

"Off where?" I asked, feeling a chill sweeping my spine.

He met my gaze, and beneath the fury, I read the fear in his eyes. "That is the question."

The clandestine deliveries of potatoes and meat continued into autumn. Every Friday at lunchtime, the lorry pulled up to the delivery entrance at the back of the kitchen where I stood as lookout while the food and sometimes other supplies were unloaded and carried to the shed.

A few days later, Jean-Claude took me aside. "Meet me at the garden shed. *Dix minutes*," he added before walking off.

I grabbed Neil's old high school letter sweater from the staff breakroom and took the elevator down to the kitchen.

Jean-Claude was waiting when I walked up, his lab coat replaced by a worn tweed jacket with patches on the elbows.

"The Germans are planning a surprise inspection," he told me.

"Can you stop the delivery?"

He shook his head. "It is too late. And the patients need the food."

Thinking of the emaciated soldiers languishing on their hospital cots, I had to agree. "What do we do?"

Rather than answer immediately, he unlocked the shed and ducked inside. Coming back out, he held a shovel in either hand. "We dig."

When the truck arrived, instead of hiding the salt pork and potatoes in the shed as usual, we wrapped them in burlap and buried them in the garden. We barely had time to fill in the hole and cover it with straw when a contingent from the *Feldgendarmerie*, German police headquarters, showed up to search the building and grounds.

"What is this?" the German police captain demanded of Jean-Claude, testing the patch of freshly turned topsoil with the toe of his boot.

I held my breath.

"Cabbages," Jean-Claude answered, perfectly straight-faced.

"Cabbages?" the German echoed.

Jean-Claude nodded. "Fall is the best time for planting them."

It was a relief to see their backs. Watching them tromp off an hour later, taking several cases of our wine with them, I sank down on the ironwork bench.

"Cabbages, really? It's a good thing that police captain wasn't in on the joke, or they might have hauled you off along with the wine."

He shrugged. "The Boches are not known for their sense of humor."

I looked out onto the garden plot. "Now what. Dig it back up?" I asked, fingering the blister on my palm.

He dropped down beside me on the seat. "Sometimes they come back to check. It is better to wait until tomorrow."

I caught him eyeing me, a smirk on his face.

"What?" I demanded, giving his shoulder a nudge.

"You are certain you work in fashion?" he asked.

It took me a minute to realize he was teasing.

I swatted his arm. "I love this sweater. It belongs to my brother. I made him give it to me before I left New York."

Turning serious, he took my hand. "You are close?"

I nodded. "We're not even a year apart. Irish twins, they call it. Growing up, we used to tell each other everything."

"That has changed?" he asked, picking up on my wistfulness.

"Before I left New York, Neil dropped out of art school. No explanation; just showed up back home. We were all shocked. Art school was his dream. He's been sketching ever since I can remember. At least he's dating someone, *finally*, though mom and dad still haven't met her." Seeing an opportunity, I slipped in, "Speaking of secrets, is there anything *you'd* like to tell me?"

"I do not think so," he answered evenly.

His expression stayed matter-of-fact, but by then I knew him well enough to see through the mask. Keeping things from me was his way of protecting me, I knew, but that didn't mean I had to accept it.

Looking around to make sure no one was nearby, I lowered my voice and said, "Pork and potatoes aren't all you're trafficking. You're smuggling out POWs, aren't you?"

A heavy breath, a muttered expletive in French, and finally, a whispered admission. "Not every patient who leaves the morgue with a toe tag is dead, only dead to the Nazis."

I didn't hesitate. "Let me help."

His features firmed. "If the Boches catch us, they will not bother to check for passports. Anyone involved could be shot, even an American who imagines she is invincible. Your life is too high a price. I will not pay it."

As chilling as the prospect was, the recent run-in had boosted my confidence. Working together, the two of us had bested the Nazis. Though it was only pork and potatoes at stake, fighting back felt *good*.

"If it comes to that, I'd rather be shot saving a soldier than burying a pig."

He cut me a dour look. "You say that now."

"Which patient is it?" I persisted, reasonably sure I knew everyone by his chart.

"The patient on the Jaw Ward."

"The millworker from Pantin who fell face first into a grain grinder?"

Head and face bandaged, the poor man had been languishing in his hospital bed since before I'd started back volunteering in early August.

"An RAF fighter shot down over the Ardennes," he admitted. "After the field hospital was disbanded, we brought him here. It has taken all these months, but we finally have a plan in place and people to get him out."

"How will you do it?" I asked.

By then, Neuilly was a hornet's nest of Nazis, with the American smack in the center. In addition to German police headquarters across the street on rue du Château, both the German army post and the Gestapo were around the corner on boulevard Victor Hugo.

He hesitated as if weighing how much more to say.

"Next Friday at four o' clock, an ambulance will arrive to pick him up and take him to a safe house in the Dordogne Valley. When he is well enough, one of our men will guide him across the Pyrenees into Spain and from there Lisbon and back to England."

"Who else's in on it?" I asked.

"*Personne*. Nurse Betty used to help us sometimes, but she is back in America. It will be the man driving the ambulance and me, *nous deux, c'est tout*."

Us two, that's it.

I thought back to the letter I'd sent from Vichy and the recent heated telephone conversation with my mother. Both times I'd insisted I was staying on to serve Paris in her hour of need. To make a difference. So far, I'd helped hide some pork and potatoes. A benefit to the patients and staff receiving the food, but hardly bringing down the hammer on Nazism. I had more to give, more to *do*, and I knew it.

I slipped my hand in Jean-Claude's. "Now it's the three of us."

Chapter Twenty-Six

Fridays were among my usual days working at the boutique, but I'd asked Bridget to cover for me so that I could leave early for my "date" with Jean-Claude. It was a date, in a manner of speaking, just not the sort she thought.

At a quarter to four, I changed into a spare nurse's uniform from the supply closet and met Jean-Claude in the Jaw Ward. The RAF pilot lay in his solitary cot amid the rows of empty beds, his head wrapped up like a mummy's, his right leg in a plaster cast.

"This is Archie," Jean-Claude told me. "Be careful with him. His broken leg is real, and so are the burns on his back. Earlier, I gave him another blood transfusion to help boost his immune system against infection. Under the circumstances, it is the best I can do." To the pilot, he said, "Remember, not a word until you are inside the ambulance."

Beneath the bandages, the airman nodded.

Between us, we got him onto the gurney and wheeled him through the hallway and onto the lift. Stepping off onto the ground floor, we headed outside to the ambulance pickup.

At four o' clock on the dot, a battered Ford ambulance rumbled through the hospital's arched entrance and pulled up to the curb.

Nervous, I started pushing the gurney toward it too fast, as if it held a slab of salt pork instead of a living person with wounds not yet healed. I hit a rut on the path, and the gurney bucked.

"Blimey!" my patient exclaimed.

A few paces ahead, Jean-Claude turned and gave us a black look.

I made myself slow down. "You're doing terrific, Archie. Hang in there, we're almost to the finish."

"You're American," he whispered.

"As apple pie."

"What are you lot still doing in Paris?" he asked, his East London accent even broader than Bridget's.

Pork on the brain, I said, "Saving your bacon, it seems."

He chuckled. "If you really want to help, tell your President Roosevelt to get off the stick and join the war."

I smiled. "I'll fire off a telegram to the White House just as soon as we get you in the back of that ambulance."

The driver, dressed in a medic's uniform, got out from behind the wheel, opened the ambulance back, and brought out a stretcher.

"Wish me luck, Apple Pie?" Archie said. I imagined him winking at me beneath the bandages.

"*Bonne chance.* And *bon voyage*," I whispered.

I stood off to the side as the driver and Jean-Claude got him off the gurney and onto the stretcher. They'd just lifted the stretcher into the back of the ambulance when the distinctive sound of hobnailed boots striking pavement sent my heart sinking. I looked across the front lawn as a half-dozen German police marched toward us, led by the police captain from the other week.

Drawing up, the German police captain looked among the three of us. "Late for a patient transport, is it not?"

"I had to stop and change a flat tire," the ambulance driver answered.

"Who do we have here?" he asked, flagging a hand to indicate Archie in the ambulance back.

"A gristmill worker from Pantin," Jean-Claude answered, "injured when he lost his footing and fell into the blades."

"So, you say." The police captain jerked his head toward his second-in-command. "Search it."

The Germans fanned out around the ambulance, kicking tires and pulling open doors.

Heart pounding, I spoke up, "You might want to keep your distance. This patient has tuberculosis."

The Germans froze.

"We're transporting him before he infects the entire ward," I added, by then knowing how paranoid the Nazis were about contracting any kind of disease.

The police captain looked at Jean-Claude, the attending physician in charge. "Is this true?"

Jean-Claude gave a vigorous nod. "We are transporting him to Dordogne. The country air is his best hope for recovery. See for yourself."

He held out Archie's chart or rather the chart for the injured granary worker he was supposed to be.

The police captain grabbed it from him and gave the notes a cursory glance over. The chart was all in French, and I suspected he was too proud to admit he couldn't read it.

He shoved the chart back at Jean-Claude. "You cannot transport patients to the Free Zone without the permission of the Ministry of Health."

Beneath his lab coat, Jean-Claude's shoulders squared. "This hospital operates under the *Croix Rouge* by direct order of Pétain. If you do not like it, take it up with him."

I held my breath as the two men stood toe-to-toe, gazes in a lock hold.

The German was the first to look away.

"Let them go," he called out to his men. Turning back, he stuck his face up close to Jean-Claude's. "I have my eye on you, *Jude*."

He signaled to his men, and they turned in unison and marched off.

Jean-Claude closed the ambulance back. "*Va, vitement*," he called out to the driver, already back behind the wheel.

I stood with him watching the ambulance drive through the arched gateway. Now that the immediate danger was behind us, it was an effort to hold myself up.

"I'm lucky the hemline on this uniform is so long. My knees were knocking together the whole time," I admitted.

Reaching out, Jean-Claude took my chin in his fingers and gently turned me to face him. "You were *merveilleuse*," he said as if seeing me with fresh eyes.

The praise brought a warm sting to my cheeks. "I am glad you let me help."

"If you had not spoken up to stop the search, they would have found contraband medical equipment and supplies and ... more."

I opened my mouth to ask what kind of more, then stopped myself. Maybe I didn't need to know everything, at least not all in one day.

Instead, I said, "I should get back. Bridget thinks we're on a date, an early rendezvous before your shift."

He frowned. "I do not want you on the roads alone after dark."

I hated to admit it, but he wasn't wrong to worry. The stories of girls and young women cornered and harassed by Nazi soldiers or worse were sobering. "What do you suggest?" I asked, thinking he would see me home.

He skimmed my arms, his hands cupping my elbows. "Why not let your friend think the date went well? *Très bien*," he suggested with a smile.

"Jean-Claude?"

In the waning light, his gaze held mine. "Stay the night. With me."

Chapter Twenty-Seven

We took the staff elevator up to the fourth floor, only instead of climbing the stairwell to the roof, he led me along the hall with numbered doors on either side similar to a hotel.

"*Voilà*," he said, holding the door for me to enter.

Inside was more of a bedsit than a bedroom, the furnishings modest but well-appointed, everything well-ordered and scrupulously clean. Along with an iron fourposter and nightstand, there was a small study with a cabinet of books, all medical texts, and a kitchen area with a hotplate, a shelf for dishware, and a small painted table with two chairs.

Jean-Claude hung his lab coat on a hook and busied himself with making dinner, the mainstay of which was a leek soup from the hospital kitchens. He poured it into a pot and set it atop the burner.

"Can I help?" I asked, amused to see this domesticated side of him.

He shook his head. "You are my guest."

Rather than ask twice, I walked over to the French doors and stepped out onto a small balcony. Standing at the wrought-iron railing, I looked beyond the manicured hospital grounds to the rooftops of sprawling villas, now seized as housing for Nazi officers and senior officials.

"*Ouf.*"

I glanced back at Jean-Claude sucking his finger, soup streaming the sides of the pot.

I went back in and walked over. "I'm sure it's not that bad. Here, let me taste."

He handed me the wooden stirring spoon, and I took a cautious sip. "Well?" he asked.

"I thought Parisians were known for their cuisine."

He grimaced. "I am more gourmand than gourmet."

My traitorous gaze took him in. There wasn't an ounce of fat on him and hadn't been even before the war. Rather than make a fool of myself by saying so, I focused on the soup. "It's only … mostly burned on the bottom."

Burned or not, compared to what many Parisians were getting by on it was a feast, and we were lucky to have it.

There was a half-loaf of bread as well, the crust tough as nails, and a hunk of molded cheese that might have been brie. When I picked up a paring knife and started to trim off the spoiled bits, he clicked his tongue.

"It's molded," I protested.

"Penicillin too is mold," he countered, whisking it away and putting it on a plate with the bread.

I carried the bowls of soup over, and he brought out a dusty bottle of wine and uncorked it. Quite a contrast to the first time we'd sat down to supper in the Marais. Then I'd been a girl he'd felt guilty for wanting. Two years later, the soup was burned and there was no apple tart to follow it, but none of that mattered because I was a woman who'd proven herself his equal.

"*Santé,*" he said, sloshing red wine into our water glasses.

"*Sláinte*." Seeing his furrowed brow, I explained, "Irish Gaelic for health."

We took our seats, with him holding out my chair as though we were in a fancy restaurant rather than the staff quarters of a hospital.

He began slicing cheese, serving me first, taking care to give me the non-molded parts, I noticed. Not wanting to be rude, I took a cautious nibble. He was right. The brie wasn't half bad.

"Your family is Irish?" he asked, and the question brought home just how little time we'd had for ordinary conversation.

I picked up my spoon and slipped it into the soup. "Mostly, yes. My grandmother came from Inishmore, an island off the coast of Galway. And my Grandpa Joe was Irish too, though he was born in New York."

The corners of his mouth tipped up. "That explains it, then."

"Explains what?" I asked.

"Why you are so stubborn," he said. "And so fearless."

The latter landed like a compliment. Never good with those, I felt my face flush up. "Good thing I am. You needed me and my stubbornness today."

"And you were there. You are always there when I need you."

He *needed* me. Our eyes locked, and I felt a floodgate of feelings open.

I spooned up another mouthful of the soup, burned but edible. "It's growing on me." Seeing his confused look, I clarified, "It means it's not so bad."

He snorted. "Drink more wine, and it will taste even better."

He topped off my glass and then his. "You were good with the airman. Kind and encouraging. Funny. You calmed him, otherwise he might have panicked and given us away."

"Does that mean you'll let me help you again?"

He cut off another hunk of stale bread and passed it to me. "It means ... I am thinking about it."

We finished the meal, mopping our bowls with the last of the bread, the cheese devoured to crumbs.

He poured out the rest of the wine and stood. "Do you like jazz music?"

Of all the questions he might have asked me, that was the last I'd expected.

I stood with him. "I do."

He walked across the room to a record player. I hadn't noticed it earlier.

I put down my glass and followed him over. "You keep a Victrola here?"

"Music helps me relax," he admitted.

He lifted the top. A record was already on the turntable. "Stardust" by the American composer Hoagy Carmichael. Reading the label, I saw this was the Tommy Dorsey version featuring the band's girl vocalist, Edythe Wright.

He pressed the tonearm's cueing lever and set it on the record so that the needle fit the first groove.

After the initial scratchiness, there was an instrumental intro, and then Miss Wright's plaintive voice filled the room.

"Sometimes I wonder why I spend
The lonely nights
Dreaming of a song.
The melody haunts my reverie
And I am once again with you."

Jean-Claude held out his hand to me. I took it and stepped into his arms, thrilling to the warmth of his hand settling onto the small of my back, his wine-spiced breath striking the side of my face, making me dizzy with wanting to kiss him.

> "When our love was new, and each kiss an inspiration.
> But that was long ago, and now my consolation
> Is in the stardust of a song.
> Beside the garden wall, when stars are bright
> You are in my arms
> The nightingale tells his fairy tale
> Of paradise where roses grew.
> Though I dream in vain, in my heart you will remain
> My stardust melody
> The memory of love's refrain."

I must have listened to the song a hundred times at least and yet dancing in Jean-Claude's arms, my cheek resting on his chest, the cornball lyrics didn't feel cornball at all. They felt … real. There might be a war on and people dying all around us, and yet what I most wanted was for that moment, that feeling, to stretch out forever.

"This is nice," I said, setting my free hand atop his shoulder, thrillingly firm beneath the moth-eaten sweater.

"Hmm." He buried his face in the curve of my shoulder.

> "And now the purple dusk of twilight time
> Steals across the meadows of my heart
> High up in the sky the little stars climb
> Always reminding me that we're apart

*You wander down the lane and far away
Leaving me a song that will not die ..."*

"The music makes me forget," he murmured, his warm breath striking the side of my neck.

I pressed closer. "Is that so bad?"

When his hand slipped inside my blouse, I didn't stop him.

*"Love is now the stardust
Of yesterday
The music
Of the years
Gone by."*

The song ended, but we stayed as we were, his circling thumb wreaking havoc with my senses, his mouth brushing the side of my neck.

Abruptly, he let go of me and stepped back. "Forgive me, I forget myself."

I shook my head, still in the clouds, or better yet the stars. "I like it when you forget yourself."

Rather than answer, he turned away, busying himself with lifting off the playing arm and drawing down the lid. "It is late. We should go to bed."

Loosened up by the wine and the dancing, I was ready for anything, or so I told myself.

"You take the bed." He crossed the room and pushed the two straight back chairs together.

I did my best to hide my disappointment. "You can't possibly sleep like that."

He looked back at me. "When I was an intern, I learned to sleep anywhere under any condition. Once during rounds, I was so exhausted that I fell asleep on my feet."

"You're making that up."

"*Je te jure*," he said, laying a hand over his heart.

Lost to lustful longing though I was, my full bladder chose that moment to make itself known.

"Is there a ..." I trailed off, embarrassment getting the better of me.

"Take the hallway to the end. It will be on the right." He handed me a towel and opened the door.

By the time I returned, Jean-Claude had taken off his necktie and shoes and stockings but not much else.

He looked away while I got out of my dress. With my bladder emptied, desire returned, and I had half a mind to ask him to help me with my zipper. At the last minute I chickened out, my latent Catholic guilt getting the better of me. That, and I'd never undressed for a man before.

I stepped out of my dress, rolled off my precious silk stockings, and laid them across a chair. Still in my slip, I crawled under the covers.

"I'm decent," I called out.

He walked over and for a few thrilling seconds I wondered if he had changed his mind about joining me.

"*Bonne nuit,* Daisy." He bent and brushed his mouth over mine.

"*Bonne nuit,*" I answered my pulse fast and fluttery.

Straightening, he reached out and pulled the chain on the floor lamp, dousing us in darkness.

I lay in bed listening to the scraping of chair feet and the creaking of wood as he settled his long body between the chairs.

Watching shadows slip across the ceiling, I called out softly, "Jean-Claude?"

"Hmm?"

"Have you thought about leaving France? After the war, I mean. I'm sure any modern hospital would count itself lucky to have a specialist in facial reconstruction on staff."

Several esteemed New York institutions sprang to mind.

"Paris is my home," he said. "I was born here."

"Yes, of course. But working with so many American surgeons here, surely one of them could recommend you for a position in the States. Dr. Bove is from New York, isn't he?" I asked, already knowing the answer. "I'm sure he'd write you a reference."

As the former chief surgeon of the American, Dr. Charles Bove's recommendation would go a long way in opening doors for a promising young surgeon, and Jean-Claude was certainly that.

"For the right opportunity, I suppose it is possible," he conceded.

Possible. Given the helter-skelter world we were living in, I couldn't ask for more.

I spent the next several minutes breaking my promise to myself and daring to imagine the future life the two of us could make. Me working with Gran at Kavanaugh's, Jean-Claude at New York-Presbyterian Hospital or another such temple to healing. Meeting up at home in the evenings and sharing our workdays over candlelit suppers. I'd just moved on to imagining the beautiful children we'd have – two, no more than three – when a snore broke the stillness.

I sat up, pulled the lamp chain, and looked over. Jean-Claude's boast was borne out. Arms folded across his chest and the rolled-up lab coat pressed into service as a pillow, he was sound asleep.

I turned the light off and settled onto my side, pressing my face into his pillow. Tucked into his bed, the mattress a lot less lumpy than the one I slept on at Madame LeBrun's, wrapped in sheets scented with his skin, I joined him in drifting off.

Chapter Twenty-Eight

December 1940
Another bitterly cold winter descended. Many Parisians faced choosing between putting food on their tables and coal in their furnaces. The Christmas season came, but few had the heart or means to celebrate.

With the petrol shortage, taxis disappeared, and bus service fell off. The only vehicles on the road were black Mercedes-Benz Wehrmacht staff cars and green and gray army trucks. Those who had kept automobiles before the Occupation put them on bricks and brought out their bicycles. On Friday evenings, I often saw Dr. Jackson pedaling past the hospital gates on his way home to his family, his head covered in an aviator's helmet, his big hands stuffed into fleece mittens.

It wasn't only food, wine, and artwork the Nazis diverted to Germany. Medical supplies and medicines, especially insulin, were siphoned off as well, setting off a national health crisis. Rubber and tin, the mainstay materials for many medical tools, were seized for the Wehrmacht war machine. At the American, Jean-Claude, Dr. Jackson, and the head nurse, Elisabeth Comte, risked their lives to take back what they could. I helped however I could but with the worsening shortages it never felt like enough.

As conditions under the Nazis deteriorated, people began banding together to fight back, *resist*. Rumor had it that a group of doctors in Paris had formed a Resistance group called Vengeance. I suspected Jean-Claude was part of it, though when I asked him point blank, he denied it. Given how well we'd worked together in the past, hiding the food supplies and then smuggling out the downed pilot, I was hurt to be shut out though I knew he was only thinking of my safety.

By mid-December, the inaugural issue of *Résistance* was released, one of several anonymously published underground newspapers clandestinely circulated, the name a callback to General de Gaulle's June 1940 BBC address. I came across a copy shoved into my locker at the hospital and couldn't put it down. Reading the mimeographed broadsheet top to bottom, I was shocked to learn that Nazi atrocities against French civilians were even worse than I'd realized.

There was the recent case of Jacques Bonsergent, a twenty-eight-year-old French engineer who'd been coming home after curfew from a wedding when he and his friends ran afoul of a German patrol party. A brawl broke out, and he was arrested and sentenced to death.

For residents of the Ritz, life continued much as it always had. Buffered from the brutality, Chanel and her set continued to enjoy the usual pleasures – smokes in the Psyche Salon, dinner in the Grille Room, and a nightcap in Frank's bar, no matter that there were Nazis there. According to Chanel, one could simply choose not to notice them.

"That does something to them," she told me, looking satisfied with herself. "When a woman who still has something left ignores them completely."'

She certainly didn't ignore von Dincklage, who seemed to have made the Ritz his second home. Every time I dropped by to say hello to Frank, Blanche and Jacques or to telephone my family, I spotted him holding court in the smoking lounge or at one of the bar tables. According to Frank, no matter how crowded the bar was, he and Mademoiselle Coco invariably ended the night at each other's side. By then it was an open secret that he spent most nights in her room. It wasn't my place to judge her and yet that she was almost certainly sleeping with the enemy caused her to slip from the steep pedestal I had always put her on.

Since the disappointing trip to Vichy, and her taking up again with von Dincklage, our relationship had cooled. She rarely invited me to join her for drinks at the Ritz and our cozy afterwork chats in her atelier apartment likewise had fallen off. No matter where she was, her conversation always came around to André, still a prisoner in Germany. Freeing him had become an obsession, which I told myself was only natural. He was her blood, after all, more a son than a nephew, as well as seriously ill. So far, all her highly placed connections in Vichy and Paris seemed to have led nowhere. Not even von Dincklage had been able to secure his release. I wondered whether it was ever a bone of contention between them.

On Christmas Eve, Otto Abetz, the German ambassador to the Vichy government, and his French wife, Suzanne hosted a dinner party at the German embassy housed in the Hôtel Beauharnais. General Rudolf Schleier, the German consul in Paris, and Luftwaffe General Friedrich Hanesse were the guests of honor. Chanel was invited, and I felt certain she would attend on von Dincklage's arm.

She summoned me to her room at the Ritz to drop off her ensemble for the evening. The decor was still on the spartan side, though she had brought in several Coromandel screens as well as the gilded dressing table from the duke.

I found her sitting in front of the triple mirror in her cream-silk robe applying lipstick.

Hanging the garment bag outside her closet, I said, "I suppose you heard Jacques Bonsergent was executed."

Blotting her lips on a tissue, she said, "Who?"

Coming up behind her, I met her gaze in the mirror. "The engineer arrested for coming home after curfew. The Nazis put him in front of a firing squad yesterday."

"*À la guerre comme à la guerre.*" She opened a drawer to her right and began combing through her jewelry. "Before you leave, I want to discuss the new shipment of No. 5. It will arrive after the New Year."

Von Dincklage arrived as we were finishing up. The Occupation seemed to be agreeing with him. Even I had to admit he cut a dashing figure in his evening wear.

"Mademoiselle Blakely, how delightful to see you again," he said.

Feeling the opposite reaction, I acknowledged him with a nod. "Baron."

Bypassing me, he crossed the carpet to where Chanel sat on the tufted beige dressing stool.

Sweeping her hair to the side, he dropped a kiss on the curve of her shoulder. "Hmm, this delightful perfume never gets old."

"The scent of eternal youth, that is the point," she replied with a smile, picking up her eyebrow pencil.

Straightening, he looked over at me. "Will you be joining us this evening, mademoiselle?"

"I won't," I said, wishing I had managed to miss him.

Chanel spoke up, "Marguerite is brooding over an executed French *résistant*. She would make poor company."

His gaze flickered over me. "I take it you mean Monsieur

Bonsergent. He was found guilty of 'an act of violence against a member of the German army.' We cannot keep the peace if we turn a blind eye to terrorism."

"There was a scuffle," I said, recalling the account I'd read in *Résistance*. "According to the testimony of his friends, he didn't so much as raise a fist."

He behaved as if I was boring him. "They would claim that, wouldn't they? Terrorists do cover for one another."

Though I was tempted to rebut him, doing so could be dangerous. By then, I suspected he was higher up in the Nazi chain of command than he had let on. Given my clandestine activities at the hospital, I was better off not poking the bear.

Instead, I wished them both a happy Christmas and let myself out.

I rode the elevator down to the rue Cambon lobby to find Blanche so that I could make my telephone call home for the holidays. As luck would have it, I caught her walking out from the ladies' lounge where she had a regular bridge game going.

She took a ring of keys from her pocket and unlocked the manager's office. "Your timing couldn't be better. Popsy's making his rounds," she said, her pet name for Claude, whose heart had gone *pop* when he first saw her, or so he had confided in the early days of their marriage.

Now those halcyon days were over, and the Germans had invaded not only Paris but their beloved Ritz.

"Thanks, Blanche, you're the bee's knees," I said, whisking inside.

The call was patched through, and Gran picked up on the second ring. "Oh Daisy, I do wish you'd come home," she said, sounding as worried as I'd ever heard her. "From what we read in the papers things are dreadful over there."

The whole family was gathered at her and Grandpa's Gramercy Park townhouse, everyone eager to have their turn to talk to me.

Mom, Dad and Neil wrestled the phone back and forth, their jumbled, intercut conversations taking me back to the chaos of mornings at our kitchen table, the four of us rushing off to jobs, school, and various appointments and yet always managing to come together as a family.

Grandpa Adam got on the line last. "Get back here, kid. You're giving us all gray hair."

"It's not so bad," I assured him, crossing my fingers to make up for the fib. "We Americans are mostly left alone."

It was Bridget I worried about. Being British, she was considered an enemy combatant though the only "weapons" she ever fired were atomizers of No. 5. As she had pointed out, she was safer in Paris than she would have been in London, now in its fifth month of nightly air raids.

The call ended with choruses of Merry Christmases and more pleas for me to stay safe.

Stepping out of Claude's office, I spotted Fritz entering the hotel, not through the swinging doors that Chanel and other guests used but the service entrance.

I considered ducking back inside, but it was too late. His lifted brows confirmed he had seen me, too.

Heart pounding, I waited for him to walk up.

"Are you Germans taking over this side of the hotel, too?" I quipped.

It was the first time I had spoken to him since we had run into one another in the elevator on my first day back in Paris. I had kept up the cold shoulder treatment, though doing so had turned out to be a lot tougher than I had imagined. Many times, I had found myself wanting to go find him and tell him this or that, to share an amusing story from the boutique or the burden of a difficult day at the hospital, only to remember that I couldn't. He was the enemy. Whenever I felt myself on the verge of weakening, I reminded myself of the atrocities the Nazis were perpetuating in France and on her people, Jews especially, though Blacks, the Romani and the infirm were also targets. I wasn't built like Chanel or her actress friend Arletty, living openly with her Luftwaffe officer at the hotel. I couldn't turn a blind eye to injustice and suffering as they seemed to. And yet hypocrite that I was, I still held onto the copy of *My Ántonia* I'd bought for him on the quay. Every time I went to toss it out, something held me back.

Fritz looked past me to the door of Claude's office. "You are fortunate it is me who saw you. You should be more careful."

Rather than reply to that, I glanced down at the briefcase, which he was gripping so tightly his knuckles were white.

"No rest for the wicked, I see. The baron is keeping you busy. Seizing all those textiles for the German army must make for mountains of paperwork if that is indeed what he does."

He didn't answer, not that I'd expected him to.

"You have plans for Christmas?" he asked, switching subjects.

"The usual cozy celebration at ours under Nazi rule," I answered with an eyeroll. "My roommate and I are pooling our ration tickets, so it should be *quite* a party. I suppose you're off to the big shindig at the German embassy."

He nodded. "Later, yes. It is not how I would choose to spend Christmas, but it is expected."

I snorted, far from caring how unladylike I sounded. "You not having a choice, that's rich. From what I've seen, you Nazis have nothing but choices. The tragedy is you impose yours on the rest of us."

His gaze scanned the area, catching on a German guard stationed at the far end of the Hallway of Dreams.

He turned back to me looking like he'd have liked to shake me. "I know you are angry; it is understandable. But in such times as these, the wise know to hold their tongues – and when necessary, their noses."

"Kick up your heels while others are starving, you mean?" I demanded, though that time I lowered my voice.

He answered with a sigh. "For your own sake, try to find a little peace. It is Christmas."

Von Dincklage had said something similar. Pleas for peace, coming from the mouths of Nazis. It was almost too much.

Eyeing him, I asked, "What are you really doing on the civilian side of the hotel?"

The tips of his ears turned bright pink. He hadn't wanted to be seen any more than I had. That was interesting.

"Seems we're both where we're not supposed to be," I concluded.

He stayed silent.

"Tell you what, I'll keep your secret if you keep mine. Deal?" I held out my hand.

He took it, his big hand engulfing mine. Feeling the warm press of his skin to mine, a memory flashed back to me: Fritz stroking my hair in the Luxembourg Gardens a few days before war was declared. Cheek pressed against his chest, I hadn't wanted to say goodbye to my friend. Not then. Not ever. But too much had happened since to return to such tender times, and I doubted I was the only one of us to know it.

"*Ja*, we have a deal," he said firmly, looking and sounding exactly like who and what he was.

A German soldier.
Breaking hands, he turned and strode off toward the stairs.
I stood there a while longer, waiting to see if he would look back.
He didn't.

Chapter Twenty-Nine

January 1941

The day after New Year's, I was working in the boutique helping Bridget with the annual inventory when a surprise visitor strolled in.

Josephine Baker.

Wearing a full-length mink coat, she walked up to the perfume counter. "*Bonjour*, ladies. I'm a Guerlain girl myself, but maybe you can help me pick out something else, something special. I'll know it when I see it."

Mesdames Millet and Aubrey and Bridget fell over each other in their rush to wait on her. Madame Millet helped her off with her mink and took it to be hung up while Madame Aubrey procured a chilled bottle of black-market champagne from somewhere upstairs and presented it in a baccarat crystal flute carried in on a silver tray.

"Champagne, madame?"

"*Merci*." Miss Baker accepted the fizzing flute and looked toward the mirrored stairs. "Where is Mademoiselle Coco?"

"Mademoiselle is out at an appointment," Madame Millet told her.

Miss Baker paused in sipping her champagne and chuckled. "An appointment between the sheets if I know Coco. And believe me, I know Coco."

Thinking of the last time I'd seen Chanel and von Dincklage together in her suite on Christmas Eve, I admitted to myself that she probably wasn't wrong.

"I'll need someone to help me. Hmm, who shall it be?" She looked between Bridget and me. "I pick you, Red."

Out of the side of my eye, I saw Bridget's face fall.

I stepped forward, wondering if she remembered me from the hospital. "*Avec plaisir, madame.* What would you like to see first?"

"Everything." She handed off her half-finished glass to Bridget and hooked her arm through mine.

I showed her around the shop, though she seemed to know it as well as I did, pointing out where a display had been expanded or moved since her last visit, pausing to try on a hat or slip on a glove.

Once we were out of the earshot of the others, she dropped her voice and said, "Thought you might like to know the eagle has landed."

"Sorry?"

"The downed bird you helped has been nursing his broken wing at Les Milandes, my château in the Dordogne."

Josephine Baker's was the safe house Pilot Archie had gone to! This impressive lady had more layers than an onion.

"I just received confirmation he made it safely back to England," she added, holding her voice to a whisper. "Before he left, he asked me to be sure and let Nurse 'Apple Pie' know."

I smiled. "That's wonderful news. Thank you for telling me."

"This was my last chance to stop by. I'm leaving at the end of the week on a tour of French Africa and Southern Europe."

"How long will you be gone?" I asked.

"I start out in Casablanca and from there I'm booked for shows in Tangiers, Lisbon, and Madrid."

Casablanca, the main port city in Morocco, was the most important Vichy-controlled naval base after Toulon as well as the European gateway to Africa. If the Allies could drive fascist Italy out of the African continent, the road would be clear for an invasion of southern Europe. Josephine's performing there could be a coincidence – but I doubted it.

"I can't blame you for wanting to get out of France," I said, thinking of Jean-Claude, who I wished would consider doing the same.

As a Jew, he would need a false passport and travel visa to leave the country, but surely someone among his Resistance contacts could provide him with those. The few times I had forced the subject, we had come close to quarreling.

"I'll be back," Josephine assured me. "'*J'ai Deux Amours*' isn't just a song to me. My two loves really are France and Paris. This country, this beautiful city, welcomed me with open arms when my own turned me away. No matter where I am in the world, everything I do, I do for them. I have a feeling you're the same."

She wasn't wrong, only I had *three* amours: France, Paris – and Jean-Claude. For as long as I had breath in my body, I would do whatever it took to defend them.

"If you ever find yourself in a tight spot, you can get word to me through my manager at the club. And know that you and yours are always welcome at Château des Milandes."

Out of the blue, I found myself blinking back tears. Though I hadn't known her for long, or very well, she'd made an impression on me that I suspected would last a lifetime. "I don't know what to say."

"Say you'll be careful. In this war, we're all playing the long game."

Catching the concern in her eyes, I said, "I'll be as careful as I can." It was the same promise I'd made Gran.

Her gaze traveled over me. "The first time I set eyes on you, I sensed we were kindred spirits."

I shook my head, feeling far from worthy. "You've risked your life airdropping supplies to refugees and opening your home to downed airmen. I'm just … an American heiress in Paris."

Her features firmed. "Don't sell yourself short. You've got a lot to give, Daisy Blakely, and my prediction is you're just getting started."

She hugged me, and though I'd only met her properly once before, I felt myself tearing up again.

"Take care of yourself, Daisy."

Stepping back, I managed a watery smile. "Go safely for now, Jo."

Chapter Thirty

June 1941

My twenty-first birthday arrived, my fourth birthday in Paris and quite a contrast to the splashy week I'd spent with Gran. Remembering how eager my eighteen-year-old self was to reach my majority, I felt old indeed. But then the war and Occupation were aging all of us beyond our years. I didn't feel twenty-one. I felt thirty.

That evening, I celebrated with Bridget at the Ritz bar, her first time there, with Frank treating us to his delicious signature cocktails. Midway through our first round of drinks, Mademoiselle Coco walked in with von Dincklage. When she heard it was my birthday, she insisted on sending over a bottle of the bar's best champagne and then joined us for a glass.

The following Sunday at sunset, Jean-Claude and I held our own celebration on the hospital rooftop with a bottle of wine from the hospital's inventory and what was coming to be known as "war cake." Egg-less, milk-less, and butter-less (lard was used instead), it was delicious. Between the two of us, we devoured every morsel.

"*Bon anniversaire, chérie.*" Brushing a crumb from the corner of my mouth, he leaned in to kiss me.

Melting against him, I tried not to think about where any of us might be in another year or even month.

That spring, the Vichy government had enacted yet another new "law," this one forbidding Frenchmen from seventeen to forty years old from leaving the country other than to go to work in German factories. Jean-Claude's window for escape was closed.

A few weeks later, I went up to Mademoiselle Coco's apartment in search of an invoice we were missing for the inventory. Having searched everywhere, I had to think it was among the papers on her rolltop. The mirrored outer doors to the apartment were locked but by then I had a key to every door in the atelier.

After my light knock went unanswered, I let myself in. Moving through the foyer, muffled voices reached me. Realizing my mistake, I started backing away, but too late.

"Who is there?" Mademoiselle Coco called out.

Caught, I walked into the parlor. Mademoiselle Coco sat on the beige suede sofa with von Dincklage. Seated in an armchair across from them was a third man I hadn't met before. Pudgy, in his late thirties with thinning strawberry blonde hair and dandified clothing, I would have remembered him.

Noting the papers poured out over the coffee table, I said, "I do apologize. I didn't realize anyone was up here."

Von Dincklage was the first to recover. He swept the documents into a stack and stood. "Mademoiselle Blakely, permit me to introduce Baron Louis de Vaufreland."

He gestured to the other man, who rose and turned to me. "*Enchantée*, mademoiselle."

"Mademoiselle Blakely is Coco's American apprentice," von Dincklage continued. "And one of the rare Americans to intrepidly hang on through the war. Apparently, her loyalty has earned her the keys to the kingdom." He cut Chanel a sharp look.

From behind black-framed glasses, Chanel sent me a glacial glare. "The next time knock first."

Not so very long ago, she would have invited me to join them, maybe even asked my opinion. André's continued captivity was taking a tremendous toll, causing her to lean on people like von Dincklage, who I strongly suspected had his own agenda.

"I will," I promised, declining to point out that I had knocked. But then I was already in enough hot water.

Cheeks burning, I closed the door and cut through the foyer.

A few weeks later, Mademoiselle Coco began talking about making a trip to Madrid. Though Spain was a neutral nation, traveling there would require a government approved visa, scarce as hen's teeth and by then impossible to obtain without a connection to the Nazi higher-ups. I presumed von Dincklage would provide it.

"I think I will open a boutique there," she told me, my barging into her apartment by then water under the bridge. "It is an opportunity to improve No. 5 sales in the Spanish market."

Since closing the atelier, her perfume business had become even more of an obsession, second only to getting André released.

The trip was planned for early August. I was shocked to hear that de Vaufreland would be her travel companion.

"Are you certain you can trust him?" I asked, blunt as I never would have dared be before the Occupation.

Overnight, Baron de Vaufreland had become a fixture at the Ritz as well as a frequent visitor to the atelier, though I never saw him walk out with so much as a scarf. Whenever I encountered him, he was the soul of patrician politeness, and yet beneath it all, something about him struck me as oily and false.

She shrugged. "He is half Spanish. His aunt is the Duchess of Almazan, and I am relying on him to make the necessary social introductions. His fluency in Spanish and German will be of great help at the border checkpoint at Hendaye. A woman traveling alone in these times …"

She left the thought unfinished, and I didn't press her, neither of us wanting to dwell on the atrocities that girls and women suffered all too often in wartime.

A few days later, I heard her on the telephone talking to Tiny.

"*T'inquiète, chérie. Ton père retournera chez toi bientôt.*"

Don't worry, darling. Your father will return home soon.

It was the sort of well-meaning platitude that adults often said to soothe a worried child. But Chanel had sounded more than soothing.

She had sounded certain.

Chapter Thirty-One

Later that June, *Résistance* reported that Vichy's new Ordre des Médecins, the national governing body of physicians, had capped Jewish doctors at two percent of the physician population. Out of nine hundred Jewish doctors in France, only one hundred and ten were permitted to continue practicing.

My thoughts flew to Jean-Claude. Medicine was more than a profession to him. It was his calling, deeply rooted in his family's personal pain. His patients adored him and so did the medical staff, deservedly so. He was at the beginning of what ought to be a long and laudatory career.

Fibbing that I had a cold coming on, I left the boutique at lunchtime, got on my bicycle, and raced off to Neuilly. I whizzed past the decommissioned *Octroi de Neuilly* and the black, white, and red German sentry box announcing the entrance to the suburb. Birds warbled from the leafy canopies of the trees bordering both sides of the broad boulevard, but like the blister building on my big toe, I ignored them and pedaled on.

Coming up to the hospital's arched entranceway, I scanned the area, girding myself to see ... Gibbets set up on the front lawn? A guillotine getting busy? Instead, the hospital buildings and grounds looked as they did any other day, opulent and serene. An orderly pushed a patient in a wheelchair. A pair of nurses sat on a stone bench on the lawn having their lunch. A gardener in overalls and a broad-brimmed hat clipped the boxwoods. In every way, a normal day and yet unsure of what I would find once I went inside, my pulse raced a mile a minute and pearls of sweat popped out on my forehead.

I entered through the emergency room entrance, unlocked the wire mesh cage and hung my bicycle on an empty hook, and then took the patient elevator up to the surgery floor. Stepping off, I headed to the admittance desk where several nurses congregated speaking in hushed tones.

When I presented myself to the older French nurse, she waved me back without a word, her eyes suspiciously damp.

Voices filtered out from his closed door, Jean-Claude in conversation with another man, an American.

I recognized the New England-accented voice as Dr. Jackson.

"This is a setback, nothing more," he said, with such steely assurance that I came close to believing him myself. "Roosevelt won't sit on the sidelines forever. America *will* join the war, and then we'll win this thing and send the Germans packing. And you, my friend, will be back where you belong."

My heart dropped. My fears were confirmed. Jean-Claude had been cut.

"Thank you, Doctor Jack," Jean-Claude said. "It has been an honor working under you." His solemn tone told me how touched he was. And how hurt.

"The honor's all mine, son," Dr. Jackson assured him. "You lay low and stay safe. France needs young doctors with your talent and passion. You're the bright future of French modern medicine and don't let anyone make you believe otherwise."

I ran into Dr. Jackson on his way out. Over six feet with massive shoulders, bushy brows, and a strong-featured face, there was no slipping past him.

"Daisy, it's not your regular day, is it?" he asked, down-to-earth as always.

I shook my head. "I came as soon as I heard about the new order."

He glanced back at Jean-Claude's closed door. "It's a damned dark day for the hospital and for French medicine. Do what you can to cheer him up?"

"I'll do my best, sir."

I entered Jean-Claude's office as he was pulling heavy medical tomes from the shelves behind his desk and laying them in a box. Several half-full file boxes sat in a corner.

I hurried over and put my arms around him. "I just heard. I'm so sorry."

For a moment, he leaned in and let me hold him.

Pulling back, his miserable eyes met mine. "*Je suis fini*. I am finished. Done."

"But this is the *American* Hospital. Surely that must mean something," I said.

"The American Hospital *in Paris*," he emphasized. "Like the rest of France, it belongs to them now. The Boches can do what they want with it, with us. At hospitals throughout France, doctors have been let go. Nurses and administrative staff as well. For being Jews."

"Surely something can be done, the decision appealed or—"

"Dr. Jack wrote a letter on my behalf, stressing that maxillofacial surgery is a 'critical field' for the war, but the committee would not budge."

One of the nurses I knew from working on the ward poked her head inside. "I just heard, Dr. Jacob. *Je suis desolée.*" Her damp gaze circuited the torn apart office. "Do not bother with this. I will have your books and other things sent to your home."

Jean-Claude nodded. "*Merci.*"

She nodded and backed out.

He looked back at me. "It seems there is no reason to stay."

He crossed to the front of the desk and took off his lab coat. Heart in my throat, I watched him clasp it in both hands.

"I remember the first time I put this on. Even then there were those who felt there were too many Jewish doctors in France. I had to study hard and fight harder. But I did not care what it took. I was determined. And proud to be working at a modern hospital. Proud to be a part of something bigger than myself."

The bicycle ride back to the city was a somber affair. Midway there, the heavens opened, the drenching downpour forcing us to take cover under a footbridge. Jean-Claude insisted I wear his jacket and rather than stand on the roadside arguing, I took it and slipped my arms into the too big sleeves.

We reached rue Saint-Lazare just as the streetlamps were shutting off, the only light coming from the closing cafés.

I looked over at Jean-Claude. "Any chance you still have your *laissez-passer*?"

From the early days of the Occupation, the authorities had permitted doctors to circulate after curfew. If he were stopped on his way back to the Marais, he could say he'd been making an emergency house call.

"I had to turn it in," he admitted, looking almost embarrassed about it.

Thinking of Monsieur Bonsergent, I suppressed a shudder. "In that case, you'll have to stay over."

Inside the apartment house, I sneaked him up the stairs.

Bridget met us at the door, hair in curlers and face covered in cold cream.

"It's after nine. I've been worried sick," she whispered, ushering us in and closing the door behind us.

"Bridget, meet Dr. Jean-Claude Jacob. Jean-Claude, my roommate, Miss Bridget Ponsby."

"The dishy doctor Daisy's always mooning over," Bridget announced with a grin, clearly getting a kick out of embarrassing me. "We've met before when you came by the boutique, though I don't expect you remember me."

Never one for flattery, he settled on a hesitant smile. "*Enchantée*," he said.

Changing the subject, I said, "We'll have to put Jean-Claude up on the sofa for the night. I'll slip him out in the morning before anyone's the wiser."

I was asking a lot, and I knew it. If we were found with a man in our room, we could both be tossed out. But if Jean-Claude were caught out after curfew, he faced far worse – arrest, imprisonment and possible deportation to a labor camp in Germany. I couldn't let him risk it.

"I'll put the kettle on," Bridget said, unflappable as always.

"You're the best, Bridge," I said, thanking my lucky stars to have a friend and roommate who always had my back. Promising myself I'd make it up to her, I turned back to Jean-Claude. "Go into the bedroom and get out of those wet clothes. You can wear my robe. It's hanging on the hook."

He did as I asked. When he came out again, he was wrapped up in my housecoat, the v-neckline showing a tantalizing triangle of black-brown hair, and carrying his sodden clothes, which I draped over the heating grate.

"Toilet's down the hall on the right," Bridget called out from her post at the hotplate.

"*Merci*," he said, looking relieved.

He struck out into the hallway while I stood guard at the door. If not for the predicament we were all in, the sight of him padding barefoot in my floral print quilted housecoat, the hemline hitting just below his knees, would have had me in stitches.

I turned back to Bridget, who handed me a folded pair of my pajamas. "I don't know what I'd do without you." I gave her a quick hug.

"Through thick and thin." She squeezed me back. "Wake me before you go. I'll be your lookout."

Jean-Claude returned just as I was finishing buttoning my pajama top.

Bridget handed him a cup of tea, black and unsweetened as we'd all learned to take it. "I'll leave you two lovebirds to it." She headed off to our bedroom.

I took a pillow and blanket down from a shelf in the closet and settled Jean-Claude on the couch.

"Have everything you need?" I asked.

Hands laced around the steaming teacup, he nodded. "*Oui, merci*." He drained his cup, set it on the table and settled onto his side.

"*Bonne nuit*." I pressed a kiss to his temple and started for the bedroom.

Midway there, I stopped. Now that he was no longer at the hospital, who knew when we'd be alone like this again.

I circled back to the sofa and spooned in beside him.

It was a sorry excuse for a sofa. In better times, it ought to have been thrown out. Plastering myself against him, I felt every faulty spring and lump. Given the narrowness of the cushion, it was a miracle I didn't fall onto the floor. But Jean-Claude anchored me tight against him, his arm beneath my breasts. I settled my head on the inside of his shoulder and breathed in the scents of vanilla, lavender, and rainwater.

His breath struck the side of my neck. "You realize I have no position, nothing to offer you."

"You heard what Dr. Jack said. Soon the Nazis will be routed, and you'll be back where you belong."

"Sumner does not have a crystal ball any more than you or I do," Jean-Claude countered.

"Maybe not, but he believes in you. I believe in *you*. This war will end and once it does, we'll ... start again. Make plans."

Whether we lived in Paris, New York or Timbuktu no longer mattered, not to me. So long as we were together, I would be content.

I woke up to a dark room and the rusty ringing of my alarm clock. Disentangling myself from Jean-Claude, I grabbed for the clock, not wanting to wake Madame LeBrun or Olivier sleeping below.

He sat up beside me, swinging his long legs to the floor. With his rumpled hair and pillow creased cheek, he looked younger than his thirty-two years, boyish and vulnerable and sweet.

We retreated to separate sides of the room to dress, with him putting on his stiff but mostly dry clothes. I slipped on a wrap dress I only ever wore in the apartment and the bulky cardigan from my brother.

Bridget was still asleep when I looked in on her. I thought about waking her as we'd agreed, then decided not to. If we were caught, at least she wouldn't be blamed.

When I walked back into the main room, Jean-Claude had his jacket on.

I led us down the front stairs, every creaking floorboard throwing my heart into flights of panic. Stepping off the landing, I spotted him watching me from the side of my eye and quickly smoothed out my expression.

We tiptoed through the front hall to the kitchen in the back. When I'd first come to Paris, the pantry had overflowed with good things to eat. Now even the breadbox was bare.

I opened the rear door leading out to the muse and poked my head out. Peering through the gray mist, I whispered, "Coast is clear."

I struck down the back stairs, and he followed me.

Shoving my hands in my pockets, I asked, "What will you do now?"

His features firmed into the familiar stubbornness. "This is my country. I will stay and fight for it."

"Fight with the Resistance, you mean?" When he didn't deny it, I went on, "Let me help like I did with the airman. You said so yourself, I'm good at it."

His face softened. "You are good at many things. This thing, it is too dangerous."

"I don't care."

"But I *do* care. You are neither Jewish nor French. This isn't your fight."

"Isn't freedom and justice everyone's fight?"

Rather than reply, he took me in his arms and rested his forehead against mine.

The tender gesture sent tears spilling down my cheeks. "This is *not* goodbye. I won't let it be," I said, my declaration no less fierce for being whispered.

The crooked smile he sent me didn't reach his eyes, weary yet stark with longing. "Unfortunately, it is not up to us."

On impulse, I shucked off Neil's cardigan and gave it to him.

"But you love this sweater," he protested.

I love you, I started to say but superstition got the better of me and I held back, afraid to jinx us.

Instead, I mustered a smile. "You can give it back to me when I see you again."

He hesitated and then shook his head, the look on his face sending daggers into my heart. "Being seen anywhere near the Marais, anywhere near me, will only bring you danger. And pain. Promise you will stay away."

"For how long?" I asked, my voice coming out as a broken whisper.

"For as long as it takes."

I pressed a hand to his chest, both a nudge to go and a last chance to touch him. "Go safely for now."

Chapter Thirty-Two

November 1941

Summer slipped into fall. I hadn't seen Jean-Claude since that June morning when he'd tried talking me into giving up on us, as if I ever would. His absence left a huge hole in my life. And heart.

Worse even than missing him was the worrying. By then it was clear that the Nazis, working through the Vichy puppet government, were out to strip Jews of not only their goods and livelihoods but their humanity. Every time I walked past a newspaper stand, I braced myself, never knowing what the next draconian edict would bring.

Whenever I felt myself slipping into despair, I told myself the Occupation wouldn't last forever. Surely such evil couldn't prevail indefinitely. Once the Nazis were driven out, Jean-Claude and I would find our way back to one another. In the meantime, I honored his request to steer clear of the Marais.

Though it wasn't the same without him, I continued volunteering at the American. By then, La Muette at Drancy wasn't only a POW camp but a weigh station for civilian prisoners marked for deportation to Germany. We were flooded with patients suffering from severe malnutrition, dysentery, and tuberculosis and other maladies that came from filthy living conditions and poor diet.

That November, Chanel's niece Tiny, then fifteen years old, was staying with her in Paris. One afternoon, she ran down the mirrored stairs into the boutique and rushed up to me.

"*Papa est libre! Il vient a Paris!*"

I made my apologies to the customer I'd been helping and steered the girl aside.

"Slowly, Tiny, take a breath and tell me."

"*C'est vrai, c'est vrai!*" She took my hand and tugged me out toward the mirrored staircase.

I found Chanel sitting at the top holding a letter to her bosom, eyes shining with tears.

Since late September when she'd got back from her trip to Spain with Baron de Vaufreland, she'd been tense and snappish and uncharacteristically tight-lipped. Clearly whatever deal she'd had in the works to expand sales of No. 5 hadn't panned out. Once she might have confided in me. It seemed the closer she got to von Dincklage, the greater the gap between us.

"Why should I make even more money for those thieving Wertheimers?" she'd demanded when I'd greeted her on her first day back, eager to hear happy news.

No more was said on the subject, and I'd filed the episode away. Now as her watering eyes met mine, I felt as if we might be on the verge of returning to the old closeness.

"André is being released," she said in answer to my unspoken question. "He's coming home."

"That's wonderful." Taking a seat on the step below her, I asked, "How did it happen?"

She fluttered her hand as if my question were a fly that had sneaked inside. "Spatz made some calls on André's behalf."

At the mention of von Dincklage, I felt my ebullience ebb. Relieved as I was for Chanel and her family, I couldn't stop thinking of all the other French prisoners of war and deported Jews languishing in stalags without an influential relative to pull strings for them. Not just any strings, *German* strings.

A few weeks later, André was back in Paris, ailing with tuberculosis but safe. Despite his poor health, Mademoiselle Coco insisted on hosting a homecoming lunch at her atelier apartment. I was invited, which I took as a sign that I was back in her good graces. Joining us that afternoon were Misia, Serge Lifar, the Ukrainian born director of the Paris Opera Ballet, and von Dincklage. The baron was his usual dapper self, chatting in French and occasionally slipping into English but never German. Amazing to me was that no one seemed to bat an eye at breaking bread with a representative of the regime responsible for the guest of honor's imprisonment and ill health.

André and the others were already seated at the walnut dining table when I walked in. Until then, my only image of him had been the framed photograph of a dark-haired teenage boy in a British school blazer that Chanel kept on her writing desk. The man I met was in his early thirties, grayish pale and painfully thin, with the periodic racking cough common to tuberculosis. I had to think he would have rather been in bed than at the dining table in a suit and tie, a pillow at his back, but if that were true, he hid it admirably, answering everyone's less than tactful questions with smiles and sometimes jokes.

Given the momentous occasion, Tiny was permitted to dine with us. Seated between her recently returned papa and her beloved Auntie

Coco amid a glittering assembly of sophisticated Parisian grownups, I think the poor girl ate even less than André did.

The lunch was as lavish as any Chanel had put on before the war – pheasant soup, medallions of veal, and baked apple for dessert, the black-market delicacies brought over from the Ritz. Between courses, she kept the conversation flowing and her butler, Leon, did likewise for the wine, an excellent Château Latour 1929, Pauillac, Premier Cru Classe. After three years in Paris, I had learned to sip sparingly and keep my head. Unlike Mademoiselle, there would be no midday nap for me.

The lunch stretched into a second hour, and the voices in the room began to rise. Flush with wine, Lifar gave an animated account of his current production of *Le Chevalier et la Damoiselle* in which he was both choreographer and principal dancer. It was an open secret that he was a favorite of Hitler's right hand man, Hermann Göring, who made sure that his star continued to rise.

Chanel waxed enthusiastic about the monthly Franco-German lunches at the Ritz she had begun attending. From Blanche and Frank, I gathered the events catered to a cabal of French and German businesspeople looking for ways to profit from the war.

Once the main course was removed, she touched her spoon to the side of her wine glass, the ringing cutting through the cacophony. "As most of you know, André was director of *Les Tissus Chanel* before the war. Going forward, he will head Maison Chanel." She turned to him and patted the top of his arm. "In this way, you can take your treatments here in Paris and rest and work as you wish."

André pushed back from the table and stood. "*Un grand merci* to my dear Aunt Coco for doing me this tremendous honor and for never giving up on bringing me home. And to all of you who have come today to welcome me home, I say—"

A coughing fit cut him off. He covered his mouth with his napkin and subsided into his seat. Tiny rubbed her hand over his back and whispered soothing words.

I glanced over to von Dincklage, searching his face for a trace of remorse, but his expression stayed neutral.

Chanel called for the cheese course to be served, the heightened pitch to her voice signaling her distress. We were finishing when out of the blue, Misia, eyelids heavy and elbows on the table, looked from André to Mademoiselle Coco and announced, "I am glad to know that our dreary days in Vichy were not wasted."

The table went suddenly, starkly silent. Chanel and von Dincklage exchanged a look, and then Chanel said, "We were fortunate. *Chère* Josée spoke to Pierre on André's behalf."

That the Comtesse de Cambrun might have been persuaded to plead André's case with her father certainly seemed plausible. And yet earlier that month, Chanel had told me point blank that von Dincklage was the one who'd interceded.

Chanel turned to me. "The next time the *comtesse* comes into the boutique, put whatever she selects on the house account."

Her gaze held mine, and in her darkening irises I read a warning. While she might find my American forthrightness amusing in private, contradicting her in front of her family and closest friends would finish us.

Coffee was served. As the table sobered, small talk fizzled. Poor stalwart André finally succumbed to exhaustion and slumped in his chair, sweat beading his brow. Chanel had Tiny take him across the street to her room at the Ritz where she'd had a daybed brought in for him.

It was a relief to get up from the table and go back to work, though whether I was rearranging a display of gloves or tidying up the dressing room after a messy client, I couldn't stop thinking about the awkward lunch, and the lie I'd caught Chanel in. By then, I knew her to be a frequent fibber, embroidering facts to better fit her legend. But altering the circumstances of André's release went beyond a white lie. The nagging voice inside me demanded to know why she had done it.

I went back over what little I knew of her trip to Spain. She and de Vaufreland had stayed in Madrid through to the end of September, a considerable time abroad for a soured business deal. Now, less than two months later, André was free. Had de Vaufreland helped Chanel with more than Spanish translation and social introductions? If so, what had he, and von Dincklage, expected in return?

As soon as I could get away, I bundled up and rode my bicycle to rue des Rosiers, to hell with my promise to stay away. Jean-Claude and I belonged together. From the time we had hidden the pork and potatoes in the shed at the hospital, we had proven we were stronger together than apart. Once I told him about the lunch, surely, he would see that I was too valuable to continue keeping in the dark.

Stopping across the street from his building, I got off my bike and looked up to the fourth-floor balcony. The shutters on the front facing window were still drawn. With all the crackdowns on Jews, the family probably felt safer without people from the street looking in.

Battling a bad feeling, I secured my bicycle, entered the building and took the stairs to the fourth floor. My repeated knocks on the Jacobs' apartment door went unanswered.

Across the hall, a door opened, and an elderly neighbor poked her head out. "*Vous cherchez la famille Jacob?*"

Frantic, I turned to her. "Yes, the Jacob family, do you know when they'll be back?"

Her rheumy eyes met mine, and she gave a grim shake of her head. "*Pas sorti, parti.*"

Not out. Gone.

Chapter Thirty-Three

December 1941

December brought gunmetal gray skies and frigid temperatures. It wasn't uncommon to see housewives combing through garbage bins scavenging for scraps to feed their families. Like food, coal was scarcer than ever. But on rue Cambon, you would never have known a war was on. As in previous years, the Chanel boutique was packed with holiday shoppers, only now they were almost all wives and girlfriends of German officers.

Across the street, the Ritz was decorated to the hilt. In the grand salle on the Place Vendôme side, a pianist played Christmas carols as guests gathered to sing along in German. Meanwhile, I could barely bestir myself to help Bridget hang stockings and scatter holly around our apartment. Whether I was at the boutique, hospital or home, I couldn't get Jean-Claude and his family off my mind. More than once, I glimpsed a tall, dark-haired man in the street or on the Métro and thought it was him only to be disappointed.

By then, Jewish families in Paris were disappearing in droves. I consoled myself that Jean-Claude had colleagues in his corner who would do their best to protect him, including Dr. Jackson, almost certainly one of the doctors aligned with Vengeance. That Jean-Claude still hadn't gotten word to me hurt, but I also knew that his silence was for my safety. That didn't keep me from planning out all the choice words I would have for him when I saw him again, which I told myself I would. Soon. The alternative was too heartbreaking to bear considering.

In the meantime, I kept my head down and carried on, continuing to divide my days between the boutique and hospital where I had added several more shifts. And yet every time I got my hands on a new issue of *Résistance*, I couldn't fight the feeling that I ought to be doing more.

The first Sunday in December began as any ordinary start to the week with me spending the day at the American. As always seemed to be the case, our patients' needs outstripped the available medicines and supplies, but we banded together and did our best by them.

Given how cold it got once the sun went down, I had started leaving earlier to get home before dark. Still, by the time I reached Madame LeBrun's, my teeth were knocking together.

Our apartment wasn't much warmer than outside. Bridget had a light supper of leek soup waiting. Wearing our winter coats and gloves with the fingers cut out, we carried our supper over to sit by the wireless. At six o' clock, we switched on the BBC and learned that imperial Japan had bombed U.S. naval bases in the Pacific, including Pearl Harbor on the island of Oahu in Hawaii.

Shocked, I set my soup aside and leaned in to listen. The United States was still officially neutral. Even after Japan had joined Germany and the Axis powers, a direct strike on American soil had never entered my mind.

Now Japan had declared war against both the United States and

Britain. In response, President Roosevelt had ordered the mobilization of the United States Army.

By the time we switched off the radio, I was in tears thinking of the servicemen and women on the blown-up bases, their grieving families, and my own family in New York. They'd been so intent on me coming home but as the Pearl Harbor attack bore out, no one was entirely safe anywhere. Above all, I thought of Neil, who would almost certainly be called up to fight.

Bridget put her arm around my shoulder. "Chin up, Daise, now that America's in, we're going to beat these Boches to a bloody pulp. It's what we've been praying for."

"You're right, it is," I said, wiping my eyes on my coat sleeve. "I just never imagined it happening like … this."

PART THREE: 1942–1944

"We are never so defenseless against suffering as when we love."

Sigmund Freud

Chapter Thirty-Four

Once the calendar turned to 1942, the Nazi occupiers scuttled any pretense of civility. The draconian measures imposed made the previous two years look like a dress rehearsal. Signs declaring "Access forbidden to dogs and Jews" cropped up everywhere, at the entrances to cafés, theaters, and public parks, the ugly words stamped in thick, Gothic script. Ordinary people suspected of aiding the Resistance were arrested and tortured for information. In the Métro stations, posters warned *résistants* that their families would be executed in retaliation. Guerilla attacks on the Wehrmacht exacted a heavy price: one hundred French lives for every German soldier killed.

Ever since I had opened the inaugural issue of *Résistance* in December 1940, I had been determined to find a way to do more to help. When the first transport of more than one thousand Jews left the internment camp at Compiègne at the end of March bound for the Auschwitz concentration camp in occupied Poland, it was the final straw.

The following Sunday as my shift was winding down, I knocked on Dr. Jackson's office door.

Wearing an old olive-green army sweater beneath his lab coat, he looked up from the patient chart he'd been poring over.

"Daisy, this is a treat. What can I do for you?"

I came straight to my point. "I need to see him, Dr. Jack. And please don't pretend you don't know who I'm talking about."

He fiddled with his fountain pen, rolling it on the desk blotter and finally sticking it back in the holder. "You know he's trying to keep you safe by staying away."

Recalling how Chanel had brazened her way back into the Ritz at the start of the Occupation, I squared my shoulders and lifted my chin.

"I do know that, yes. But living under Nazi rule, none of us are safe. I've already proven myself by helping smuggle out a downed airman from this very hospital, and I'm prepared to do a great deal more. I understand that you're his mentor and friend, and that you're naturally reluctant to break your word to him, which is why I haven't come to you before now. But I'd hope that as a fellow American who's also chosen to stay on here, you might understand how *I* feel about this city, this country, this *man*, and help me. But if you feel you can't, I'll understand. I'll keep asking around until I either find someone who will help me or get myself arrested, whichever comes first."

The next day, I took my bicycle to the *Oeuvre de Secours aux Enfants*, the Children's Aid Society. According to Dr. Jack, once Vichy's *Statuts Juifs* went into effect, the OSE had begun recruiting Jewish doctors barred from practicing. Jean-Claude was one of them.

I stopped across the street from the building to wait. A while later, the main door opened, and a tall, thin man in a newsboy cap and a coat with the yellow Star of David sewn onto the left breast pushed his bicycle out. It took me a moment to realize it was Jean-Claude. Relief rushed me, followed by blood-boiling fury at what the Nazis had done to him simply because he was a Jew.

He spotted me and quickly crossed the street.

"I'll have Sumner's head for this," he whispered.

Despite the harsh words, his eyes looking back at me were liquid with longing.

Taking heart, I said, "Don't blame Dr. Jack. I didn't leave him much of a choice. I needed to talk to you."

He darted a look around, scanning the vicinity. "Not here. The Gestapo has spies everywhere." He jerked his head toward a slim strip of alleyway wedged between a shuttered wineshop and a cobbler's. We leaned our bicycles against the side of the building and entered it.

Amid graffiti, garbage and peeling posters, Jean-Claude turned me in his arms and kissed me deeply.

"*Mon Dieu*, you smell good." Lifting his mouth from mine, he nuzzled my neck.

I tilted my head back, my lower belly fluttering like a butterfly beating its wings. "So do you."

He scoffed. "I smell like a goat."

I laid my hands on his shoulders, sharper than I remembered them being. "How is your family?"

"Rachelle is still in Paris. We managed to get *Maman* out. She is staying with a Christian family in the Zone Libre."

"And you?"

He hesitated. "The work helps. We treat adults as well as children, anyone in need. Every day there are more patients waiting than the day before. Almost all suffer from malnourishment. Dr. Jack gives us what medicines and supplies he can spare."

"I want to help."

He looked at me as though I'd grown a second head. "Daisy, you cannot volunteer at a *Jewish* hospital."

"I don't mean that kind of help. I want to help with … the Resistance," I said, lowering my voice though there was no one to overhear. "With Vengeance if that's the group you're with."

His featured firmed. "You are helping already by working at the American."

I eyed him. "Am I? By patching up prisoners so the Germans can deport them to their labor camps?"

For once he didn't have an answer.

"I know you have a Vengeance meeting today. Don't bother denying it. I have it from the horse's mouth."

His eyes widened. "Sumner knows better than to have told you that."

"What he knows is that I'm loyal and resourceful, and an asset to the cause. And that I despise the Nazis as much as you do. Take me with you, introduce me to the other members and let them decide."

He lifted a brow. "You realize if they decide no, they will have to shoot you?"

If he was trying to scare me, he was going to have to do a lot better than that.

"Then let's hope they vote me in," I said.

He locked his eyes on mine. "You are very stubborn."

"And you aren't? All this time, you've refused to let me help even though I've *proven* I'm good at it."

"Perhaps I care for you too much to risk you."

It was as close to a declaration as I'd ever gotten from him and after five months apart, months during which I'd sometimes worried he might have moved on from me, it was heartening to hear. Under better circumstances, I would have taken time to savor it. But like coffee or sugar and bread made from real flour, time was a commodity in short supply.

Instead, I said, "I know you've tried to protect me by staying away, but I'm a grown woman, and this is my decision and nobody else's. You want to fight the Nazis and take back France? Well, so do I."

I swung away and walked back out to the street, leaving him to follow.

The bicycle ride to Saint-Trinité church in the ninth arrondissement went without a word. Jean-Claude pedaled ahead of me, a good thing because it meant he couldn't see my face. I was about to take a big step, and I knew it. Once I did, there would be no turning back. Despite my tough talk earlier, a part of me worried I had bitten off more than I could chew.

The church was beautiful, as all churches in Paris are, and new by European standards, having been built in the middle of the previous century, with a tall bell tower and a large rose quatrefoil stained-glass window above the main entrance. Two smaller domed bell towers flanked the sides.

We got off our bicycles and pushed them across Place d'Estienne d'Orves to the boxwood-bordered front garden. Inside the church gate, I stowed my bicycle next to Jean-Claude's and followed him to the adjacent presbytery.

At the entrance, he paused. "Let me do the talking."

He led us into the parish office, the smell of old books bringing me back to my first time stepping inside Shakespeare and Company. Then I had been blissfully ignorant of the dark days ahead, over the moon to be in the City of Light and utterly certain that my purpose in Paris revolved around Maison Chanel and its fascinating founder. How far away and long ago those dreamy days seemed.

Nine people of various ages and walks of life sat around a large library table, Dr. Jack at its head. To his right was a late thirtyish man in a priest's collar. I knew several of the others by face if not name as medical and administrative staff from the hospital. My walking in caused a stir though not as big a one as I had prepared myself for. I surmised Dr. Jack had let the others know to expect me.

Jean-Claude's sister, Rachelle, turned away from the window she'd been looking out and walked over.

Ignoring me, she looked from Dr. Jack to Jean-Claude. "How can we be certain she is not a collabo?"

The one time we'd met before, I'd sensed she disliked me. Now her question confirmed it.

Jean-Claude blew out a heavy breath. "She helped me smuggle out a downed airman from the American. And before that, to conceal food and other clandestine deliveries."

A man in his mid-forties with a laborer's callused hands turned to me, and I recognized him as the delivery driver, who went by Pierre.

Addressing the group, he said, "*C'est vrai*. Every Friday, she helps carry in potatoes and meat from the farm and hide them."

Dr. Jack scraped back his chair and stood. "You've heard from Jean-Claude and Pierre and now I'll add my two cents. I've known Daisy as a volunteer at the hospital since before the Occupation. She's one of our most dedicated volunteer aides, and one of a handful of Americans who've chosen to stay in France despite the danger. If that's not a testimony to her character and bravery, I don't know what is."

I could see his opinion carried considerable weight among the group. Heads nodded; shoulders relaxed. Gazes wandered back to me, more curious than suspicious.

Seizing my moment, I launched into making my case. "As

Mademoiselle Chanel's apprentice, and confidante, I'm privy to all the atelier's comings and goings, including hers. Since the start of the Occupation, she's become quite … friendly with a Baron von Dincklage."

Pausing to read the room, I got the impression that von Dincklage was a familiar name.

Encouraged, I continued, "Last August, she took a trip to Madrid with the baron's associate, Louis de Vaufreland. Supposedly he went along to introduce her to Spanish investors who might have an interest in helping her expand her perfume business in Spain, but nothing ever came of it."

I paused there, locking eyes with each *résistant* in turn, ending at Rachelle. Meeting her gaze, that time I read in it a grudging respect.

"I have reason to believe the baron may have helped Mademoiselle Chanel with getting her nephew released from a German stalag, and that now she may be under some sort of … obligation to him."

"You are on … cordial terms with Baron von Dincklage?" the priest asked.

"Not particularly," I admitted, steeling myself to lay out my trump card, hoping it wouldn't cost me the man I loved. "But prior to the war, I met a German officer assigned as his private secretary at the German embassy. We struck up a friendship and though I broke things off once the Germans invaded, I have reason to believe he would be open to … rekindling our relationship."

Out of the side of my eye, I saw Jean-Claude stiffen.

Fording on, I said, "His name is Fritz Eberhardt and he's the only one the baron seems to trust with his documents. He goes back and forth between the Hôtel Lutetia, where he's billeted, and the Ritz, almost always carrying a brown leather attaché case."

"Everyone knows the Lutetia is the headquarters for the Abwehr," Rachelle put in, referring to the German military intelligence service that worked closely with the Nazi Schutzstaffel, or SS, the paramilitary organization aligned with the Gestapo.

I nodded. "I just need to get close to him, and I can get access to those papers, I know it."

Jean-Claude spoke up. "Do you not think he will notice that his secret documents are missing and his new girlfriend with them?"

Fortunately, I'd anticipated the question and had done my homework. "I can take snapshots with a Minox spy camera and then put the documents back before he realizes they're missing."

Jean-Claude looked like a man ready to murder, not the Nazis but me. "While he sleeps, you mean?"

Shocked as I was by his frankness, I was determined not to show it. "I'll put knockout drops in his schnapps," I tossed out, no matter that I'd never seen Fritz drink anything stronger than champagne.

He dragged a hand through his hair. "If you are caught, do not think they will go easy on you because you are a woman."

Determined not to let him or anyone else around that table underestimate me, I lifted my chin. "You think I'd break. I wouldn't."

He skewered me with a look. "Everyone breaks. Tell her, Rémy," he said, addressing an older man who'd so far sat silent.

Rémy scraped back his chair and stood. Though probably around my father's age, his haunted eyes, sunken cheeks, and slouched posture gave him the appearance of an old man.

"Last September, my daughter Marie rode her bicycle to Place du Trocadéro to deliver a message to one of our contacts. Gestapo agents were waiting when she arrived. They took her to their headquarters on rue des Saussaies. The torture went on for days, weeks.

Finally, they let her go. A beautiful girl, my Marie. Beautiful and so full of life. Now she screams every night in her sleep. And makes my wife cover all the mirrors. After what the Boches did to her, she will never be beautiful again." He took his seat, a tear tracking down his creased cheek.

Knowing nods traveled the table. From the side of my eye, I saw Jean-Claude watching me and did my best to put on a poker face.

Rachelle stood next. "They are not wrong. But there are strategies to minimize the damage. When you're first brought in, they'll beat you to soften you up. Make a show of resisting and then pretend to falter. Give them something close to the truth but not the truth. Once they realize the information is false, they'll come back to you. I won't lie, it will be bad. Try to hold out for twenty-four hours. That will give anyone working with you time to get away before you give them up. And if it is too much, there is this."

She lifted the chain around her neck, brought out the locket hidden under her blouse, and opened it. Sheltered inside the chamber like a pearl was a capsule.

"What is it?" I asked, though I had a pretty good idea.

Jean-Claude answered for her. "Cyanide, a lethal dose."

"We all carry them." She snapped the locket closed and held it out for me to take.

I took it and slipped it over my head. Raised Catholic, I'd been brought up to believe suicide was a mortal sin. If it came to it, could I really kill myself? Joining the Resistance meant putting myself in a position where I might have to make that choice. Was Jean-Claude right? Was I making a mistake?

Freedom must always be defended, Daisy.

I heard Gran's voice inside my head, a snippet of memory from that long ago day when we'd stood inside Shakespeare and Company waiting for Miss Beach. Now much more than the publication of a banned book stood at stake. What I wouldn't give to have Gran's arms around me for even a minute, to lay my head on her shoulder and soak in all her love and wisdom. Or even to hear her voice over the crackle of a telephone line. Once the United States had declared war, the transatlantic calls home to New York had stopped.

Rachelle broke into my brooding. "This German, exactly how will you approach him and renew your ... friendship?"

Luckily, I'd given some thought to that, too.

"Von Dincklage uses Mademoiselle Chanel's rooms at the Ritz as his own. Fritz ... Hauptmann Eberhardt is often called there to meet with him."

"First you will need to train," Jean-Claude said, voice flattened with what I recognized as resignation. "And to choose a codename."

I thought for a moment, and then it came to me. "Call me Apple Pie."

Chapter Thirty-Five

Early 1942
My first Vengeance meeting and the others that followed ended with the same parting pledge: *Vivre libre ou mourir*. Live free or die, the motto of the Resistance.

I spent the remaining winter months preparing for my new role as a *résistante*. As I quickly learned, everyone in Vengeance had a unique skill they brought to the group. The priest, Père Rafe, helped create false identity papers. Rémy sent coded messages to a contact in Vichy, who forwarded them to de Gaulle's Free French in London. Pierre's food deliveries were far from the only drop-offs he made. Explosives to sabotage railways and disrupt communication lines were hidden in produce crates in the back of his lorry. When Jean-Claude wasn't working at the Children's Aid Society, he helped Dr. Jackson treat other *résistants*, sometimes performing surgeries in a group's encampment or hideaway under the most primitive conditions.

Rachelle was a whiz at anything mechanical. She took it upon herself to train me to pick various varieties of locks – deadbolts, padlocks, barrel bolts and others I recognized by sight if not by name. At first, I was butterfingers, but gradually I got the hang of it and let the device "speak to me," as she put it. How I would perform under actual pressure remained to be seen.

As winter softened to spring, I felt myself growing antsy, impatient to prove myself, worried that after all my big talk I wouldn't get the chance. My success hinged on finding a way back to Fritz. I had seen him a handful of times in passing, always at the Ritz with von Dincklage but never alone. Given the frosty way we had left things, I couldn't very well march up out of the blue and ask him out. For my mending fences not to arouse suspicion, I needed something or someone to provide a believable cover.

Ironically, that someone turned out to be Mademoiselle Coco. For the first time since the outbreak of war, she was designing again, not an entire line but a single showstopping creation, a gown to complement a "comet" brooch by Van Cleef & Arpels. Both the brooch and dress were to be unveiled in an exclusive show at the Ritz that April. The partnership with the luxury jewelry design firm was the fruit of one of the Franco-German lunches at the Ritz and consequently had the Wehrmacht's blessing. Chanel's "cher Spatz" had seen to it personally that the restriction on fine fabric was lifted for the occasion.

The gown's creation consumed the atelier for months, breathing life back into the silent, dusty workrooms. Madame Millet hired back a half-dozen *petites mains* to help bring Chanel's vision to life, everyone sworn to secrecy about the design, which like its namesake brooch, was meant to be kept under wraps until its unveiling at the Ritz.

With a bit of luck and planning, the event would provide me with an opportunity to catch Fritz alone and off guard. I just had to make sure he would be there. Unfortunately, the guest list, compiled by Madame Aubrey, was as closely guarded as the gown was. I considered trying out my new lockpick skills on her desk drawer but every time I came close to working up my nerve, someone or something interrupted.

Two days before the show, Mademoiselle Coco called me into the atelier to view the finished gown.

Circling it on its form, she asked, "The fringe, it is too much?"

"It's perfect. An absolute dream of a dress," I said sincerely.

The comet gown was the most gorgeous evening dress I'd ever set eyes on, designed to make the wearer feel like a princess. The deeply décolleté bodice had triple shoulder straps of ruby velvet ribbon with floor-length streamers in the back, invoking a comet. But the gown's glory was the skirt, a heavy crinkled crêpe in a glorious, shimmering emerald-green that changed hue depending on the light.

She paused from pacing. "That is good because you will wear it tomorrow evening."

Her statement floored me. "I'm not a model," I protested. "Surely, Yvette or Sophie would be a better choice."

Both experienced mannequins, they had modelled several Chanel collections. Yvette, I knew for a fact, was still in Paris.

"For the wearer of this gown, I do not look for experience. I look for originality. You, Marguerite, are an *originale*."

It was one of the nicest things she'd ever said to me and having put myself forward to spy on her and her Nazi lover, it landed as bittersweet. Unsure of how to answer, I went momentarily mute, a situation she seized on.

"It is settled." She turned on her heel and walked off, leaving me alone with the dress.

As much as I adored fashion, wearing a pretty dress for a party or date wasn't the same as parading in front of a room of strangers. And not any room but the Ritz's grande salle. How was I supposed to finagle my way back into Fritz's good graces with everyone watching me?

Amid pacing the atelier with sweaty palms, it struck me. Everyone watching meant *Fritz* also would be watching. Chanel had handed me the golden opportunity I had been waiting for. It didn't matter if Fritz was on the guest list. As the mannequin for the comet gown, *I* would invite him.

I let the atelier clear out and then sneaked upstairs and "borrowed" one of the blank cream and gold invitations sitting out on Madame Aubrey's desk. Inside, I drew what hopefully passed for an olive branch and signed my name, then took it to the Ritz and had it couriered over to Fritz at the Hôtel Lutetia.

That evening, I met Jean-Claude and Rachelle at Saint-Trinité, not in the presbytery but in one of the side chapels lining the nave. Slipping into the wooden pew beside Rachelle, I whispered my plan.

"It is not bad enough you work for one of France's greatest anti-semites, now you must model for Nazis as well," Jean-Claude hissed over his sister's head.

Lacing my hands, supposedly in prayer, I said, "I don't think Mademoiselle Chanel dislikes Jews more than she does anyone."

From everything I'd seen and heard over the past four years, she dished out her vitriol in equal measure to all.

Jean-Claude shook his head. "Your eyes will open. And maybe then you will not be such a hypocrite."

I felt my face flame. "Me a hypocrite? How so?"

His blazing gaze bore into mine. "Admit it, you cannot wait to be paraded about with everyone's eyes on you."

Outraged, I shot back with, "I admit nothing except being sick to my stomach with stage fright."

Caught in the middle, Rachelle intervened. "Daisy is right. It is an opportunity to get close to Eberhardt and through him von Dincklage." She turned her head to me. "Keep your eyes and ears open. Even the slightest detail could help save lives."

The night before the show, I was racked with nerves, mostly about the modeling aspect of my mission. On Bridget's suggestion, I practiced smiling in the mirror and walking back and forth across the apartment while attempting to balance a dictionary atop my head. Sitting on the sofa like a judge in a beauty pageant, she critiqued my performance and offered suggestions for improvement, some helpful – "smile, it's a fashion show, not a funeral," others humorous – "imagine the audience in their knickers."

The next day, the atmosphere in the atelier was as tense as if we were launching an entire collection, not one dress. Then again, the green comet gown wasn't any dress. It was *the* dress, a wearable work of art. Having an entire evening riding on a single garment, and model, was daunting for all of us, no one more so than me.

The afternoon of the event, our entourage of six: a hair and makeup stylist, two *petites mains*, Madame Millet and me, with Mademoiselle Coco, bumped along rue Cambon from atelier to hotel, the comet gown concealed inside an oversized garment bag hanging from the bar of our luggage trolley. Mademoiselle Coco directed the gown's transport like an army general, stopping every few steps to point out a puddle or give a dark warning about garbage in the gutters. By the time we whisked the cart inside the swinging doors of the hotel's rue Cambon rear entrance, I felt like the hired muscle assigned to protect a movie star.

The other star of the evening, the Van Cleef & Arpels comet pin, had arrived already and was under lock and key in the safe in Claude's office. Except for Mademoiselle Coco, who had previewed it to design the dress, none of us had seen it before. Though it wouldn't be officially unveiled until later that evening, Blanche ushered us inside for a quick look, locking the door behind her.

Claude stood at his desk guarding a jeweler's case embossed with VCA, an obelisk stamped between the second and third letter. He waited for us to gather around and then slipped on a pair of white-cotton gloves to prevent smudging, as Blanche explained into my ear, opened the trifold case, and laid the brooch on a black velvet liner, all with the solemnity of a priest performing a mass. The brooch didn't disappoint. Though I had been to the private rooms of Tiffany & Company in Manhattan a handful of times, I had never seen anything like it. Avant-garde in style, it had an enormous diamond at the center surrounded by rays of rubies, emeralds, jade, and large pearls finished in pearl-shaped pendants. A long, supple fringe of jewels suggested a comet's tail.

Afterwards, I was spirited off to an empty suite on the Place Vendôme side to get ready. Given the fanfare surrounding the event, and the money involved, the *Kommandant*, Colonel Speidel had granted us special permission to cross over to the Wehrmacht wing for one night only. I spent the next several hours being painted, coiffed, and lastly, poured into the dress. Chanel stayed with me the entire time, overseeing every detail, fluffing the full skirt and adjusting the angle of the matching headdress of looped ruby velvet ribbons.

Catching my reflection in the full-length mirror, I felt as if a stranger stared back at me. American as apple pie Daisy was gone. In her place was French Marguerite, an exotic confection of womanhood I'd never met before but badly wanted to get to know. Feeling like I had stepped into a movie, I held out my arms to the two *petites mains* who slipped on the ruffled green suede opera gloves designed to go with the gown.

Resting a hand on her hip and holding a cigarette in the other, Chanel slowly circled me.

"*C'est bon*," she finally said, coming back around to my front, and I hid a smile, knowing that "good" from her counted as quite a compliment.

A few minutes before the event was to start, I was led out to the top of the grand staircase, the two *petites mains* carrying the gown's enormous train to keep it from dragging. Chanel stood with me out of sight. Below, the parquet tiled foyer was covered in white cloth covered tables, every one of them filled.

From the lower landing, Claude gave his short speech, welcoming everyone to the Ritz and acknowledging several distinguished guests, most of them German. Finished, he signaled to the pianist, who began playing, a classical piano sonata by some long-dead German composer, as formal and stiff as our occupiers were.

Recognizing my cue, the nerves I thought I had conquered hit me like a brick. Heart hammering, I clenched the shiny-black wrought-iron rail and looked down to a sea of searching faces all staring upward.

Chanel's voice called me back to myself. "Remember to go slowly. You are not walking, you are floating. And breathe."

Mouth dry, I managed to nod.

I recalled Bridget's advice from earlier. Imagining the audience stripped down to their underclothes was oddly calming. As was reminding myself that for the next few minutes I wasn't Daisy, I was her alter ego, Marguerite. I struck a smile and started down, my high heels sinking into the royal blue carpet. Tempted as I was to rush and get it over with, I made myself go slowly, the gown's long train and full skirt hiding my knocking knees.

Halfway down, I spotted Fritz at a table with von Dincklage. His gaze slipped over my face and down to my gown's plunging neckline, and then snapped back up, his cheeks stained with a blush to rival Schiaparelli's signature pink.

Reaching the bottom, I stepped off the landing and struck the pose I'd practiced in the mirror, what I'd come to think of as the Chanel stance. One foot forward, hips forward, shoulders down, hand on my hip. Holding my smile, I lifted my chin and waited.

Thunderous applause broke out. The room rose to its feet. Calls of "*brava*" and "*magnifique*" and "*wunderbar*" carried over the clapping. Chanel's comet gown was a triumph and apparently so was I.

Men and women crowded around me, remarking on my beauty and grace. Sasha Guitry likened me to Hollywood screen siren, Myrna Loy, also a redhead, and asked if I had ever considered acting. Shooting me dagger looks, Arletty gripped the arm of her Luftwaffe officer boyfriend and steered him away.

White-jacketed waiters circulated with trays of champagne. Someone pressed a fizzing flute into my gloved hand. Parched, I downed half the glass in a single swallow. Behind me, one of the *petites mains* bent to bustle my train.

Von Dincklage commandeered the stairs to propose a toast to Chanel, lauding her extraordinary talent and taste and vision. And yet even in my dazed state, it wasn't lost on me that it wasn't Chanel everyone was looking at.

It was me.

Peering over the tops of heads, I spotted Fritz hanging back by the piano. I tried to maneuver my way toward him, but the heavy gown wasn't made for moving. Before I could take another step, air raid sirens sounded. Feeling like Cinderella caught out after midnight, I gave up my glass, lifted my heavy skirt in both hands, and made my way down to the cellar with the others.

Bottles of wine and casks of cognac lined the cave-like room. On Claude's order, silk Hermès sleeping bags and fur rugs were unfurled over the bare floor. Several guests, still with drinks in their hands, hunkered down to continue the party.

A boom shook the air, followed by the whistles of bombs dropping in the distance. Wine bottles rattled in their racks. The ceiling beams trembled, raining dust on our heads. Chanel's maid, Germaine, hurried over with her gas mask. My mind circled back to Jean-Claude's gallery of broken faces, all casualties of war, and for a queasy, dizzying few seconds I thought I might lose my champagne all over Chanel's beautiful creation.

Fritz materialized at my side, looking concerned. "You are unwell?"

Amid my mounting terror, I saw an opportunity and seized it, throwing myself against him. For a fraction of a moment, he hesitated and then wrapped his arms around me.

We stood there like that, not speaking, his gloved hand tracing soothing circles on my bare back as blast upon blast rocked the walls.

Finally, the salvo subsided. I unpeeled myself from his dinner jacket and stepped back, taking a few deep breaths to get my bearings.

"I'm sorry. I don't know what came over me," I said, reaching up to straighten my hair fascinator.

"An understandable reaction when bombs are dropping over one's head. You are better now?"

Reading the concern on his face, it was hard to look at him and see what I knew I should see. An enemy. "Much, thanks."

It was my first time seeing him out of uniform since the Christmas Eve party in 1938. Taking in his perfectly fitted white dinner jacket and black trousers tailored to emphasize his trim waist and narrow hips, I felt swept back to that sparkling, lovely evening.

"*Gut.*" He glanced around the cellar where guests were brushing themselves off and picking debris out of each other's hair, a few giving in to nervous laughter. "Now the danger is past, the champagne is flowing, and our masters seem to have forgotten us."

I followed his gaze over to Mademoiselle Chanel and von Dincklage sipping champagne in a corner and talking among themselves as if no one else existed.

"Shall we rejoin the party?" he asked.

I reached out and took his hand. "I have a better idea."

By the time we reached the reception area, the lights were back on. Hotel employees swept up broken glass, righted overturned canapé carts, and ferried fresh drinks to the guests emerging from the cellar. Sidestepping the mess, we crossed the Hall of Dreams to the rue Cambon side, the German sentries too busy to bother with us.

Frank was already back behind the bar brushing debris into a dustpan.

"Mademoiselle Daisy, Herr Eberhardt, what's your pleasure?" he asked as if it were an ordinary evening.

"I'll have the Bee's Knees," I said.

Out of the side of my eyes, I caught Fritz's look of surprise. The last time we had lifted a glass together, I had still been getting used to champagne.

"The same," he said, ironing out his features.

Frank left us to make our drinks. As the only other people in the bar, we had our pick of tables.

"I hope you don't mind standing," I said, glancing back at my voluminous bustle. "You may have left your uniform back at your hotel, but I'm still wearing mine."

My cheeky comment earned his chuckle.

Turning serious, he said, "I was surprised to receive your invitation."

I steeled myself. "And pleased, I hope?"

"Pleased yes, but also curious. Why did you ask me tonight?"

It was a reasonable question and fortunately I had my reply ready.

"If this war has taught me anything, it's that life is precious and sometimes short. I don't want to waste any more of mine staying angry at a friend."

Strangely enough, it was more truth than lie.

From the other side of the hotel, piano music reached us. Without lyrics, it took me a minute to place the song. Once I did, my heart gave a lurch. "Stardust." Ever since the night I'd spent in Jean-Claude's room at the hospital, I'd thought of it as *our* song, to be played for our first dance at our wedding and then taken out and dusted off for anniversaries and special occasions over the years.

Interrupting my thoughts, Fritz asked, "Does your dress allow for dancing?"

Brushing off guilty feelings, I flashed a smile. "I think that could be arranged."

He smiled back. "*Gut*. But I wonder if first we might …"

He flagged a hand to indicate my fascinator, the beautiful, beribboned monstrosity held in place with a profusion of lethally sharp hatpins.

"Oh, of course. But you'll have to help me off with it. And try not to mess up my hair. It took *hours*."

"You are fortunate I have a sister," he said, the wry remark reminding me of why I'd always found it so easy to like him.

I bowed my head, and he pulled out the pins one by one, slipping them into his pocket, and lifted off the hat.

Holding it up, he made a face. "Why do women wear such things."

I took it from him, blew off the dust, and set it on an empty table, arranging the streamers to cascade over the side so they wouldn't crease. "I'll have you know this particular *chapeau* fetches more francs than most French make in six months." I almost added "under the Nazis" but stopped myself in time.

He held out his hand, and I took it, slipping into his arms.

His palm rested on my waist; his other hand cradled my wrist. I set my gloved hand atop his shoulder, surprised at how easy it all was, how natural it felt to be in his arms, how seamlessly we moved to the music and with each other.

How easy it would be to fall back into friendship with a Nazi.

I closed my eyes and set my cheek against his shoulder, savoring the lemony scent of his aftershave or maybe it was his bath soap, the reassuring warmth of his big, strong body. Unlike Jean-Claude, unlike most French by then, he was well-nourished, a perfect balance of flesh and bone. A man who wouldn't "blow away in a puff of wind," as Gran liked to say. What a novelty in these hungry times.

"I have missed you, Daisy," he said, his lips in my hair, which I no longer cared about messing up.

Not having to meet his eyes helped. "I've … missed you, too."

I *had* missed him. I hadn't realized how much until then.

When our love was new, and each kiss an inspiration.
But that was long ago, and now my consolation
Is in the stardust of a song.

The lyrics rushed back to me, bringing with them buried, bittersweet memories. Our first shy peck on New Year's Eve at the Ritz. Winter walks in the Luxembourg Gardens when the blustery weather had given him an excuse to put his arm around me. The passionate goodbye kiss we had shared when I had been certain I would never see him again. And now here we were together again, he as an occupier and me as a spy for the Resistance. How crazy, and cruel, life could be.

Fritz broke into my reverie. "I am glad we are friends again."

I lifted my head from his chest and looked up at him, wishing that were so. "I don't know if I can be friends with Hauptman Eberhardt," I replied, remembering the adage that the best lies are based on truth. "But I am very happy to have Fritz Eberhardt back in my life."

Chapter Thirty-Six

The next morning, the fashion columnists for all the major newspapers reported not only on Chanel's comet gown but also its model, "Mademoiselle Daisy Blakely of Manhattan, New York, granddaughter of Mrs. Rose Kavanaugh's Blakely of Kavanaugh's Department Store." A few added the sobriquet, "*La Star De La Ville*."

The Toast of the Town.

Flowers flooded the boutique, roses and camellias for Mademoiselle Chanel. Standing out among the latter was a simple bouquet of marguerites, daisies, the accompanying envelope addressed to me.

I opened it and slid out the notecard penned in English.

May I have the honor of taking the Toast of Paris to dinner?
Maxim's, seven o' clock. Fritz.

Bridget came up beside me and snatched the note out of my hand. "So, Miss Toast of Paris, are you going?"

"As a matter of fact, I am," I answered, taking the card back.

"Good for you. It's about time you gave up moping over You Know Who."

She meant Jean-Claude, of course.

Rubbed raw from his recent remarks though I was, still I couldn't resist defending him. Lowering my voice, I said, "It's hardly his fault Jews aren't allowed to socialize outside the ghetto."

Catching my look, she backed down. "I'm just saying a night out on the town wouldn't kill you even if it is with a Boche. I have a drinks date after work, otherwise I'd help you get ready."

She plucked a daisy from my bouquet and walked off humming.

With the comet gown launched, and no new designs planned for the foreseeable, there was nothing to keep me late. I closed the shop and went home early, drew a bath and washed my hair, giving it time to dry before heating the curling iron to create the soft waves that were all the rage. Still new to applying makeup, without Bridget to help me, I left my eyes natural and settled on raspberry lipstick and a hint of rouge and powder. After the previous night, slipping on my little black dress felt anticlimactic even if it was Chanel. For the finishing touch, I dabbed No. 5. behind each ear, in the hollow of my throat and lastly between my breasts.

At twenty minutes to seven, a black Mercedes rolled up to the front of Madame LeBrun's to collect me. The driver, thankfully in plain clothes and not a Nazi uniform, stepped out to open the rear door for me. Sliding into the backseat, I reminded myself that if I was going to win back Fritz, I had better get used to playing the part of a Nazi officer's girlfriend.

I arrived at the restaurant a few minutes early. My driver had just drawn up to the curb outside 3 rue Royale when a liveried doorman vaulted into the street and whisked me inside the red-canopied entrance.

The restaurant's opulent interior was unlike anything I had ever seen even before the war. The stained-glass ceiling and window panels bathed everything in a lush, rosy light, a respite from the gloom that shrouded the rest of Paris. After handing off my wrap to the cloakroom attendant, I followed the maître d' into the dining room. Weaving through the closely placed tables, I took in the fanciful frescoed walls, mahogany volutes, beveled mirrors, and bronze sculptures, feeling as if I had entered a fairy land.

Fritz sat at a table for two tucked beneath an enormous gilt-framed mirror with elaborate flourishes of flowers, leaves, and fruit. He stood when I approached, and I slipped into the velvet-covered banquette across from him.

"The restaurant is lovely. I've never been before," I admitted.

That pleased him, I could tell. He smiled, unearthing a dimple in the center of his squared chin.

"I wanted to take you somewhere where we could truly be alone," he said. "A night outside the Ritz fishbowl."

The Ritz was certainly that, especially the bar where French and German intelligence operatives socialized cheek by jowl, each side invoking booze and bonhomie as weapons to try and loosen the tongue of the enemy.

My gaze snagged on a stunning blonde in a white satin evening gown at a nearby table. I had noticed her when I first walked in but hadn't wanted to gawk.

Turning back to Fritz, I whispered, "Is that—"

"Marlene Dietrich, I believe so. And if I am not mistaken, her escort for the evening is the French actor, Jean Gabin."

Champagne sat chilling in a footed silver ice bucket at Fritz's side. A waiter in tails approached, poured a measure into his flute and, once he'd approved it, filled both our glasses.

"Does monsieur wish to order?" he asked Fritz.

Fritz looked over at me. "Do you know what you would like?"

I hadn't so much as opened my menu.

"Why don't you do the honors," I suggested, mostly to make him feel manly and in charge, though it wasn't lost on me that like Jean-Claude, he'd asked me first.

He gave our order in flawless French. Afterward, the menus were whisked away, and we raised our glasses.

Sipping my champagne, I asked, "How is your sister, Klara? Is she still in school?"

Maybe it was a trick of the low lighting, but a cloud seemed to pass over his face.

"She is in her last year of Gymnasium and kept quite busy with her BDM activities."

"BDM?"

"*Bund Deutscher Mädel.* The German League of Girls," he explained.

He took out his billfold and passed me a photograph. It was of a tall blonde girl of fifteen or sixteen wearing a white blouse, dark tie, and dark skirt, her hair braided into twin pigtails. In the background, two other girls dressed in the same uniform stood at a paddock fence feeding carrots to a pony. The pastoral scene might be the basis for a Nazi propaganda poster.

"Very pretty," I said, hiding my disgust behind a smile.

Passing back the photograph, I made a mental note to mention Klara to Jean-Claude and Rachelle when I saw them next. Though Fritz's sister was still a child, it seemed she was well on her way to being poisoned by Nazi doctrine.

Fritz slipped the photograph back into his wallet, a slight frown furrowing his forehead. "I worry that all the sporting and agricultural competitions are interfering with her studies, but she loves it and has made many friends."

Nazi friends, I added to myself.

Our consommé came, an opportunity to change the subject. I sipped the cold fish soup from my spoon and contemplated what my next move might be.

"What of your family?" he asked. "They must worry for you being in France."

"They do," I admitted, reminded of the stricken look on my parents' faces when I'd finally scraped up the courage to tell them I was going back to Paris.

I found myself telling him about Gran's close call on Fifth Avenue two years earlier and how it had taken me going back to realize that Paris felt more like home than New York did. Naturally I left out any mention of Jean-Claude. Instead, I focused on my volunteering at the hospital and the satisfaction it brought me even with all the shortages.

I stopped there. For someone who'd set out to be the Resistance's eyes and ears, I was doing an awful lot of the talking. But then I had always found Fritz to be a good listener, perhaps too good. Going forward, I would do well to remember that he wasn't my friend, not anymore. He was an asset. As bad as I felt about using him, my loyalty was to the Resistance and de Gaulle's Free French. I eased my conscience by telling myself that a decisive Allied victory would save lives on both sides.

A junior waiter approached to clear our bowls and refresh our champagne glasses.

"I am glad your grandmother is recovered." Fritz said, his clear blue eyes looking into mine. "I know you are close with her."

"You remember that?" I said, surprised and moved.

"I remember everything of our time together. I was lonely in Paris. Having you to talk to helped make the loneliness less."

The second course arrived, Lobster Newburg, an American delicacy.

"I thought you might enjoy a taste of home," Fritz said.

"I'm sure I will." Touched by his thoughtfulness, I forked up a morsel of lobster in puff pastry dressed in rich sherry cream sauce. Delicious. I looked over at his plate, the same dish as mine.

Following my gaze, he said, "I enjoy American culture very much, or at least what I know of it from books. I hope to visit someday, New York especially."

Seeing an opening, I jumped on it. "I'd love to show you around after the war. Will it go on much longer, do you think?"

It was as if my question raised a wall between us.

His guarded gaze met mine. "All wars end eventually. How soon is for the politicians to decide."

Sensing that the smooth reply was all I'd get from him, for the night at least, I steered the conversation to more neutral topics, offering up harmless, hopefully humorous antidotes from the boutique as well as Bridget's and my cat-and-mouse brushes with Olivier, who hadn't entirely given up his peeping. Every time I interjected something about the war, hoping to plumb him for information, he clammed up, silent as the Sphinx.

Our plates were cleared, and dessert brought out, Dame Blanche for us both. As far as I could tell, it was a fancy version of a hot fudge sundae. By the time it arrived, I admitted to myself that spying took a lot more patience than I had imagined.

The meal ended with espressos, made with real coffee, not the awful ersatz stuff we drank elsewhere. I stirred in a cube of sugar and savored it in small sips.

Afterward, Fritz paid *l'addition*, and we rose and went to collect my wrap from the coat check.

Standing outside the restaurant, his car pulled up. When he slid in the backseat beside me, his hip briefly brushing up against mine, I didn't move away.

I waited for him to suggest continuing the evening at a nightclub or cabaret. Instead, he directed the driver to take us to Madam LeBrun's.

Once we were underway, he reached across the seat and took my hand. "Thank you for making my last evening in Paris a memorable one."

My heart dropped. "You're leaving?" I asked, unprepared for the rush of disappointment I felt and not only because I hadn't gotten anywhere near his briefcase.

As much as I had resisted enjoying our dinner, I had enjoyed it, very much. And not only on account of the food and wine, sublime even by pre-war Parisian standards. Compared to Jean-Claude, whose moods could be almost as mercurial as Mademoiselle Coco's, Fritz was easy company.

"In the morning," he admitted, tracing circles on my palm with his thumb.

Sitting beside him in the back of the darkened car, I thought of the Minox I had tucked into my evening purse, the pocket-sized spy camera purchased on the Black Market with Frank's help. If Fritz was leaving in the morning, tonight was my one chance to get a look inside his briefcase. Perfect gentleman though he'd always been with me, he was still a man. If I asked him outright to have the driver turn around and take us to his hotel, I doubted he would turn me down.

But despite my tough talk at the Vengeance meeting, I wasn't altogether sure I was ready to go through with it. Unlike Bridget, who had

had several boyfriends since coming to Paris and didn't seem to take any of them too seriously, I was still a virgin. Before the Occupation, I had planned to stay one until I got married.

We pulled up in front of Madam LeBrun's. Fritz told the driver to wait, and then got out and came around to open my door.

He walked me to the entrance. I felt deflated, and not only because I had failed in my first Vengeance mission. Like it or not, the time I had spent with Fritz had meant something to me and probably always would.

We reached the front steps, and I climbed the first one and turned back to him. Being a step above him put us at eye level. If he wanted to kiss me, I would make it easy for him.

"I'd ask where you're going, but I don't expect you'd tell me."

"I do not expect I would," he admitted. "That does not mean I do not wish to. Or that I am looking forward to leaving you."

"At least tell me when you'll be back," I wheedled. "You are coming back, aren't you?"

He hesitated. "I hope so, but I cannot say."

"Meaning you don't know, or you won't tell me?"

He looked at me, his expression wistful. "Both, perhaps."

Despite chickening out in the cab, when he reached out and cupped my cheek, I closed my eyes and leaned into his hand.

Soft lips brushed my forehead. I opened my eyes, surprised and, if I were honest with myself, disappointed, too. The goodbye kiss we had shared in the Luxembourg Gardens before the war had proved that Fritz was more than capable of pleasing me. With Jean-Claude's stinging remarks at the church still fresh in my mind and fed up with his stubborn insistence that we had to wait until after the war to be together, I was willing to give Fritz a chance to prove himself again.

Instead, he stepped back, his gaze brimming with what I flattered myself was regret. "*Bonne nuit*, Daisy. Until we meet again, take good care. Paris can be ... a complicated place." A last, lingering look and then he turned to go.

I watched him get back in the Mercedes, sad to see him go and not only because his leaving left my mission in limbo. With the war on, none of us ever knew when a goodbye might turn into a farewell. For all I knew, this might be the last time I ever saw him.

Clapping drew my attention to the alleyway running alongside the apartment house. Terrified, I spun around, expecting to see Gestapo agents closing in.

Instead, Jean-Claude stepped from the shadows, a lit cigarette wedged into the side of his mouth.

"What are you doing here?" I demanded, angry but excited, too, my heart fluttering in that funny way it always did whenever I first laid eyes on him.

Rather than answer, he tossed the smoke on the street and came toward me. Closing the distance between us, he sealed my mouth with a hard kiss.

Chapter Thirty-Seven

His mouth was warm and moist, his kiss flavored with tobacco and wine and anger. He sank a heavy hand into my hair and pulled my head back, sending pins peppering the pavement. I moaned against his lips, and he kissed me deeper, tonguing me until my knees went weak.

When he finally let me go, every inch of me was shaking. I opened my mouth to say ... something, but before I could, he took hold of my arm and towed us along the street. I didn't ask where we were going. I was past caring at that point. All I knew was that the waiting was finally over. After that kiss, I *had* to be with him.

We turned the corner onto rue Bourdaloue as the street went dark, the lamps shutting off for the commencement of curfew. Drawing up beneath the sagging canopy of a closed café, he took a key from his pocket and unlocked the door.

Inside, he pulled out a flashlight and switched it on. Dust floated in the still, sour air, the battered floorboards creaking beneath our feet. Keeping hold of my hand, he led us through the long bar and small, rustic kitchen and then down a flight of narrow stairs. Reaching the cellar, he let go of me and slid a heavy rack of wine to the side, revealing a small door cut into the limestone.

Ducking, I followed him through. We were in a stone-walled chamber that must be part of the maze of tunnels that ran beneath the city. A pallet and blanket took up most of the earthen floor. On a small side table, a razor and shaving soap sat beside a tin cup and two earthenware pitchers, one for water, the other wine.

I shivered in the chill, loamy air. "Is this where you've been—"

He killed the flashlight and pulled me roughly to him, backing us up until my spine slammed against the stones.

The pitch blackness made it easy to be brave. I set my hands on his shoulders and gave him my mouth again, welcoming his kiss, rough and raw and bruising. His hand covered my breast, and I wasn't cold anymore. Deft fingers undid the front of my dress and slid my bra straps off my shoulders, the chill air making my nipples stand out. His first grazing touch nearly dropped me to my knees.

A fierce urgency seized me. Suddenly, I couldn't wait to learn him. I pulled at his jacket and shirt, popping buttons in my hurry. My eager hands trailed his flesh, the bones close to the surface, the skin toughened in places, smooth in others. He reached down between us and found me with his fingers, raising a beautiful, budding ache that built until my hips and all the rest of me strained to reach a place I'd never been before. And then suddenly something inside me snapped, all the exquisite tension streaming out in the space of a scream.

I'd barely come back to myself when he pulled off my panties and lifted me against him, my dress riding my waist.

"*Oui?*" he asked, the first he'd spoken since he'd seen me.

I wrapped both arms around his neck and cinched my legs around his hips. "Yes."

The first blunt breach nearly knocked the breath from my body. I dug my nails into his back and ground against him, the pain warring with the pure thrill of him filling me. With each thrust, the shock faded. I opened to take him deeper until we rocked in a rhythm that I had to believe was entirely our own. Suddenly he went taut, then bucked, releasing himself with a groan, our damp bodies clinging together, his head sinking into the curve of my shoulder.

"*Bonne journée.*"

I opened my eyes to Jean-Claude beside me, propped up his elbow, his cheek resting in his palm, the thin blanket at his waist.

Expression sheepish, he said, "Last night, I was not a gentleman."

I turned onto my side and touched a scratch on his shoulder. "I don't suppose I was much of a lady either."

"And this morning? How do you feel?" he asked.

After making love, we'd retreated to his pallet and almost immediately fallen asleep in each other's arms. For once my dreams were free of wailing air raid sirens and barking German shepherd dogs and Gestapo agents in black leather trench coats.

"Good. A little sore."

"Only a little?" He eyed me.

"Maybe more than a little," I admitted, looking away.

The damp café basement was a far cry from the white wedding and gold bands I had envisioned for us but bringing my gaze back to Jean-Claude's, I couldn't bring myself to regret any of it. As the chain around his neck holding what I knew to be cyanide attested, the world was falling apart around us. At any moment, Gestapo agents might break down the door and take us off to be tortured and shot or deported to their filthy internment camps. Who could fault us for grabbing hold of what happiness we could?

"I have a remedy. I will show you if you like," he offered with a smile.

At my nod, he eased me onto my back. Starting at my lips, he kissed a path down my body, stopping at my waist, his mouth blessing each hip in turn. Then his head disappeared between my thighs, and I forgot to breathe.

We had just finished his "remedy" when three sharp knocks sounded outside the door. I bolted upright and grabbed the blanket.

"That will be the café owner's son come to wake us," Jean-Claude assured me, dropping a kiss on my shoulder.

I wrapped the blanket around myself while he pulled on his pants and went to answer.

A boy of about fourteen stood outside holding a wooden tray. His curious eyes took me in, and I pulled the blanket tighter.

Jean-Claude took it from him. "*Cinq minutes, merci.*"

He shouldered the door closed and carried the tray over to me. It held a chipped plate with two slices of unbuttered bread and two cups of coffee. The burned acorn smell announced it was the ersatz kind.

"*Manges.*" He picked up a piece of bread and held it to my lips.

Guilty thinking of the lavish supper I'd had, I moved his hand away. "You have it. I'm the one dining at Maxim's."

The instant the words were out, I regretted them.

His face darkened. "With your Nazi boyfriend, you mean?"

For a sickening few seconds, I wondered if last night's lovemaking had been more to do with propping up male pride than it had his feelings for me.

I reached for my dress and pulled it on over my head. "He's not my boyfriend. He's my asset. Whatever you think you saw last night, I was only acting," I added, as much to convince myself as him.

I *had* felt something for Fritz, an attraction that went beyond liking, and yet those feelings paled compared to what I had experienced the previous night and that morning with Jean-Claude. Now that Jean-Claude had let me into his life, *really* let me in, I didn't want to be with anyone else. Not even when he was being a horse's ass as he was then.

"You think I am jealous?" he asked.

I got the dress on and stood, shaking out the wrinkles. "Aren't you?"

"Of course, I am. But I am also afraid. More afraid than the first time I saw my father's ruined face and refused to cry."

Softening, I looked over at him. "We're all afraid of the Nazis. I don't know anyone in their right mind who isn't."

"It is not them I fear. It is you."

Whatever I had steeled myself to hear, it wasn't that. "Me?"

He framed my face between his hands. "If they hurt you, it would break me."

He took me in his arms, and I tucked my head beneath his chin. For a few minutes more we stood together like that, his arms encircling me, his heart drumming against mine.

"*Je t'aime*. I love you," I said, done with holding back. "I've loved you since the day I walked onto your surgical floor and your hair was sticking up like a porcupine's quills. Heck ... *hell*, I even love the infuriating way you have of shrugging all the time and raising your right eyebrow like a stern French schoolmaster."

He lifted his head to look at me, expression tender. "Daisy, I—"

Three sharp knocks outside the cellar door brought us back to ourselves. We broke apart, running hands through our hair and checking our buttons.

Assured we were decent, Jean-Claude turned away from me and called out, "*Entrez*," before either of us could lose our courage.

Chapter Thirty-Eight

By the time I got back to the flat, Bridget had left for work as I should have done. There wasn't time for a proper bath, so I made do with washing up in the sink. Rushed as I was, I couldn't resist stopping to study myself in the mirror. Did I look as different as I felt? Would my kiss-swollen lips and the beard burn branding my cheeks reveal me as a scarlet woman?

I dressed, dusted my face with powder, and put on a little lipstick, then hurried downstairs. Stepping off the landing, I ran into Madame LeBrun standing at the front door seeing Olivier off to school.

"You had a late night, *mademoiselle*?" she remarked, gaze raking me over.

"I overslept," I lied, though really, what business was it of hers?

She still didn't budge.

Once such a run-in would have intimidated me, but two years under Nazi rule had toughened me up. As had working for Chanel.

"I really must be going. *Bonne journée*," I said firmly and that time she moved away and let me pass.

I got to the atelier as Chanel's lawyer, René de Chambrun, was leaving, his fleshy face flushed and his silk tie askew. Other than accompanying his wife on the occasional shopping trip, I hadn't seen him in a while. Being the son-in-law of Pierre Laval, the most egregious collaborationist politician in France, must keep him busy.

Brought face to face, I had no choice but to speak to him. "Comte de Chambrun."

"Mademoiselle." He acknowledged me in passing and went on his way.

I spotted Bridget in the back folding scarves. Seeing me, she beckoned me over.

She took me by the elbow and whisked me behind the counter with her. "I'd ask how your date with the Boche went but since you didn't come home last night, I suppose I have my answer. So, how was he?"

I hesitated. Of course, she would think I'd spent the night with Fritz. I *needed* her to think that. And yet I didn't like lying to her.

"A lady doesn't kiss and tell," I settled on saying.

The prim reply earned her eyeroll, but at least it got her to drop the subject for the time being.

I looked up at the mirrored stairs. "Guess I'd better go and face the music."

Having never been late for work in my life, I wasn't sure what to expect.

Bridget shrugged and reached for another scarf. "With all the fuss earlier, I doubt anyone even noticed."

"What fuss?" I asked.

"Mademoiselle is up in arms again over the Wertheimers."

Mindful of a customer over in jewelry, a Nazi officer's girlfriend I had seen a time or two at the Ritz, I lowered my voice. "The last I heard, Pierre and Paul Wertheimer had fled with their families to New York. I can't imagine that, being Jewish, they plan to return to France anytime soon. Certainly not while we're under Nazi rule."

"Being in New York doesn't stop them from manufacturing and selling No. 5," Bridget whispered back. "The talk is they have a factory in Hoboken, New Jersey where they're churning it out like jars of jam."

That made sense, I supposed. Chanel had partnered with the Wertheimers in the first place because they could provide a large factory and distribution network through their Bourjois cosmetics company. What I didn't understand is how they could produce the perfume in New Jersey when the main ingredient, Jasmine Grandiflorum, was found only in France.

I left her and took the mirrored stairs to Chanel's second-floor apartment, carrying my handbag with me rather than taking time to stow it downstairs. Finding the doors ajar, I knocked loudly and then let myself in. Coming into the living room, I found Chanel supine on the beige suede sofa, an arm draped across her eyes like the femme fatale in an old silent movie. Other than slipping off her shoes, she was fully dressed, her clothes somehow still looking as if they'd come off a laundry press. A crystal ashtray overflowing with cigarette stubs stained with red lipstick sat out on the side table.

"Marguerite," she said, lifting her arm to look at me. "My head, it is splitting. Bring me an aspirin. The bottle is in my desk."

"Of course," I said and went into the alcove to fetch it.

Pulling up the rolltop on the desk, I saw a half-finished letter lying out. Growing up, I had been raised to believe that nosing through others' personal correspondence was an eighth deadly sin, but I reminded myself that I was working for the Resistance now.

I looked down at the cream-colored vellum, wishing I'd thought to bring my Minox camera with me instead of leaving it in my evening purse.

The addressee was Kurt Blanke, the German lawyer in charge of enforcing the Nazi Aryanization laws related to the seizure of Jewish businesses and property, who operated out of the Gestapo headquarters at the Hôtel Majestic.

> *Cher Herr Blanke,*
>
> *Parfums Chanel is still the property of Jews ... and has been legally 'abandoned' by the owners. I have an indisputable right of priority. The profits that I have received from my creations since the foundation of this business are disproportionate, and I appeal to you to help repair in part the prejudices I have suffered in these seventeen years ...*

Disgusted, I tried telling myself I shouldn't be so shocked. Hadn't Chanel boasted of harassing the Wertheimers for more than a decade, until they had been forced to retain a lawyer to respond to her many lawsuits? Now she had the Nazis and their antisemitic edicts on her side.

"Marguerite, the aspirin," she called from the adjacent room.

Seeing red, I left the bottle where it was, picked up the letter, which she hadn't bothered to hide, and walked back to her.

I flagged the letter in her face. "Siding with the Nazis against Frenchmen, how could you?"

She lifted her head from the sofa arm and looked over at me. "Fashion is a business, and sometimes business requires sharp elbows. Your grandmother did not teach you this?"

She had disappointed me before, starting with her taking up with von Dincklage. But this time was different. What she was doing was calculated, vicious, beyond forgiveness. All for the sake of a fragrance.

Staring at her, I felt a stab of genuine loathing. "My grandmother is nothing like you."

She sat up, swinging her legs to the floor. "Do you imagine, if our positions were reversed, that the *frères* Wertheimers would hesitate to use the laws against me?"

"Having never met them, I can't say if they would or wouldn't but that doesn't make what you're doing right."

She stood. "Tell me, were the Wertheimers right to send their spy, Herbert Gregory Thomas, to France to steal my formula and ingredients and take them back to the States?"

I didn't have an answer for that.

Stepping into the silence, she clicked her tongue. "When I was your age, I was a woman making my way in life. I forget that you are a little girl still."

Once the criticism would have crushed me. But I was no longer the same starstruck eighteen-year-old who'd first come to Paris with Gran and seen the city, and Chanel, through rose-colored lenses.

Refusing to be derailed, I continued, "You signed a contract, legally binding and of your own free will, granting them the majority stake in your perfume company."

Jabbing a finger in my face, she demanded, "What do you know? You were not there, I was. These men, these *Jews*, they tricked me."

Like breaking a pencil, something inside me snapped. My thoughts flashed to Jean-Claude coming out of the Children's Aid Society in his worn coat with the yellow Star of David stitched over the heart. To the ugly signs with their ugly message, "*Interdit aux Juifs*," posted outside the city cafés and restaurants, cinemas and theaters and gardens. To the Jewish passengers crowded like cattle onto the last cars of the Métro, now the only ones they were allowed to ride, fear on their faces every time the car doors opened.

Meeting Chanel's defiant face, I no longer saw the world's greatest fashion designer, a living legend, the idol of my girlhood. Instead, I saw a bigot and traitor.

A collabo.

I closed the distance between us, the table with its overflowing ashtray the only thing stopping me. "You made a bad deal. If you're so desperate for someone to blame, look in a mirror."

There was a flash of a hand and then a loud *crack*. It took several seconds for my baffled brain to register what had happened, and then I reached up to my flaming cheek. It was my first time being slapped. For a handful of heartbeats, it occurred to me that maybe I ought to cry. But living under the Nazis, there was a lot more to cry about than a slap on the face.

Oddly calm, I looked her in the eye and said, "*J'ai fini ici.*"

I'm done here.

I wheeled away to the door.

"Marguerite, come back."

I descended the staircase, the mirrored panels reflecting her handprint on my cheek. Ignoring the stares of Bridget and the collabo customer, I cut across the boutique floor and headed out the door.

By the time I got home, the mark had faded but not my outrage.

I had been deluded in thinking I was special to her, more than just another of her *filles*. Too late I understood that all of us, the *petites mains*, the mannequins, even the old timers like Millet and Aubrey were nothing but pawns to be manipulated to serve her needs.

Whatever love she still had in her she saved for her nephew, André, Tiny and perhaps her dog. Even her affair with von Dincklage seemed mostly to do with propping up her ego. They were using each other, a situation that seemed to suit them both.

My discovery of her letter was a watershed moment in my Paris life. Until then, Chanel and the city had seemed almost one and the same to me. Whatever personality flaws I had overlooked in consideration of her charm, élan, and undeniable genius, whatever allowances I had made in consideration of her fears for her nephew, were over and done.

What I would do with my newfound insight remained to be seen. All I knew then was that when the opportunity presented itself, I wouldn't hesitate.

I would be ready.

Chapter Thirty-Nine

July 1942
That Bastille Day was the grimmest yet under the Occupation. Picking up on the sullen faces and murmured conversations in the streets, I couldn't help thinking back to how joyously we'd all celebrated my first two years in Paris with parades, and fireworks, and parties on houseboats.

Two days later, French police arrested thirteen thousand foreign-born Jews and herded them into the Vél d'Hiv where Bridget and I had roller skated before the war. According to Rachelle, who was friends with a Polish girl who had been taken, the internees had endured five days without food, water or facilities. Those left alive were transferred to La Muette at Drancy to await deportation to internment camps in Poland.

Since the start of the Occupation, Hitler's second-in-command, Hermann Göring had traveled between Berlin and Paris where he had become a fixture at the Ritz, almost always carrying his gold and diamond-studded marshal's baton custom-made by Cartier. Along with being the architect of the London blitzkrieg, he oversaw enforcement of the *Einsatzstab Reichsleiter Rosenberg* – ERR – the Nazi taskforce responsible for seizing Jewish-owned art and valuables. In

Paris, the confiscated paintings and other artwork were stored in the Jeu de Paume, a former indoor tennis court in the north corner of the Tuileries Gardens, until they could be transported to Germany.

Not all that was stolen made it to Berlin. According to Blanche, who had heard it from Claude, the walls of Göring's suite were papered in priceless paintings, the closets stuffed with women's silk clothing and furs. But jewels were his obsession. His most recent acquisition was a collection of emeralds taken from Mrs. Corrigan, the wealthy American widow he'd booted out of the Imperial Suite.

Though the Ritz was officially neutral, I had observed enough goings on to surmise that most of the senior staff were helping the Resistance in one way or another. Frank ran a clandestine mailbox from behind the bar. I'd seen him palm more than one sealed note and slip it in his pocket only to bring it out later and pass it to another customer under the cover of a bar napkin. Anyone else who noticed would assume he was continuing his illegal betting operation, which he had run before the war. According to Blanche, he also acted as a middleman helping the desperate to obtain forged passports and other falsified identification papers. She knew because he had helped her once.

By then, she and I were good enough friends that I had been let in on her secret. She was Jewish, born Blanche Rubenstein, though official documents, forged courtesy of Frank, gave her maiden name as Ross. By day, she put on a smile and played the part of the gracious hostess, chatting up the Germans in the bar as if they were regular guests. But by night ... On at least one occasion, she had deliberately left on the lights in the kitchen basement of the Place Vendôme wing during an air raid, essentially putting a pin in the map for the Allied bombers flying blind at night. As much as I admired her bravery, I worried that one of these days what she called her "chutzpah" would catch up with her.

Beneath his stuffy exterior, Claude was no slouch. He had come up with a simple but ingenious system for alerting the Allies when the hotel hosted high-ranking Nazis. Each visiting German military or political dignitary was assigned a codename based on a fruit or vegetable – Göring was "potato" – and had persuaded managers from many of the other Paris hotels to join him.

Surrounded by such courage, how could I do less?

A week after the incident with Chanel, I admitted to myself that I had been foolhardy to quit. With Fritz out of France, her atelier was my sole conduit for gathering information on von Dincklage. It was also my sole source of income. Soon, I would have to break my promise to myself and tap into the family money in my bank account. Several times, I considered swallowing my pride and asking Chanel to take me back but from everything Bridget had said, she was still furious with me, banning anyone on staff from speaking my name.

Amid berating myself for my hotheadedness, it struck me that a much bigger nest of Nazi activity was right under my nose and had been all along.

The Hôtel Ritz.

At my first opportunity, I sought out Blanche. Claude stood beside her at the reception desk glancing over the guestbook, perhaps with an eye to alerting his network about a new delivery of "vegetables." I knew for a fact that Herr Potato himself, Hermann Göring, was back in the city, having spotted him drunkenly weaving through the Place Vendôme the day before, waving his Cartier cane like a cheerleader's baton.

Blanche and I exchanged the usual pleasantries and guest gossip and then I came to my point. "You were a film actress, weren't you, Blanche?"

From across the counter, I sensed Claude flinch and gathered he didn't appreciate Blanche's acting past being brought up.

Blanche, however, lit up like a billboard in Times Square.

"In the twenties, I had small parts in several motion pictures, including the "Perils of Pauline" serials with my good friend, Pearl White. My career was just taking off when I came to Paris to rendezvous with an Egyptian prince who wanted to make me a movie star. Instead, I met Popsy, and he talked me into trading in the silver screen for a gold wedding ring."

I spotted Claude's mustache twitch and surmised he didn't remember the story in quite the same way.

Blanche continued her reminiscence. "Not that I regret it ... much," she qualified, cutting Claude a sideways smirk. "In many ways, the Ritz is the greatest show on earth."

Seizing my segue, I said, "About that, did you happen to hold onto any of your old makeup and costumes? If you did, I'd love to have a look."

Eyeing Claude, she admitted, "I might have saved a few mementos. I'll get someone to cover the desk and show you."

A short while later, she led us through the staff service area up to the attic. Heavy furniture was crammed inside, most of it covered in dustsheets. Looking closer, I saw that several walls had built-in cupboards.

Following my gaze, she said, "The late founder, César Ritz, had closets built all through the hotel, not just up here but in all the guest suites, a rarity at the time. Since the Occupation, they've been a godsend for us and our guests to stash valuables and ... other things. It's been a while since I was up here."

She walked up to a particular cupboard and pulled at the door, the warped wood giving way with a groan.

Standing back, she said, "Artifacts from my glory days."

Looking inside, I saw that the shelves were filled with theatrical props and costumes. Women's wigs on forms. Long-waisted flapper style gowns hanging on hooks. Cases holding prosthetic noses, facial hair, and even fake sets of teeth.

She took out a handled case covered in Morocco leather, set it atop a table, and opened it. "My pride and joy."

It was a tiered cosmetics case of the type that theater people used to take with them when they were on the road, the yellowed satin-lined interior divided into custom compartments for lip paints, pancake makeup, pots of rouge, cakes of eyeshadow, and various sized brushes.

Looking back at her, I said, "This is amazing."

She nodded. "Claude hates this stuff. He's always after me to throw it out. I tell him when he gives up his tramp mistress, I'll give up my warpaint. We've been at a stalemate for almost twenty years." She cracked a laugh, but her brown eyes looked sad. "Daisy, what is this really about?"

I confessed my plan to sneak into Göring's suite and see if I couldn't find the manifest of stolen artwork.

She stared at me as though I'd sprouted a second head. "You'd be taking a huge risk. He's a monster even by Nazi standards. Are you sure about this?"

I didn't have to think twice. "I want to help. I *need* to help. Along with you and Claude and Frank and everyone here at the hotel, I have a brother fighting in this war. I don't want to look back someday and kick myself for sitting on the sidelines."

I didn't mention Jean-Claude. There were some things not even Blanche needed to know.

"I can see your mind's made up," she said with a sigh. "To pull it off, you're going to need to change your looks starting with hiding your biggest giveaway." She reached out and lifted a copper curl from my collar.

Later that evening, I stood in the hallway outside the Imperial Suite wearing a chambermaid's uniform and pushing a catering trolley of champagne and caviar which Göring had ordered from the kitchen. According to Blanche, the Reichsmarschall had taken morphine since being wounded in the First World War and was addicted. Presently, he was undergoing one of his periodic detoxifications, which centered on a regimen of hot baths and mysterious injections administered by a doctor who visited him at the hotel. Whatever was in the shots made him ravenous. Trays with plates of half-eaten black-market oysters, pâtés and foie gras, and dishes of sugared nuts littered the four corners of the suite. If my stomach hadn't been clenched with nerves, I would have been salivating. When my first few knocks went unanswered, I took out Blanche's master key and let myself in.

I parked the cart inside the foyer and looked around, taking a minute to get my bearings. According to Blanche, the sprawling suite, the largest in the hotel, comprised three bedrooms, several salons, a dining room, a boudoir, and maids' quarters. Blanche hadn't exaggerated. The walls really were plastered with priceless paintings, several of which I recognized as Old Masters from my time visiting the Louvre with Gran. Unlike the curated displays I'd seen there, these seemed haphazardly hung, various periods and styles crammed together. It seemed Göring gorged himself on fine art the way he did food. Indiscriminately.

Sloshing water and offkey humming brought me back to myself.

I grabbed the tray with the champagne and caviar and followed the sounds through the lavish boudoir to the en-suite bathroom.

The door stood open. Scented steam wafted out, not No. 5 but a cloying floral fragrance that had me fighting a sneeze. Unlike Mademoiselle Coco's stark white bathroom, here the walls were paneled in ornately carved oak. A crystal chandelier that looked like it belonged in a banquet hall descended from the soaring ceiling. Set beneath it was the biggest, gaudiest bathtub I had ever seen, topped in pink-marble and fitted with gold faucets, custom built to accommodate the Reichmarschall's bulk.

Göring reclined in the sudsy water, hair plastered back from his bloated face, bubbles brushing the tops of his meaty shoulders. He sat up when he saw me, sending suds sloshing onto the monogrammed towels spread over the floor tiles, the bathwater dipping to mid-chest and revealing the start of a substantial mound of stomach. The sight of so much shiny white blubber made me think of a whale in its tank, but I reminded myself that Hitler's right hand wasn't a captive but a predator.

"The caviar and champagne you ordered, *général*," I said in French, keeping my eyes modestly lowered as a young maid would.

He pulled a fleshy, bejeweled hand from the water and waved it toward the gilt-trimmed dressing table. "Set it there."

Heart drumming, I carried the tray over and put it down. Feeling his gaze boring into my back, I left the domed lid on the caviar and lifted the open bottle of champagne from its bucket of shaved ice.

"Shall I pour the champagne, *général*?" I asked, watching him in the fogged mirror.

"First, come here," he said, beckoning me over.

I put the bottle back on ice and walked to the side of the tub, perspiration pooling in my armpits and not only because the room was like a sauna.

He raked his cold, appraising gaze over me, lingering on my bosom, accentuated by the darts sewn into the uniform, a size too small for me but the best Blanche could come up with on such short notice.

"You're pretty little thing. I have seen you before?" he asked, though it didn't sound like a question.

Over the past two years, we had in fact passed each other many times in the hotel's hallways and public rooms, especially the bar when I'd accompanied Mademoiselle Coco. Fortunately, he hadn't been in residence during my modeling the comet dress. Still, I'd been thorough in my disguise. Wearing one of Blanche's wigs, a sleek black chin-length bob, and prosthetic teeth that changed the shape of my mouth, I told myself not even my own mother would know me.

Keeping my gaze lowered, I shook my head. "I am new on staff."

"I never forget a face," he insisted, his porcine one pouring sweat. "What is your name?"

"Françoise," I answered, feeling my knees start to shake.

He reached for my hand, dwarfing it in his wet bearpaw. "You do not speak like a Parisian. Where are you from?"

Ordinarily hotel guests treated the rank-and-file staff as invisible. I hadn't expected him to drill me, which was why I hadn't given much thought to coming up with a cover story. A mistake I wouldn't repeat – assuming I left the suite alive.

"Alsace-Lorraine," I blurted out, remembering Fritz mentioning his mother was from there.

"Tell me, Françoise, do you like pretty dresses?" he asked, playing with my fingers.

"I do," I said, not caring for where this was leading.

He lifted my hand and pressed a sloppy kiss to my palm. "These closets are filled with a king's ransom in minks and sables and silk kimonos and gowns trimmed in jewels," he bragged, "all of which would suit you much better than that dowdy uniform." He slipped his hand up to my forearm and pulled me down to him, his rings biting into my flesh. "Take it off."

Forced to my knees, I fought against crying out. "Please, I'm just a maid."

He brought his face up to mine, and I smelled the stale wine on his breath. "I am prepared to be generous with you, *fräulein*, but first you must be generous with me."

Abruptly he let me go.

I stumbled to my feet and took a shaky step back. "As you wish, *général*. But perhaps you would enjoy a glass of champagne while you er, watch?"

"Pour yourself one as well," he said magnanimously, leaning back with a smile.

I went back to the vanity and crushed two sedatives from my pocket into the bottom of the coupe. To hide the bitter taste, I added a sugar cube, then poured in the champagne.

I carried the glass over and passed it to him.

He took a healthy slug and then gestured toward me with the half-full glass.

Face burning, I undid the top two buttons at my collar.

"*Schön*," he said, taking in my cleavage with an appreciative eye.

"Take another sip, and I will look even better," I quipped, striking a tart tone.

It worked. He swallowed more champagne and leaned back to look at me.

I dropped another button and then another, going slowly to give the drug time to take effect.

He drained his glass and lifted his hairy arm from the bubbles. "Enough of your teasing. Take it all off," he demanded, sounding like a petulant child tired of playing a game.

I slid the dress off my shoulders and over my hips. It landed at my feet, leaving me in my slip and underwear. Face burning, I reached up and pulled the slip over my head, careful not to knock my wig crooked.

Stripped down to my brassiere and panties, I felt panic take over. Why was he still awake? From everything I'd learned from administering medicine to patients at the hospital, the tranquilizer should be taking effect by now. Given his girth and history of morphine use, maybe I'd underestimated his tolerance.

"Allow me to refresh your drink," I said, whisking away his glass.

Hands shaking, I crushed another capsule into his glass when snoring sounded.

I swung back around to the bathtub. Göring's chin rested on his beefy shoulder, his eyes closed, his mouth slack, saliva dribbling out. I could have wept with relief, but I reminded myself I wasn't out of the woods yet.

I poured the drugged champagne down the sink and went over, nudging him so that his head was pillowed on the porcelain. Not that the world needed Hermann Göring in it, but if he drowned under the Ritz roof, the entire staff would answer for it, starting with Claude and Blanche.

I pulled on my clothes and hurried back for the Minox. Retrieving it from the bottom of the catering cart, I began going through rooms, opening drawers and closets, all while praying my sleeping whale wouldn't wake up anytime soon.

314

I found his desk in a side parlor, a gilded French affair that probably went back several centuries. Taking the lockpick from my pocket, I plied the key lock as Rachelle had shown me. Shuffling through papers, I came across several pornographic postcards showing nearly naked women doing disgusting things with dogs, personal correspondence, mainly letters from his wife, and finally the manifest marked "Jeu de Paume." The five-page typed document meticulously cataloged each piece of stolen artwork by date of receipt, painting title, artist, description, lot number, and collection of origin, as well as the date for its train transport to Berlin.

Heart hammering, I laid the document on the green baize desk blotter and photographed it page by page, making sure to advance the dial on the camera after each click. A bead of perspiration rolled off my nose and landed on the last page, making a blot in the ink. *Merde*. Finished, I put it and the other papers back exactly as I'd found them, closed the drawer, and locked it with the dummy key from Blanche.

Out in the main room, I wrapped the Minox in a dinner napkin and put it back in the cart. Stepping out into the hallway, I took a moment to do up my buttons. If anyone saw me, they'd assume champagne and caviar weren't all I'd served Göring. What they wouldn't assume was that I'd been spying on him.

I started to roll the cart to the elevator when I remembered Blanche mentioning Göring kept a stash of morphine tablets, one of several drugs the American was in dire need of. Thinking of all the brave French and British POWs moaning in pain on their cots, I left the cart out in the hallway and went back in. Rushing from room to room, I came across a wingchair flanked by two small side tables, one holding a big crystal bowl filled with sparkling gemstones and the other a twin bowl brimming with capsules. I scooped up a handful of pills and stuffed them in my pocket. Tempted as I was to take more, I stopped, not wanting to press my luck. If Göring noticed the bowl was running lower than usual, hopefully he'd think he'd gone on a binge and blacked out.

Later that evening, I stood from the library table in the presbytery of Saint-Trinité and briefed the other Vengeance members. By the time I set the double-spooled film on the polished tabletop, even Jean-Claude was speechless.

Dr. Jack was the first to recover. "This is wonderful work and beyond brave. We'll take it from here."

Pierre took the film and slipped it in his pocket. "I will pass this onto our man at the SNCF," he said, referring to the *Société nationale des chemins de fer français*, France's national railway service.

Though forced to transport weapons and other supplies for the Wehrmacht, many railway workers were loyal to de Gaulle's Free French and had formed a Resistance group of their own.

"Before I forget, I also took these." I reached into my pocket and brought out Hanna's drawstring pouchette.

Jean-Claude took it from me and poured several morphine capsules into his palm.

Cracking one open, he moistened his index finger and tasted a small amount of the powder, then nodded to Dr. Jack.

Dr. Jack beamed at me. "These are as precious as any painting."

The meeting dispersed. One by one, Vengeance members walked up to me and kissed my cheeks or patted me on the shoulder.

Rémy, father of the tortured Marie, clasped both my hands in his. "*Chére* Apple Pie, you have restored my faith that these Nazi *salauds* will get what is coming to them."

On her way out, Rachelle paused and turned back to me. "That was good work, *shiksa*. I was wrong about you."

Coming from her, it was high praise.

When Père Rafe excused himself as well, it was down to Jean-Claude and me.

Looking out the window, he still hadn't spoken a word to me.

"You're mad at me," I said, breaking the silence between us.

He crossed the carpet and took hold of my upper arms. "Do you realize you could be in rue des Saussaies or avenue Foch now, being tortured like Marie was. For paintings."

"And morphine," I reminded him.

He gave me a light shake and that time I winced.

Pushing up my right sleeve, he took in the bruises on my arm, the largest one the circumference of Göring's thumb.

He blew out a heavy breath. "You are lucky these bruises are all you got. Do not think you are out of danger. If Göring realizes it was you—"

"He won't."

"But if he does …" He left off there, and I understood that he wasn't so much angry as he was afraid. "Promise me you will never risk yourself like this again."

"Françoise the chambermaid is officially retired," I said.

I didn't say anything about Daisy Blakely.

Three days later, French newspapers ran the story of how "terrorists" had planted explosives along a stretch of northbound railway lines to Germany. When the German soldiers accompanying the transport of "liberated artwork" went to unload the cargo from the derailed train, only empty picture frames remained.

Chapter Forty

September 1942

With America's entry into the war, it wasn't long before the Nazis began targeting Allied civilians left in France. Once a week, Bridget and I reported to our local *commissariat de police* where we answered the same silly sounding questions – did we keep a horse, *really?* – and signed our names in the ledger of "enemy aliens." Remembering how Jean-Claude and his family had been made to register, I couldn't shake the foreboding feeling that we expats were all on borrowed time.

Toward the end of September, Dr. Jackson was arrested. Gestapo agents showed up at the hospital and pulled him out of a patient appointment. As it was a Wednesday, I wasn't there, but the staff was still buzzing about the episode when I showed up for my regular Sunday shift. Well-liked and respected, Dr. Jack exuded an aura of invincibility and optimism that buoyed us all even in the lowest times. Seeing Gestapo agents take him away had shattered everyone's fragile sense of safety.

Two weeks later, he was back at the hospital, brushing off the ordeal as if it were little more than a hiccup and recalling the excellent lunch that he and his fellow prisoners had been served at the holding center in Saint-Denis, much better than our hospital food. The real torture, he assured us, a glint in his eye, had been the reams of paperwork the Nazis had made him fill out.

Such were the times we were living in.

That fall, the Nazis put out the lie that German women in America were being interned and brutally mistreated. In retribution, they decreed that any British or American women still in France would be rounded up and interned for the duration of the war.

I thought I'd prepared myself for the knock on my and Bridget's apartment, but when it came, I felt my knees go weak.

I opened the door to two helmet-headed German soldiers and Madame LeBrun with them.

"*Je suis desolée, mademoiselle.* I had no choice but to let them in."

"Don't distress yourself, Madame LeBrun." I looked at the soldiers. "Give me a few minutes to pack a bag."

"*Nein.* You will come with us now."

"Not without a change of clothes, I won't," I insisted, recalling Chanel demanding to bathe before going to see Colonel Speidel about her suite.

Heart pounding, I left them standing out in the hallway and went into the bedroom to pack.

They entered, and I heard them banging around the main room, opening cabinets and drawers though I'm not sure what they hoped to find.

One soldier followed me into the bedroom. For a minute I froze, imagining the worst, but fortunately he seemed more interested in my things than me.

Fuming, I held my tongue as he rummaged through Bridget's and my shared closet and dresser. He grabbed a lacy brassiere and held it up, sending me a leering look. I snatched it away and shoved it into the bag I was packing.

Taking in the two beds and second comb and brush set atop the dresser, he demanded, "Where is the other girl?"

Fortunately, Bridget was working at Maison Chanel. Given Chanel's relationship with von Dincklage, I suspected the Nazis would avoid making any arrests at the boutique.

"No other girl, just me," I answered, schooling my features not to show the fear I felt.

I could see he didn't believe me.

"I did have a roommate, but she left Paris a while ago. Last I heard, she was in the Free Zone."

Still skeptical, he picked up Bridget's brush, bright blonde hair caught in the bristles.

"She left that to cover her share of the rent. The silver backing makes it valuable."

"*Ja*, it does." He shoved it into his pocket.

Not knowing how long I'd be away or where, I slipped on my winter coat and grabbed my overnight bag, purse, and hat. When the soldier guarding me was called into the main room by his fellow, I reached beneath the mattress, took out the necklace with the cyanide capsule, and slipped it over my head.

They hustled me down the stairs and outside to where a bus waited.

Stepping aboard, I saw that the benches were filled with all women, most of them Americans. Several I knew by face if not name. Scanning the half-full seats, I confirmed Bridget wasn't on the bus. Relieved, I took a seat toward the back, wanting to be as far from the soldiers as possible.

The bus trundled along the Paris streets, stopping at each residence where an Allied woman was known to live. Leaving the rest of us under guard, the same two soldiers who had arrested me would go inside and bring the unlucky woman out. Sometimes they would return grim-faced and empty-handed, shaking their heads at the driver and muttering among themselves in German. In those instances, we all sent up a loud cheer, refusing to be silenced even when one of the soldiers took out his revolver and fired onto the truck roof.

By the time we turned onto rue de l'Odéon, we were nearly full up. When our bus pulled up at Shakespeare and Company, my heart dropped. The bookstore's glass storefront was stripped bare. Even the sign was blacked out.

Once again, the two soldiers climbed out and walked up to the entrance. The door must have been left unlocked. When one soldier tested the knob, it swung open. They disappeared inside. Digging my nails into my palms, I kept my eyes peeled, hoping Miss Beach had got away.

Time crawled by. I glanced at my wristwatch. Fifteen minutes had passed but it felt like hours. Finally, the soldiers emerged with Miss Beach between them, hat askew, wearing a velvet Spanish-style cloak and carrying a purse in one hand and an overnight case in the other. How small and fragile she appeared in contrast to the Nazi brutes bracketing her, her face thinner and more lined than I remembered it from the times I'd dropped by with Fritz, and yet she held her head high and her back straight.

She stepped onto the bus, giving the driver, a Frenchman, a piece of her mind and then continued down the aisle between seats, pausing to greet a friend or offer words of encouragement to a frightened, tear-stained stranger.

I waited for her to reach my row in the back, and then I hailed her. "Miss Beach ... Sylvia."

I shifted over to make room, and she slipped in beside me, setting her case on her lap. "Lovely to see you again, m' dear, despite the deplorable circumstances."

I waited until the bus started up, trusting the rumbling engine to cover our conversation. "I can't believe the Germans looted your shop, though I suppose at this point nothing they do should surprise any of us."

She answered my sympathy with a chuckle, and for a minute, I wondered if nerves had gotten the better of her.

Bending her head to my ear, she confided, "The Boche haven't gotten their grimy mitts on so much as a single book or stick of furniture, that I promise you."

She went on to recount how a few weeks earlier a German officer had spotted her last copy of Mr. Joyce's *Finnegan's Wake* in the bookshop window and demanded to buy it. When she refused, he'd stomped off swearing he would be back to confiscate it and the rest of her stock.

"It's my last copy, and you're not having it," she'd told him, and I was reminded of the copy of *My Ántonia* Fritz had asked her to order but which inexplicably had never come in.

"All my French friends rushed over to help. In two hours, not only *Finnegan's Wake* but all the books disappeared. We piled them into clothes baskets and carried them up the stairs to an empty apartment. I even had the housepainters paint over the sign and the carpenters take down the shelves!"

She acted as if our being rounded up was a joke, which helped me feel slightly more at ease, though thinking of the poor souls taken to the Vél d'Hiv in July, I kept my guard up.

Inside the bus, we couldn't see where we were going. Demands to be told our destination were met with tight-lipped silence. More than any taunts or brutishness, the soldiers' refusal to answer unnerved me. I imagined being sent off to a labor camp or factory in Germany, never to see my family again. Or Jean-Claude. All this time, I had worried about him being deported, and now it seemed I was the one of us on track to be sent away. I wondered how long it would take for him and the other Vengeance members to hear I'd been arrested. And Fritz. I could have used his help, but he still wasn't back in Paris.

They took us to the botanical gardens, le Jardin d'Acclimatation. From bicycling back and forth between Paris and the American, I knew we were near Neilly-sur-Seine. Being close to the hospital made me feel a bit better. When I didn't show up for my Sunday shift, my absence would be noted. Dr. Jack would get word to the other Vengeance members, including Jean-Claude.

Other buses drew up into the lot as well and more women piled off, some dazed, others irate, still others bored or affecting boredom. In such fraught situations, everyone finds their own way of coping. Mine was to be a silent observer, opening my eyes and ears to all that was going on around me and making a mental map of the area.

Once the vehicles were emptied, we were lined up and led into a former zoo building. Almost immediately, we dubbed it the monkey house. Though any animals were long gone, the stench of urine and feces lingered. Several cutups in our group amused us all by making apelike noises and gestures, drawing the soldiers' stern admonitions to be silent.

Eventually, we were herded into a large room filled with about two hundred cots and each assigned a bed and given a blanket and thin pillow. I stuck close to Miss Beach in the hope that we would be assigned adjacent cots, which we were. At that point, no one spoke beyond a few necessary words, likely because there wasn't anything to say. We'd been brought here as prisoners, "enemy aliens," and there was nothing to do but try and make the best of it. For the next half hour or so, the room filled with the sounds of settling in – the opening and closing of suitcases, the squeak of mattress springs, the plumping of pillows.

Later, before lights out, I spotted Fern Bedaux holding court from her cot, sharing a box of black-market chocolates with several other women. Seeing her, my heart dropped. If the wife of a French collaborationist millionaire who'd had Herman Göring as a dinner guest couldn't slip the noose, what hope did the rest of us have?

The first night was the worst. Between the water dripping down on us from the roof and the German guards in the gallery above shining their flashlights in our faces, I didn't sleep. I doubt anyone did. The next day, we were all bleary-eyed and dragging. Even Fern lacked her usual élan.

The dullness of our days left plenty of time for thinking. When I had first met Sylvia, she'd mentioned that the American expat community in Paris was close-knit. I hadn't given the remark much thought at the time. I did now, especially as we were literally living on top of each other.

Once a day, we were allowed to walk in the fenced outdoors. Being penned like a zoo animal wasn't an experience I wished to ever repeat, but at least it was a reprieve from the unpleasant odors.

On my second day there, I spotted a striking blonde standing off to herself smoking a cigarette. Not only striking in looks but strikingly familiar. The last time I had seen her, she had been larger than life, projected onto a movie theater screen. Drue Leyton, from the popular *Charlie Chan* detective films, it had to be!

When I had first arrived in Paris, she'd been broadcasting for the

Voice of America, quite a departure from her glamorous Hollywood days. Sometimes she had brought guests on her program. One of her most interesting celebrity interviews was with Josephine Baker. What a small world Paris was. The Occupation had made it even smaller.

I approached, clearing my throat to get her attention.

She looked me over, her dark brown eyes guarded. "Do I know you?"

"No, but I'm a big fan of your films," I gushed albeit in a whisper. "I admire all you've done for France and raising awareness of what's been going on here among the folks back home."

Even before the invasion, Leyton's scathing on-air criticisms of the Nazi regime had earned her a promise of execution announced on Berlin radio.

"Thanks, that means a lot." She darted a look around before continuing with, "These days, I go by my married surname, Tartière. Only Sylvia knows me from before and now you. I'd appreciate it if you'd help me keep it that way."

"Of course. I won't breathe a word," I said, thinking that Sylvia Beach must indeed know every American left in Paris.

Though I never crossed paths with her again, the brief encounter with Drue Leyton breathed new life into me. Though interred, I wasn't alone. Or powerless. I could still be of use to Vengeance even from the inside of a prison. Rather than spend my days wringing my hands, I'd take the opportunity to determine who among my countrywomen could be trusted. Mrs. Bedaux already bore a blackmark for her husband's business dealings with the Nazis. Those more covert in their collaboration would be harder to root out.

Chapter Forty-One

On the morning of the tenth day, the guards got us up earlier than usual and ordered us to dress and gather our things. As soon as breakfast was over, an unappetizing gray gruel that any French cook would have been embarrassed to serve, they marched us outside and loaded us back onto the buses.

Throughout the half-hour drive back through Paris, I sat with my hands clenched, certain the Boches must be deporting us to Germany after all. When I stepped off the truck and saw the imposing façade of the Gare de l'Est train station, I nearly lost my breakfast.

Fortunately, it wasn't as bad as I'd feared. Our captors weren't sending us to Germany but to Vittel in the Vosges mountains in northeastern France. Like Vichy, Vittel had been a spa town patronized for the health benefits of its mineral spring. Now its splendid mountains vistas were viewed through a screen of barbed wire.

Once there, guards marched our group inside the lobby of the Grand Hôtel, one of six hotels used to house non-Jewish prisoners. A small, informal welcoming committee of fellow inmates had gathered to greet us. I was shocked to see Bridget among them.

We rushed into each other's arms, hugging as if we hadn't seen each other in years.

Stepping back, I said, "I told the soldiers you were in the Free Zone. What happened?"

"Sneaky Boche bastards came for me at the boutique while Mademoiselle Coco was having lunch at the Ritz," she told me, cutting a look to the two stone-faced guards posted at the entrance.

My attempts at shushing her drew a sly smile.

"Relax, Daise. Roughing us up wouldn't look good for the cameras."

"What cameras?" I asked, looking around.

She hooked her arm through mine and steered us toward the staircase, the carpet bearing tracks from the crush of German jackboots. "I'll show you around and catch you up."

It was immediately evident that the Nazis meant to put forth Vittel as a model camp. The International Committee of the Red Cross was allowed in to conduct regular inspections, and we prisoners received weekly ICRC care packages. We got to wear our own clothes and keep personal possessions. German documentary filmmakers captured us on camera enjoying outdoor sports including tennis, golf, and swimming. In the evenings, we were encouraged to put on plays, lectures, concerts, and even séances. No matter how politely I was asked, I always declined to be interviewed and held my hands up to my face whenever I felt a camera veer my way. Thinking back to the Pathé newsreels I had once watched, I balked at participating in any Nazi propaganda.

Materially, we were much better off than the average Parisian, but we were still prisoners. I couldn't think of anything beyond getting myself out and back to Paris, and Jean-Claude.

Poor health was by far the best chance for early release, but illness wasn't as easy to fake as one might imagine. Unlike the American

Hospital where a doctor might sign a waiver stating that a patient's tuberculosis made him too ill to work in a German factory, here the two French doctors staffing the clinic, Dr. Jean Levy and Dr. René Pigache, were prisoners themselves. Like the rest of us, they were kept under close watch. Even Miss Beach, who boasted that she had been instrumental in getting the Gestapo to release the British theatrical theorist, Gordon Craig and his family from prison, so far hadn't been able to manage the same for herself.

At the start of my second week in Vittel, a guard informed me I had a visitor. I couldn't think who it could be. Every American and Brit left was either here or at one of the municipal prisons in and around Greater Paris. Other than Jean-Claude, gone to ground to avoid Jewish roundups, I didn't have anyone in France to turn to. Unless Fritz was back. If he was, I had to believe he would do everything in his power to help me.

I made the guard wait while I ran a comb through my hair and refreshed my lipstick, then followed him out to the visitor's lounge.

Entering, I felt my excitement shrivel. Instead of Fritz, a short, balding man in an expensive suit stood with his back to the door, hands laced at his back. He turned to greet me, and I couldn't have been more shocked.

"Comte de Chambrun?"

"Mademoiselle Blakely, I trust you are not feeling too unwell?" he asked in a solicitous voice, glancing over at the guard.

His question struck me as strange but then so did his being here. What was the son-in-law of Pierre Laval doing in an internment camp for Allied women?

"I'm as well as can be expected under the circumstances. What brings you here, *monsieur le comte*?"

"You do, mademoiselle. I promised Mademoiselle Chanel I would handle your case personally."

"My case?" I echoed, wondering if he was playing with me.

"I have explained your ... medical condition to the authorities—"

"My *medical condition?*"

"Ah *oui*, your medical condition. Once I produced the documents detailing the severity of the ... cancer, the authorities agreed to release you into Mademoiselle Chanel's custody. As soon as the paperwork is signed, I will accompany you back to Paris."

Recovering, I asked, "And my friend, Bridget Ponsby? The British girl from the Chanel boutique," I added when his expression stayed blank. "She's here, too."

I had left Bridget behind once before, at the start of the German invasion when Chanel had insisted on taking me with her to Corbère. Even though it had all worked out, I still felt guilty. I wasn't going to make the same mistake again, not if I could help it.

He shook his head as if I was a spoiled child demanding a second serving of dessert. "Mademoiselle Blakely, it is nothing less than a miracle that I am able to secure your release."

Not about to give up so easily, I lowered my voice and demanded, "How much is it costing Mademoiselle for the forged medical certificate and bribes to get me out?"

He hesitated, then leaned in and whispered the sum into my ear.

My jaw dropped. Considering how I'd left things with Chanel, I was surprised she wasn't paying the Nazis to *keep* me in prison.

Recovering, I said, "I have that much in the Bank of France and more."

Unfortunately, the Nazis had frozen my account as they had done for all Allied expats.

"If you can get my money unfrozen, I'll gladly hand it over to whatever authorities are in charge in exchange for Bridget's release. With a generous commission to yourself, of course," I added, knowing how he and his wife enjoyed the high life.

He hesitated, licking his lips. "I can only promise to try," he finally said. "But you must prepare yourself that what you ask may not be possible."

I felt my lip curl. "You are the son-in-law of Pierre Laval, the second most powerful Frenchman in France, some would say the *most* powerful. For you, there is very little that is not possible."

Two hours later, I was on a train back to Paris, seated in a *première classe* car with Chanel's lawyer. After weeks of living under lock and key, the speed of my release was dizzying, so much so that I had trouble believing I was really free. Officially, I had been released into the comte's custody on the condition that I resume work at Maison Chanel. A part of me wondered whether I had exchanged one jail for another, but for the moment I had bigger worries weighing on me, namely springing Bridget from Vittel.

Before leaving, I had insisted on saying goodbye to her. Amid hugging her and promising to write, I had slipped her a note scribbled on the hotel stationery explaining I was working on getting her released.

I looked over at the comte, his nose buried in an edition of *Le Jour*, an antisemitic rag even before the Nazis had arrived.

"Once you have my money unfrozen, how soon can you get my friend out?" I asked.

He took his time in answering, wetting his index finger and turning the newsprint page. "A month if we are lucky."

"And if we are not lucky?"

He gave the newspaper a shake, rattling wrinkles out of the pages. "This is a delicate matter, mademoiselle. First, we must have your money released. Only then can we proceed with contacting the appropriate authorities. Until then, Mademoiselle Ponsby is not in the worst of places. A former resort makes for a pleasant prison, I imagine."

"It's still a prison," I replied, not bothering to sugarcoat my bitterness. "Consider yourself fortunate that you can only imagine it."

He scowled. "And now, through the kindness and generosity of my client, Mademoiselle Chanel, you are free again. A word of advice, mademoiselle: these are dangerous times. Use your freedom wisely."

Six hours later, our train pulled into Gare de l'Est in Paris. We parted ways outside the station, with me promising to report to Maison Chanel first thing in the morning.

When I got back to my apartment building, Madame LeBrun intercepted me in the front hallway.

"You have a visitor. A gentleman," she said.

My heart stopped. Surely Jean-Claude would have sufficient sense not to show up here. My thoughts again flew to Fritz. Perhaps he was back in Paris after all.

Recovering, I snapped, "Another soldier, perhaps?" It wasn't fair of me, but I still hadn't gotten over that she'd shown the Nazis to my door.

For once, she had the grace to look away. "I put him in the *salon*."

Heart in my throat, I followed her into the parlor.

A man sat on the edge of the threadbare petit point sofa, immaculately dressed, head hung, hat in his lap. Hearing our approach, he looked up, then leaped to his feet.

"Daisy, thank God!"

I blinked; half afraid I might be hallucinating. "Uncle Blake!"

Chapter Forty-Two

I extracted my uncle from Madame LeBrun's parlor and brought him upstairs to my apartment, still a mess from the Nazi soldiers tossing it.

He looked from the overturned lamp back at me. "Your landlady told me you were in prison."

"I was, though in fairness it was converted from a hotel. Mademoiselle Chanel arranged for my release." Too tired to go into the details, I steered him to the sofa. "I'll make us coffee. It's ersatz, and there's no sugar or milk to put in it, but it'll warm us up. In the meantime, why don't you tell me how you got here?"

Moving to the kitchen area, I filled the coffee urn with water from the taps, set it on the hotplate to heat, and took out two brewing bags of the roasted peas that passed for coffee, all while listening in shocked silence as my by-the-book uncle filled me in on how he'd asked Gran for her Irish passport and had it altered with his photo and birthdate. Ireland being a neutral nation in the current war, he'd had next to no trouble coming into France.

A short while later, we sat sipping our coffees, my usually taciturn uncle pouring out his soul. Hattie had left for Paris not long after

Gran got out of the hospital. When the Nazis invaded, she'd stayed, not sure where to go or how to get out.

I thought back to our brief meeting in Gran's hospital room when I had purposefully dismissed the dangers of wartime Paris so as not to worry the family. Had I inadvertently encouraged Hattie to follow in my footsteps?

Feeling guilty, I asked, "Why did she come without you? Did you two have a falling out?"

The question came out harsher than I'd intended. But I'd seen her and my uncle together in New York and my uncle had worn his heart on his sleeve. So had Hattie, or at least she'd seemed to.

His miserable look left me regretting my bluntness. "Nothing like that. But Mother was still getting back on her feet, and Hattie … she wants more from life than she or any other Black performer can hope to have in New York or anywhere else in America, for that matter. Asking her to wait didn't feel fair. When she wrote me saying she'd landed a job in the chorus at Chez Joséphine, I told myself I'd done right to push her to go."

Since the start of the Occupation, foreign-born Blacks living in France had been the first to be interned. Josephine, by then a French citizen, had announced that all live performances would cease at her club until France was free again. But rather than closing and laying off her staff, as Chanel had, she had kept the club going and found her dancers other jobs.

He raked his fingers through his hair. "I pushed her to come here. Hell, I bought her the boat ticket. Paris was supposed to be her shot at having the life she's always dreamed of. Instead, she's in hiding."

I reached over and touched his shoulder. "She can still have that life. You both can."

He exhaled as though he carried the weight of the world. "If we're lucky enough to get out of this, no more beating around the bush. I'm asking her to marry me and that's that."

"You *will* get out of this. For this to work, you have to believe that."

He nodded, gaze dipping to his coffee.

"Do you have a recent picture?" I asked.

Setting the cup aside, he brought out his wallet and took out a photo portrait of Hattie.

"How's her French?" I asked.

"Fine, I guess. Why do you ask?"

"I'm just thinking ... what if she wasn't American? What if she had identification papers saying she was French. Or French North African. Algerian, say? Any of those would keep her clear of the roundups."

He brightened. "These papers, how would we go about getting them?"

"I know someone who might be able to help, but it's going to take money. Mine's still frozen."

"I brought cash. It's sewn inside my clothing," he said, patting his coat pocket.

"Good. Until we figure out a plan, we'll have to keep her hidden. Both of you." I paused. "Where is she now?"

"Holed up in the wine cellar of Chez Joséphine. The staff has been hiding her since things got bad."

I took a moment to think. Josephine was still out of the country touring, but I had a way to reach her, as well as her promise of sanctuary.

Taking advantage of Madame LeBrun's momentary guilty feelings, I arranged with her to have Uncle Blake stay in Monsieur Levy's vacated apartment. I wasn't sure I trusted her, not a hundred percent, but given that she'd already seen Blake, and heard his American accent, I figured the cat was out of the bag. I left him with assurances that I'd be back as soon as I could, stuck on a wide-brimmed hat to hide my hair, and went to find Jean-Claude.

The café on rue Bourdaloue was the likeliest place to start. Rather than head straight there, I took a roundabout route in case I was being followed, making a show of window shopping the department stores on boulevard Haussmann. Circling back to the café, I found Jean-Claude at a table in the back, the newsboy cap drawn low over his brow.

"*Dieu merci*," he said when he saw me, leaping up to pull out my chair.

We took our seats without embracing, never knowing who among us might be an informant. In such desperate, hungry times, a food coupon or loaf of bread could buy a lot of loyalty.

Beneath the table, his hand gripped mine.

"When did you get back?" he asked. "You are all right? They did not …" He looked me over me as if searching for whip marks and missing teeth.

Aching to kiss him, I settled for giving his hand a squeeze. "A few hours ago, and no one laid a finger on me. The Nazis have set up Vittel as a model prison to showcase to the world how compassionate and forward-thinking they are," I said with heavy sarcasm. "The worst torture was having to listen to Fern Bedaux warble out 'Stormy Weather' in the talent show. It's a good thing that woman married money."

We ordered two more glasses of wine, and I filled him in on Uncle Blake and Hattie and the predicament they were in as well as my fledgling plan for getting them out of Paris.

When I'd finished, he said, "It could work. The Resistance has used Josephine's club before. Her manager, Louis, is one of ours. We should speak to him as soon as possible. Tonight, I think."

We let the café clear out, then slipped behind the bar to the stairs leading down to the cellar. Jean-Claude shouldered the door closed and took me in his arms, kissing my eyelids, the tip of my nose and finally my mouth.

Lifting his lips from mine, he sighed. "*Mon Dieu*, I've missed you."

I stroked his cheek, leaner than before I'd been taken. "Good, selfishly I'm glad. I hope you were every bit as miserable without me as I've been without you."

Tempted as we were to pick up where we'd left off our first night together, there wasn't time. Instead, we left and took the tunnel to Montmartre. Jean-Claude led us on a zigzagging course through the sewers, not once stopping to consult the hand drawn map in his pocket.

We came out at Montmartre where a low-slung door was carved out of the side of the butte. Entering through it, we stepped into a wine cellar.

"*Voilà*, Chez Joséphine," Jean-Claude announced.

Since the club wouldn't open for several more hours, we went above where Jean-Claude introduced me to the manager, Louis. He took us to Hattie's hideaway, a storage room leading off from the kitchen. Recognizing me, she threw down the book she was reading and leaped up from her mattress on the floor.

"Blake said you'd know what to do!" she said, throwing her arms around me.

Hoping he was right, I hugged her back, then pulled away, gesturing toward Jean-Claude. "This is Jean-Claude. He knows the Paris tunnels like the back of his hand." Pride had me adding, "He's also a surgeon, a brilliant one."

"I will help in any way I can," he said. "Daisy has come up with a plan to get you and her uncle out of Paris. I think it is a good one. We hope you will think so, too."

Hattie beamed at us. "I'm willing to try almost anything at this point. If I stay cooped up much longer, I'll go Looney Tunes."

I turned to Louis. "Can we draw the blinds and get her above ground for a while?"

"*Bien sûr*," he said.

A short while later, we four sat around one of the club tables sipping glasses of wine and going over my plan, which hinged on Hattie and Blake masquerading as cabaret performers.

Finished, I asked, "Do you think Blake's up for it? He's always been … on the reserved side."

She smiled. "Don't you worry about him. I'll get him up to speed."

Afterwards, we walked through the club, both the front and back of the house, including the backstage lift, choreographing their escape as if it were a play. We settled on a Friday, two weeks away, sufficient time to have Hattie's false papers made and for Louis to promote the event.

It was a bold, brash plan with every opportunity to fail and one big reason to succeed.

My uncle and Hattie were head-over-heels.

Knowing that feeling all too well, I was determined to do everything in my power to give them the chance at the happily ever after I so desperately wanted for myself and Jean-Claude.

Chapter Forty-Three

I finished my first night back in Paris alone in mine and Bridget's bedroom, which felt forlornly quiet and eerily empty. Though I would have much rather stayed with Jean-Claude in his café cellar hideaway, I didn't feel right leaving my uncle on his own. I made us a simple meal on my hotplate, and then helped settle him in Monsieur Levy's old apartment down the hall.

Despite being exhausted, my buzzing brain wouldn't let me sleep. Along with going over the plan to get my uncle and Hattie out of Paris, I kept circling back to my release from Vittel. As much as I hated being beholden to Chanel, her bailing me out presented an opportunity.

The next morning, I bathed and dressed and then took the Métro to the Louvre station from where I walked the few blocks to rue Cambon. Entering the boutique, I presented myself to the *vendeuse* hired to take Bridget's place, who had never heard of me. It took several tries before I persuaded her to pick up the house phone and call up to the atelier.

Stone-faced, Madame Millet met me at the front counter. "Mademoiselle will receive you in her apartment," she said with frosty formality.

I thanked her and made my way to the stairs.

I stepped off onto the second floor and headed for the mirrored double doors to the apartment. Heart hammering, I raised my hand and knocked.

From inside, Chanel called out, "*Entrez.*"

I found her sitting at her rolltop writing desk, fitting I supposed, considering that our falling out had started with a letter. She finished whatever she was scribbling, slipped the fountain pen back in its stand, and slid the stationery sheet in the drawer before turning her chair to face me.

"You will be happy to hear that the Wertheimers have found a way to thwart justice yet again," she announced, regarding me from behind black-framed eyeglasses.

"How's that?" I asked, careful to keep my tone neutral.

Taking off her glasses, she rubbed the bridge of her nose. "Before Pierre and his brother fled France, he transferred their interest in *Parfums Chanel* to Félix Amiot, a French businessman and a Christian. Amiot is under contract to make airplanes for the Germans, which makes him—"

"Untouchable," I finished for her, interrupting as I never would have dared do before.

"*Oui.*"

I waited for her to say more. Instead, she studied me, her steady gaze and uncharacteristic silence more straining than any insults she might have hurled.

I cleared my throat. "Thank you for getting me out of Vittel. Why did you?"

She shrugged. "I made your *grand-mère* a promise."

I shifted my feet. As much as I still despised her amoral opportunism,

I couldn't entirely forget my early days in Paris when she'd taken me under her wing.

"Well, I'm certain she will be very grateful." Pride had me adding, "I have money of my own. It's frozen now, but *monsieur le comte* is working on getting it unfrozen. Once he has, I'll pay you back every franc."

She snorted. "I do not want your francs. I want your loyalty."

"I don't understand," I said, feeling a stab of fear that she'd somehow found out I was working for the Resistance.

"You will resume your apprenticeship until the war is over and you can go back to New York. Or you can go back to Vittel. It is your choice."

Despite her matter-of-fact tone, I didn't miss a certain gleam in her eye. Seeing it gave me the courage to ask, "Why would you even want me back?"

She thought for a moment. "It amuses me to have you here. You add … *un petit quelque chose en plus*."

Like the flourish of silk camellias on a gold lamé gown, I was "a little something extra." Something to light up the atelier during the dreary Occupation years.

Whether a compliment or an insult, her answer struck me as at least honest. Even so, the younger version of me, the Daisy who'd first come to Paris, very well might have marched back to prison rather than humble herself to accept. But I'd done a great deal of growing up over the past four years. Too many people were counting on me, my uncle and Hattie among them, to let pride stand in the way.

I began peeling off my gloves. "Where would you like me to start?"

* * *

In early November, American and British forces landed in French

North Africa, opening a new front against the Axis powers and clearing a path for an Allied invasion of southern Europe. Finally, the Nazis were on the defensive. Three days later, 200,000 Wehrmacht troops marched into Vichy and took over the government. The so-called Free Zone was no more.

Practically, that meant no more smuggled letters home to Gran and the family, not even to let them know Uncle Blake had made it to Paris safely. As much as I ached to ease their minds with a phone call, knowing that Helga the Nazi switchboard operator at the Ritz listened in on every conversation, I didn't dare risk it.

Amid everything, Bridget came back from Vittel. One day she simply showed up at the apartment. René de Chambrun must have come through more quickly than I had dared hope. Wondering what his cut was, I made a mental note to check my bank balance once Blake and Hattie were safely away. From Blake I had learned that *Life* magazine had included de Chambrun in its blacklist of French collaborators. I wondered if Chanel knew and whether she worried that her associations with collaborationists and Nazis might blow back on her after the war. Once I would have asked her outright, warned her, even.

But grateful as I was for her getting me out of Vittel, I couldn't forget, or forgive, her willingness to use the Wertheimers Jewishness as a weapon. Nor, I suspected, could she set aside what she saw as my disloyalty. There were no more invitations to drinks at the Ritz or cozy after-hours chats in her apartment. I was, after all this time, just another of her *filles* albeit one with a rich grandmother.

The night of Blake and Hattie's escape arrived. I had come home from the Ritz where I had picked up Hattie's – now Delphine's – forged papers from Frank. Bridget wasn't at the apartment, which was just as well. She already knew something was up, and that getting Blake and his girlfriend out of Paris was part of it. With the three of us sharing a bathroom, I couldn't very well keep her in the dark entirely, but the fewer details she knew the safer she'd be if the plan went sideways.

Blake was already at Chez Joséphine getting ready for the big night ahead. I used the time by myself to prepare physically as well as mentally. Unlike my escapade with Göring, I didn't have to pretend to be anyone other than myself. I made up my face and pinned up the front of my hair in the victory rolls popularized by Hollywood actress, Betty Grable, then slipped on my Chanel little black dress and Bridget's black velvet pelisse. Satisfied I looked the part of an American heiress out for a night on the town, I was almost out the door when I remembered and retraced my steps to the bedroom. I retrieved Rachelle's necklace with the cyanide capsule from under my mattress and put it on, concealing it beneath my clothing.

I was on my way out the door when Bridget walked in, her eye makeup smeared and her hair a rat's nest of tangles.

Taking one look at her, I said, "Bridge, what's wrong?"

She shook her head. "I'm only tired. Sick and tired of this bloody war."

"Mademoiselle Chanel won't take you back?" I asked.

She hesitated, and then shook her head. "She says she can't afford to pay a second *vendeuse* with business at the boutique being so slow these days."

"I'm sorry. You'll find something soon and even if you don't …" Knowing how touchy she could be about money, I stopped there and settled for a quick hug.

She pulled back, giving me the oncever. "You're so dressed up."

Reading her hurt look, I felt like the worst friend in the world, ostensibly going off to kick up my heels and leaving her miserable and alone. If only I could confide in her like I used to, what a weight off that would be.

Instead, I said, "I borrowed your pelisse. I hope that's okay."

She shrugged. "Always did look better on you than me."

There was an awkward pause, with her no doubt wondering why I didn't invite her along.

"Well, see you later," I said, feeling like a heel.

I hated brushing her off, but I had to get myself to the club and in my seat before the curtain went up.

On my way out, she caught my arm.

"Don't go out tonight, Daise. I've only just got back. Let's stay in and be cozy. We can drink tea and eat Bovril on crackers and gossip like we used to. Those were good times, weren't they?"

"The best," I assured her. "But I have … people waiting for me."

Her hand fell away, her eyes suspiciously bright.

I would have given an eyetooth to be able to tell her the truth but doing so would endanger her, too. I promised myself I'd come clean just as soon as Blake and Hattie were safely out of Paris. Until then, the less she knew, the safer we'd all be.

"We can stay in tomorrow night and play cards and listen to the radio, how's that sound?" I said, imagining us hugging things out and maybe having a good laugh, too.

She gave me a tight smile. "Peachy."

Chapter Forty-Four

The atmosphere at Chez Joséphine was more subdued than when I'd visited with Bridget before the war, the tables only half-full, mostly with German soldiers. Without Josephine, the place felt like a glittering but hollow shell.

Tonight was to be the first cabaret performance since the invasion. Her club manager, Louis, had put out the word that Chez Joséphine was bringing back music for one night only in honor of a very special guest performer.

I found Jean-Claude nursing a beer at a table in the back. Despite the eyeglasses and false mustache, borrowed from Blanche's theatrical stockpile, I spotted him straightaway.

I slipped into the empty seat beside him. "I feel like the entire Wehrmacht is here," I said under my breath.

Beneath the table, he took my hand. "Sometimes hiding in plain sight is the best way."

I bit my bottom lip, then remembered I was wearing lipstick, red no less. "Let's hope this is one of those times."

He laced his fingers through mine. "*Bon courage*. It is a good plan. Trust it."

He was right. It was a good plan, but like any clandestine mission, it was far from foolproof. I wasn't worried about Hattie. She *was* a cabaret performer. Uncle Blake was my concern. A born introvert, he had shunned the spotlight all his life. When push came to shove, could he really carry off all we were asking of him?

A drumroll from the orchestra pit brought everyone's attention to the stage where the velvet curtains parted.

Louis, dressed in a top hat and tailcoat, walked up to the microphone. *"Mesdames et Messieurs, je vous présente La Belle d'Algérie, le toast de Montmartre, Mademoiselle Delphine du Lac."*

The orchestra struck up a bluesy beat and the houselights dimmed. The spotlight homed in on a slender figure perched atop a tree branch. Hattie as Delphine wore a skimpy bra top, heavy necklaces, and a girdle of faux bananas, a version of the costume that had catapulted Josephine to stardom. Judging from the *ooh la las* echoing through the audience, the act hadn't gotten old.

Uncle Blake, aka Bastien St. Cloud, strode out onstage in a safari suit and pith helmet, netting covering his face. He gave an elaborate yawn, took off the hat, and sank down onto a bed of palm fronds to sleep.

So far, so good.

The music picked up, my heart rate with it. Hattie/Delphine climbed down and sprang onstage. She nudged the sleeping explorer awake, pulled him to his feet and danced around him, shimmying her shoulders, thrusting her hips, and shaking her buttocks like Josephine did in her *"danse sauvage."*

The audience, especially the Germans, roared.

Circling to the explorer's front, she ripped off one shirt sleeve, then the other, the tearaway seams giving way. Looking over her shoulder at the audience, she gave an exaggerated wink and then ripped off his shirtfront, showing off a buff, bare chest and trim waist.

Uncle Blake?

The pants were the last to go, leaving him in tight shorts like a boxer would wear.

Equal parts impressed and mortified, I glanced over to Jean-Claude for his reaction, but his expression stayed neutral. Then again, it wasn't his uncle stripped down to his skivvies.

They segued into a kicky dance number, Charleston moves interspersed with swing steps, their bodies moving in perfect time to the music and each other. For the grand finale, dramatic drumbeats brought them backing apart and backing away from each other until they stood at opposite ends of the stage. All at once, Hattie ran toward Blake at full tilt. Sensing what was coming, I tensed, steeling myself for him to miss.

Instead, he caught her by the waist and lifted her high in the air, the toes of her right foot resting on his chest, her other leg extended like a ballerina's.

The audience stood, clapping ferociously.

Holding hands, the duo bowed as coins and flowers pelted the stage. Shouts for an encore came in French, German and English.

They took a final bow and exited stage left.

A magician came onstage next. Jean-Claude and I got up and headed for a side door that led to the service entrance at the back of the club. We'd just stepped outside when a truck barreled over the cobbles toward us, Pierre at the wheel. Over the running engine Jean-Claude rapped on the club door. Dressed in street clothes, Hattie and Blake poked their heads out.

"Your carriage awaits," I whispered.

We put the two of them in the back of the truck, covered them with a tarp, and squeezed into the front seat with Pierre.

Sitting between Pierre and Jean-Claude, I spent the half-hour drive to the train station nibbling my nails. By the time we pulled up outside Gare Montparnasse, I vaulted out of the seat like a Jack-in-the-box.

After checking for German patrols, we opened the truck back and helped Hattie and Blake out. Pierre drove off, and Jean-Claude and I walked them inside the station.

"Almost to the home stretch," I whispered to my uncle.

We descended to the ticket hall. Jean-Claude reached into his pocket and pulled out an envelope with their train tickets, and we passed through the turnstiles to the passenger platforms.

Two patrolling German soldiers approached and demanded to see our papers. I held my breath as Hattie handed over her forged documents, and then Blake.

The one soldier studied her open passport. Looking at the photograph on the document and then back at her, he broke into a smile. "The show, we wanted to go, but we were on duty."

The second soldier spoke up. "May we have your autograph, Fräulein du Lac?"

"Why, of course, boys. Where would you like it?"

Pen and paper were produced, and she signed using one soldier's back as a surface.

The two Germans walked off, and we let out a collective breath.

Turning to Hattie, I said, "You're a born star." I looked at Uncle Blake. "And you, I've never seen you so much as twostep. I'm impressed."

"I had a top-notch teacher." He sent a warm look to Hattie, who smiled back.

She didn't know it yet, but he'd be proposing once they reached Josephine's estate in Dordogne. It went to show that war tore people apart, but it brought them together, too. If not for Hattie striking off for France and being in danger of internment, Uncle Blake almost certainly would have stayed in New York carrying on with his staid, cautious life. Seeing them together gave me hope that Jean-Claude and I had a similar happy future in store.

The train rumbled into the station.

Waiting for the passengers to step off, Hattie asked, "Sure you won't come with us to Les Millandes?"

"Thanks, but we're needed here," I said and left it at that.

There would be plenty of time for war stories in the years ahead. For the moment, keeping my uncle and the rest of the family in the dark about my involvement with the Resistance was the kindest thing I could do for them.

I watched them disappear into the train car, my emotions a mix of sadness and relief. Who knew when we'd see each other again? Probably not until the war was over. Since the Allied invasion of North Africa, most *résistants* including Dr. Jack talked as if an Allied invasion would happen at any time. Hopefully, they were right, and soon we could all go back to our normal lives. After living so intensely, I wasn't sure I remembered what normal felt like.

With almost an hour until curfew, Jean-Claude and I took the Métro back to Montmartre. We would return to the club and follow the tunnels back to his hideaway under the café on rue Bourdaloue. With Blake and Hattie on their way to safety, there was no longer any need to postpone our reunion.

When our Métro train stopped at Abbesses station, two Gestapo agents waited on the platform, sticking out like sore thumbs in their fedoras and black leather trench coats, one man wearing an eyepatch. More German soldiers stood sentry at the turnstiles, cutting us off from the street.

Jean-Claude pulled on the brim of his hat and sank lower in his seat. "We can get off at the next station," he whispered.

Two armed soldiers boarded the adjacent train car. Walking along the aisle between seats, they stopped at each row, peering into passengers' faces and checking papers. It was only a matter of time before they came to us.

Mouth dry, I looked over at Jean-Claude. He took my hand, and we leaped up, bolting for the doors.

We stepped off onto the platform, the car doors smacking closed behind us.

The agent with the eyepatch nudged his comrade and both men stared straight at us.

Jean-Claude tightened his hold on my hand. "Run!"

We tore off toward the platform edge, the Nazis in pursuit.

"*Halte an!*"

A shot rang out. Jean-Claude stumbled, his grip slackening. Looking down, I saw the blood on his pants leg and swallowed a scream.

"*Vas!*" He threw me in front of him.

At first, I thought he meant for us to jump onto the tracks, then I spotted the ladder. I climbed down, and he followed, dragging his hurt leg.

An oncoming train gave us cover. Jean-Claude shoved me under the lip of the platform and covered me with his body. I closed my eyes, prepared for us to be crushed like insects. Instead, the train barreled over, the jarring vibrations pummeling my body, the deafening noise making my ears ring.

Afterwards, we made our way single file through the two-way train tunnel, Jean-Claude limping ahead.

Pulling back from me, he let out a breath. "If another train comes, you know where to go. And watch out for the third rail."

Shaken, I managed to nod.

We continued following the tracks, sloshing through garbage and decaying animals and foul, ankle-deep water.

Passing through the tiled tunnel arch, he pulled the handle to a side door and drew me in with him.

Inside, he took the flashlight from his pocket and switched it on. We were no longer in the station but in a much older-looking tunnel, the walls carved from limestone and trickling moisture.

We came to the top of steep stairs, the circular stone steps wide enough for us to go down together. I wrapped my arm around his waist, feeling sweat soaking through his wool jacket.

"I am slowing you down. Go on without me. You must," he insisted.

"Fat chance."

I wrapped my arm around his waist, and we started down, descending into chilly, loamy air. More than once, we looked over our shoulders, expecting to see Gestapo agents bearing down on us.

Midway down, he motioned for me to stop, the sweat streaming his face causing the fake mustache to droop. "I will meet you at the bottom."

"Not on your life." *Or mine*, I silently added, knowing better than to believe him.

I slipped off his glasses, and we continued down, me softly counting out each step.

One hundred and thirty-one steps later, we reached the bottom. Jean-Claude shone his flashlight around. We were in a grotto, with a decently high ceiling and nubby stones for walls. A conical tower took up a quarter of the space. As my eyes adjusted to the near darkness, a chill swept through me.

We stood inside a mass grave.

The walls weren't made of quarried stone but of human skeletons. Skulls perched atop stacks of femurs and tibia bones, with Christian crosses set in the center. A bone archway led to an adjoining gallery where yet more remains were arranged in a fanciful fashion. Even the "tower" was composed of bones.

Mouth dry, I whispered, "What is this place?"

"The Catacombs," Jean-Claude answered, yanking off his mustache and stuffing it into his pocket. "Built in the second part of the eighteenth century to house the human remains overflowing the city's cemeteries."

I had heard of the Catacombs – everyone in Paris knew about them, including the Germans – but I had never imagined them quite like … *this*.

"The tunnels run one hundred fifty miles beneath the city," Jean-Claude said, still catching his breath. "Entrances are hidden in the basements and cellars of schools, hospitals, cafés, church crypts, sewers, even the Eiffel Tower."

"Don't forget Métro tunnels," I said.

I leaned him against the wall, took off my Chanel silk scarf, and fumbled in my evening bag for a pen.

Watching me, it didn't take him long to guess what I was trying to do. "Have you ever applied a tourniquet before?"

Fishing out the fountain pen, I shook my head. "No, but fortunately I know a doctor who can talk me through it."

He shone the flashlight on the area. "You want to place it above the joint."

I knelt at his feet. Sticky blood ran to his ankle, the metallic smell filling my nostrils. Fortunately volunteering at the American had cured me of my squeamishness. I lifted his pants leg to look at the wound. As best I could tell, the bullet had struck the crease of the knee and lodged there. I knotted the pen on the outside of the material to create tension, and then slowly twisted it, tightening the cinch.

I tied off the knot and stood. "What now?"

"We wait," he said. "If we are lucky, they have decided I am not worth the trouble and have given up."

I didn't ask what would happen if we weren't lucky.

Thinking back to our near capture at the station, I said, "They weren't just checking papers; they were looking for us. Do you think someone tipped them off?"

"It is possible," he admitted.

My mind raced through the Vengeance members I had met, asking who might be an informer. Surely not Rémy whose daughter had been scarred by torture or Pierre, who had repeatedly risked his life to deliver contraband food, medical supplies and later, explosives. Rachelle would swallow a sea of cyanide capsules before she let a single name slip, certainly not her own brother's. The priest, perhaps? Père Rafe hadn't been seen in several weeks, though we hadn't heard he'd been picked up by the Gestapo.

"Will we have to spend the night?" I asked, dreading his answer and not only because our haven was a cold, dark crypt.

From volunteering at the hospital, I knew that a tourniquet was meant as a temporary triage. After two hours, nerve damage could set in. Mind racing, I ran through the possibilities. I could leave Jean-Claude here, take the flashlight and make my way out to bring back Dr. Jack. If need be, he could remove the bullet right here.

Propping a shoulder against the wall, he shrugged. "As a boy, I once spent a night down here on a dare."

"Hopefully you brought a blanket." I rubbed my upper arms, wishing I'd worn something warmer than Bridgette's pelisse.

He wrapped his free arm around me and sighed. "Always so brave, my Daisy. You should not have to be."

Voices in German brought us breaking apart. Jean-Claude killed the flashlight.

"*Vas!*" He dug into his pocket and pressed a wilted square of folded paper into my palm.

His map of the underground.

He tried handing me the flashlight as well but instead of taking it, I wrapped my arm around him. "We'll hide," I whispered.

We ducked behind the bone tower, flattening our backs against it. I slipped my hand in his.

He squeezed it. "*Je t'aime*," he whispered, so softly I almost didn't hear him.

I swallowed against my throat's cinching and promised myself I wouldn't cry.

Jackboots struck the stone steps, the same ones that moments ago I'd counted as we descended. Heart hammering, I silently counted them again now. With every ringing footfall, I felt my hold on Jean-Claude, and the hope of our happy someday together, slipping farther away.

They reached the bottom in a fraction of the time it had taken us. Someone had left an old kerosene lantern hanging on a hook. I had noticed it when we had first entered. One of the Germans must have spotted it, too. I heard the scratching of a match being struck, and then light streaked through the chamber.

One of them called out, "We know you are here. Surrender and it will go easier for you."

They jangled the lantern, casting macabre shadows on the bone walls.

Jean-Claude shoved the flashlight at me.

I grabbed his sleeve, but he threw me off and limped out into the open, hands in the air.

The agent with the eyepatch grabbed him by the collar and smashed his face into the wall, then patted him down for weapons. The other grabbed a hank of his hair and lifted his bloodied face to the light.

"*Jude*," he smirked.

He drove his boot into Jean-Claude's wounded leg, sending him folding to the rough floor.

I shoved a fist into my mouth to keep from screaming.

"Where is the woman?" the second soldier demanded in his ugly, guttural French.

Jean-Claude shook his head. "No woman, only me."

"There *was* a woman," the first agent insisted, then followed with another vicious kick to the ribs.

Drawn onto his side, Jean-Claude ground out, "Search if you like. You would not be the first to lose their way in these tunnels and never come out again."

That seemed to give them pause. The one-eyed agent said something to his fellow in German. Silent tears streaming my cheeks, I watched them haul Jean-Claude to his feet and drag him up the steps and into the darkness.

Chapter Forty-Five

Even with the flashlight and map, it took me a while to find my way back above ground. Once I did, I walked the streets, too reckless in my grief to care about the curfew. A part of me wanted to get caught. I had just hidden in the shadows while the man I loved was brutally beaten and borne away. As cowardice went, it didn't get any yellower.

Less than a block from Madame LeBrun's on rue Saint-Lazare, a patrolling German soldier stepped into my path.

"Heil Hitler."

"Heil Hitler," a familiar voice echoed.

I turned to see Fritz approaching. Relief rushed me. I hadn't heard he was back in Paris. He must have been waiting for me outside Madame LeBrun's.

He reached us, and more odious salutes were traded.

Fritz glanced at me. "I see you've met my secretary. I sent her on an errand, and the foolish woman forgot her pass. How many times must I tell you, *fräulein*, keep your pass in your handbag," he said, sounding stern.

The sentry scrutinized me, but thankfully it was dark. Too dark to see Jean-Claude's blood on my black dress.

I turned to Fritz and struck a smile. "Really, darling, is a secretary *all* I am to you?"

I caught the guard's smirk. "I see how it is." He looked from Fritz to me. "You were fortunate tonight, *fräulein*. Next time, do not forget your pass."

"I won't," I promised.

He waved me on.

Trembling, I turned back to Fritz.

He bent his head to my ear. "They are watching. Take my arm and walk with me but not too fast."

I slipped my arm through his, and we took the block back to Madame LeBrun's at a stroll.

"I didn't know you were back in Paris," I said.

"I got in this morning." He turned to face me. "What were you doing out after curfew?" Though his voice was mild, I detected a note of jealousy.

"I lost track of the time."

The lame excuse earned me a look. I was going to have to do a lot better.

I paused, weighing how much to say. "A friend was arrested tonight for violating the curfew." The truth but not the whole of it, just as Rachelle had taught me.

He studied me. "Does this friend have a name?"

I hesitated. Did I dare? As far as I knew, Jean-Claude hadn't been flagged as a member of the Resistance. By then, it was enough of a crime to be a Jew in hiding.

"Jean-Claude Jacob. He's a surgical resident at the American Hospital, or at least he was."

"Jewish?"

"Yes. Could you find out where they've taken him?"

He eyed me. "If I did, what would you do with the information?"

I didn't falter. "I would tell his family." Another half-truth.

"I will see what I can find out," he said.

"Thank you," I said, that time sincerely.

We came up to the apartment house, and he walked me to the front steps. "This friend, you were with him when he was taken?"

I resisted the impulse to look away. Liars looked away. Honest people looked you in the eye.

"We went to a cabaret in Montmartre."

"Now that I am back, perhaps you will permit me to take you there sometime?"

Kicking up my heels was the last thing on my mind, but with Jean-Claude arrested, I needed Fritz in my corner more than ever.

"That would be nice," I said. "Thanks for coming to my rescue."

I turned to go inside, but he touched my sleeve.

"I am sorry about your friend."

"So am I." I headed up the steps, haltingly as if my legs were made of lead.

Feeling his gaze on my back, I unlocked the door and slipped inside.

Entering the apartment, I felt as if lifetimes had gone by since I'd left instead of only hours. In the space of an evening, I'd lost Jean-Claude and regained Fritz. My emotions were a muddle of fear and fury and fledgling hope. With Fritz back in Paris and in my corner, maybe Jean-Claude could be saved.

The main room was pitch dark, which struck me as off. Ordinarily when Bridget or I went out on our own, the other made sure to leave the kitchen light on. I pulled the lamp chain, turned on the taps, and drew myself a glass of water. Standing at the sink, I gulped it down it, wondering how much to tell Bridget. The blood on my dress would be hard to explain away.

I found her in bed, the covers pulled up to her chin.

Seeing me on the threshold, she screamed and bolted upright.

I hurried over. "Bridge, it's me."

Switching on the bedside lamp, I saw that her eyes were red, the skin beneath puffy and smudged.

She raked a trembling hand through her hair, which she hadn't bothered to brush from earlier. "You gave me a start." Her gaze went over me. "You look a fright. Is everything all right?"

I hesitated, then shook my head. For all I knew, rooming with me might be putting her in danger. If so, she had a right to know.

"The Gestapo arrested Jean-Claude."

Saying it aloud made it *real*. I felt splashes on my cheeks and realized I had started crying.

She moved over to make room for me on the mattress. "I'm so sorry, Daise."

I squeezed in beside her, and she wrapped her arms around me.

Head on her shoulder, I said, "Two agents were waiting at the Abbesses station. It's like they knew we'd be there."

She stiffened. "Why would you say a thing like that?"

I paused, my inner voice giving off a murmur of misgiving. "When we stepped off the train, one pointed right at Jean-Claude. We tried outrunning them, but Jean-Claude was shot in the leg, so we hid in the tunnels, but they found us. Oh, Bridget, he gave himself up to save me. If he's deported to Germany, I don't know how I'll ever live with myself."

If I hadn't brought Jean-Claude in to help me get Blake and Hattie out of Paris, he would still be here, in hiding but free.

"It's not your fault," she said, rocking me like I was a little child.

I lifted my head from her shoulder and sat up, the knot in my gut refusing to let go. "Where were you off to this afternoon? You never said."

Without the boutique to go to, I was reasonably sure she'd had nowhere to be.

She looked down at her hands, several of the pretty oval nails bitten off. "I went for a walk to clear my head."

Bridget never went for walks for the sake of walking, certainly not once the weather turned chilly.

I slipped off the side of the mattress and stood. "Where to?"

"I dunno, I don't remember. Why are you ... *interrogating* me?" she snapped, her voice cracking on the word.

It wasn't like Bridget to be evasive. Earlier I'd wondered about a possible informer. It struck me that I might have the culprit in front of me.

I grabbed her by the elbows and hauled her off the bed. "Someone tipped off the Boches that we'd be in Montmartre. It was you, wasn't it?" I gave her a shake.

Anguished eyes met mine through a waterfall of tears. "I tried to hold out. I meant to. I did, for a while."

"Tell me *everything*." When she didn't answer right away, I shook her again.

"After you left for work this morning, two men in black leather trench coats and fedoras came for me. They put me in the back of their Mercedes and drove me to their headquarters on avenue Foch."

I knew what went on at 82–84 avenue Foch. The stately manse requisitioned by the *Sicherheitsdienst*, the Gestapo's counter-intelligence branch, was one of several torture centers scattered throughout the city. Most civilians who entered never came out again. Neighbors reported being awakened by screams in the night.

"They took me to an office on the fourth floor, cuffed me to the chair and then an agent started firing off questions."

"What kinds of questions?" I demanded.

"Mostly about … you. Your comings and goings. Was I aware of you harboring any enemies of the Reich? Had I seen any suspicious messages passed on? Did you … associate with any Jews?"

Heart drumming, I demanded, "And what did you say?"

"I played dumb, swore that we were roommates, not friends, and that I mostly saw you coming and going. After about an hour, they stopped asking nicely. They slapped me around a bit and then took me up to the sixth floor where they keep prisoners. There was a woman inside one of the cells, maybe our age, it was hard to tell. She was chained to a big iron ring in the wall. They tore open her blouse and showed me what they do to girls like me, girls who don't talk."

By then, her eyes and nose were streaming. A better friend would have hugged her and then found her a hankie, but I wasn't a friend at that moment. I was an operative for the Resistance. Beyond all, I was a woman in love.

Shoulders shuddering, she shook her head. "I had to give them someone. It was either you or—"

"Jean-Claude."

A miserable nod answered. "I overheard you and your uncle talking about getting him and his girl out of Paris, and that your plan had to do with putting on a show at Chez Joséphine. The advert posters are in all the Métro stops, so I knew it was tonight. It was an easy bet that Jean-Claude would be there, too."

Until then, I thought I'd done a pretty good job of covering my tracks.

"Why's that?" I demanded. "You haven't seen him around since the night he stayed over."

She wiped her nose on the sleeve of her pajama top. "When you didn't come home from your date with the Boche, I knew you too well to believe you'd sleep with him out of the blue after all this time. Jean-Claude's a different story. You've been head-over-feet for him since you two first met. I figured he was still in the picture."

I stared at her. My best friend, or so I'd believed. Now I couldn't stand the sight of her.

I backed away to my bed, tore off the blanket, and headed into the living room.

She followed me out. "What are you doing?"

I sat down on the sofa and pulled the blanket over me. "What does it look like?"

She stood over me, eyes swimming. "Daisy, please, you're my best friend."

The last time I'd spent the night on the couch, I'd had Jean-Claude with me, his arms anchoring me to him, his lips in my hair. Sick with imagining what the Nazis might be doing to him, I could barely bring myself to look at her.

Arrowing my gaze on her, I said, "As soon as the curfew is up, I'll be going out. If you're still here when I get back, I'll turn you over to the Resistance myself."

Chapter Forty-Six

Early the next morning, I went to Dr. Jackson's apartment, hoping to catch him before he went to the hospital. He had an in-home practice where he also saw patients, providing the perfect cover for any clandestine comings and goings.

I entered through the gated garden and knocked.

His wife, Toquette, answered, still wearing her housecoat.

"I'm so sorry to trouble you, I know it's early, but is Dr. Jack in? I need to speak to him. It's about Jean-Claude ... Dr. Jacob."

"Of course, come in."

She ushered me through their modest but well-appointed apartment to his medical office. Leaving me there, she went to fetch her husband.

Too antsy to sit, I paced the worn carpet.

A few minutes later, Dr. Jackson entered, hastily dressed in an old army sweater and trousers, his hair uncombed, with what looked like a pillow crease on his left cheek.

"Daisy, what's happened?" he asked, taking me in, a mess of tangled hair and ruined makeup and rumpled clothing, though I'd dispensed with the bloodied cocktail dress.

I told him everything, starting with my scheme to smuggle out Blake and Hattie and ending with Bridget's betrayal.

"He turned himself in to those monsters to save me." My voice, which had held steady until then, broke.

He scraped a hand through his hair, making the ends stick up worse than they were, the gesture reminding me of Jean-Claude.

"I'll see what I can find out. They'll probably take him to Drancy if they haven't already."

Feeling helpless, I wrung my hands. "If they deport him ..."

While Jean-Claude remained in France, there was still hope. Guards could be bribed to look the other way. Keys could be smuggled in. But if he were sent out of the country to Auschwitz or another concentration camp, I'd probably never see him again.

Dr. Jack put his arm around my shoulder. "Jean-Claude is an extremely resourceful young man. If anyone can figure out how to keep alive, my money's on him."

I nodded, doing my best to believe him.

"I know I'm asking a lot," he continued, drawing his arm away, "but with the Gestapo watching you, try to treat this as any other day. Go about your normal routine. And steer clear of any Resistance activities for the foreseeable."

He stepped behind his desk and reached for his prescription pad. I wondered if we were going to prescribe me a sedative. I could have used one.

He wrote something down, tore off the sheet, and handed it to me.

"What's this?" I asked, not bothering to try to decipher his handwriting, almost as bad as Jean-Claude's.

"A prescription for iron pills. If anyone questions your coming here, show them that. Now go home and try to get some rest."

When I got back to the apartment, Bridget had cleared out. Other than an earring dropped under the dresser, there was no trace of her. Looking around, it hit me. I'd lost my lover *and* my best friend, both within a single night. Fritz was back in Paris, and clearly eager to resume our relationship, but after being chased through the tunnels with Jean-Claude, it was hard to see beyond his uniform.

For the first time since I'd come to Paris, I was all alone.

I sank to my knees in the center of the carpet and cried as I hadn't done since I was a little child, howling my hurt without a care for who might hear me.

Eventually I exhausted myself. Throat raw, I got up, stripped down to my slip and climbed into bed.

A few days later, I packed up and moved into a room on the rue Cambon side of the Ritz. By then, I was done with feeling sorry for myself. Jean-Claude didn't need my tears. He needed my strength. Though my money remained frozen, Blanche assured me I could postpone paying until the war was over. I decided to hold onto the rue Lazare apartment for the time being, though I didn't see how I could ever live there again. Those four walls with their watermarked wallpaper held far too many memories, the happy ones the hardest of all.

I gave myself another few days to settle in before contacting Fritz. When he invited me to afternoon tea in the hotel dining room, I accepted even though it meant sitting on the German side. He waited until the tea was poured and the tiered tray of dainties served before telling me his news.

"I am afraid your friend, Dr. Jacob was taken to La Muette," he said, his expression grave.

My stomach knotted, but I forced down a sip of tea. "The Gestapo shot him in the leg. Do you know if he's received any medical treatment?" If they sent him to the American or another hospital, there might be a chance of smuggling him out.

He hesitated. "There is an infirmary at the prison but ... I cannot say what care he might receive there."

"Will they deport him?" I asked, dreading his answer.

He set his chinaware cup down on its saucer. "He is Jewish, so it is a possibility. But if he is unable to work ..."

The honest answer only worsened my worries. By then, we'd all heard of incidences where prisoners had been taken out and shot, either because they were too ill to transport or in retribution for a Resistance hit on a Nazi.

Doing my best to behave as though Jean-Claude was a friendly acquaintance and not a lover, I put on a smile. "Take me dancing tonight? You did promise me a night out in Montmartre," I reminded him.

He studied me, his gaze thoughtful. "You are certain?"

Despite Dr. Jack warning me off Resistance work, with Jean-Claude imprisoned, I couldn't sit on my hands and do nothing. I was more determined than ever to see inside Fritz's brown briefcase. If what I found saved Jean-Claude or even one Allied life, whatever happened to me afterwards would be worth it.

Thinking of how Bridget might handle such a situation, I reached across the table and slipped my hand in his. "I'm certain I want to drink fountains of champagne and eat mountains of fresh oysters and dance until the cork soles of my shoes wear out." Holding his gaze, I lowered my voice and added, "Certain that afterward, I want you to take me back to your hotel room and make love to me."

Predictably, his pupils widened. "Daisy?"

"I've missed you, Fritz. And I've already wasted too much time blaming you for a war that isn't your fault. Whatever time we have left, let's enjoy it."

Later, as Fritz was paying *l'addition*, Mademoiselle Chanel passed by our table, von Dincklage with her. When the baron moved to exchange a few words with Fritz, she seized her opportunity.

"I see you are learning to bend, Marguerite," she remarked, expression smug.

Though I'd never wanted to slap a face more, I forced a smile. "Like a reed in the wind, mademoiselle, I bend but I don't break."

Later that night, after dinner and dancing, Fritz and I stepped into the lobby of the Hôtel Lutetia. Unlike the Ritz, which had a very special relationship with the Wehrmacht, the Lutetia was fully requisitioned, meaning that the management was no longer allowed to accept civilian guests. Remembering Gran and I eating macarons in her suite, it was hard to believe the hotel was now the Paris headquarters for the Abwehr.

As Fritz's date, I was spared being searched, a good thing given what I'd brought with me in my evening purse. Ignoring the guards' lewd looks, I held onto Fritz's hand as he led us through the reception area to the elevators. As the car rose, I told myself I wasn't betraying Jean-Claude. I was fighting for him with the only weapon I had.

Once inside the room, like pulling off a Band-Aid, I couldn't wait to get it over with. Fritz had barely got the door closed when I threw myself against him, wrapping my arms around his neck and smashing my mouth against his.

He gently drew down my clinging arms and pulled back to look at me. "Why such a hurry?"

"It's just ... we've waited such a long time," I said, hoping my haste hadn't ruined things already.

A tender look answered. He lifted my hand and pressed a kiss inside my wrist. "All the more reason to go slowly. I want ... to make it good for you."

I bit my lip. He assumed I was still a virgin. Given how long I'd put him off, why wouldn't he?

Fritz was nothing if not a generous lover. Unlike the first time I'd been with Jean-Claude, our fevered passion making animals of us both, he was slow, deliberate, thorough. Turning me to face away from him, he started on the zipper at the back of my dress, his knuckles gliding down my spine to the small of my back. I felt a brush of cool air against my bare skin as the dress opened, then fell away, and suddenly everything was warm again. Warm and wet and succulent, his patient, *knowing* lips trailing kisses along my neck, the tops of my shoulders and the sides of my breast. Nuzzling my neck, he unclasped my brassiere and slid the straps off my shoulders, then reached around to cup me, teasing and testing until I gave in and arched back against him, silently begging him to take me.

Afterwards, he fell asleep almost immediately, his soft, rhythmic snores punctuating the stillness. Lying in bed beside him, I stared up at the ceiling, tears sliding out the sides of my eyes and soaking into the pillowcase. Not because Fritz had hurt me. He hadn't. But because I hadn't hated it, or him, no matter how much I had wanted to.

I slipped out of bed, found his discarded shirt on the floor and put it on. Drying my eyes on the back of his sleeve, I tiptoed out into the main room where I'd left my evening clutch with the Minox camera lying out on the console table. I found Fritz's brown attaché case parked in the back of a closet in the corner, hidden behind a duffle bag of dirty laundry.

Setting it atop the table, I confirmed it was locked as I'd expected. The tumbler combination lock was the kind I'd practiced on, only Fritz's case had four dials instead of three. Taking a breath, I reviewed everything Rachelle had taught me, starting with gently applying pressure to the shackle and turning the dials until I heard a click. Once I got all the dials to the point where they clicked, the case should open. The key was to apply the right degree of pressure. Too much and the dials wouldn't turn, too little and there would be no click. Multiple clicks in a single dial meant there were false gates designed to defeat thieves and interlopers like me.

It took the better part of an hour to get the thing open. By the time I lifted the lid, I'd sweated through Fritz's shirt and gray light streaked through the Venetian blinds.

Fritz would be up in another hour, maybe less. I had to work quickly. There were at least a dozen folders, the documents grouped in two-ring brass binders. Photographing them all would take hours, which I didn't have. I would have to prioritize and wait for my next opportunity to come back. Keeping an ear cocked for Fritz, I flipped through but unfortunately all the writing was in German. I kept on, searching for anything that might include photographs or drawings. Finally, my patience was rewarded with a map detailing German gun emplacements along the Atlantic.

I took out my Minox camera and got to work.

Chapter Forty-Seven

1943

By 1943, the Germans were on the defensive. The fresh-faced young soldiers from the early days of the Occupation were mostly gone from Paris, reassigned to fight on the Front. In their place, middle-aged men with receding hairlines, paunches, and brutish bearings patrolled the city.

That April, Chanel made two trips out of the country, both with Spatz, though she was too cagey to say where they had gone. From pumping her maid, Germaine, I had learned that warm winter clothes were packed as well as sturdy boots.

In July, Italy surrendered. Mussolini and his fascist government were out. The reinstated Italian king and prime minister joined the Allies and declared war on Germany.

At the Ritz, the Wehrmacht leaders in residence congregated in the bar and on the German side of Monsieur Dabescat's dining room, speaking in nervous whispers.

Dining with Fritz, I often saw Carl von Stülpnagel, the military governor of France, his cousin and chief of staff, Cäsar von Hofacker, and Hans Speidel, the *Kommandant*, with their heads together, wearing worried looks.

By then "*Le Boche est fini*" was a whispered prayer on nearly every Parisian's lips. But the Nazis weren't about to go down without a fight. Gestapo placards in Métro stations and at bus stops offered a bounty of 50,000 francs for any Allied airmen dead or alive. Pierre Laval instituted the *Relève*, which made it mandatory for Frenchmen between seventeen and fifty years old to be sent to work in German factories, cogs in the Wehrmacht's war machine. He also formed the Milice, a fascist militia of native Frenchmen tasked with rounding up Jews and routing out *résistants*, using the most brutal means possible.

Nazi barbarism only made us that much tougher and more determined to fight. By the summer, our Vengeance group had grown from a hundred volunteer operatives to more than twenty thousand strong. Funding poured in from London from the British government and de Gaulle's Free French. They supplied Vengeance and other Resistance networks with weapons, clothes, medical supplies, canned food, and cash, and even vehicles, parachuted in during nighttime drops in countryside.

In the fall, British and American aerial bombings intensified. We became accustomed to the rumble of planes overhead, the screeching of air raid sirens, and explosions rattling the windows, welcomed them, even. By then, I don't think anyone believed Germany could win the war, least of all the Germans.

When I received a note from Dr. Jack – Sumner, as I now called him – asking me to stop by his avenue Foch practice that afternoon, I surmised it was about Jean-Claude. With the Gestapo breathing down our necks, we didn't meet unless it was necessary for a mission.

Mrs. Jackson greeted me at the front door. "He's expecting you," she said, her usual calm self though I sensed sadness behind her welcoming smile.

She ushered me to his medical office, the door standing open.

"I'll be in the kitchen if I'm needed," she said, then left us.

Sumner stood from behind his desk. His lab coat gaped open at the front, enough for me to see the holes in the army pullover sweater he had on beneath.

"Daisy, good of you to come. Please, have a seat."

He gestured to the visitor's chair, but I shook my head. "Thanks, but I'll stand, if you don't mind. You have news for me?"

To his credit, he didn't beat around the bush.

"I do but not the news any of us were hoping for, I'm afraid."

Heart in my throat, I said, "Go on."

"According to our intelligence, it looks like Jean-Claude was one of seven prisoners taken from La Muette to Mont Valérien and … shot."

I felt my chest seize up.

"With his leg wound, he wouldn't have been any good to them at a labor camp," he added.

I remembered Fritz saying something similar. "He was expendable, then. Expendable and Jewish," I said, my bitterness welling up.

He crossed to the front of the desk. "My dear, I'm so sorry. He was a brilliant young surgeon and a good friend. His death is medicine's loss. And ours."

I nodded. "Thank you for telling me."

I left and spent the next few hours walking along the quay. By the time I got back to the Ritz, I had decided.

I would no longer be satisfied with helping repatriate stolen

Jewish artwork or even passing on maps of Nazi missile launch sites. For my next mission, and for as long as I had breath in my body, I would devote my every waking moment to taking out as many Nazis as I could.

Chapter Forty-Eight

1944

A few days after the New Year, Chanel made a second trip to Madrid, supposedly another stab at setting up a Spanish boutique. This time, the venture was to be managed by her old friend Vera Bate Lombardi, recently returned to Paris. A childhood chum of Winston Churchill, Vera had promoted Chanel's London boutique back in the twenties before leaving to marry an Italian cavalry officer in Mussolini's army. With the fascists deposed, and her husband cooling his heels in a prison camp outside of Rome, Vera was at loose ends and presumably looking for a project.

Instead of Baron de Vaufreland, Von Dincklage accompanied them. By then, no one left France without a visa issued by the Nazi higher-ups, in this case, the Paris Gestapo chief. That Spatz had arranged visas for both women as well as used his connections to clear up Vera's passport troubles I didn't doubt. I only wished I knew what he was getting out of the arrangement. When I fished for information from Fritz, he was frustratingly tight-lipped, which only raised my suspicions that boutique business wasn't all the trio had been up to.

Chanel returned less than a week later, as close to hysterical as I'd ever seen her, swearing that everyone she'd ever loved and trusted had abandoned her. Fortunately for those of us around her, she never stayed in one mood for very long. After the first few fraught days, she threw herself into finishing the costumes for her friend, Jean Cocteau's latest staging of *Antigone* at the Paris Opera.

While Chanel and her friends pursued their artistic passions, the rest of us struggled to stay alive and out of Nazi prisons. By the spring of 1944, Gestapo arrests had reached a sickening crescendo. It was as if knowing they were losing the war made the Nazis more determined to take as many of us *résistants* down with them as they could.

One day in early May, I received an unsigned letter in my morning mail at the Ritz:

If you pass by avenue Foch don't visit the people you know there.

I thought I recognized the penmanship as Toquette's and told myself she wouldn't be writing if she and Sumner had been arrested already. Regardless, I took the warning seriously and shared it with Pierre to spread the word among other Paris based Resistance networks, especially the Goelette and Prospero groups, which both used the Jackson's residence as a meeting spot and mailbox.

When I went into the American the next day for my volunteer shift, the atmosphere was tense, everyone talking in whispers. The Gestapo had sent a car to take Sumner from the hospital to his home, and no one had seen or heard from him since.

After spending a sleepless night, I couldn't hold off any longer. I had to see for myself. Taking a page from Chanel's playbook, I tied a scarf over my hair and put on a pair of dark sunglasses before taking the Métro to avenue Foch.

Coming up on the Jackson's apartment at No. 11, I spotted the potted plant in the window, one of several signals we had worked out to telegraph danger. Toquette's prize daffodils still bloomed in the garden, but the apartment windows were dark. The Jacksons were gone. Taken.

Sumner's loss was a shocking blow to the medical Resistance and to me personally. Though he wasn't the first *résistant* physician to be interred, to many of us in the movement, he had stood out as larger than life. Invincible. With Rachelle off fighting with the *maquis* in the countryside, he was also my last living link to Jean-Claude. Now they were both gone.

Since the Occupation, the Germans had used the French state railway system to move war materials produced not only in France, but also Portugal and Spain, to the Reich. When our Vengeance group received word from London alerting us to an impending Allied amphibious and airborne invasion by way of the Normandy beaches in northwest France, I buried my grief and threw myself into helping with the operation.

Our orders were to partner with Résistance-Fer, the Resistance group of national railway workers, to sabotage the German munitions trains supplying German troops sent to repel the Allied invasion. Set for June 5th, the mission would be the most audacious strike against the Nazis I had ever been part of, and the most lethal. Until then, I had never taken a life, had never imagined that I would have to. That was about to change.

That evening over a candlelight dinner in my room, Fritz told me that he would be leaving Paris for a week, maybe longer, to accompany a convoy of textiles to Bayeux. When I heard his destination, I nearly dropped my teeth.

Bayeux was the nearest station to Normandy, as I well knew. Just as I knew it wasn't fabric Fritz would be accompanying. It was munitions. On the very train I had pledged to intercept.

"Textiles?" I repeated, needing a moment to gather myself.

"For uniforms," he confirmed, gaze on the black-market steak he was cutting into.

"Can't Baron von Dincklage send someone else?" I asked, kicking myself for the question coming out as shrill.

His mouth tightened as it did whenever he felt like I was asking him to choose me over his country. "Daisy, you know I cannot refuse. I have my orders." Softening, he reached across the table and took my hand. "Once I am back, I will make it up to you, I promise."

Arguing with him would get me nowhere. When it came to doing what he saw as his duty, he was intractable. Instead, I nodded and managed to choke down a few more bites of supper. Later that night as I sat up watching him sleep, his loathsome uniform hanging in my clothes closet, I tried seeing him as any other German soldier. An upholder of the same murderous regime that had killed Jean-Claude and so many other good people. I shouldn't care what happened to him. I *didn't* care.

But of course, that wasn't true.

The man whose life I should be ready to take without a second thought wasn't just any German soldier. He was Fritz. Fritz, who gave his chocolate rations to hungry French children and saved scraps from his plate for a stray dog that had begun hanging outside the kitchen door of the hotel. Fritz, who held me and made love to me so tenderly that sometimes I felt like whatever was left of my broken heart, a heart I had taken such pride in hardening, must be pulverized to powder. Fritz, who I couldn't imagine ever hating or hurting anyone, and yet upheld a regime dedicated to hating and hurting hundreds of thousands, maybe *millions* of Jews.

For a handful of heart wrenching moments, I considered calling off the mission. I would come up with an excuse, any excuse. I was ill, the materials for the explosives hadn't come in, Chanel or one of her collaborating friends had found me out and now I was compromised.

But no, I couldn't possibly cancel, and not only because Rachelle and Pierre and the others would be within their rights to take me out to some remote spot and shoot me in the head like a rabid dog in need of putting down. Too many lives hinged on those weapons never reaching the Germans at Normandy. French lives. British lives. American lives, including my own brother. Though Mom would never admit it, Neil was her favorite. If anything happened to him, she would curl up and die, I knew it.

Not just France but the fate of the free world hung in the balance. If I let that train through, the war would go on that much longer. There would be more battles, more deaths, more roundups of Jews.

Eventually I went to bed and spent what was left of the night tossing and turning while Fritz snored peacefully beside me. By the time dawn broke, I had decided. There was only one thing to do.

I had to keep Fritz off that train.

The mission day arrived. Nerves a jagged mess, I rose before Fritz did, called down to the kitchen, and ordered breakfast brought up, including Fritz's favorite: hot chocolate.

Pacing the suite, I waited for the food to arrive, more nervous than I was about the actual mission, which wouldn't take place until that evening. Finally, I heard the light rapping outside the door. A sleepy-eyed waiter wheeled in the food trolley.

I thanked him, reached for my purse, and sent him off with a tip.

Hurrying over, I took the lid off the chocolate pot, reached into my robe pocket, and brought out the syrup of ipecac I'd taken from the pharmacy at the hospital. Unscrewing the top, I poured in the entire bottle, stirred it, and then hurried back to the bedroom.

"Fritz, breakfast," I said, shaking his shoulders, for the first time ever waking him before his alarm clock went off. "I ordered your favorites."

Flopping onto his back, he sent me a sleepy smile. "You are my favorite."

He reached out to pull me back into bed with him, but I moved away before he could.

"Please, it's getting cold," I said, tossing him a robe.

"What is the occasion?" he asked, coming out into the main room as I was dragging his chair up to the table.

"No occasion. I'll miss you, that's all."

He hesitated and then sat. "We will celebrate when I get back," he promised, his solemn look making me want to burst into tears. "Maxim's, I think, unless there is another place you would prefer to go."

"Maxim's sounds lovely," I said, thinking of our first "date" which unbeknown to him hadn't been a real date at all but the start of my spying career.

I poured the hot chocolate and passed it to him, my shaking hand sending the cup rattling in its saucer.

"*Danke.*" He lifted the cup and took a sip.

Seeing his face pucker, my heart dropped. "You don't like it?"

"It is ... a bit bitter," he admitted.

"It's probably ersatz," I said. "Put some sugar in it." I dropped a sugar cube into his cup without him asking and stirred it with a spoon. "Try it now."

"Aren't you having any?" he asked.

Heart hammering, I stuck on a smile. "I already had mine," I lied. "While I was waiting for you, lazybones, to get out of bed."

He drank some more. "You are certain nothing is wrong?"

Reminded that the best lies are partway true, I stopped fighting myself, stopped fighting the truth and the tears, and let it all pour out of me.

"*Everything* is wrong," I exclaimed, starting up from my seat and waving my arms like a wild woman. "You're leaving, and I'm going to miss you, but I don't want to miss you. I *hate* that I'll miss you. That I miss you already. All I want is to look at you and see ... and see a filthy Boche, a Nazi *salaud*, a henchman for Hitler, and yet even when you're wearing that goddamned uniform, I still can't look at you and see anything but ..."

"But?" he asked, regarding me with wary eyes.

I dropped my arms. "I can't see anything but ... *you*. My friend. My *lover*."

He swallowed hard. "I am all of those things and still there is more I wish to be to you." He got up from the table and came around to comfort me, his arm wrapping around my shuddering shoulders, his kisses drying my tears.

Suddenly he stiffened and stood back. "I ... I do not feel very well."

He turned away and hurried to the bathroom.

Twenty minutes later, he was still on his hands and knees on the bathroom floor vomiting into the commode.

"Stay put, I'll have some tea sent up and be sure there's someone to check in on you," I said, speaking through the closed bathroom door. "Oh, and I'll leave word for Baron von Dincklage that he'll have to find someone to replace you."

On my way out of the hotel, I found Blanche and brought her in on my plan, admitting Fritz was my asset.

"You didn't seem the type to take up with a Kraut," she said when I had finished.

Rather than reply to that, I passed her a second bottle of ipecac, which I'd wrapped in a napkin.

"Make sure he gets a dose of this every other hour until the evening," I said, trusting her to find a way.

"I'll spoon-feed him laced bone broth and sugared tea myself. Don't you worry, I'll kill him with kindness." She shot me a wink.

"Maybe don't go that far," I joked, relieved to have such a good friend on my side.

Unlike Bridget, Blanche was as dedicated to fighting the Nazis as any of us were. Being the de facto doyenne of the Ritz made for the perfect cover. Perfect but not foolproof. I was asking her to risk herself to save a German, a Nazi, no less.

Dropping her voice, she said, "Seriously, Daisy, keep your mind on your mission and come back to us. Too many good people have been lost in this fight already. When the Americans break through, I plan on getting rip-roaring drunk, and I want my pals right there with me."

That night, I laid on my belly in the bushes of a hillside in Creully near Bayeaux with Pierre and Rachelle. Caps on our heads and dirt scrubbed into our faces, we pinned our gazes on the lonely stretch of railroad track below.

Not lonely for long.

The bombs, five in all, were Rachelle's babies, loving creations fashioned of battery, rolls of wire, metal hooks with cables attached, the gelignite strangely pleasant-smelling, like almonds, hidden in boxes and tucked into the rails like Easter eggs waiting to be found.

"The hard part is over," Rachelle whispered to me, excitement in her voice.

I didn't really believe it and neither, I think, did she.

"It is your first time," she continued, the whispered words an unaccustomed kindness. "It will get easier."

It was funny how gentle she was with me now that Jean-Claude was gone, almost like a big sister though we were the same age.

"Murdering people?" I asked, mindful of the cyanide capsule nestled between my breasts.

She scoffed. "The Nazis are the murderers, not us."

Pierre consulted his timepiece, his lucky timepiece, which his father had carried in the Great War. "It is almost time. *Deux minutes.*"

Two minutes.

He held the detonator out to me.

Everyone in our immediate Vengeance group had voted that as Jean-Claude's lover it was my right to do the honors. As if there was some kind of nobility in pressing a switch and killing total strangers from more than a mile away.

A train whistle sounded. Below, the train steamed through the tunnel, the engine's headlamp cutting through the murky twilight.

Seeing it round the bend on the thin ribbon of track, it didn't seem real, more like a little kid's model locomotive, lovingly assembled, glued together and painted.

I watched it snake along, feeling like I was watching a movie. The train that Fritz would have been on if I hadn't found out in time to stop him. The train that someone else's Fritz, or Hans, or Heinrich was on right now, not suspecting that life, theirs, was down to two minutes. Just two minutes. Less than that now.

I still hadn't made a move to take the detonator Pierre held out.

"If it's too much, I can do it," he said.

That time, I reached for it, the device sticking to my sweaty palm.

Rachelle's eyes met mine. "*Prête?*"

Pulse pounding, I nodded and set my thumb on the switch.

She began counting. "One, two …"

Instead of thinking about the soldiers on the train, I would think of Jean-Claude as I had last seen him, hobbled and bloodied.

"… Three."

I closed my eyes and pressed down firmly.

Chapter Forty-Nine

The next day, June 6th, the BBC broadcast the Allied D-Day invasion live from Normandy. Under the command of Dwight Eisenhower, Allied Expeditionary Force Supreme Commander, Operation Overlord landed 150,000 troops on five beaches in Normandy, the largest amphibious invasion in the history of warfare.

Later that day, Blanche's chutzpah finally caught up with her. According to Claude, stiff-lipped but clearly heartbroken, she had celebrated the D-Day invasion with a champagne lunch at Maxim's, accompanied by her friend, Lily Kharmayeff. As the bubbles flowed, Blanche began letting off four years' worth of steam. In the middle of a dining room packed with German officers, she'd tipsily sung the "*La Marseillaise*" and backtalked a German officer, then slung her glass of champagne in his face. She and Lily were arrested and trucked to the municipal prison at Fresnes. So far, Claude hadn't been allowed to see her. As one of the few Ritz regulars let in on her secret, I could appreciate the agony he must be going through.

And the fear.

If they tortured her into naming names, we would all be in deep trouble.

Knowing the Nazis' days were numbered, Parisians began reclaiming their city and their national pride. That Bastille Day, one hundred thousand people took to the streets, facing down panzer tanks and gunshots fired into the sky and setting celebratory bonfires around the city.

On the steamy evening of July 20th, I came in from Maison Chanel to meet Fritz for drinks and found the hotel swarming with SS men. My first, heart-dropping thought was that Blanche had broken. As her arrest showed, even with the Allies on French soil, none of us were out of the woods yet.

Feeling perspiration pooling underneath my arms, rather than retreating to my room, I made myself cut through the rue Cambon lobby and head into the bar. Fritz wasn't there yet, but I spotted a few regulars sipping cocktails and speaking in whispers, their bug-eyed gazes darting to the door when I entered, then relaxing in relief when they saw it was only me.

Frank stood behind the bar, his usual cucumber-cool self, though I didn't miss the dark circles under his eyes.

I pulled up a stool and sat. "What's going on?" I asked, careful to keep my voice low.

He laid a fresh bar napkin in front of me. "A cadre of officers in the German high command tried to assassinate Hitler."

I picked up a menu and pretended to study it though I knew the offerings by heart. "Tried?"

Frank poured me a flute of champagne without my asking. "They planted a bomb in a briefcase and put it under the conference table at Wolf's Lair where Hitler was supposed to sit. Someone moved it at the last minute."

Mindful of watchful eyes, I picked up my drink and took a sip. "Wolf's Lair is in northeastern Poland. Why are the SS *here*?"

"Three of the suspected co-conspirators, Carl von Stülpnagel, Cäsar von Hofacker, and Hans Speidel, are Ritz residents."

"When you said 'high command' you weren't kidding."

Frank gave a grim nod. "All three used my behind-the-bar mailbox to pass on messages, which means the Gestapo is likely on to me."

My thoughts flew to Fritz. It wasn't like him to be late. "Have you seen Hauptmann Eberhardt?"

"A package is waiting for you. In your room."

"A package?" I repeated, holding his gaze.

"The material is marked urgent."

I slid off my seat and stood. "In that case, I'd better go and have a look."

Taking the back stairs to my suite, I passed more SS and Gestapo coming and going. Reaching the third floor, I ran across a bullet-headed brute with an eyepatch on his way down, and for a few seconds my heart stopped. One of the two Gestapo agents who'd chased Jean-Claude and me! Praying he hadn't gotten a good look at me that night, I held my breath and walked past him.

When I opened my door, Fritz's deer-in-the-headlights gaze met mine.

Weak with relief, I pulled the door closed behind me and bolted it. "I just heard about the assassination attempt on Hitler."

"They meant to eliminate Göring, too," he said, "and negotiate a neutral peace with the Allies."

I took that in. With the Allies on track to win the war, I didn't see Churchill and Roosevelt accepting anything less than an unconditional surrender.

"Are you ... involved?" I asked.

"In the plot, no. But of watching the men involved in the plot, yes."

"Watching for who exactly?"

He hesitated. "I cannot answer that now. But trust me, Daisy, we are on the same side. And it is only a matter of time before they come for me. Stülpnagel has already received orders to return to Berlin."

It was my turn to pace. If the Boches took Fritz, they wouldn't execute him by firing squad as they had Jean-Claude. That would be too quick, too clean, too merciful. For a traitor within the Abwehr, only a slow, agonizing death would do. Strangulation by piano wire was the wretched death reserved for high-level traitors. I'd already lost Jean-Claude to the Nazis. I wasn't about to stand by and lose Fritz, too.

I whirled back to him. "You can't stay here."

He winced as if I'd slapped him. "I was wrong to come here. I have put you in terrible danger. Such weakness, such cowardice, is inexcusable. Forgive me."

He started for the door.

I grabbed his sleeve. "Whoa, what I meant is we have to get you out of Paris. Out of France. But first, we need to get you out of that uniform."

A six foot two German with movie-star looks wasn't going to fade into the woodwork just because I put a beret on his head. More than a change of clothes, an invisibility cloak was called for.

He shook his head. "My clothes, everything I own, are at the Lutetia."

"You can't go back there, that's the first place they'll look." I thought for a moment. "Wait here and don't open that door for anyone but me."

I went back downstairs and walked up to the reception counter.

Claude was manning the front desk, ordinarily Blanche's post, the dark circles beneath his eyes there for good reason. With the Nazis still holding his wife, he would have little love for collaborators.

"*Bonsoir,* Monsieur Auzello. I need to borrow a key."

Unfortunately, my lockpick tools were back at Madame LeBrun's hidden in my mattress. In those days, grand European hotels like the Ritz kept the key to each guestroom behind the front desk. When you left for the day, you gave your key to the staff attendant and then retrieved it on your return.

"Of course, mademoiselle." He reached for mine, but I stopped him.

"The key to No. 227–228, *s'il vous plaît.*"

He turned back to me. "That is Mademoiselle Chanel's room."

"It is," I said.

We held a look.

He took down the key and handed it to me. "*Bonne chance.*"

I dropped the key into my pocket and headed back to the bar.

"Find your package?" Frank asked.

"I did but it needs new ... wrappings, including a passport, preferably Swiss."

I waited, letting that land. Frank and I were pals, but with the Gestapo already watching him, I was asking a lot, and I knew it.

Finally, he said, "My man, Greep is snowed under with similar requests, but I'll see what I can do."

I blew out my breath. Père Rafe, our Vengeance forger, hadn't resurfaced, which meant he was probably dead. If Frank had turned me down, I wouldn't have known where to turn.

"I won't forget this. Thank you."

"Don't thank me yet. It will cost one hundred U.S. dollars. And he has a month backlog."

"Tell him I'll pay double that if he can do it in two weeks or better yet, one."

He picked up a damp cloth and slowly, meticulously wiped away the water ring left on the bar. "It may take me a few days. Anything else?"

I eyed him. He was of medium height and on the doughy side, but his shoulders were decently broad and his upper arms firm, presumably from all the cocktail shaking.

"Any chance you've got a change of clothes you can spare?"

Back in my room, I handed Fritz the Ritz shopping bag from Frank. "Civvies, courtesy of Frank."

He quickly changed, shucking off the detested feldgrau uniform for Frank's white dinner jacket, shirt and black pants, the Ritz barman uniform. The only thing Frank hadn't been able to come up with on such short notice was shoes. Fritz would have to wear his jackboots and hope that no one was overly observant.

I rolled up his uniform and stuffed it under the mattress. As much as I would have liked to have tossed it in the trash or, better yet, burned it, it might come in handy down the road.

Lastly, I focused on his hair, mussing it a bit to make it look less military.

Satisfied, I headed for the door. "We have to move."

"Where?" he asked.

"You'll see."

I opened the door, poked my head outside, and confirmed all was clear. Once I did, I beckoned for him to follow me down the hallway to Chanel's room. I knew for a fact that she wasn't there, otherwise her key wouldn't have been at the front desk. I gave the perfunctory knock anyway, counted silently to five, and then took out my borrowed key.

"Are you mad?" Fritz whispered.

"Just enough." I opened the door and slipped inside, pulling him in with me.

The reek of No. 5 crowded every nook and cranny.

I remembered the secret stairs to the attic that she'd bullied the staff into building for her on our return to Paris in 1940. Now that same attic crawl space would hide Fritz, at least until the downstairs went dark and the SS men left.

I went up the pulldown steps first, Fritz following. A dresser, a trunk stuffed with God only knew what, and a strong scent of moth balls crowded the low-slung space. Taller than me, he had to hunch to keep from hitting his head on the beams.

We hunkered down, sitting cross-legged on the bare floor.

Fritz's voice struck a doleful note in the stillness. "I cannot hide here forever."

"You won't have to. The bar closes at nine o' clock. Once things go dark downstairs, we can take the staff lift down to the wine cellar. There's a door that leads from the cellar to the underground. We'll take the tunnels to my apartment in the eighth."

"You risk a great deal for me," he said.

"You said we're on the same side. I'm giving you the chance to prove it."

An hour later, we were making our way through the tunnels, the loamy scent and my own fast-beating heart taking me back to my last night with Jean-Claude. Since then, I'd made a point of memorizing his map, the underground passageways mostly following the streets aboveground. We emerged at the French railway headquarters at No. 88 rue Saint-Lazare, a few blocks from Madame LeBrun's.

"If we run into any patrols, pretend to be drunk," I whispered, reasoning that a drunken German weaving along the Paris streets wouldn't raise any eyebrows.

Spotting a soldier ahead, I threw my arm around Fritz as if he needed support. "Lean on me and sing."

"Sing what?" he whispered.

"I don't know, anything. Don't you know any beer hall tunes?"

"I do not go to beer halls," he said, expression solemn.

Keeping an eye on the German soldier, I said, "Fine. *Il est des nôtres*, then."

The song, "He's one of us," was a popular French drinking ditty and, thanks to Bridget teaching me the words, one I could come up with on the fly.

Clearing my throat, I launched in with, *"Il a bu son verre comme les autres."* He has drunk his glass like the others.

Fritz joined in with, *"C'est un ivrogne."* He's a drunkard.

Together, we sang, *"On le reconnaît rien qu'à sa trogne."* You can see it from his face.

We took the last several blocks singing at the top of our lungs. Several passersby slung insults my way. *Salope*, slut, was the favorite. Parisians were getting bolder, no doubt about it.

Thankfully, by then we were at the entrance of Madame LeBrun's.

She met us in the front hallway dressed in her robe with a hairnet covering her hair. Her gaze froze on Fritz, whom she'd met when he'd come to pick me up on Sundays before the war.

"*Putain.*" She lobbed me a loathing look and stomped up the stairs.

I waited for her door to slam shut, then turned back to Fritz. "Follow me."

Upstairs, I unlocked the door to my apartment and entered. Since moving to the Ritz, other than paying the rent, I hadn't been back much. Once the host of happy times, filled with warmth and girlish giggles, now it had the sad, stagnant atmosphere common to forgotten, unloved places.

I reached into my handbag and took out a bottle of schnapps.

"From Frank." I handed Fritz the bottle, then went to the cabinet and took out two glasses.

"*Danke*." Fritz poured out the drinks and handed me mine.

"He says it may take two weeks to get your forged passport or even a month," I admitted. "Apparently, there's no shortage of people looking to leave Paris, some of them even Germans."

The attempted joke fell flat.

We carried our drinks and the bottle over to the sofa.

Sinking down on the lumpy cushion next to me, Fritz asked, "What shall we toast to?"

Putting my feet up on the ottoman, I shrugged. "Blue skies and better days?"

"And a Free France?" he suggested.

We touched glasses and drank deeply.

Expression doleful, he shook his head. "Daisy, I don't know what to say, how to repay you."

I turned my head to look at him. "I'll settle for the truth."

Swirling the schnapps in his glass, he said, "I was recruited by the Deuxième Bureau before the war, in 1937."

"You've been working for French military intelligence?" All this time, I'd struggled to reconcile the good, kind person I knew him to be with his Nazi affiliation. The two never had summed for me and now I understood why.

Half afraid to believe him, I pressed, "But I thought the Bureau was disbanded when the Germans invaded."

"Officially, yes, but certain former operatives continued in the shadows." He took another sip, then set his glass aside. "When we first met, I told you that I come from an old Prussian military family. Even before the war, many from the former Weimar Republic did not support the Reich and its fascist fanaticism."

I took a moment to absorb that. "I take it requisitioning textiles for the German military isn't all Baron von Dincklage has been up to."

"It is a cover, of course, the latest of many. He reports directly to Joseph Goebbels, Reich Minister of Propaganda, and has since before the war."

I'd never believed von Dincklage's assertions of being a humble fabric broker for the Wehrmacht, but nor had I imagined he was so high up in the Reich's food chain.

"You've been spying on him all this time?" I asked.

He nodded. "The Christmas Eve you caught me entering the civilian side of the hotel, you assumed I was going to see the baron, but you were only partially correct. I have had Mademoiselle Chanel's room bugged for some time. I was going to the adjacent room to spy on them. There is a very small hole drilled into the wall behind a mirror."

No wonder he had looked so startled to see me coming out of Claude's office.

"The Bureau has been watching the baron since the early thirties when he was sent to spy on the French war fleet at Toulon. But his main talent is recruiting assets from among the French elite." He paused. "Women especially."

"Women like Mademoiselle Chanel, you mean?"

He picked up the bottle and topped off our glasses. "Last April, she made two trips to Berlin with von Dincklage. On at least one occasion, they met with the *SicherheitsDienste* intelligence chief Walter Schellenberg."

Stunned, I thought back to Chanel's travel over the past two years. The warm clothing and boots packed in April 1943 must have been in preparation for visiting a bomb-riddled Berlin. The second trip to Madrid in January with Vera Bate Lombardi and von Dincklage was still a riddle, but I'd bet my last franc it was about more than a second try at opening a Spanish boutique.

"What would Schellenberg want with a couturier?" Feeling like my head must be spinning, I took another sip of schnapps.

He shrugged. "Mademoiselle Chanel knows a great many influential people, many of them members of the British aristocracy. German intelligence assigned her a codename, Agent Westminster, after the pro-Nazi duke who was once her lover."

Not yet ready to let him off the hook, I asked, "What were you doing with a map of German gunneries in your attaché case?"

He knocked back his drink. "I had intended to pass them on to London, but you saved me the trouble."

"You left the case for me to find!?"

He smiled. "Behind some laundry and locked, of course. I did not wish to insult you by making it *too* easy."

So much for my grand espionage triumph.

Turning serious, he said, "Many times, I wished to tell you ... everything, but doing so would have meant putting you in danger. Now I have done so anyway."

"You haven't done anything. Hiding you is my choice. No matter what happens, I'd do it again. In a New York minute."

He set his glass down and turned to me. "I think you are the bravest woman I have ever known. I also think I would very much like to make love to you, this time as your ally, not your asset."

Learning that he wasn't a Nazi, I felt as if invisible weights were lifted from me. Jean-Claude was gone, dead. Soon Fritz would be gone, too. The war drove home how precarious and precious every moment was. Years from now, I didn't want to look back and regret wasting this one.

I grabbed his shirt with both hands and pulled him to me. His lips met mine, his familiar, gentle kiss quickly becoming urgent, his hands moving over me as if seeking to memorize every curve and angle and hollow of my body.

He lifted me into his arms and stood. I wrapped my arms around his neck and let him carry me into the bedroom. Reality dissolved to the weight of him pressing me into the mattress. The hot brush of his mouth on my neck. His stubbled jaw grazing the inside of my thighs. The thrill when he shifted onto his back and lifted me atop him, his big hands bracing my waist, guiding me to cover him. His muted groan when he came inside me.

The peace suffusing his face when he settled my head onto his shoulder. Unlike all the times before when I'd lain awake, my guilty conscience demanding to know how I could love one man and make love to another, a Nazi no less, I followed him into a peaceful sleep.

Chapter Fifty

The next morning, I was the first of us to wake. I slipped free of Fritz's arms, got up, and put on the quilted floral housecoat I kept at the apartment. Remembering Jean-Claude wearing it, I wondered what he'd think if he could see me now? What would Dr. Jack think? Rachelle? Last night, I hadn't slept with Fritz to get information or to keep up my cover as his girlfriend. I had slept with him for one reason only.

Because I had wanted to.

A yawn announced Fritz was awake. He got out of bed and walked over. Stopping behind me, he wrapped his arms around me and pulled me back against him.

"Guten morgen, liebling," he said, kissing the side of my neck.

It was one of the few times he'd spoken in German to me but then he didn't have to hide who or what he was anymore and neither did I.

I turned to face him. "Before I forget, I have something for you, a present."

"I thought last night was the present." His aquamarine eyes darkened, and he dropped his gaze to my breasts.

I smiled. "Then I suppose this will be your *second* present."

I crossed back to the bed, opened the nightstand drawer, and took out the copy of *My Ántonia* I'd bought for him five years ago. There had never seemed a right moment to give it to him until now.

He took it. Smoothing a reverent hand over the brown dustcover, he said, "You remembered."

I nodded. "I see why you love it so much. It's beautiful and hopeful and tender and ... true."

Cather's novel, written as a man's poignant recollection of his childhood friendship turned to first love with a Czech immigrant girl on the Nebraska plains, had torn up the heart I hadn't thought I still had.

He looked into my eyes, the expression on his face more worthy of precious gems or gold bullion than a musty old book. "I don't know what to say."

"It's nothing, just a book," I said, more moved than I'd meant to be. "We have a lot to do to get you ready. I'll make us breakfast."

Once we were dressed, I was determined to be all business. Fritz's life depended on him being prepared for whatever came his way. It was my job to make sure he was.

I fixed a simple breakfast of ersatz coffee and toast, all that I had in an otherwise bare pantry.

As soon as we had finished, I stood from the table. "I've got to go out. Sit tight. I won't be long."

I came back an hour later with a brown paper *pharmacie* bag and found Fritz sitting at the kitchen table reading his book.

He had done the washing up, the dishes left to dry in the rack by the sink. The domesticity struck me as sweet, endearing really. In another time and place, we might be any young couple setting up housekeeping, starting our life together. Would we be happy? After last night, I had to think we would.

He closed the book and set it aside. "What do you have there?" he asked, gaze going to the bag.

I took out the box of Marchand's hair rinse No. 4. "Something to make you less handsome."

He smiled, the skin at the corners of his eyes crinkling in that oh so delicious way. "You think me handsome?"

I rolled my eyes. "Stop fishing and grab that chair, would you?"

I sat him down at the kitchen sink, draped a towel around his shoulders, and had him lean back into the basin. Turning on the taps, I wet his hair, then used a pocket comb to part it.

"I like the view," he remarked, gazing at the gap in my blouse.

Pouring on the rinse, I resisted the urge to swat him. "I'll bet you do. Keep your eyes closed, so the solution doesn't get in them."

He dutifully closed his eyes, but his mouth stayed smiling.

Following the instructions on the box, I saturated the strands, using my fingers to work the solution into his scalp.

He let out a sigh. "That feels *gut*."

I snorted. "Don't get used to it."

Another sigh. "I would like to get used to this. I would like it very much."

Hearing the wistfulness in his voice, I knew a scalp massage wasn't all he meant.

I added the rest of the rinse to the strands and used my fingers to pull it through to the ends of the hair.

Afterwards, he surveyed the results in the hand mirror I brought over. "It is very … brown."

With his hair darkened, he looked different, older, if not exactly transformed.

He still had the sculpted features of a classical statue, but Blanche's cache of theatrical makeup props would take care of that.

"Stand up," I said. "We need to do something about your Prussian posture."

He stood. "What is wrong with it?"

Circling him, I said, "You carry yourself like a military man, that's what."

"I *am* a military man."

"Not anymore, you're not. Hunch your shoulders."

He lapsed into an exaggerated slouch, leaning forward as if he carried a cord of wood on his back. I couldn't tell if he was serious or clowning around. Either way, we didn't have time for antics. He had to get this right. His life depended on it.

"*Gut?*" he asked, loping across the carpet.

"Not good. You look like a bad impersonation of Quasimodo. Instead, maybe try for a half-starved Parisian beaten down by four years of Nazi occupation."

He rolled his eyes. "Very funny."

"I'm a regular Milton Berle." I stood on my toes and pulled back his shoulders. "Better." Though tempted to kiss him, I reminded myself we were working.

He glanced over at the paper bag. "What else do you have in there? Or am I ugly enough?"

I opened my mouth to fire back a zinger, but the desire in his eyes stopped me.

Holding his gaze, I said, "Not ugly at all."

I set my hand on his chest, savoring his warmth, his scent, the harnessed strength of him. Strength that by then I knew how to dismantle with a look, a touch, a word.

I had never undressed a man before and suddenly I very much wanted to. Not any man. Fritz. I wanted to strip him bare and see him weak. To make him tremble and moan and beg. Just a little.

Just enough.

When he moved to embrace me, I shoved his arms down to his sides and tore at the buttons of his shirt. Opening it, I feathered kisses over his pectorals, following the dusky gold queue disappearing into his trousers.

He sucked in a heavy breath. "Daisy—"

I reached down and unbuckled his belt.

"Daisy, I want you to know—"

Before he could get any more words out, I slid my hand inside his waistband and fitted my hand around him.

Frank came through with Fritz's forged passport in ten days instead of the promised two weeks. When I got the message, I had mixed emotions. Relief but also sadness. Even before I'd known the truth, that Fritz wasn't on the side of the Nazis, he had been more to me than just an asset. The days spent holed up together in my apartment had brought us even closer. Saying goodbye to him was going to hurt.

Pierre showed up at my door at the agreed-upon hour.

"*Nous sommes prêts?*" he asked, looking beyond me to Fritz, with his new dark hair, prosthetic nose and padding beneath his shirt to make it look like he had a paunch.

"Almost ready," I answered, ushering him in.

I'd managed to barter for an old pair of hiking boots to replace the jackboots that would have given Fritz away. They were at least a size too small, but with leather being second to gold, they were the best I could come up with. Fritz sat on the sofa and squeezed his feet inside, doing up the laces without a word of complaint.

Next, I handed him the forged passport and travel visa. "Once you step out that door, Fritz Eberhardt ceases to exist. You are Franc Egger, a wine merchant from Lausanne."

Looking it over, he nodded his approval. "A nice touch, to let me keep my initials."

"The best lies stick close to the truth." I glanced at Pierre. "Give us a moment?"

He nodded and made himself scarce.

Fritz followed me into the bedroom, the sheets still mussed from our early morning lovemaking.

I closed the door behind us, and he took me in his arms.

Laying my cheek against his chest, I said, "Pierre will get you as far as Besançon. From there, a guide will take you over the Jura Mountains into Geneva. Lay low until the Allies break through."

"And what of you?" he asked. "What will you do?"

I didn't have to think about it. "Stay in Paris and keep fighting until France is free."

He let out a heavy sigh. "The leaders of the *Wehrmacht* have been trained that failure is not an option. Desperation drives such men to do terrible things." Catching my look, he amended, "Even more terrible than what has been done."

"I'm on the winning side, remember? In case you haven't heard, *Le Boche est fini*." Stepping back, I tried for a smile.

His somber eyes held mine. "It was not a coincidence that I became ill on the day I was to accompany the shipment of weapons to Normandy, was it?"

I shook my head.

"You did not know then that I was working against the Wehrmacht, and yet you spared me."

"I did," I admitted.

"What would your Resistance comrades do if they found out that you kept me off the train?"

I didn't have to think about it. "They would execute me, naturally."

He cupped my cheek. "Strong, brave *and* beautiful. In better times, I would ask you to come with me. As my wife."

"In better times, I might say yes."

"Might?" His aquamarine gaze probed mine.

Pierre calling out from the main room saved me from answering. "*C'est l'heure. Nous devons partir.*"

It was time for Fritz to go. Time for us to say goodbye. Instead, I slipped my arms around his waist and held myself tightly against him.

Resting his chin atop my head, he sighed. "I dislike goodbyes."

Throat thick, I said, "Then we won't say goodbye. We'll say go safely for now."

He pulled back to look at me. "Another of your American idioms? I do not know this one."

I managed a watery smile. "Not American, Irish. It means ... Until we meet again."

For a moment, the clouds in his eyes lifted. "I have always wanted to see New York. Perhaps, after the war, I will come to you there?"

"Perhaps," I said, no longer sure where I belonged.

Rather than press me, he tipped up my chin and brushed a last kiss across my mouth.

I didn't walk out with him. Instead, I waited for the outer door to click closed before coming back into the main room. My eye caught the copy of *My Ántonia* lying open on the kitchen table. My first thought was that he'd left it by mistake, then I saw the note inscribed.

Whatever we have missed, we possess together the precious, the incommunicable past — FE

I touched my fingertips to the perfectly penned script, which I recognized as a paraphrased passage from the book.

Tears slid down my cheeks, splashing onto the page and blurring the ink. Once Chanel had said to me that a woman who couldn't cry had given up on happiness. Another of her maxims. I hadn't given it all that much thought at the time. I did now.

Thanks to Fritz, I hadn't given up on happiness after all. Being with him had helped bring me back to life after losing Jean-Claude. If we were meant to be, we'd find each other after the war. If not, I'd always look back on our time together for what it was.

A gift.

Chapter Fifty-One

By the middle of August, American and French troops had fought their way to the Seine. Six days later, the last cavalcade of Germans rolled out of Paris. People streamed into the streets and squares, cheering and chanting *vivre libre ou mourir*.

At nine o'clock on the morning of August 25th, French and American tanks, jeeps, and other armored vehicles poured into Paris. The city exploded in a frenzy of joy. French flags hung from windows and balconies. Women kissed every soldier they could get their hands on. Kids ran around torched German tanks and gobbled Hershey Bars pitched into the crowds by American GIs. The bells of Notre Dame, silent since the invasion, once more rang a joyous peel. Whistles blew, people danced and drank wine in the streets, passing around dusty bottles tucked away in hope of this day. Swastikas, German street signs, and other despised trappings of the Third Reich were torn down and burned. The French Tricolor and the Stars and Stripes flew side by side on the Eiffel Tower.

At the Ritz, Claude had the French flag hoisted as soon as the Germans drove off. The scarlet swags of swastikas and other Nazi symbols were likewise taken down.

I wondered what Jean-Claude would make of it all. I had always envisioned us sharing this happy day together. I was finding it harder and harder to remember his face, the sound of his voice, his scent. I clung to what memories I could conjure. The habit he had of raking his hand through his thick hair and raising funny looking furrows. The warmth of his hand on my waist when we'd danced. Our bicycle ride back from the American in the rain. The adorably funny picture he'd made wearing my floral bathrobe.

Like Jean-Claude and so many dear friends and brave heroes of the Resistance, Dr. Jackson and his family weren't there for the victory celebrations. According to our intelligence, the Jacksons were interned in Germany, Sumner, and his son Pete at Neuengamme concentration camp in Hamburg and Toquette at the women's camp at Ravensbrück north of Berlin. Hard as it was to think of them behind barbed wire, at least they were alive.

I joined the crowds packing the square outside the recently liberated Hôtel de Ville, now the headquarters of the National Council of the Resistance, where General de Gaulle would deliver his victory speech.

At 7 p.m., de Gaulle appeared on the balcony to address a jubilant crowd, a tall man with a long, thin face and prominent nose and wearing his brigadier general's uniform.

"Paris! Paris outraged! Paris broken! Paris martyred! But Paris liberated! Liberated by itself, liberated by its people with the help of the French armies, with the support and the help of all France, of the France that fights, of the only France, of the real France, of the eternal France!"

It was a corker of a speech, as Bridget might have said, and though I personally thought it shabby of him not to acknowledge the contributions of Great Britain and the United States, after four years of occupation, Parisians went wild.

Afterwards, he continued to the Ministry of War, where he was installed as provisional president of France.

The next day, I stood among the tens of thousands of proud Parisians lining the Champs-Élysées for the victory parade, holding up banners that read "*Vive de Gaulle*" and waving miniature French tricolors. Towering over everyone else, the general led his entourage on foot from the Arc de Triomphe down the Champs to the Place de la Concorde and from there to Notre Dame cathedral for a thanksgiving mass.

Straining to see over the people in front of me, I was reminded of the Bastille Days I'd celebrated with Bridget before the Occupation. I hadn't seen or heard from her since I'd kicked her out of our apartment the morning after Jean-Claude's arrest. At the time, her betrayal had seemed so black-and-white but, in hindsight, the gray areas seeped through. The Nazis had thrived by turning neighbor against neighbor and friends into foes, making animals of us all. Facing torture, most in Bridget's shoes would have acted as she had. In giving up Jean-Claude, she'd sought to save not only herself but me as well.

Later in the Place de la Concorde, I spotted Sylvia Beach and Adrienne Monnier standing across the square by the obelisk. I'd heard Sylvia had been released from Vittel after five months on a ticket of poor health, though she looked sound enough to me. I caught her eye, and she beckoned me over. I'd taken a few steps to join them when firecracker-like sounds sent me dropping.

Bullets sprayed the square. People leaped off their bicycles and scrambled to squeeze under the existing wood and barbed wire barricades. Others made a run for rue Saint-Florentin or ducked into doorways. I took refuge behind the sandbags at the base of one of the fountains. Covering my head with my hands, crazy thoughts crossed my mind. I thought of Jean-Claude and wondered if I'd be seeing him soon in whatever Afterlife awaited. I thought of Gran and the rest of the family and how devastated they'd all be if I died. I thought of Neil fighting somewhere in France and prayed that he was staying safe. Mostly I thought of myself and what lousy luck it would be to cash in my chips just as Paris was liberated.

Eventually the sniping stopped and the shrieking quieted. When I lowered my stiff arms and peered out, the dead and wounded were being loaded onto stretchers.

I stood and brushed off bits of gravel from my knees, then made my way over to the ladies, disheveled and shaken-looking but seemingly unhurt.

Miss Beach clasped her companion's arm in the crook of hers. "Leave it to the Boches to go out with a bang."

Though the Germans had surrendered the city, as we'd just discovered for ourselves, scattered pockets of holdouts remained to be routed. Picking us off had been like shooting fish in a barrel.

"Will you come back to ours and take tea?" Sylvia asked me.

"Ersatz coffee," Mademoiselle Monnier corrected her.

"Thank you, but I think I'll head home," I said, scanning the rooftops for more possible snipers.

Sylvia nodded. "Another time, then. Please give our regards to Madame LeBrun."

"I moved into the Ritz a while ago," I admitted and left it at that.

Sylvia's brow lifted. "Oh, then you must not know?"

She and Adrienne exchanged a look.

"I'm afraid I don't," I admitted.

"*Pauvre* Madame LeBrun lost her son," Adrienne said.

"Olivier?" I asked, hoping I'd misheard.

Sylvia sighed. "He and a schoolfriend were caught scribbling anti-Hitler slogans on the station walls at Place de la Madeleine. When the German patrolmen called them out, they took off. Olivier panicked and jumped onto the tracks. Passengers on the platform tried to pull him out but before they could—"

"The train came," Mademoiselle Monnier finished for her.

"That's horrible," I said sincerely.

I had never cared for Olivier, but even so, he had been an innocent child. Now he was yet another casualty of the Nazis. Ordinarily I would call on Madame LeBrun and pay my respects, but since she'd seen me with Fritz, and assumed I was a Nazi collaborator, I suspected I was the last person she'd want darkening her door.

I said my goodbyes and made my way back to the Ritz on foot. All around the city, ecstatic Parisians were holding rooftop parties. Reaching rue de Rivoli, I remembered Misia Sert had an apartment at No. 252. Giving into whim, I stepped into the street and looked up.

Chanel stood at the balcony railing, holding a miniature French tricolor on a stick in one hand and a cigarette in the other. With her, I spotted Jean Cocteau, who had attended social functions at the German embassy throughout the Occupation, and Serge Lifar, who had cooperated with the Nazi censors to keep his ballets going. With de Gaulle's Free French in power, all three had reason to worry.

Absent was von Dincklage. The baron, along with other senior Nazi officials, had fled Paris in July.

Seeing me, Chanel raised her brow. Her scarlet mouth slanted in what might have been a smile, and she waved her flag to me.

I lifted my hand and waved back, then walked quickly away.

Coming onto Place Vendôme, I skirted the square to rue Cambon when it struck me. With the Nazis gone, there was no civilian side of the hotel to stick to, no need to show anyone my pass. I backtracked and entered through the main entrance, stopping to exchange a few pleasantries with Jacques, restored to his post.

Cutting through the grande salle, I heard my name and turned around.

A tall, blond GI in olive drab twill stepped out from behind the tabletop display of fresh cut flowers. I blinked and then blinked again.

Neil's hesitant smile stretched into a grin, and he opened his arms. "Happy Liberation Day, sis."

Chapter Fifty-Two

A short while later, Neil and I were tucked into a table in the Ritz bar, thronged with thirsty war reporters keeping both Frank and Georges busy making martinis.

Serving with the 4th Infantry Division under Major General Barton, my brother had plenty of his own war stories to tell.

"Golly, sis, if only you could have seen it. Landing on D-Day at Utah Beach, the Battle of Normandy, and now liberating Paris. It was raining cats and dogs when we broke camp at Carrouges on the 23rd. When we got to the assembly area forty miles southwest of Paris the next day, my dogs were barking. Hem was with us for most of it," he added, gesturing with his beer glass to a barrel-chested, gray-bearded man standing at the center of the reporters, his khaki shirt opened to show off a mat of curly white chest hair.

Amused, I asked, "You call Ernest Hemingway Hem?"

"Sure, all us fellows do. He's covering the war for *Collier's*."

Gathered around the celebrated author were the prizewinning Hungarian American war photographer, Robert Capa, Chicago *Daily News* reporter, Helen Kirkpatrick who had ridden into Paris in a tank with General LeClerc's Second Armored Division, and Lee Miller, a former fashion model turned photojournalist for *Vogue*.

Sipping the ginger ale I had ordered to help settle my stomach, I pointed out a busty, pixyish blonde in a tightknit top sticking close to Hemingway's side. "That's Mary Welsh, a reporter with *Time Life*. According to the Ritz rumor mill, she and Hemmingway are knocking boots, though they're both married to other people. Speaking of which, how's *your* love life? Last I heard you were seeing an Italian girl named Maxine. Is it serious between you two?"

My sisterly snooping sent his gaze dropping to his beer glass. "It is," he admitted.

"Well, don't just sit there like a stone," I pressed. "I want to hear everything."

He picked up his beer and took a deep drink, then wiped foam from his upper lip.

"I met Max working on the loading dock at Kavanaugh's."

"I didn't know Gran had women working on the loading dock," I said, though I supposed it made sense. Since the war, Allied women had taken over all sorts of manual labor jobs traditionally reserved for men.

Looking away, he shook his head. "Max is short for Massimo."

Despite my uneasy stomach, I wished I had ordered something stronger than soda pop.

"He's a waist gunner with the 100th Bomb group in East Anglia," Neil continued, staring into his beer. "Never held a gun in his life until basic and now he's firing off a machine gun at 35,000 feet in the air, go figure." Despite the pride in his voice, he still hadn't met my eye.

"Do mom and dad know?" I asked.

"I'm planning on telling them once I get back. And introducing them to Max, if they're up for it."

"Once they get used to the idea, I'm sure they'll want to meet him."

His gaze edged back up to mine. "What about you?"

I reached over and squeezed his hand. "Of course, I want to meet him. If he makes you happy, then I'm happy."

"Really?"

I rolled my eyes. "Yes, really." I paused. "I love you, lamebrain."

He leaned back in his chair, looking as if the weight of the world had been lifted from his shoulders. "What about you? Going through the French countryside, the stories we heard, the stuff we saw, looked like things have been rough over here under the Krauts."

I had carried my secrets for so long, I wasn't sure how to put the past four Occupation years in words. But I supposed I had to start somewhere.

"It was rough," I admitted, "and it got worse every year. No food, no fuel, no basic amenities unless you bought them on the Black Market. But the worst part was not knowing who to trust. Some people became informers to get by, but others made enormous sacrifices to do their part," I added, thinking of Jean-Claude, Blanche – back from Fresnes but a shell of her former bubbly self – and the Jacksons, still interred in Germany.

At least Fritz had made it through. Pierre had sent word that he'd arrived safely in Switzerland.

He studied me. "I get the feeling you were in the second group?"

Clasping my drink, I admitted, "After the German invasion, I helped smuggle in food and supplies, hide downed airmen, that sort of thing." For whatever reason, staring into my glass made it easier to get the words out. "When the Jewish deportations started, I joined a Resistance group called Vengeance. We gathered intelligence and passed it on to London, provided medical support to *résistants*, and did whatever we could to strike against the Nazi infrastructure. A lot of that work went on in this very bar."

Looking up, I peered around the barroom packed with press. The Nazis had cleared out just days ago, and yet the stories from the war had taken on a fuzzy feeling, as if they were already part of the past.

Neil lifted his beer. "To my sister, the Resistance fighter."

Touched, I saluted him with my ginger ale. "To my brother, the war hero."

We each took a sip, then set our drinks down.

Neil's expression turned thoughtful. "For two sheltered rich kids from Manhattan, we did okay over here, didn't we?"

For the first time since Fritz had gone, I found my smile. "We sure did."

Chapter Fifty-Three

September 1944
Paris was free, but the deprivations of four years of Occupation didn't disappear overnight. Owing to retreating German troops burning the grain mills in Pantin, bread lines were longer than ever. Heating fuel and petrol stayed scarce. The Métro only ran a few hours a day and rationing remained in place. And the war was still on. Starting on September 3rd, we endured periodic strafing from German V-1 rockets, our ears attuned to their distinctive buzzing sound.

Throughout France, people accused of collaborating with the Nazis were called to task in *épurations*, purges. The Vél d'Hiv stadium, notorious as the site of the first Jewish roundup, was now a detention center for collabos. "Horizontal collaborators," women accused of sleeping with Nazis, were the lowest hanging fruit, and not even *Le Tout* were immune. Arletty had her head shaved and was sentenced to eighteen months' internment at Fresnes for living at the Ritz with her Luftwaffe officer. I worried Chanel might be next. Despite the dirty pool she'd played against the Wertheimers, I still had a soft spot for her.

Earlier that month, the first U.S. troops had crossed into Nazi Germany. Thinking of Neil fighting with the 4th, I was riding my bicycle back from the Hôtel Lutetia where a repatriation center had been set up to reunite survivors of the camps with their families. Knowing it was a longshot, still I had gone in the hope of speaking to someone who might have crossed paths with Jean-Claude at La Muette. One survivor I had met remembered a man coming in with a hobbled leg who fit Jean-Claude's description, but he couldn't say for certain if he was among the prisoners who'd died of fever, were taken out to Mont Valérien and shot, or put on a convoy to Auschwitz. Though disappointed, I was determined to keep trying.

I had just turned onto rue de Rivoli when a disheveled scarecrow of a woman shrilled, "*La Pute Américaine.*" The American whore.

Lost in thought, it took me a minute to realize she meant me.

Madame LeBrun darted into the street in front of me. I slammed on the brakes to keep from hitting her, nearly sending myself flying over the handlebars.

"*Salope, putain,*" she shouted again, pointing at me, hate blazing from her red-rimmed eyes.

"Madame LeBrun, please, you are not well." I tried edging the bike around her, but she grabbed the handlebars and held on.

People began drifting over. A grocer threw down his broom and headed into the street. A young mother handed her baby to the older woman with her and joined him. Two teenage boys abandoned their game of boules and came over. A waitress at a sidewalk café serving a table of GIs set down their food, tore off her apron, and took off toward me.

In frantic French, I pleaded, "Please, there's been mistake. I'm not a collabo."

"No mistake," Madam LeBrun hissed. "I saw her with my own eyes. She was sneaking a Boche into her room. Later, she helped him escape."

"Her mistake was thinking she could get away with it," the young mother said.

A man I hadn't noticed before spoke. "I saw her get out of a Nazi Mercedes to dine with her Boche boyfriend."

It took me a minute to place him in plain clothes, but once I did, I recognized him as the doorman from Maxim's.

By then, the spectators had grown to a dozen.

Hemmed in, I gripped the handlebars of my bicycle to keep my hands from shaking. "Please, I'm not a collabo. I'm a *résistante*. I worked for Vengeance."

"Now that the Boches are gone, *tout le monde* is with the Resistance," the grocer snickered.

I shook my spinning head, their odors overwhelming. The young mother was hatless; I could smell the grease in her stringy hair. The café waitress had wine on her breath. The grocer was overly fond of garlic. Madame LeBrun emanated a vinegary reek. For a frightful few seconds, I was sure my lunch would come up.

I took a breath and tried talking my way out of it. "Send someone to 12 rue de l'Odéon. Mademoiselle Beach at Shakespeare and Company will vouch for me."

"An *intellectuelle*," someone spat, as if it was a dirty word.

Then again, considering how many of their French artistes had betrayed them by collaborating, or at least cooperating, with the Nazis, perhaps it had become one.

"The Ritz, then. Ask for Madame Auzello at the desk. Or Monsieur Meier at the bar."

"We are wasting time. Take her!"

Someone kicked my back tire. The bicycle fell over, taking me with it. I hit the street hard, scraping the side of my face, my right arm twisted beneath me. Surrounded by feet, I panicked and tried to scramble up. Before I could, the toe of a dusty boot slammed into my breast. I cried out and curled onto my side, covering my stomach.

"*Salope, salope, salope …*"

Rough hands hauled me upright. Lost to a sea of shoving, slapping, punching, and hairpulling, I was borne along, one boy beating me with a stick every time my steps lagged.

We crossed the Pont au Change to Île de la Cité and came to the Palais de Justice. A large group gathered outside the Seine-facing side of the courthouse. An acrid stench filled the air. Someone had gotten a fire going in a trash bin.

Seated on a stool outside the gate, a grandmotherly woman was having her steel-gray hair shorn off by a barber plying his shaver. Two men stood on either side of her holding her arms, pistols stuffed into their belts and FFI tricolor armbands on their left sleeves. A small boy who couldn't have been much older than six gathered up the fallen hair and threw it in the makeshift firepit.

Catching snippets of rapid-fire French, I gathered she'd billeted junior German officers in her boarding house and had accepted ration cards and money in return. That she likely hadn't had a choice didn't seem to matter to anyone. The mob wanted vengeance and now that the Nazis were gone, they'd take it out on their own.

Two more FFI agents approached me. My tormentors turned me over to them and fell back. I repeated my plea to send someone to the Ritz for Blanche or Frank to vouch for me, but they likewise ignored me. Instead, they each took my arm and pulled me toward a parked lorry. A half-dozen women with shaved heads hunched in the truck bed, some crying, others staring numbly ahead, one with her chin defiantly tipped up. The younger ones were stripped down to their slips; several had swastikas marked on their foreheads.

One of the men gave me a shove. I managed to climb up and haul myself over the side, landing on my hands and knees.

A hand tipped in oval-shaped nails reached down to me.

I grabbed it and looked up.

A short, curvy girl with a gap between her front teeth stood over me, her shaven scalp gouged and bleeding in spots, a swastika marked on her forehead in red lipstick.

"Bridget?"

She guided me over to the pile of rags serving as seating.

"Shove over," she said in English and the other women shifted to make room for us.

Head spinning, I dropped down beside her. Thinking of the laughing, giddy girls we were before the war, it was hard to believe we'd come to this.

Lowering my voice, I said, "I know I ... said things, terrible things, but I didn't mean them. I was out of my mind with worry over Jean-Claude and desperate for someone to blame. I would *never* give you up to the Resistance, I swear it."

She didn't blink. "I know you didn't turn me in. I did."

Staring over at her, I felt my mouth fall open.

"I told the *épuration* committee how I spilled the beans to the Gestapo about Jean-Claude and got him arrested."

I was aghast. What Bridget had admitted was a far more serious crime than horizontal collaboration. It was treason. People were being shot for less.

Finding my voice, I said, "If you hadn't, they would have tortured you horribly. Anyone in your circumstances would have done the same."

She turned to me. "You wouldn't have. You'd have let them pull out every tooth and toenail before you talked. And yet here you are, in the same boat as the rest of us collabos. What happened?"

"Madame LeBrun saw me sneaking Fritz up to the apartment and called me out."

One sandy brow lifted. "So, you knocked boots with the Nazi after all?"

"Fritz isn't a Nazi. He's been spying on the Abwehr, and von Dincklage, for the Allies since before the war."

She took that in. "Suppose we all have our secrets." She moistened her cracked lips. "Ever ask yourself how I got out of Vittel so quick?"

"I promised René de Chambrun money to get you out," I said, wondering what she was getting at.

She snorted. "In a week? He's a barrister, not a magician."

I thought back to that tumultuous time. So much had happened so quickly. Coming back from Vittel and finding my uncle in Paris. The fevered plan to get him and Hattie out of the city. Jean-Claude's arrest. It wasn't until weeks later that I'd checked my bank details and realized that no money had been drafted. At the time, I'd wondered if Chanel had paid for Bridget's release, too, as a way of making amends.

She lifted her chin. "I didn't need your bloody money. I got myself out by promising to keep an eye on you. One 'enemy alien' keeping tabs on another seemed an easy enough deal to strike. I couldn't think there'd be much of anything to report. Then I got back to Paris and there was all that business with your uncle."

"You *informed*?!" That time, I didn't bother dropping my voice.

"I really did try to convince the Gestapo there was nothing going on but it seems I'm not the ace liar I fancied myself."

I stared, not at her hacked off hair and marked forehead but at her eyes, which met mine without a trace of shame.

She ran a hand over her head, shiny as a billiard ball. "The FFI man who had at me was so drunk, I'm lucky he didn't lop off an ear. They'll do better by you. Brought in a proper barber to do things right."

I didn't know what to say to that, so I settled on silence.

"Seeing as I'm clearing the air, you should know it was me who put the flask of No. 5 in your bag."

All this time, I'd been so sure it was Millet and Aubrey. Instead, the culprit had slept in the bed next to mine, my best friend, or so I'd thought.

"Why?" I asked, feeling as if I'd entered one of Jean Cocteau's absurdist plays.

"Sounds silly now, but I was jealous of that Polish girl. You were always inviting her to lunch with us; every time I turned around, she was there, tagging along. I didn't fancy being replaced."

I couldn't believe what I was hearing. "Hanna and her family fled Poland with nothing. She was in a foreign country and could barely speak the language. I felt sorry for her."

"St. Marguerite," she said, and her tone told me it wasn't a compliment. "When she went on admiring your Chanel handbag, I *knew* you'd give it to her."

Before I could think what to say to that, my name was called.

"Marguerite Blakely, for horizontal collaboration and acting against the national interest."

Acting against the national interest – the French euphemism for spying!

Bridget sent me a sympathetic look. "*Bon courage*, as the Frenchies say. My advice: stay still and don't make a fuss. Goes quicker that way."

The two FFI fighters who had brought me over returned for me.

Knowing that putting up a fight would only provide the sadistic satisfaction they craved, I climbed down on my own and let them walk me over to the shearing area.

They shoved me into the still-warm seat. Clumps of brown, blonde and black hair littered the ground at my feet. I expected them to turn me over to the barber and get on with it. Instead, they seemed determined to stretch out the ordeal, one man pulling my curls this way and that while the other made crude comments about my hair color for the amusement of the crowd. One of them grabbed a fistful of my hair and yanked my head back, so forcefully that I felt snapping in my neck.

The first strafe of the shaver against my scalp was a shock I'll never forget. Hanks of hair slipped down the sides of my face like tears, hitting my shoulders and landing in my lap. Rather than toss them into the firepit, the boy snatched them up and started handing them out as souvenirs.

Tears pushed at the backs of my eyes, but I was too stubborn to shed them. It was only hair. It would grow back. With Jean-Claude dead and Fritz in Switzerland, it wasn't like I had anyone to doll myself up for.

Out of the side of my eye, I saw the FFI man tending the trashcan walk toward me, the firestick in his mitted hand. I tried twisting my head to better see what it was, but the barber admonished me to stay still.

He waited for the barber to finish, then drew up in front of me. That's when I saw that the stick that he carried wasn't a stick at all.

It was a branding iron.

Chapter Fifty-Four

"*Arrêtez!*" Stop!

I looked out to Josephine Baker cutting through the crowd, which parted for her like the Red Sea had for Moses. Watching her bound up onto the platform, I wondered if I was hallucinating. The last I had heard she was entertaining the troops in North Africa. I hadn't known she was back in Paris.

Reaching me, she elbowed one of the FFI man aside and helped me up. "I got you, honey."

She wrapped her arm around my waist and turned us to look out onto the square.

"This woman, an American like me, is not a collaborator. She's a hero," she said in French, her trained stage voice carrying to the far reaches. "She didn't have to stay and suffer through four years of Occupation. She chose to stay because, like me, she has two loves – France and Paris. Because of the work she did for the Resistance, countless lives were saved. Jewish lives. French lives. Allied lives. Everything she did, she did at great personal cost and terrible danger, in the service of a free France."

The heckling quieted. Scornful faces softened.

Seizing on the shift, Josephine laced her fingers through mine and raised our joined hands high into the air.

"*Vive la liberté. Vive la France.*" She turned to me. "*Vive la Marguerite.*"

The same onlookers who a moment ago had been only too happy to watch me shaved and branded erupted into cheers. Several men standing in the front started up the platform to hoist me onto their shoulders. I shrank back, terrified of being touched.

Before anyone could get their hands on me, Josephine whisked me offstage and through the crowd. Occasionally she stopped to scribble an autograph or accept a hearty "*bon retour*" but even then, she kept a steadying hand on my elbow.

It wasn't until I settled into the front passenger seat of her sleek black-and-white Delage that my numbness began to crack. I rested my head, my *bald* head, against the sunbaked snakeskin and felt tears stinging my scraped cheeks.

She passed me a hankie embroidered with her initials, then gunned the engine.

"One of my contacts tipped me off that you were on the purge committee's list. I got down here as fast as I could. Sorry I didn't make it sooner."

I used the hankie to blot my eyes. "Don't be sorry. You saved me from branding and maybe worse."

"I'll send you to my *perruquier*. Best wigmaker in Paris and smoking hot. Could be just what the doctor ordered."

At her mention of doctor, I choked back a sob.

"Oh dear, there I go shooting off my big mouth. Things didn't work out with the delectable Dr. Jacob?"

"Jean-Claude's dead," I admitted, marveling that it was still so hard to say the word.

She turned her head to look at me. "Oh, baby girl, you've had one hard knock after another. Come back to my pied-à-terre. We'll clean you up and then pop open a bottle of bubbly and get rip-roaring drunk. How's that sound?"

"Thanks, I appreciate it, but I think right now I need to be alone. I have a room at the Ritz," I added.

"No worries, I understand. Some hurts run so deep they need time to heal."

Eyeing her profiled face, I said, "Sounds like you're speaking from experience."

Motoring through the mostly empty streets, she filled me in on her past three years. I'd heard she'd been ill but hadn't realized how serious it was. Or that a miscarriage had been involved.

"I'm so sorry, Jo," I said when she'd finished. "I had no idea."

Sniffing, she nodded. "S'okay. I realize now that God has a different plan for me. I'm going to adopt a beautiful Rainbow Tribe of orphaned babies and little kids, not just from France but all over the world, and we're all going to live at Les Milandes, one big, happy family."

"They'll be lucky to have you," I said sincerely.

She turned onto Place Vendôme and slowed to a stop at the hotel entrance.

"Sure you're up for being alone?" she asked.

"I'll be all right."

I tried giving her back the hankie, but she shook her head.

"Keep it. A little something to remember me by."

"Les Milandes isn't *that* far," I pointed out.

"True, but New York is. I'm not likely to go back there anytime soon. But I have a feeling you might."

Rather than answer, I reached over to hug her, inhaling her wonderfully woodsy, spicy scent, not Chanel No. 5, but Guerlain Sous Le Vent.

"Take care, Josephine, and thank you for everything you've done, not just for me and my family but for France. You ought to get a medal."

She cracked a laugh. "Just one?" Sobering, she said, "If you ever need me, promise you'll look me up?"

"I will, I promise."

I opened the car door and got out. At the hotel entrance, I turned back and glimpsed her blowing me a kiss.

She tore off, tires screeching. I stood watching until the Delage turned the corner and disappeared. Without knowing why, I sensed it was the last time I would ever see her.

Back in my room, I drew myself a hot bath and climbed stiffly in. Though I scrubbed my bruised skin until it was raw, it was no use, I still felt dirty. Finally, I gave up and got out, put on my pajamas and crawled under the bedcovers.

By then, I had decided. There was nothing and no one left for me in Paris, or in France, either, for that matter. Josephine was right.

It was time to go home.

Chapter Fifty-Five

At ten o' clock the next morning, I finally got out of bed, so stiff and sore I felt like a lorry had hit me. Not yet ready to face curious eyes, instead of calling for room service, I stayed in my pajamas and put on a pot of chicory coffee using the drip coffeepot I'd brought over from Bridget's and my old apartment. I was filling the well from the sink in the bathroom when I heard knocking outside my door, not the politely restrained rapping of a Ritz staff member but heavy, determined pounding. The FFI come back to finish me off?

I stared at myself in the wall mirror and took a few deep breaths. The other day, I had been easy pickings, but I wouldn't make the same mistake again. Until I could arrange to get out of Paris, I would have my guard up.

The knocking kept up. I set the coffee urn down and came out from the bathroom. Peering out the keyhole, I saw Chanel's maid, Germaine, standing in the hallway.

"What is it, Germaine?" I called out.

"Please, mademoiselle, I must speak with you. It is urgent."

"*Attendez.*" I went in search of a scarf, a Chanel design like the rest of my wardrobe, and tied it around my head.

I opened the door and ushered her in. If she noticed my missing hair, she was either too polite or too distraught to point it out.

"Mademoiselle Coco has been taken. By the *Fifis*," she said, using Chanel's word for the FFI.

I led her over to an armchair and sat her down. Between hitching breaths, she managed to tell me what had happened.

At eight-thirty that morning, a hotel porter had knocked on Chanel's door and informed her that two men, FFI agents, requested her presence below.

"'Germaine, go to rue Cambon, to my writing desk, and bring me the letters from Churchill,' she told me," Germaine recalled. "'The letters from Winston only. Leave the others behind.' Then she went into the bathroom to dress."

What others? I wondered, reading between the lines.

Before Germaine could leave to fetch the letters, the agents themselves showed up at the suite door. Unflappable as ever, Chanel had emerged from the bathroom dressed and dry-eyed and went off with them to the prefecture of police on Île de la Cité.

"That was *two* hours ago, mademoiselle." Germaine reached into her skirt pocket for her handkerchief and mopped her streaming eyes.

"Did you find the letters?" I asked, my heart hammering so hard I half-expected it to punch a hole in my chest.

Germaine nodded. "They were in the writing desk in her apartment as she said."

She dug into her pocket and took out a packet of letters tied with a black ribbon.

"Leave them with me," I said. "I'll see that they're placed in the proper hands." I offered up a reassuring smile and held out my hand.

"*Merci, merci, merci!*" The poor woman got up and launched the letters and herself at me, kissing both my cheeks. "I knew you would know what to do." Stepping back, she looked at me with grateful, trusting eyes.

"Go back to Mademoiselle's room and wait for her there," I told her, steering her toward the door.

I went through the Churchill letters, six in all, mostly chatty correspondence that read like a social diary, confirming the dates and times of personal meetings and occasionally recalling their halcyon days of fishing and hunting parties. The oldest was dated 1936 when Churchill had brought his grown son, Randolph, with him to Paris, and the last referenced his November 1939 visit when he was Lord of the Admiralty. Certainly, they proved that Chanel and Churchill were friends, or at least friendly acquaintances, though I couldn't say to what degree that would sway the *épurations* committee in her favor.

I dressed quickly, left the hotel, and cut across the rue Cambon. The boutique was shuttered but I had kept my key. I hurried up the stairs to the second floor and let myself into the apartment, heading for the rolltop desk. I opened all three drawers, lifted the dividers and shook them, and even flipped through the stack of cream-colored stationery stock.

On the verge of giving up, I picked up Chanel's little black address book to put it back. A folded sheet of paper fell out. Opening it, I saw that it was a handwritten letter penned on Ritz Madrid stationery.

Hôtel Ritz, Place del Prado, Madrid
6 January 1944
c/o Sir Samuel Hoare, British Ambassador, Madrid

My Dear Winston,
    I hope this letter finds you well, dear, and not too terribly torn asunder by this dreadful war business.

*You can well imagine that after years of occupation in
France it has been my lot to encounter all kinds of people!
Living in close quarters with the Germans, I can assure you
that they are in no means unified behind Monsieur Hitler.
En fait, it has come to my attention that certain high-ranking
German officials wish nothing more than to see him removed
and a speedy and peaceful resolution to hostilities with
Britain and her Allies.*

*You know far better than I, my dear, the disaster that
would befall us all if a weakened Germany were to fall into
Soviet hands.*

*I trust you know me well enough after all these years to
understand that I want only to be of service. Should this letter
find your favor, I stand willing to make whatever introductions you deem helpful and fitting.*

I remain always affectionately…
Coco Chanel

I tucked the letter in with the others and made my way back to the Ritz. Climbing up to Blanche's portion of the attic, I helped myself to the black wig I'd worn for Göring along with some pancake makeup to cover my more dramatic bruises. My bicycle was long gone, but Jacques came to my rescue and let me borrow his.

I reached the prefecture of police on Île de la Cité. The big, stone-clad building had been liberated the previous month when striking police had joined the FFI in reclaiming it and other government buildings from the retreating Germans. I secured Jacques' bicycle outside and entered through the main door.

Inside the central court, men and a few women milled about,

the men wearing FFI armbands and serious faces. A large Cross of Lorraine, the double-barred cross that had been the symbol of de Gaulle's Free France since 1940, was mounted over the main door. Thinking of Jean-Claude and all the brave *résistants* who hadn't lived to see this day firmed my resolve to see justice done.

I walked up to a harried-looking secretary typing on an old Contin typewriter, the black phone on her desk ringing off the hook.

Pitching my voice above the shriek, I said, "I need to see Pierre Latour. Please tell him Daisy Blakely ... Apple Pie is here. I have critical information about a woman brought in for interrogation."

She looked up, expression frayed. "He is very busy, mademoiselle. Leave your message with me, and I will see that he receives it."

In the middle of my arguing with her, Pierre stepped out from an interior office. At first, he didn't recognize me, but I flagged my hand and called out his name.

"Pierre, a word ... in private, *s'il te plaît?*"

He led me into an empty office. Instead of Pétain's portrait, a framed photograph of General de Gaulle hung from the gray wall behind a desk piled with papers and files. A pair of scarred desk chairs sat across from it, one with handcuffs dangling from the mid rail.

Suppressing a shudder, I stayed standing. "I'm here about Mademoiselle Chanel. I know your men came to the Ritz this morning and brought her in for questioning. Before you go any further, you need to see this. I found it among some letters in her desk."

I opened my handbag and took out Chanel's last letter to Churchill, written from Spain.

"As you'll see when you read it, in this letter to Winston Churchill, Mademoiselle Chanel tries talking the prime minister into accepting a conditional peace with the Germans, a deal that would remove

Hitler but leave the Nazi regime intact. It's all here, in black and white, written in her own hand."

I held out the paper, my own hand shaking.

He still made no move to take it.

Confused, I rambled on. "I don't know if Churchill ever received it, perhaps Sir Samuel refused to send it on, but that's not the point, is it? The point is Chanel is on the hook to the Abwehr, to Baron Spatz von Dincklage, and has been for years."

I was talking a mile a minute like Sylvia did, but I was too weary and wound-up to care.

"And I have it on good authority, unimpeachable authority, that last spring she and von Dincklage traveled to Berlin – *Berlin*! – twice to meet with Himmler *and* Walter Schellenberg." I stopped for breath, feeling like I'd run a race.

"Daisy, please, sit. Let me get you a glass of water."

I didn't want to sit. I didn't want a glass of water. I wanted Jean-Claude back, here with me, to share this day and all the ones that came after. But if I couldn't have that, him, and I couldn't, then I'd settle for justice.

"Pierre, what are you not telling me?" I demanded, not understanding what I was missing, why he couldn't seem to look me in the eye.

"We had to let her go."

"Sorry?" I reached out, grabbing hold of the chairback.

Grim-faced, he admitted, "She was released an hour ago. We had no choice. Duff Cooper called on her behalf."

During the war, Alfred Duff Cooper, the Viscount Norwich, had served as the British government's liaison to de Gaulle's Free French. Since the Liberation, he'd been appointed ambassador to France's provisional government.

"Monsieur Cooper relayed the message that Prime Minister Churchill personally requested Mademoiselle Chanel's release."

"So, Churchill came through after all," I said, more to myself than him.

Chanel had spent most of the last four years under von Dincklage's thumb, working for the Abwehr, and yet all the Nazis' elaborate schemes to get her to Churchill had gone nowhere. Ironically, all she'd had to do to catch his attention was get herself arrested.

Pierre shrugged. "*Peut-être* he has fond memories of their youth when she was mistress to his good friend, the Duke of Westminster?"

"Perhaps," I echoed, though I doubted a statesman of Churchill's stature would be swayed by sentiment.

More plausible to me was that Chanel knew where the bodies were buried, specifically the pro-Nazi dealings of certain members of the British elite, including her old lover, the Duke of Westminster, and the Duke and Duchess of Windsor.

Finally, he reached out for the letter. I was about to hand it over, but at the last minute something stopped me. An inner voice that cautioned it might come in handy someday.

I slipped it back into my bag. "*Merci*, but I think I'll hold onto it for now."

Some survivors of war take relics to remember. A bullet casing, a pebble from a razed stronghold, or more macabre, a tooth or lock of hair from a felled enemy. My relic would be this letter. Who knew, maybe someday in the far future I'd turn it over to a reporter to publish. More likely I would burn it and carry Chanel's secrets and mine to the grave.

Chapter Fifty-Six

Deflated, I got back to the Ritz and returned Jacques' bicycle. Habit had me entering the hotel through the rue Cambon side.

Blanche stood at the porter's station directing the stacking of several large crates. Her naturally dark hair was back to blonde though it had thinned in patches. Seeing her reminded me not to feel so sorry for myself. During her two months at Fresnes, she had lost her best friend, forty pounds, and very nearly her life. A shaved head and Chanel's slipping the noose were small potatoes in comparison.

Her haunted eyes widened when I walked up. "This is a new look."

I reached up to make sure the wig was on straight. "I hope you don't mind me borrowing it. I'm going to need to wear it ... for a while," I added, then filled her in on my recent run-in with the FFI.

"Those fucking FFI vigilantes are almost as bad as the Boches," she said though I could tell from her face she didn't believe it, and neither did I.

I glanced around. "Don't tell me we're shipping the furniture to the Germans, too," I asked, only partway joking.

Other than the portrait of César Ritz still hanging in the main salle, the fleeing Germans had taken whatever wasn't nailed down, including clearing out the display cases in the Hall of Dreams.

She leaned closer, near enough that I caught a whiff of vodka on her breath. "That bitch, Coco, is finally leaving and good riddance."

"Leaving?"

She nodded. "Got back an hour ago, packed her bags, released her room, and ordered her furniture and those damned Chinese screens she's so crazy about to be shipped to the Beau Rivage Palace Hotel on Lake Geneva."

Neutral Switzerland – the perfect place for an accused Nazi collaborator to wait out the war.

I left Blanche and headed out the swinging double doors to rue Cambon. Approaching No. 31, I saw a line of American GIs stretching more than a block long. I cut to the front and spotted the reason: a handwritten sign in English taped to the main shop window.

Chanel No. 5 free to any American soldier.

Drawing a hail of dirty looks, I cut the line and went inside.

Chanel and Madame Millet stood at the perfume counter handing out bottles of No. 5.

"*Un grand merci pour vôtre service*," Chanel said, passing a small black-and-white store bag to a freckle-faced American corporal.

He looped the black handle over his wrist. "Much obliged ma'am. I don't know what you just said, but this here's gonna make my mama's year."

Chanel flashed him a smile and switched to English. "Having you safely home will be your mother's true reward. When my André was taken prisoner by those nasty Boches, all the *parfum* in the world could not make life sweet again."

He tipped his cap and turned to go, grinning from ear to ear.

I waited for the door to close behind him before walking up. It took both women a moment to recognize me.

"Très chic," Chanel remarked, "though I prefer you as a redhead."

"Seems we both fell out with the FFI," I said.

She looked from me to Madame Millet. "Leave us."

The head seamstress nodded and crossed to the front of the counter. "*Bonne chance*," she whispered to me in passing and though we weren't friends and never would be, I sensed she had stopped being my enemy some time ago.

I waited for her to disappear through a side door, then turned back to Chanel.

"I heard you were taken in for questioning."

She shrugged. "The Fifis came for me, we had a conversation, they found nothing and now I am free again."

"They found nothing because they were told to stop looking. Churchill came through after all. Brava, Agent Westminster."

I'd expected her to deny it. She didn't.

"In terrible times, we do what we must to survive. What right do you have to judge me? You spent the last year with *your* German."

"I was working for the Resistance. And my German, as you call him, was helping us."

She sucked her teeth. "I was helping, too, working to bring about peace between Germany and Britain."

"A conditional peace."

She shrugged. "Peace is peace. Think how many lives might have been saved if I had succeeded. French lives. Allied lives. German lives."

"And the Jewish lives?"

She looked away. "I am leaving in a little while for Lausanne. Larcher is driving me."

"Give my regards to Baron von Dincklage. On second thought, don't."

That she didn't answer beyond a tight smile as good as confirmed that Spatz would be joining her in opulent exile if he wasn't there already.

"What will happen to Maison Chanel?" I asked.

What once had seemed a temple to fashion now struck me more as a funhouse, an elegant distortion, a carefully curated lie.

She blew out her lips. "I have worked every day of my life for thirty-five years, ever since I opened my first hat shop on boulevard Malesherbes. I have earned my retirement."

A snort escaped me. "You, retired? I can't imagine it."

Improbably, she smiled. "I am not certain I can, either. But we will see."

On the walk over, I'd rehearsed what I would say to her, the righteous tirade I would unleash. Now none of that seemed to matter. No words could bring back Jean-Claude or the tens of thousands of Jews deported to German concentration camps, or the brave Resistance fighters tortured and killed. No words could undo the last four years or erase her part in it. And yet, like a cat on her ninth life, she had survived it all.

But so had I.

"I hope you left room in your luggage for these." I reached into my handbag, took out the packet of her letters and dropped it on the counter.

She glanced down but made no move to reach for them. "They are all there?"

I held my gaze on hers. "All but one."

"Hmm," she said.

I glanced out the window where the line of American soldiers had lengthened. "I'll let you get back to it. Bon voyage."

I turned to go, but she called me back.

"Go home to New York, Marguerite. Marry a beautiful man, make beautiful babies and when the time comes, run your beautiful department store. And someday when you are old, perhaps you will think of me and your days on rue Cambon and not be so angry anymore."

Rather than answer, I took a last look around. The displays of chic hats and jewelry and scarves. The mirrored staircase with its plate glass panes placed to mimic the facets of a diamond. The scent of her namesake fragrance, Chanel No. 5, hovering over it all like an oppressive, opulent cloud.

And at the center of it all, the *Grande Mademoiselle* herself, wearing her signature simplicity like a suit of armor, her scarlet lipstick perfectly applied, her hair dyed as dark as the day I'd first set eyes on her, an awestruck eighteen-year-old eager to embark on a fairy tale adventure. An arrow of sunlight chose that moment to strike through the window. It hit Chanel full-on, and in that stark, unforgiving light I saw her for what she was: a selfish, ruthless, loveless old woman.

Chanel's voice broke through my reverie. "*Adieu*, Marguerite."

I locked my gaze on hers. If Paris – and Chanel – had taught me anything it was to be entirely myself without explanation or apology.

"My name is Daisy."

Chapter Fifty-Seven

By mid-September, General de Gaulle's provisional government had set up courts to stem the vigilante violence. As autumn descended, the heavy pall of war began to lift from Paris, though the fighting kept on elsewhere. The owners of houses and shops threw off their heavy shutters, the streetlights came on again, and dogs and children went back to playing in the streets. Women once again window shopped, haggled at markets, and met friends at cafés, the shaved ones hiding their fuzzed scalps beneath glossy new wigs.

The lines of American GIs outside Maison Chanel dwindled. Chanel herself was gone, settled in Switzerland for the foreseeable. Though her boutique stayed open, I only ever saw a handful of customers straggle in.

With nothing in Paris to hold me, I began making travel plans of my own. After six years away, it was time to go back to New York. When I had last visited, I had felt like a foreigner. Hopefully settling in with my family would help make the city feel like home again.

Blake and Hattie saw me off at Le Havre.

"Promise you'll come back to visit once the baby's old enough?" Hattie said.

My heightened sensitivity to smells had been the first tipoff. Bouts of morning sickness followed. By then, the shock had mellowed to happy anticipation. Though I had never set out to be a single mother, I counted my blessings. Unlike Gran, who had come to New York pregnant and alone, I had a loving family to lean on.

"*Visit?* You're not getting rid of me that easily. Once we open the Paris Kavanaugh's, the baby and I will be living here at least part of the year."

How I would manage to crisscross the Atlantic with a baby I couldn't say. But considering my mother had taken Neil and me with her to the office, clearing out a file cabinet as a makeshift cradle, I knew I'd work out a way.

Uncle Blake's smile thinned, suggesting that he hadn't thrown caution to the wind completely. "You might want to give the French economy time to recover."

"After four years of occupation, Parisians are starved for a little luxury. I should know," I couldn't resist adding, a less than subtle reminder that he was still a visitor here.

He shook his head, knowing better than to debate me. "Still our Daisy. I was afraid the war might have changed you," he said and though I smiled with him, I felt a lump rise in my throat.

I had changed, profoundly, in ways I couldn't begin to put into words. My hair was the least of it. I had given up wearing wigs before the first peach fuzz appeared. Rather than seeing my shorn scalp as a mark of shame, I'd come to consider it a badge of honor, a testimony to all I'd lived through. Not just lived through.

Survived.

I gave them both a hug and shooed them off. "Run along, you two. I hate goodbyes. Besides, I'll be seeing you lovebirds in New York for your wedding."

A summer wedding was in the works, the reception to be held at Kavanaugh's. Though I hadn't yet been let in on all the details, I suspected Gran and Mom would recruit me to help with the planning once I was back and settled.

I waited for them to walk off, then made my way over to the quayside café and bought myself a cup of tea. I'd just sat down to drink it when I heard my name called.

"Daisy? *Daisy*!"

I turned toward the ticket window, raising my hand to shield my eyes from the sun glare off the water. A tall, scarecrow of a man in a worn hat and shabby suitcoat skirted the line of waiting passengers and hurried toward me, his crutch scarcely slowing him down.

Squinting, I took in the dark hair grown past his collar, the proud set of his shoulders, the elegant, long-fingered hand holding the crutch, and leaped up, spilling my tea over the table.

Rounding it, I ran to meet him.

"Jean-Claude!?"

We fell into each other's arms, hugging so hard I marveled our bones didn't break. Kissing his mouth, burying my face in his neck, running my hands along his back, I still couldn't believe he was real.

Finally, we pulled back to look at each other, stupid smiles on our faces.

Framing his thin face between my hands, I took note of the new lines at the corners of his eyes and the strands of silver threading his hair. "I thought you were dead. Dr. Jack heard you'd been taken out and shot."

"I nearly was. My name was on the list. By the time I got to Drancy, the infection had set in. I was too ill to stand, let alone survive a train to Germany. When I admitted to the camp doctor that I was a surgeon at the American, he decided I was too valuable to let die. He removed the bullet and treated the infection with what little supplies he had."

"That was good of him," I said, horrified at all he'd suffered, but beyond grateful to have him back.

He snorted. "Good, maybe. Selfish, too. Once I recovered, he put me to work helping him in the camp infirmary. The conditions were terrible, worse than any field hospital I've ever known, but it was the only medical care prisoners received, and I like to think I helped save a few lives."

"I *know* you did."

His dark gaze skimmed over me. "All I could think was to stay alive and come back to you."

He kissed me again, long and slow and sweet. Our lips were the same perfect match they'd always been, but nearly everything else had changed.

I pulled back. "I'm not the same person you left in the tunnels."

He gestured with his crutch. "As you can see, neither am I."

"It's more than that. I'm … I'm pregnant."

His smile flattened.

"The father is the German lieutenant who reported to von Dincklage," I admitted.

"Your asset?"

I hesitated. "He started out as that. It wasn't until the assassination attempt on Hitler that I found out the truth: he'd been working for the Allies all along."

He took that in. "Where is he now?"

"Pierre and Frank Meier and I smuggled him out to Switzerland."

"He is gone, then?" he asked.

Meeting his gaze, I knew he was asking about more than geography. "He is."

I still cared for Fritz. In another life, I could see myself looking him up after the war, inviting him to visit me in New York and meet my family. After all we'd been through together, he held a place in my heart and always would. But Jean-Claude *was* my heart. My soulmate.

"And you are going as well?" He glanced back at my suitcase, spilled tea dripping down the sides.

"I was going back to New York. I told myself Paris was over for me, that I had nobody left here. That everyone I cared about, loved, was gone." Unexpectedly, my voice broke.

He swallowed hard, the muscles of his throat working. "And now? *Tu m'aimes encore?*"

I didn't have to stop and think. "Of course, I still love you! With all my heart. I have since the first time I walked into your exam room, and you were rude to me."

He shrugged in that oh-so-French way, one of so many things I'd missed about him. "*Alors, ça suffira.*"

"Will it be enough, though? After everything that's happened, can you honestly love and raise the child of a German officer?"

His jaw firmed. "I can and *will* love any child of yours as my own." Ever practical, he added, "We should marry as soon as possible."

I hesitated. "You're certain about this?"

His gaze stayed on mine. "Certain that I want to spend the rest of my life with you? To be a family with you? *Oui*, I am."

More than any declaration, it was the fierce love in his eyes that won me over.

"My grandmother will want us to have a Catholic wedding," I said, our different faiths one of several hurdles ahead.

He smiled. "Then we will marry twice, here in the Grande Synagogue de Paris, and again when we arrive in New York."

It took me a moment for his meaning to sink in.

"But France, Paris, is your home. You said so yourself."

He cradled my fuzzed head between his calloused hands and drew me gently to him. "*You* are my home."

His mouth met mine, and I drank him in, this beautiful, impossible, brilliantly flawed man who was my soulmate in every way.

Ours wasn't the starry-eyed love story I had fantasized for myself when I had first come to Paris. The war had left both of us dented but not broken, hardened by loss and horror and yet willing to open our hearts and learn to live again. Unlike the couples in Hollywood movies, Jean-Claude wasn't my knight in shining armor nor was I his damsel in distress. We were two battle-scarred warriors who had fought their way out of the darkness and found each other again. Fortunately for us, our love wasn't the stardust of yesterday; the music of years gone by.

Instead, it held the promise of many happy years to come.

THE END

Selected Bibliography

The following books and resource materials were invaluable in researching *Stardust*.

> Hampton, Ellen. *Doctors at War. The Clandestine Battle Against the Nazi Occupation of France*. Louisiana State University Press: Baton Rouge. 2023.
>
> Hemingway, Ernest. *A Movable Feast*. Scribner: New York. 1994 (Restored Edition).
>
> Lewis, Damien. *Agent Josephine. American Beauty, French Hero, British Spy*. BBS Publications/Hachette: New York. 2022.
>
> Picardie, Justine. *Coco Chanel. The Legend and the Life*. Harper Collins: New York. 2010.
>
> Mazzeo, Tilar J., *The Hotel on the Place Vendôme. Life, Death, and Betrayal at the Hotel Ritz in Paris*. Harper Collins: New York. 2014.
>
> Sylvia Beach Interview on James Joyce and Shakespeare & Company, for the opening of the Martello Tower in Sandycove in Dublin as a museum. (June 16, 1962). Manufacturing Intellect via YouTube.

The American in Paris (2017). [Documentary film]. Written and directed by Antony Easton. Paris: Passion Pictures.

Vaughan, Hal, W., *Doctor to the Resistance. The Heroic True Story of An American Surgeon and His Family in Occupied Paris*. Potomac Books, Inc.: Washington: DC. 2004.

Vaughan, Hal, W., *Sleeping with the Enemy. Coco Chanel's Secret War*. Alfred A. Knopf: New York. 2011.

Author's Note

While some French doctors collaborated or at least cooperated with the Nazis, many more took part in the Medical Resistance, putting their careers and lives on the line. Medical Resistance activities might be as discreet as falsifying a medical record to keep a patient from being deported to a German labor camp or as all-consuming as running the medical service for the maquis, rural guerrilla bands that literally took to the hills to fight the Nazis. Labeled by the Vichy government as abetting "terrorists," medical resistants risked torture, internment, and death.

Dr. Sumner Jackson, the Maine-born chief medical officer of the American Hospital in Paris, shouldered such risks throughout the Occupation years, including hiding a B-17 tail gunner in his family's ground floor apartment at 11 avenue Foch in Paris, smuggling other downed Allied fighter pilots out of France, and with his Swiss wife, Charlotte (nicknamed Toquette) opening his home as a meeting spot and mailbox for at least two Paris Resistance groups. In the waning years of the war, the Jacksons and their teenage son, Pete, were arrested and interned. Dr. Jackson died at Lubeck Bay on May 3, 1945, when the German prisoner transport ship he and Pete were on was hit by friendly fire. The next day, Germany surrendered. Today, a bronze plaque in the hospital's main building commemorates his selfless service.

An American expat, and international celebrity, Josephine Baker was an Honorary Correspondent for the Deuxième Bureau, the French foreign military intelligence service that operated in the shadows after the Nazi invasion. After the war, Baker was awarded the Médaille de la Résistance avec Palme, the Croix de Guerre, *and* the Legion of Honor, France's highest decoration for military service. As of this writing, many of the war records detailing her extraordinary courage and daring espionage activities in the service of the Allies and a free France are still sealed by the French government.

The story of Sylvia Beach's run-in with a German officer over her copy of James Joyce's *Finnegan's Wake* is faithful to Beach's account as recalled in a 1962 interview filmed for the opening of the Joyce Tower and Museum in Sandycove, Dublin.

And then there's Gabrielle "Coco" Chanel[1]. A half-century since her death, the *Grande Mademoiselle* of fashion still fascinates. We know for fact that she attempted to use the Nazi "Aryanization" laws to reclaim her perfume company from the Wertheimers only to be outwitted by them yet again. In the book, her letter to Kurt Blanke, the Nazi lawyer in charge of the economic persecution of French Jews, is faithful to her actual one whereas the letter from her to Churchill at the end of the book is entirely made up. I did, however, look at other correspondence between the two to capture her unique communication style as well as to map the boundaries of their unusual friendship.

Since 2011, it's come to light that Chanel undertook espionage

---

[1] Chanel designed her "comet" gown in April 1940, before the Nazi Occupation, not in April 1942 as I've written here.

activities during the Occupation years in service to the Abwehr. Sometime in 1941, she was enrolled in the Abwehr's Berlin registry as Agent F-7124, code name Westminster, a reference to her former relationship with the Duke of Westminster. Beginning in late 1941, she undertook the first of three missions on behalf of her Nazi handlers, none of them successful, and all reliant on her connections to highly placed British aristocrats, notably Churchill. After the liberation of Paris, she was taken in for questioning by representatives of General de Gaulle's provisional government but freed after a few hours, ostensibly at Churchill's request.

On April 16, 1946, a French court issued a warrant to bring her before French authorities after discovering she had been teamed with French traitor Baron Louis de Vaufreland, referred to as "V-Mann" in official Abwehr documents, on a 1941 mission to Madrid meant to provide cover for Vaufreland's spying work. Once again, she was let off for lack of solid evidence. Had the judge, Roger Serre, been privy to the full story, including the transcript of the British interrogation of Count Joseph von Ledebur-Wicheln, an Abwehr agent and defector, the court might have arrived at a very different verdict.

In 1944, von Ledebur-Wicheln told MI6 agents that Chanel and von Dincklage, aka Abwehr agent F-8680, had traveled to a bombed-out Berlin in 1943 to offer Chanel's services to SS Reichsfuhrer Heinrich Himmler. Ledebur also revealed that Chanel, after visiting Berlin, undertook a second mission to Madrid for General Walter Schellenberg, Himmler's chief of SS intelligence. Fortunately for the Allies, Chanel's clumsy attempts at spy craft were more in the vein of the Keystone Cops than James Bond.

Chanel had two longtime atelier employees who inspired supporting characters in *Stardust*: her chief seamstress, Madame Manon, and her right hand, Mademoiselle Angèle Aubert, both with her for decades. In the book, I cast these characters as meanies, but I have come across nothing in the archives to suggest that they were anything other than dedicated employees. Rather than defame the dead in the service of storytelling, I have altered the names to create the fictitious mesdames Millet and Aubrey.

Meanwhile, Stateside …

Rose's accident is modeled on Winston Churchill's near brush with death. In December 1931, Churchill was in New York for the start of a forty-city lecture tour of the United States, accompanied by his wife Clementine and daughter Diana. At 10:30 p.m. on December 13, 1931, the then fifty-seven-year-old former Chancellor of the Exchequer was crossing Upper Fifth Avenue, then a two-way street, when he was struck by a truck driven by a young Yonkers man, Edward Cantasano. Distracted by searching the street numbers for the home of financier Bernard Baruch at No. 1055, Churchill had forgotten to look right. Afterwards, Cantasano drove Churchill to Lenox Hospital where he was hospitalized for ten days with a sprained shoulder, cuts on his face and more seriously, pleurisy.

Churchill took full responsibility for the mishap, twice inviting Cantasano to tea with his family. Mrs. Churchill tried giving Cantasano, who was unemployed, a sizeable check for his troubles, but he turned it down on principle. Churchill was released in time to spend Christmas with his family in their suite at the Waldorf-Astoria. Had he been more seriously injured or killed, the world map might look *very* different today.

Acknowledgments

My interest in the Second World War began late one night when, as a high school student, I interviewed my father for World History class. My assignment, due the next day, *naturally*, was to gather an oral history from a family member who'd lived through a flashpoint event in modern history. Over cups of Sanka instant coffee, for the first time he opened up to me about his wartime experience – serving on an American-built airfield in Corsica in 1943 where he was tasked with bearing away the wounded and dead from the B-17s that limped back to base, receiving the news that his own father had died of a heart attack, and coming back to his hometown of Baltimore, Maryland where he and his fellow former GIs met up at German beer halls like Blob's Park in Jessup, Maryland to eat sauerbraten, sip steins of German beer, and tap their toes to "oom pah" bands, seemingly without a trace of irony. Daddy, thanks for the stories and the box of wartime photos, doubly precious now that you've passed.

Many thanks to the talented team at Joffe Books, especially my wonderful editor, Rebecca Slorach, Head of Choc Lit, and freelance editor, Katie Seaman, both of whom shepherded *Stardust* from a rather unwieldy first draft to an actual novel.

Writing any novel but especially an historical saga is a marathon not a sprint. To my dear friends, both writers and nonwriters, whose support helped me stay the course throughout writing *Stardust*, I am so grateful to have each and every one of you in my life.

A very special shoutout to my Ocean Grove, New Jersey friends and neighbors, who threw their support full steam behind the first book in the American Songbook series, *Irish Eyes*, including Dr. Maureen Edwards, Damaris Adamo, Jane Johnson, Michael McGraw, Maryan Giachetti, Donna Fox, and Stacey Kane. Stacey passed away during the writing of *Stardust* and is much missed.

Chin scratches to my darling feline fur baby, Daisy, who passed over the Rainbow Bridge in 2023, and whose indomitable spirit is reflected in my heroine.

Last but never least, love and gratitude to my husband, Raj Moorjani, who wears many hats, including digital geek squad, talented collaborator and all-around best friend. I am so very lucky to get to walk through Life with you.

Hope C. Tarr, New York, New York

About the Author

Hope C. Tarr is a multi-published author, screenplay writer and journalist whose articles have appeared in *The Irish Times*, *Baltimore* magazine and *USA Today*. *Stardust* is the sequel to her critically acclaimed historical fiction debut, *Irish Eyes*, and the second book in her *American Songbook* series.

Prior to commencing her writing career, Hope earned a Master of Arts degree in Developmental Psychology and a Ph.D. in Education, both from The Catholic University of America. She is a founder and curator of the original Lady Jane's Salon® reading series in New York City (2009 to 2020), which donated its net proceeds to survivors of domestic abuse and homelessness.

Hope divides her time between Manhattan and the New Jersey Shore with her husband and their rescue cats. Visit her at https://hopectarr.com and https://hopectarr.substack.com where she writes *History with Hope*.

Book Club Guide

1. Daisy undergoes dramatic changes over the course of her six years in Paris. Were her actions during the Nazi Occupation justified? At the end of the book, are you still able to root for her?

2. During France's four years under Nazi rule, some French cooperated and collaborated with the occupiers while others risked their lives working for the Resistance. Did people like the film actress Arletty deserve what they got or were their punishments too severe?

3. In the aftermath of the Allied liberation of France, an estimated 10,000 French women and girls were accused of "horizontal collaboration," sleeping with the enemy, and had their heads shaved. Some *femmes tondues* (shaved women) were also beaten, branded, and killed. Almost exclusively, men were the ones who carried out these punishments. Considering the "Me Too" movement and shifting attitudes toward gender relations, what is your take on these punitive measures targeting women?

4. Coco Chanel remains a controversial figure in France's World War II history. She left Paris in September 1944 and self-exiled in Lausanne,

Switzerland for ten years, returning in 1954 to restart her fashion business. For Chanel, whom today we would be safe in calling a "workaholic," might opulent exile have been a form of imprisonment?

5. Daisy's involvement with the Resistance leads to her making several morally compromised choices. She's in love with Jean-Claude but sleeps with Fritz to get access to his briefcase. Later, she develops feelings for Fritz though as a Nazi officer he represents everything she's fighting against. Do you agree with Daisy's decisions – do the ends justify the means – or could she have made different choices and still achieved her objectives?

6. What do you make of the character of Bridget? Were you surprised by her admissions at the end of the book? Do you think she cared for Daisy as a best friend or was her attachment more to do with possessiveness?

7. The Medical Resistance in France during the Occupation years arose in part as a response to the collaborationist Vichy government's crackdown on Jewish doctors. Were you surprised to learn that some of the antisemitic restrictions imposed on Jewish physicians, and Jews generally, in France predated the Nazi takeover?

8. *Stardust* is sprinkled with historical figures, from boldfaced names like Coco Chanel, Josephine Baker, Sylvia Beach, and Drue Leyton, to lesser-known heroes like Dr. Sumner Jackson. How do you feel about encountering real-life people in historical fiction? Does it enrich the central story or distract from it?

The Lume & Joffe Books Story

Lume Books was founded by Matthew Lynn, one of the true pioneers of independent publishing. In 2023 Lume Books was acquired by Joffe Books and now its story continues as part of the Joffe Books family of companies.

Joffe Books began in 2014 when Jasper agreed to publish his mum's much-rejected romance novel and it became a bestseller.

Since then we've grown into the largest independent publisher in the UK. We're extremely proud to publish some of the very best writers in the world, including Joy Ellis, Faith Martin, Caro Ramsay, Helen Forrester, Simon Brett and Robert Goddard. Everyone at Joffe Books loves reading and we never forget that it all begins with the magic of an author telling a story.

We are proud to publish talented first-time authors, as well as established writers whose books we love introducing to a new generation of readers.

We won Trade Publisher of the Year at the Independent Publishing Awards in 2023 and Best Publisher Award in 2024 at the People's Book Prize. We have been shortlisted for Independent Publisher of the Year at the British Book Awards for the last five years, and were shortlisted for the Diversity and Inclusivity Award at the 2022 Independent Publishing Awards. In 2023 we were shortlisted for Publisher of the Year at the RNA Industry Awards, and in 2024 we were shortlisted at the CWA Daggers for the Best Crime and Mystery Publisher.

We built this company with your help, and we love to hear from you, so please email us about absolutely anything bookish at feedback@joffebooks.com.

If you want to receive free books every Friday and hear about all our new releases, join our mailing list here: www.joffebooks.com/freebooks.

And when you tell your friends about us, just remember: it's pronounced Joffe as in coffee or toffee!

www.ingramcontent.com/pod-product-compliance
Lightning Source LLC
LaVergne TN
LVHW030744060325
805264LV00005B/108